T0354557

The Range Wars

A Woman of the West

JOYCE MOON

ISBN: 978-1-4669-7801-0 (sc)
ISBN: 978-1-4669-7800-3 (hc)
ISBN: 978-1-4669-7799-0 (e)

Library of Congress Control Number: 2013901399

Trafford rev. 01/25/2013

 www.trafford.com

North America & international
toll-free: 1 888 232 4444 (USA & Canada)
phone: 250 383 6864 ♦ fax: 812 355 4082

In a dangerous, wild, and lawless country where men and women had to learn the law of survival, range wars over grazing lands and water rights was a real test on a person's strength.

Yet one woman had the courage to fight for the better; from a lonely girl to a faith-filled lady, she had the strength.

Julliannyia Hamperston went wild with excitement when her boyfriend called her out West. She couldn't be more surprised than disappointed when she became involved in a range war after finding out that her parents left her some land, very valuable land. When she meets Keith Petershire, she is torn between her desire to be her own woman and a woman in love. Julli wonders if her strength is enough to endure the savage land and win her the war. Will her newly acquired faith win her the heart of the man she loves?

DEDICATION
AND
ACKNOWLEDGMENTS

To those women whose dedication and courage helped give understanding to women and deaf people.

Dedicated to my family; my children; Shannae, Carea, Kessandra, Zhane, Emma, Duncan, Benjamin, and Peter. Also to my mother and father, Lauretta and Kenneth. Not forgetting my sisters and brother and their families. To my grandmas and grandpas, aunts, uncles, and cousins. And to those of my friends who have remained true to me, old and new.

"Beautiful Rose Song"

My beautiful rose,
Mine and mine only,
My beautiful rose.

"That's a beautiful song, Keith."

"It's for a beautiful lady. Do you have any idea who she may be?" A smile crinkled at the corners of his sensuous mouth.

"Oh, Keith, tell me who she is," Julli signed and whispered at the same time as he leaned down to look into her eyes.

"I don't need to tell you who she is, you know," he replied with one hand as he gently captured her lips in a kiss so thoroughly gentle that all she could think of was Keith and the sweet caress of his lips against hers.

Until somebody shouted, and Keith pulled away.

Signing, he said, "Zeke's homestead is ablaze!"

PROLOGUE WITH BRIONNA

Unknown Area
July 10, 1803

B rionna looked toward the huge canopy bed she shared with her big Irish husband, Colin, who was lying on the mattress, swathed in blankets despite the near eighty degrees in the room. Quickly he was dying from a fever.

Oh God, thought Brionna. *Let this man live or take me with him!*

Closing her eyes as tears slowly poured out, Brionna got up from the stool by the window and walked toward the desk. Opening the top drawer on the side, she took out a book and a bottle of ink. Reaching out, she picked up the feather by the corner and set the contents down. Arranging them where she needed them, she touched the quill and made sure it was sturdy enough for her to use. Then pulled up a chair and sat down.

Taking a deep breath, Brionna looked at the book before opening it with shaking hands. Turning to the page where she left off, she let out a silent prayer.

"Oh, Father, please listen to my prayer. My husband Colin is dying and I do not think he will last out the night. I am so afraid." Pausing, she exhaled the breath she was holding and continued with her prayer. "I am very scared and lonely. O God Almighty, give me the courage to face life alone. Please guard our child as she journeys to be with my sister in New Orleans. Father Almighty, I give my life totally to you. Please watch over me and my loved ones. Thank you, Father, for the wonderful life that I have lived. In Christ's name, I pray. Amen."

Sighing, she uncapped the ink jar and picked up the feather. After a few minutes of debating over what to write, she finally let herself concentrate on what came to her.

> Dear Journal,
>
> It is the 10th day of July of our Lord in the year 1803. Today is a very hard day. Colin is going fast and there is nothing I can do for him but pray. He may not see the dawn of marrow and I am all worn out. It has been long and the battle is not ending with the fever. I know that he has lived a good life but I am not ready for him to leave me.
>
> I want to put God down and let the devil ruin my life, but that is not what I really desire. I want the protection of the Lord. I know I have it.
>
> Aside from Colin's dying, we gave up our only child. That is another thing that has been hard for me. We sent her to my sister Bertha in New Orleans barely two weeks ago. It is difficult to believe that we were forced to send away something very precious to us after all the wonderful things God has given us.

However, with all the danger here, we know that she will be safer away until all the evil has passed.

Then we will see our precious little girl again. Colin has said that God has blessed us and that Julliannyia will inherit the blessings. I agree with him but how I ache to hold my little baby in my arms and rest my chin on her mass of curly brown hair. I do not think it good for Julli to be with my sister because she shuns God and is very egotistical. However, after deliberate prayer and fasting, I came to know that it was indeed God's will for her to go to her aunt. I know that He will care for my daughter, and send a guardian angel to help Bertha with this precious little bundle of love.

I know that blood is thicker than water, but I have my doubts on whether or not it was in Julli's best interests. She has never met her aunt. She is so young that it has to be confusing and scary to her. My heart bleeds for her in this time.

We married in Ireland at fifteen before coming to America to get away from the hardships we endured there. However, it seems that trouble followed us from our home country to here. No matter how hard we worked, we always had to struggle over something.

We tried for years to have children but when we gave up trying, God blessed us with a beautiful little girl. I am of forty-seven years and although my childbearing days are over, we are very lucky to have been able to have Julli. She is so precious and we love her dearly.

Colin and I are getting by in our years and time is just flying by fast. I know we are old enough to be her grandparents. I only have to remember that Abraham's wife Sarah was a very old woman when she bore her son, Isaac, so according to God our age doesn't matter. Just our willingness to take upon us all that he thinks we can handle. Most of all, his blessings are indeed miracles.

Julli is only three years old but I know that she will do okay and go on with her life. If anything happens to us, she will always have the comfort of a home, our home. I just hope that this place is the Promised Land for her and us as well. God forbid she gets hurt on the trip to her aunt. I just hope that Bertha will welcome her into her home even though she and I were not on good terms years ago.

Resting her head on her arms, Brionna braved a quick look toward Colin on the bed. She hoped he did not go to his Maker before she could tell him how much she loved him. Gathering strength, she pushed herself up, only to sit back down as a wave of dizziness hit her. Blinking her eyes several times, she briefly shook her head and raised her eyebrows. Placing the back of her hand against her forehead, Brionna groaned as she felt herself to be fevered. Closing her eyes and sinking wearily back into the chair, she whispered, "Oh God, I have the fever."

She let the feathered pen drop to the floor dismissively as she rested her head on the desk. She closed her eyes for a few minutes, breathing heavily, before gaining strength to get up.

Brionna slowly rose from the chair and edged her way toward the bed. The prone form of her husband registered the fact that he was dead. Looking toward his chest for any slight movement and not finding any, she continued on her way over. Brionna leaned onto his chest, but not hearing his heart beating, she placed a kiss on his chin. She reached out, brushed back his curly orange hair streaked with white, and then grabbed the sheet to cover his face.

"Now they will leave me alone and let me go from this wretched land," muttered Brionna sarcastically. She had never wanted to stay after herself and Julli had been harmed. She had begged Colin for months to sell the place and move them away from there. Brionna considered the land evil and full of despair. Sometimes she wondered if they should have stayed in Ireland, even though there was a lot of superstition and Brionna feared for her life more than once.

However, Colin had stood firm, stating that he wanted a legacy to pass on and that he liked the land they were living on. Not even when they sent Julli away would Colin budge. He was a very stubborn man and was willing to fight for what he believed was his due.

Now that Colin was dead, Bertha planned to be on the next ride out of the town. She was determined that she was going to be reunited with her daughter and sister. No matter what happened, she was going to hold her baby girl once again.

Suddenly the front door banged open. She heard footsteps stepping, and someone came into the house. She listened to see if she could recognize the sounds they were making. All she could hear was the stomping of feet and the thudding of stuff being thrown around.

The bedroom door was flung open, and Brionna saw a gloved hand aim the Winchester at the body of her husband. Before fear totally consumed her, the trigger was pulled, and she heard the blast of the rifle being shot. She looked at her husband's body and saw it jerk at the impact of the bullet hitting it.

Brionna felt herself screaming out in pain, not at her husband being shot, but as she looked at her bosom, which was now red. She had not seen the other shooter coming in and did not know that there was another gun pointed; not at Colin, but at her. In shock, Brionna watched as the attacker turned and ran out of the room, but not before she had glimpsed who it was.

Frozen and unable to move, Brionna stood there holding her bosom. She removed her hands, only to see they were covered with blood. She looked at her hands and started to feel the shock wear off. She could feel the burning pain spread through her body.

Before she realized what she was doing, she was halfway to the desk. Groaning as pain shot through her entire chest, she took a short breath while slowly inching her way across the room. She fell in the process and let out a scream as excruciating pain tore through her whole body.

Moving her hand from her chest, she saw that she was quickly losing blood and was getting weaker with every second. Closing her eyes for a minute to calm herself, she glanced at the book on the desk, and an idea came to her. Nevertheless, she had to hurry; she did not know if the attackers would come back or not.

Taking a short breath and gritting her teeth, she rolled to her right side and pushed herself up with her elbow. Keeping her eyes closed, she rose up onto her knee. With tears streaming down her face, she opened her eyes and grimaced with every wobbly knee-step she took toward the desk. Her whole blouse was covered with warm, sticky blood that was running down her skirt. Closing her eyes and placing her hand back onto her chest, groaning at every breath she took, she braved another step.

Then the room started spinning, and Brionna fell face forward on the floor. Lying there for what seemed like an eternity, she wondered if she would make it or not. Gasping and crying, she finished inching her way over to the desk, leaving a trail of blood. Very slowly, Brionna reached up and tried grabbing the journal. It fell onto the floor, and she had to reach out to bring it to her, grimacing with every effort it took. Opening it with shaking fingers covered with blood, she flipped through it and finally found the page where she had left off earlier.

Placing her hand back over her wound, she wiped off some blood with her fingers and wrote something in the book. Moaning at how much pain she was in, she swallowed carefully and took short breaths in between. She held the book open and blew on it to dry the writing. Her task done, she closed it, hoping that it would tell her story if anyone read it. Brionna picked up the book, kissed the cover, and slowly moved over to the closed drawer. She reached up, opened it, and put the book in there.

All that remained for her to do was to tell her husband that she loved him and to pray.

"I love you," she whispered as she looked toward the bed. Colin lay there, and the sight was etched into her memory. Closing her eyes and taking a long, quivering breath, she started reciting Psalms 23.

"The Lord is my Shepherd, I shall not want. He maketh me to lie down in green pastures. He leadeth me beside the still waters. He restoreth my soul. He leadeth me in the paths of righteousness for his name's sake. Yea, though I walk through the valley of the shadow of death, I will fear no evil, for thou art with me. Thy rod and thy staff they comfort me. Thou prepares a table before me in the presence of mine enemies. Thou annointest my head with oil, my cup runneth over. Surely, goodness and mercy shall follow me all the days of my life, and I will dwell in the house of the Lord forever. Amen."

With that, she closed her eyes, picturing Julli smiling at her. Brionna grinned at that hallucination and was dead within minutes.

CHAPTER 1

Day before the Birthday Party
Thirteen Years Later
June 7, 1816

Julli gasped when her aunt Bertha brought her into the living room. Julliannyia could not believe her eyes. Her aunt had gotten her what she wanted. A sapphire rock hung on a silver rope-chain. Diamonds surrounded the blue stone. She stood there looking at the window that had its curtains parted to let the sun shine on the gift. Looking at Bertha, she made the signs for "thank you!" before giving her aunt a big hug. Julli quickly strode over to the window and took down the necklace.

Julli still could not believe her aunt had actually gotten her the necklace. Julli knew that her birthday was coming up, but her aunt had not hinted at anything. Normally, her aunt gave her simple things, such as a book or perhaps even some clothes. But nothing as extravagant as a necklace. Especially an expensive one like this. Julli gazed at it and then wondered what the catch was. Besides it being close to her sixteenth birthday, Julli knew that her aunt always had a reason for something she did or said.

Lately her aunt seemed more open and human than she ever had been since Julli had come to live with her thirteen years ago. Maybe it was because Julli was growing up and her aunt was getting older and wiser. *Wiser?* thought Julli, shaking her head dismissively as she snickered at her thoughts.

From what Julli knew, it would have been worth a lot since congress passed the tariff law not too long ago. Julli could only wonder how much it cost her aunt to get such a beautiful necklace.

"How did you know?" asked Julli, signing, amazed at her thoughtfulness.

"Freddie told me," admitted Bertha knowingly. "I know that your birthday is tomorrow, but I wanted to surprise you today," signed Bertha.

"It's beautiful," Julli signed back misty-eyed.

Julli handed the necklace to Bertha, who put it around Julli's neck and clasped the ends together. She turned Julli around and smiled appreciatively at her.

"It will look good with your dress tomorrow night at your party," replied Bertha, both talking and signing, looking straight at Julli.

"What dress?" Then with a quick puzzled look, she asked another question, still signing. "What party?" questioned Julli, knowing that that was the catch.

"Why of course your party. Didn't Freddie tell you?" Her aunt gave a shocked look. For once, it surprised Bertha that Freddie had not told his favorite person the secret they had cooked up the last few days.

"What? No, he didn't say anything to me," was the remark, with hands signing and head shaking. Then it dawned on Julli that somehow her aunt had upstaged everything again and had more than likely included Freddie in her schemes. Chances were everybody on the residence was involved in some way and now Julli was going to have to go along with her aunt's plans only if to get some peace. She knew that her aunt was a very outgoing woman and loved being in charge of everything—from social circles, etiquettes, studies, even the foods the cook prepared.

"Uh-oh!" came an exclamation.

Following her aunt's eyes, Julli turned to see Freddie leaning there in the doorway. He was standing with boxes behind him, box after box. Not looking the least bit guilty, he smiled at Julli. Giving out a shout before running to him and giving him a hug, she looked at him, then hastily asked, both with her voice and hands.

"Yeah, what party?" signed Julli, placing her hands on her hips.

Freddie just smiled and patted Julli on the back, ignoring her.

Standing in front of him, she glared at him. "You were a part of this?" asked Julli, not sure she wanted to believe that Freddie had anything to do with it.

"You bet your bloomers I was," boasted Freddie, still signing to Julli as he had all the years. He turned to face Bertha when she came next to him.

"Yes, dear, Freddie has been very helpful," interrupted Bertha, signing at Freddie's side. Turning to Freddie, she asked, "Do you have the rest of the items I wanted you to get for me?"

Freddie nodded to Bertha, who moved over to allow him to bring some boxes into the room. Julli eyed them, and she knew without any doubt that it had to contain her dress and personal items since there was mention of the word "party" to her.

"Here!" signed Bertha and Freddie together.

"Another present?" at Bertha's nod, Julli squealed.

Opening the box carefully as she had learned after living with her aunt, she folded back the wrappings inside and pulled out a beautiful blue dress. Holding it up to her chest, she was glad that the dress was more modest and longer than what the other girls her age wore. There was lace on the top of the bust and skirt. Sparkly blue.

The sleeves were long and went down her wrists, even when the shoulders were puffed as was the style. There was more than enough material for the bustle underneath, which Julli was not fond of. She eyed the extra material with an arched eyebrow. Julli was not going to be restricted.

"Um bustle?" Julli asked, shocked, patting the dress and picking up the hemline. Eyeing her aunt, she knew then that they were going to have a debate over the dress.

"Yes, dear." Smiling, Bertha knew she had cornered Julli. Now came the part where Julli was either into it or not. Bertha glanced at her reflection in the window. Her own dress had the bustle underneath at the back of the skirts, and Bertha liked the style. She looked at Julli and hoped for the best.

"I don't think so," was all Julli said, shaking her head slowly.

"Yes, Julli."

Still shaking her head no, Julli wondered why her aunt was making her suffer.

Eyeing Bertha, who wore the bustle, Julli thought her aunt was beautiful but had always thought the dress made her look huge, humongously huge, like a hippopotamus.

Her aunt's short-sleeved light blue dress was breathtakingly beautiful. Puffed sleeves at the shoulders, low-cut bodice showing as much cleavage as most women in the higher-society circles. It was long even with the bustle in the back, which Julli absolutely hated. Always took up more room, even if her aunt said it helped keep her cool, especially in the summer. Julli was not going to have any of it if she could help it. She would talk to Paula about having no bustle. She did not care if her aunt was displeased later on, but Julli was not going to feel huge. She was not gonna sway her hips and act so nincompooped like the rest.

"No way!" she mouthed as she shook her head.

At her aunt's questioning look, Julli held up the dress, intent on winning and proving her aunt wrong.

"The bodice is too low. I won't show cleavage!" stated Julli, pointing to her bodice and showing how low the dress was cut.

Groaning, Bertha took a deep, calming breath, and gathering her prim and proper posture, she nonchalantly admitted, "It's the style, Julli. Every woman wears it like that. And you are about to become a woman as well." Bertha stated the obvious.

"Not me!" signed Julli, only to add, "I mean, yes, I am going to be a woman but does it have to be this low?"

"Yes, you will be a woman," stated Bertha, agreeing with her but not about to give in. "And the dress will enhance your curves."

"Uh-uh," shaking her head again as her aunt kept nodding in her perfectly poised way.

"No," snapped Julli, glaring at Bertha.

Freddie comes over next to Julli and eyes the gown, which she was still holding. He inspected the dress from the tip of the sleeves to the bottom of the gown before finally looking at Bertha, who eyed him with her brow arched.

Because Julli was glaring at her aunt, it took Freddie a minute or so to fully get Julli's attention. He finally got it by tapping her on the arm several times. "There is nothing wrong with the dress," replied Freddie, turning to Julli, trying to soothe her before the fireworks came.

"Yes, there is! I won't have some guy looking down my chest," retorted Julli, signing, her hands flying through the air in a furious gesture. She eyed her aunt's low-cut bodice, and when Bertha noticed where Julli's eyes were lingering, she self-consciously placed her hand on her chest. Now Julli was going to have to have Paula help raise the bodice so it was to the modesty scale she referred to in how she maintained her style without feeling she was breaking a rule. Julli was and always had been self-conscious about her looks and went about being scolded day by day when her aunt would catch her not following the standards she wanted Julli to follow. She expected Julli to blend in with the other people. Hearing people. Respected upper-class members of the community.

Freddie snickers and stops when Bertha turns to him, swallowing it as quickly as it came. Putting on his best stern face and ignoring Bertha's glare, he winked at Julli.

Bertha catches the wink, groans, and clears her throat. "You will wear the dress the way it is," was all she could sign to Julli.

Freddie came over to her side and handed her some navy dance slippers, hoping for once they would stop their bickering. He then glared at Bertha and shook his head.

"Your aunt had me send for them," was Freddie's only reply in signs to the delighted look on Julliannyia's face.

"All sixteen-year-olds should have a party. The party symbolizes a girl's transformation into a beautiful young lady, which I know you are. You will look beautiful. And maybe even get some fine young gentlemen callers in the process," came the remark from Bertha, who had to take her time signing the words she could and finger spelling those she couldn't, which as Freddie knew was only going to get Julli all riled up again. Not the time it took signing but the words and how Bertha put them out to Julli.

"Aunt Bertha! I do not care for boys, young or old. They are all so stupid and they make me really mad," retorted Julli, angrily flinging the dress and shoes onto the floor when she was done signing. She defiantly glared at her aunt's shocked expression. She could not seem to control herself when she and her aunt got into one of their debates.

"Julli, you'll be sixteen and you're still acting like a child!" admonished Bertha. Stepping into Julli's line of view, she continued, "It's time for you to grow up. Men are men and you are a young lady enticing to their eyes." Before Julli could protest, her aunt added firmly, signing hastily, "Julli, you will pick up the dress and Paula will make adjustments if needed tonight. No other alternating the dress."

Julli interrupted with a question, "Why can't I have my own style?"

Swallowing, Bertha was not sure why Julli would ask such a question, but that was Julli's way of getting information. Taking a deep breath, she eyed Julli and said, "Well, when the time comes, maybe you can. But for now, go and put your gown away. I will have the maid help you." Then Bertha added, stopping Julli before she turned, "And, Julli, remember to control your temper." At Julli's protest, she added, signing smugly, "You promised me."

Julli grumpily responded, "Yeah okay, Aunt B," by signing dejectedly, Forcing a stiff smile, she curtsied and left them standing there.

Freddie and Bertha watched as Julli picked up her dress and items and proceeded to take them up the stairs to her room.

Stomp—! went Julli.

They heard the door open, then shut, and waited for the bang. Right then Julli reopened them and then slammed the doors with force.

Slam—!

Next, they waited for the crashing sound of something being thrown and broken.

Crash—!

They both watched as the maid went quickly up the stairs to the room to clean up what had gotten broken. Nicole went up with the other maid to help Julli take care of her personal belongings. Bertha and Freddie knew that Julli was going to give the maids a hard time, taking her anger out on any item within her reach, which was going to be more work for them to do, having to clean up the mess. They also knew that the servants loved Julli and they would not take it personally since she would always beg for their forgiveness. Moreover, she'd end up being extra nice to them for a couple of weeks or until another fit erupted.

Crash—! again.

Freddie and Bertha exchanged glances.

Bertha said, sighing, "She'll never change."

"Give her a chance. She is still growing up. Give her time," encouraged Freddie, not about to dismiss Julli's behavior as something unchangeable.

Bertha glumly added to Freddie's remark, "Time is running out. Without becoming a responsible, respected lady, her dowry won't be much." Adding, "And her etiquette manners need improvement. Much more now than ever. It will be hard to find her a suitor, much less marrying into a respectable family."

Freddie somberly said, "She will do what you want within her means."

"Will she?" was all Bertha could ask.

"She's changed more than you realize. Do not give up on her before she has started. She needs encouragement from you now more than ever so she can think before she acts out. Julli has learned to count to ten before acting out in anger." He added, "Well, not today. Seems you made her upset enough that she forgot."

Bertha, looking directly at Freddie, could only comment with, "Not good enough."

"Bertha"—going over to her, he takes her hand into his—"you know that she is capable of doing better to meet with your standards, but you do have to give her some time to get there. She is still young."

Looking at Freddie's hand that was holding hers, she removed it and shook her head again. Freddie, not giving up, put his arms around her waist and drew her back against him. He rested his chin on the curve of her shoulder and sighed. Bertha was not helping at all.

"She takes her baths and has done a lot for you. Just remember that she even took care of you when you were sick and she missed several weeks of private tutoring. She really cares for you," admonished Freddie, straightening up. He kept his arms around her and felt her take each breath.

"Yeah, she is a darling. I still worry that somehow I failed my sister," said Bertha, still concerned about Julli's behavior. She knew that she tried her best and doted on her niece. She wondered how Julli really felt about her, being her aunt and all. It was not easy, but Bertha did put her life around Julli's to make her happy. She tried her best. Still Julli acted like she did not care.

"Brionna would not let you say that."

"But, Brionna would not be happy with her temper tantrums and I know that she would give me the look she gave when she found something she was not happy about."

Freddie leaned over Bertha and gave her a kiss on the cheek before responding with, "Brionna trusted you. Julli is a great kid. She is turning out to be a beautiful young lady. You ought to be proud of yourself."

"Thank you, Freddie. Sometimes I wonder . . ." Shrugging out of his embrace, she walks over to a chair and gently sits down, moving her skirts out of the way. "She looks much like Brionna did at that age. I cannot help but wonder what the future holds for her. It's so scary to think of," said Bertha, without much conviction that things were going to be okay.

"Yes, it is scary. But always know that Julli is of hard stock. She is very stubborn and temperamental but she is also full of grace and kindness. Julli might even surprise you. You have had years to work on her. Things are not as bad as they seem," again came the encouragement from Freddie, not letting Bertha put Julli down.

Walking over to the window and looking out, he added, "I am aware that many people still consider her deaf and dumb. You and I know she is only deaf. She's a very smart and talented young lady." Swallowing, he added, "They just don't understand her like we do. It is not as if she has a disease that could make us like her, deaf. It is a pity that people are prejudiced and make fun of her. The only thing stopping most from doing that is the fact that you have a good high-standing reputation."

Getting up and walking over to stand by Freddie, Bertha could only agree with him. She smoothed her skirts and fidgeted with the sleeves of her dress before what Freddie said made her pause and look at him.

"You'll just have to make sure Julli gets the right kind of man," was all Freddie could say. He sighed and waited for the rebuke he knew she was going to dish out.

Not easily cornered, Bertha looked at Freddie and retorted, "That is going to be harder to do than say. You know as well as I do how Julli is. You saw how she reacted about suitors. I will not be around forever to take care of her. All I want is the best for her."

"So do I. You will talk to and approve of every guy before you let them come calling, won't you?" Freddie eyed Bertha, who feigned shock at his question. "I know that you will try to keep her best interests in mind but more often than not, they end up being for you. She needs to find a man who understands her. She takes life as it is given to her."

"What can I say? She is like my own daughter," rebuked Bertha, not easily cornered.

"I know what you mean, but when you do it, just be fair," he added gently.

"Easier said than done," said Bertha, and with that she turned away from the window to sit again in the chair she recently vacated. Flicking her skirts out of the way, she sat down, only to say, "What if I can't do it? She goes against everything I try to do whether it is for her own good or mine."

"You can do it. She knows you love her and only want to make sure she is cared for properly," Freddie added, hoping Bertha for once would agree with him on that.

"You think so?" Bertha questioned Freddie with a slight crook of her head.

"Yes, she needs you to help her with that. I don't think she can do it on her own." Freddie nodded, sure of himself.

Freddie, glancing around to avoid Bertha's glare, looked at the portrait of Julli on the fireplace mantle. *Gee, she is beautiful,* he acknowledged to himself. *She is stubborn and fiercely independent. She won't give in without a fight.*

"You'll just fight with her 'til you win. You better be careful because it could backfire on you." With that he added, "Good luck!" and bowed to Bertha, trying to put an end to the conversation.

Crash—! The sound of things being thrown and broken came again.

Glancing at each other, they knew that Julli has not cooled down enough to reason with. Bertha cocked her head at Freddie and shrugged her shoulders at his way of giving up by putting his hands up above his head.

"Ha-ha. Too late." Bertha snickered.

"What do you mean?" questioned Freddie, glancing at her.

"You will help me. I do not think I can do it on my own. She pays more heed to you than she does to me. You will keep your eyes out too unless you want me to tell Julli that it was your idea for me to find her a man," Bertha answered, knowing that she had Freddie right where she wanted.

"I only meant to offer you advice," Freddie grumbled, knowing that he had gotten himself trapped in Bertha's scheme again. "Besides she is your niece. You only want what you think she wants."

"Oh really? Maybe you do not know me as well as you think you do," mocked Bertha.

Freddie rolled his eyes at that and mocked back, "You think you do, don't you?"

"I know I do and you will help me by keeping her focused like you always do," answered Bertha derisively, knowing she was trapping him.

At Freddie's grumbling, she could not resist adding, "Too bad, she has for years called you 'uncle' and thinks of you as her father, so deal with it." This came gaily from Bertha.

"Dang blast it, woman!" growled Freddie. "Why do you always have to get me to do your dirty work?" Now upset with himself, he strode over to her chair and plopped down on the arm. All respect for manners was gone. When Bertha wanted to fight, he was always caught off guard as well. Seems that Julli noticed that and used it to her advantage.

"Because I know that you love and care for Julli as if she was your own. You pretty much helped me raise her so you get some of the blame if anything goes wrong," chirped Bertha, happy not to have to bear the entire burden alone.

"Well," was all Freddie could say at the moment. Hearing the maids scuffling across the floor in an attempt to keep Julli's fit down, he grimaced when there was another *crash*—!

"See? That is not how she was raised," came sarcastically from Bertha. Calming herself even, she added, "There is no telling what will happen one day when things get too hot for her to handle. She does really need to control herself."

"She does have a temper," admitted Freddie. "Just gotta help her find her potential as a deaf person and as a woman."

"How?" inquired Bertha, willing to do what it took to help Julli be respected and treated good.

Pacing the floor, he offered, "Do things that are interesting to her. Give her a chance to find out who she is and help her use her learning to better herself. If she wants to go on a trip by herself for the day, let her. You have to show her that you trust her to make the right decisions. If she needs help, you know she will come back and ask for it. Keep her focusing on 'good deeds reap good rewards.'"

"Everything here tries to evolve around her interests." Getting her fan out, she jerks it open, fanning herself. "She changes her mind on a lot of stuff. It seems the only thing that hasn't changed is her dislike for the styles of clothes and seemingly, men as well."

"I hardly ever do things that are against Julli's best interests. It is normally you that does it," retorted Freddie, not wanting to be caught up in any of Bertha's schemes. They always had a way of backfiring on Bertha rather than arousing Julli's interest in the deed.

"What about that soldier that you had here?" questioned Bertha, not about to let Freddie get away blameless.

"Oh?" Freddie somehow knew she was going to bring up that sore subject. He had hardly ever failed to do the right thing for Julli, but that time it totally backfired on him. "So you are going to still rub in the fact that Lieutenant Megston took off running when he saw the maid signing to Julli a few months ago?" flickering his hands out in frustration at that failed attempt.

"Well, you had not informed me about him calling on Julli so I had no time to prepare the household about being discreet." Bertha shrugged.

Getting up, Freddie admitted, "Well, he came recommended as his father has several slaves that are deaf. I just assumed against my better judgment that maybe there was a man out there who could somehow relate to Julli. I did not think that even someone who grew up with the deaf would be against another deaf."

"And did Julli hold that against you?"

"Nope. She actually thought it was all your idea," admitted Freddie snidely.

"What?" thundered Bertha, shocked.

Laughing at Bertha, he admitted, "I did tell her that you were the one who wanted to set her up. Told her that you wanted her to associate with him because of his family's reputation."

Riled at what Freddie had said, she snapped at him, "You did what?"

"Well, you did not give me much choice after you blew up at Julli and Jesmaina for his abrupt departure."

"I can't believe you did that to me." Bertha shook her head dejectedly. No wonder Julli had given her a hard time with her icy glares and silence.

Looking at Bertha, he saw she was upset by that. She wiped the back of her hand across her forehead. "Okay," he lied. "No, I didn't tell her that. Don't worry I was just jesting." He had not meant for it to go that far.

"You better have been or you'll be in the slaves' quarters for the week," demanded Bertha, not going to give in without a fight. The more they argued, the more they enjoyed the making up part. Freddie always made her feel special and then would admit she was right all along.

"Not so sure you can sleep without me," came the snide remark. But before Bertha could make a comeback, they were interrupted by the maid.

"Ms. Julli asks for tea. Shall I send her down?"

The request took Bertha off guard. She had gotten into an argument with Freddie, and they had not noticed there were no more crashing or slamming noises from upstairs. Looking at the clock, Bertha noticed that it was just fifteen after four o'clock. "Yes, of course," was her only response.

Not waiting for the maid to curtsy and leave, Freddie tried sneaking out the other door before a voice brought him to a halt.

"Crikes," was all that he muttered, pausing in his attempt to sneak out.

"Thank you, Freddie. Julli and I are very lucky to have you here with us," was not what he was expecting to hear. Looking back toward the voice, he noticed that she was smiling. Thinking the worst was over, he turned and walked back into the room.

"Always in your service, my dear." Freddie bowed in front of Bertha.

"I need you to do me some favors." With that, Bertha closed her fan and pointed at him with it.

"Whatever madame requests." Freddie bowed, looking at Bertha when he straightened up.

"Since congress passed the tariff law, I need you to find out what the prices are at the warehouse and inform the bank that I will be withdrawing some money for the added costs for the party tomorrow night."

"Yes, madame. Anything else?"

"Yes. How many people exactly have been invited to the party? I would like a final head count so Cook has the number of people she has to prepare food for and dishes."

Counting mentally, Freddie paused. "I am not sure yet if several families will make it. I will have to send the errand boy to find out for sure," he admitted.

"What about the lieutenant's family?" asked Bertha, knowing that the family had been humiliated by their son's departure from society when he had refused to call on Julli. Word had spread like wildfire, and luckily, Bertha was able to contain it.

"I am not sure. Last I know Lieutenant Megston was sent out to New York City for some meetings. I think the family will come only to hold still the gossip."

"Okay. That would be one way to stop it." She paused in her thoughts, then asked, "How about Captain Hortes and his family?"

She was not sure if she really wanted them there, but it was tradition to invite all the wealthy and respected families.

"Ugh, madame!" retorted Freddie sarcastically. At the stern look on Bertha's face, Freddie bowed and said, "I will check and see what they have to say."

"There is a lot to do before the party," suggested Bertha, opening her fan and fanning herself again.

"But we will get it all done in time. Don't worry about anything," stated Freddie.

"Now that you say it, I am worried more. Do you think Julli will try to stop or ruin the party?" asked Bertha, worried. "You know she loves to have fun, sometimes too much fun."

"No. I think she will be a good girl for once. But I would not be surprised if she refuses to wear a corset and the bustle." With that he eyed Bertha's dress, which was at an awkward angle.

"She better not do anything drastic. I expect nothing less but for her to hold high to the standards I have set upon her as well as all of us," she retorted, smoothing down the skirts after she caught Freddie eyeing them.

"I know, madame. I will put it on my list to go talk to her and remind her of your expectations," answered Freddie. He bows and straightens up, feeling the air swooshing toward him as Bertha fanned them both. Seeing Freddie notice she fanned him, she stops and eyes him.

"Thank you, Freddie. That will be all." Relieved, Bertha closes the fan and lays it down on the table next to her.

Leaning over, he grabs her hand and places a kiss upon it, all the while smiling with his eyes.

"Shouldn't you get back to work?" came the coy remark.

"Uh, yeah. Uh, good day, madame." Again bowing, Freddie was relieved as he walked out of the room. Gathering the remaining boxes, he left to do his errands to get the party preparations finished.

Bertha stared at the back of Freddie as he left the room. She couldn't help but snicker at how she had made Freddie think things had smoothed over. Sighing, now tired, she leaned her head back on the cushion and folded her hands on her lap. Shaking her head slightly and closing her eyes, she was suddenly in the past some thirteen years ago. It was the day that Freddie brought her niece, Julli, into her life.

CHAPTER 2

———◆◆◆———

Freddie and Bertha with Julli and the Letter
Thirteen Years Ago
September 15, 1803

F reddie had knocked on the door that early afternoon. The maid had let him in and brought him into the greeting room. She recalled that she had sent Freddie out to her sister's when she found out that Brionna was pregnant. That had been nearly four years ago, and she hadn't expected to see or hear from him after that. Freddie looked so pale and skinny that Bertha wondered if he came home because he was sick. When she entered the room, Freddie quickly went over to her and took her hand to bestow a kiss upon it. He was just almost always a gentleman.

"Greetings, madame."

"Welcome home, Freddie," Bertha told him, gently removing her hand from his.

"Thank you, madame." The rude gesture was not lost on Freddie, who knew that Bertha was always trying to show she was above reproach. He knew it was not the case. She just could not stand to be touched by Freddie; that much he knew after she told him to leave years ago.

"What brings you back here? Is my sister okay?" Bertha was afraid it was bad news. She wrung her hands, awaiting the reply from Freddie.

"She is as well as can be expected, I guess," came the reply. Freddie did not want to be the bearer of some news that he was not sure was going to be accepted good-naturedly.

"Care for a seat, some tea perhaps?" Bertha offered, eyeing his ragged look.

"No, thank you. This is not really a social call. I am to deliver something into your possession," Freddie stated tiredly. He wiped his hand across his unshaved chin and scratched at his nose. His clothes were clean, but he felt like he should have dressed up better before he came to Bertha's house. But a promise is a promise, not meant to be broken once the word was accepted.

"Business?" asked Bertha, squinting at Freddie.

"Somewhat," came the nonchalant reply.

"Okay, let's get it over with," she said sarcastically, hating his lame replies.

Handing Bertha a letter, she saw it was addressed to her. The handwriting was familiar, and she knew it was from her sister. Opening it, she saw that it was dated nearly three months ago.

She was shocked at Freddie for taking so long. "Why, if the letter was dated a while ago, it should not have taken you that long to come here. Pray tell me what the delay was?" Bertha demanded an answer. She stood her ground, wanting an explanation as to what took Freddie so long to do a simple task her sister put to him.

"First, may I go bring in your valuable delivery?" he asked her before he answered the last question and before she could finish reading.

Nodding her head to him, giving permission for him to depart, she eyed his lanky form as it went back out. Bertha closed the letter to wait until Freddie had brought in the package. She went over to the chair in front of the fireplace and sat down, wondering what in the world her sister could be sending to her. Maybe it was some material she made or something valuable like a diamond or gold nugget. Or what?

She heard the maid opening the door at the first tap, and next she heard the footsteps coming into the greeting room. Bertha was giddy with excitement at getting something from her sister. What she was not prepared for was what Freddie brought into the room. What she was not prepared for was a child. A mere child. It was a good thing Bertha was still sitting down, or she would have been already on the floor, passed out.

"Who do you think you are bringing a child into my home?" demanded Bertha, upset with Freddie. She sat there squinting her eyes at the child.

"Meet your niece, Julliannyia Maire Hamperston," came the shocking reply. Adding, "This is what took so long to get here."

"Oh my goodness," gasped Bertha when Freddie unwrapped the little form from the blankets. Bertha stood up too quickly that she felt light-headed. She could not believe her eyes. Either she was still dizzy, or it was actually happening. The child was a miniature Brionna. Curly brown hair, big blue eyes, button nose, and a wrinkled blue petticoat. If it was possible to turn back time to when they were little kids growing up in Ireland, Bertha was sure that it did already as she looked at the child. The little bundle looked questioningly at Bertha, then to

Freddie, who got down to his knees and started moving his hands everywhere.

"What in the world are you doing?" questioned Bertha, still looking at the child Freddie introduced as her niece. She did not know if it was the shock of having her niece with her or the fact that Freddie was acting like a madman gone nuts.

"If you would be so kind as to finish reading the letter it should explain all to you better than having me doing that," answered Freddie. "And I am talking to Julli. I am telling her that she is at her aunt's house and that you are her aunt."

"What does that have to do with you moving your hands and not talking?" Bertha questioned, still piqued about what he was doing. He was on his knees, and Bertha thought she was going to have to contact the authorities to have Freddie admitted. What person flings their hands around at a child? Had Freddie lost it?

"I am signing to her. Your niece is deaf," responded Freddie, not meeting Bertha's eye. Shocked beyond words, Bertha could only stare with wide eyes at Freddie and the child. The look on Freddie's face told her that he was not kidding. Her sister had a deaf and dumb child. Bertha was shocked beyond measure. She could not figure out how they could have a child like that. No one in her family had ever had a deaf and dumb member.

So like them to send her something that they cast off. Wondering what she could have done to make them do such a thing, she stared while Freddie kept signing to the little girl. She blinked her eyes several times and opened her mouth, not daring to breathe, to say, "What? Surely you are jesting." By the look from Freddie that bordered no hint of a joke, Bertha felt as if the world had come crashing down on her. She placed her hands on her chest and helplessly stood there. She finally dared to breathe, but in her panic, she forgot to let it out, so when she tried to inhale again, she ended up coughing. When she finally caught her breath and the coughs died down, she looked again at Freddie and the child. She quickly sat back into the chair.

The little girl looked at Bertha with her big blue eyes and puckered her lips to give Freddie a kiss on the cheek, for which he smiled and which he returned.

"No, sorry. This is the real deal," he stated still, looking at Julli. Bertha watched him brush back strands of curly brown hair and tuck the wayward curls behind her ear.

"But deaf and dumb?" questioned Bertha, still not sure whether or not he was jesting.

"Yes and no. Deaf of course, but not dumb at all," snapped Freddie, looking at Bertha, then back to Julli, whom he smiled at again. The child looked adoringly at Freddie, who shared the same look.

Bertha could not resist adding something to light the fire. "Oh, I get it. A prank from Colin at a child's expense," Bertha snarled at Freddie, who continued to ignore her. "Isn't that a little too extreme?"

"I don't think so. Bertha, read the blasted letter from your sister," yelled Freddie, still signing calmly to the little girl. He got off his knees and looked directly at Bertha. Nodding at her to proceed.

"I don't think so," was all she could respond, mimicking Freddie for him yelling at her.

Looking at her new niece, she took in the clothing and the little face. Julli was wearing a flowered blue dress, blue petticoats, and black boots. Her brown hair was messed up and hadn't been braided. Strands were going everywhere, compared to Bertha's neatly coiffed hair. Bertha saw Julli looking at her, and she remembered Brionna as a little child. The child was a miniature Brionna. Julli had deep blue eyes like her mother and the brown hair as well. Bertha knew that Julli must have inherited her father's curls.

How could she resist? Bertha's heart started to feel for the little girl. She got up slowly from the chair, walking over to Freddie and the child. When she leaned over to give her a hug, the child pulled away and hid behind Freddie's back. The girl did not seem too overly fond of strangers, and Bertha knew that it would take her a while to warm up to her and vice versa.

It still did not make sense why her sister would send her child to her. They had not parted on best terms. Brionna had been the most loving and forgiving of all of them. It had come as a shock to Bertha when Brionna told her that she and Colin were leaving for America. She had wanted to go with them but had to stay and take care of things. Bertha never cared for Colin and was disappointed when they sent word that they had gotten married. Bertha was only two years older than Brionna, and she only wanted to make sure Brionna was taken care of, since their mother died years ago. Their father was a drunkard and was never around. Now Brionna sent her child to Bertha.

She did not have the faintest idea how she was going to take care of a child, especially a child that was deaf and dumb. Why was the child here? Even though the child was her sister's baby, she was tempted to tell Freddie to take the child to the nearest orphanage. What in the world was she to do?

"Did you read the letter?" came again the voice of Freddie.

"No. I wanted to see what you had to deliver to me first," she responded, looking at Freddie, who was handling the child with the utmost care. She was not sure she wanted to read the letter. If it was a prank, she was going to make her sister's life miserable, what she had left of it to live.

"Well, you better finish reading it. It will explain everything," stated Freddie, getting up, brushing the knees of his pants, and taking Julli's hand.

"What are you going to do with her?" asked Bertha, glancing at Julli, who came to stand by Freddie, holding his hand and looking up at Bertha with those big eyes of hers.

"With your permission, take her into the kitchen and get her something to eat."

Looking at Julli's wrinkled clothes and dirty hands, Bertha couldn't resist shuddering.

"Don't let her touch anything."

Freddie gave Bertha a disgusted look before he took Julli by the hand, and together they walked out of the room. Bertha watched them walk out. She stood there dumbfounded. She could not believe how her luck had come crashing down on her head. Freddie handled the little girl as if she was his own blood and flesh. *Wow!* she thought to herself. *So my sister finally had a girl and she is beautiful like Brionna but, give me a break. Deaf and dumb?*

Bertha groaned and shook her head. Still shocked beyond words, her brain was in overload. She walked back to her chair, closed her eyes, sank wearily into the cushions, and wondered what the heck she had gotten herself into. Getting out her fan, she flicked it open, only to not want any air on her face at that time, so snapping it shut seemed to make her feel a little better. Bertha took a deep breath and regained her composure, then opened the letter. Blinking to clear her eyes, she focused on her reading.

To be delivered into the care of Bertha Maire Mearse by Freddie Tahney. Julliannyia Maire Hamperston, daughter of Colin, 47 and Brionna, 47, Hamperston. Said child born the 6th month, 8th day in the year of our Lord 1800. Addressed to New Orleans 1803.

Noticing the date of birth, it was the day Brionna and Bertha's mother had died in childbirth. *Well*, thought Bertha, *at least someone recognized the date.*

To my dear sister Bertha,
June 7th, 1803

I am writing to let you know that we have really enjoyed having Freddie. He has been a lifesaver. He is a good man and brings luck to us. Our thanks for the friendship we were able to have with him. If you hadn't sent him to us, we would surely have been lost. God has blessed us all. Thank you.

Rolling her eyes, Bertha wondered what Freddie's friendship had to do with them sending their daughter to her. Then a thought came to her; maybe something had happened to them, and they were coming out soon. It would do them good to come and care for their daughter themselves instead of putting the burden on her. Shrugging her shoulders, she continued.

To get to the reason of all this, starting some three years ago I gave birth to my daughter. As you may have noticed, she was born February 8th, which as you know has always been a bad date for us. It was a very trying time for us, especially for me. Colin was like a mother hen. If I hadn't been in so much pain then, I'd have been laughing at him. Too bad you weren't here; he'd have put a smile on those frozen lips of yours. He also told me he was never going to hold my hand during labor or a crisis ever again. Poor guy, I guess his hand must have really hurt him for several days because he couldn't handle his ax very well. I hadn't expected it to be a very long labor or that painful. Nineteen hours. Can you believe it? Mother never had to suffer that long.

When Julliannyia was finally born, it felt like only minutes ago that I had just barely started to have pains. The time went by fast to my relief. Could it have been my old age that made it very hard for me? I remember being so glad, it was over. Freddie and the midwife were so helpful and made it so much easier to bear all the pain.

You know the blanket that you made and sent with Freddie? It was the first thing that your niece wore. The pinks and purples looked so good on her. It was just perfect for my little bundle of love. Thank you again for the precious blanket. It kept her warm all these long winter nights. She still has it. It is here on her bed next to ours.

Bertha, smiling, with tears in her eyes, paused to take a deep breath and wipe at the tears from her eyes. A small sound came out of her mouth when she pictured the blanket she had painstakingly learned how to make and which when she lost the chance to use it herself she then wrapped and sent to her sister along with Freddie. She felt some relief as she realized that she had done something that had been appreciated. Continuing on her reading, she exhaled and took in the next few words.

As you may now know, Julli is deaf. She wasn't always like this. Not until she was a year and half. Somehow, she got the scarlet fever and the doctor said that it was all in God's hands. She was so young and he didn't think she would survive with all the heat her body was giving off. There wasn't a thing that Colin and I could do for her. Freddie made us keep bathing her in cool water. It seemed to help for a while then we would have to do it all over again.

I don't think I got much sleep but I don't remember feeling tired or anything especially when my child was so sick and in so much pain. This was longer than my birthing pains but not as bad as they were. This was a different kind of pain. It was like a horrible dream come true. One day she's this happy chatterbox and the next day she couldn't stop crying. I felt like the worst mother.

Mother made it seem so easy when she would comfort us and we felt better real fast. I kept wondering what I was doing wrong. Julliannyia no longer acted like she did those weeks ago. She was so quiet and so pale. Colin and I kept trying to get her to eat so she would get her strength back, but she didn't seem to want anything. The only thing Freddie would give her were some herbs he put in hot water to seep. She seemed to rest better after drinking that.

Freddie said we were trying too hard. How can you try too hard to help your child get better? What did he know that I as her mother didn't?

The doctor was surprised to see her doing okay the next time he came. And he told us to let her rest a few more weeks and that he would check on her every three days.

Bertha, it wasn't 'til then that Colin and I found out she was without her hearing. You remember how Colin used to get when he was really excited? Well, he came into the bedroom one day where Julli was sleeping and screamed like a banshee.

At the mention of the word "banshee," Bertha snickered. How she and her siblings loved playing that game with Colin when they were kids. She had totally forgotten all about that. She continued with her reading, wanting to know what happened next.

Oh no, Julli loved it when he would do it since it gave her an excuse to run after him screaming her lungs out. They really loved that game although it gave me a few fake heart attacks once in a while. But that day, she didn't even move. It took him a couple of tries before she just looked at him and then that is when we realized that she couldn't hear.

Oh how Colin and I cried. I thought for sure that I would have a real heart attack. That was the day Freddie brought the doctor for a checkup. When he checked her, he was surprised that she still had her voice even if it had a very weird sound to it. He just said that the Devil had done his work on her and packed up his bag and left. The doctor told us that he was not coming back, and that we would be better off putting her somewhere where people would not fear her. I wanted to go after the doctor and box him on the ears. No man, not even a doctor should tell someone that. Especially when that someone was just a child.

Freddie went out for a while but Colin and I stayed with her. What were we to do? I felt so much like you do about God. I wondered what I had done to him to forsake my child. I have always tried to follow the commandments and we faithfully prayed and did everything from scripture studying to feeding the poor. What were we doing wrong? Why were we given this trial?

When Freddie came back, he tried calming Colin down but my husband took off leaving Freddie and I to stay with Julli. I didn't know what I or anyone was going to do. I asked Freddie to watch Julli while I went out to find Colin. Like I said, Freddie was a good friend then and still is even today.

When I caught up with Colin, he had already packed for a few days of camping. He told me to go with him so we could go figure things out calmly. Always count on Colin to remind you of God. Before we left, Colin and I had a prayer. I know you lost your faith years ago when Mother and Father both died but after I tell you what happened next, you'll see why and how I got my faith back. Colin's faith is as strong now as it was years ago, maybe even stronger now. We prayed, I mean we prayed, for his divine help. Then we went camping.

You won't believe me when I tell you what happened to us on our second day of camping. A redskin encountered us at our camp. He spoke perfect English and said that he had met some white folks years ago and they had taught him. He said that he was a scout. Colin invited him to join us but that he had to keep his weapons down. Some compromise, huh? The redskin said that we didn't have what he wanted so he wasn't going to do anything but talk. It is not often you take a redskin's word for anything. I wanted to remind Colin about a good redskin being a dead one but I just kept quiet.

I wanted to go home alive for my daughter, not make her an orphan. If you remember Colin as well as I know him, you won't be surprised to know he actually shook hands with that "thing." Can you imagine how upset I was? Mother taught us about not showing our anger to anyone that we loved. Why did it have to be okay for men to be the ones to show anger? They hardly ever show their love anyway. I never thought that was fair. Colin invited him in, yeah, I mean in our camp.

Colin and the man started talking. I overheard the redskin say he was on a spiritual journey. That was interesting. The redskin went on to say that, he knew Colin and I were going through a rough time just by the way, we carried ourselves.

Composure?? What is the meaning of being a genteel woman if you are not able to express yourself in your actions? So calm and poised? The heck with all that. I was out camping with my husband and there was a redskin there, and he didn't seem to expect me to be so prim and proper. I don't know what it was but Colin and the redskin seemed to have a bond of some sorts. They got along so well.

Anyways, he stayed there with us for three days. Colin and I got to know him pretty good. I had fun with him. He made me feel like I had a brother I could rely on. He showed us a few tricks he learned when he was younger from his older brother who I think he said was now a chief or something.

Scout also told Colin something one day and he asked me if my corset was restraining. Gee, that is what attracts men to women, isn't it? Well, I was told to take it off for the day and boy, did it feel so much better. Less confining and I could move around a lot better. Colin said I felt softer to him.

Oh anyways, to get it over with, Scout, said that we were going to have more hard times ahead of us and we had better learn how to deal with them. He asked where Julli was. We only said that we had a daughter who had been sick. I am pretty sure that Colin and I never mentioned her name. How did he know?

For three days, I did not think once about Julli. I felt like the worst mother ever. I started crying and it felt so good to be in Colin's arms and share our grief. How can a stranger make you feel so vulnerable? How could he know what we were going through? There came the question I wanted to ask him but never did, Why was he there to begin with?

He seemed to know all the right words and how we were feeling. He reminded me that he was on a spiritual journey. Colin told Scout that Julli was at home with our friend Freddie and Scout just said that he knew. That was why he was on a spiritual journey, to help his friend's friends. You have to admit that it was pretty spooky in a way.

Why didn't you tell us that Freddie was part Redskin? Did you even know? Yeah, we found out that, Scout was a friend of Freddie's and that when Freddie went into town to get supplies for us, he always went to visit his tribe. That explained why it took him so long to come home. Was Freddie ashamed of whom he was? I guess that is the price you pay for judging someone by his or her color.

Colin and I judged our own child and that was a big mistake. Scout told us to go home but before we left, he said that we needed to keep our faith and trust in the Spirit. The thing is Scout kept mentioning this word "spirit." Colin told me that it pretty much summed up what they called "Spirit" we called "God." I guess, everyone had their own name for the supreme being.

It seemed like only minutes before we were headed home after thanking Scout for his help and also for his friendship. I learned a lesson. Never judge a person by their skin color or what ailment they have. We are all children of God and he does not judge us. He is merciful and loving.

Before I knew it, we were home and Julli ran into our arms as soon as we got off the horses. She was smiling and she was so happy. Julli was hugging me. She felt the same as she did before she got sick. Colin joined us and we felt like a family all over again. It felt so good. I remember our heartfelt prayers to our heavenly Father. There was this warm and comfy feeling. Our heavenly Father really does care about all of us.

Julli got to moving her hand and we let her down only to get a frown from her. Freddie told us that he was teaching her some signs he knew and that Julli was picking them up real fast and could understand them. I told Freddie that she was not a Redskin and I would like to have known that he was a half-breed. He just said that he should have told us years ago but it was just something he liked to keep to himself and in a way protect his tribe.

Julli started moving her hands and Freddie did the same. How ridiculous they looked until Freddie started telling us what they were saying. We just stood there watching them and it felt so right.

Maybe this is what we were supposed to learn. A foreign language to help us communicate with our daughter, it looked so easy but it was sometimes hard to remember. The good side of it all was that Julli was actually talking. Her voice was kind of squeaky and Colin said that he might have to put some grease down her throat to stop the noise and Freddie told Julli. All she did was laugh and told Freddie to tell her daddy to go ahead. Yuck. They were having so much fun I could not help but laugh too.

What can compare to the joy of being able to deal with a trial and overcoming it? Well, it just felt as good as holding her in my arms after she was born.

Freddie told us that we should try communicating with our daughter. He said that we needed to think of gestures for the words we were trying to tell her. It was so amazing especially to see Colin try his hand at it. He actually told Julliannyia that he loved her. He pointed to his eye for "I" and patted his chest with his fist for "love" and just then pointed to her. Julli knew just what her papa said to her. I did the same and we were rewarded with hugs and kisses.

How often can a woman witness a man crying? It is a wonder of life. Ever since then we all have been signing, even a few of the town's folks. There are some who put us down for having her in town with us. One woman said that we were just trying to show that the devil could walk amongst us all. I cannot believe the nerve of some people.

Julliannyia is very smart. She picks up a lot of what we are saying. She has already learned to read and write. We know that she could hear before and that she knows how to say words, even if they do not sound like what normal people say. Julli can count and you would be amazed at how fast she learns what Freddie teaches her.

She is a wonderful little girl and we love her dearly. If it wasn't for Freddie, I don't think Julli would be on her way to you. Hopefully she behaves and isn't too much trouble. Freddie has said he will help you with whatever else you need.

Bertha, I apologize for not writing to you more often or keeping in touch better. I have been so afraid that you were still holding a grudge.

Life here has been rough, not just with Julli, but with the land and all. We are losing cattle and some of our workers have been hurt. Colin said that we received a threat on Julli's life. That is very bad and not safe at all. That was the final straw, so here is my daughter Julli; your niece.

Should you not feel obligated to care for her, remember we named her after you. Please I ask, no, I beg of you to keep my baby safe. Colin and I will come for her as soon as this dirty mess is over with. I know it is a lot to burden you with but I don't know where else to send her. I just want her kept safe.

Please forget the past and forgive Colin and me for the things we hurt you with. If there had been something we could have done for you back then, I wish we had the chance when we found out. I know Freddie grieves for the things that you missed out on.

I want you to know that he loves you as much as before. We too love you. You have been in our prayers for so long. I love you Sister.

God bless you and keep you all safe. In Jesus's name,

Your loving sister,
Brionna Hamperston.

Tears streaming down her face, Bertha got up and went over to the bookshelf. She took out a black bind book and put the folded letter into it. Closing and placing it back onto the shelf, she emitted a sob and broke down crying. Freddie had come into the room at that moment, and he quickly pulled her into his embrace. He handed her a hankie he had pulled out of his pocket. Bertha couldn't control her sobbing and poured out her feelings onto Freddie's shoulders. She wailed at the loss she and Freddie suffered that she did not think he knew about. For Julli's loss, being away from her parents, her hearing loss, and because Bertha was scared to do anything with her. Cried for Brionna and Colin's safety and for them to come out and get their daughter. And begged for help. Help for everything she was going to have to deal with.

Time seemed to have stopped. There was no hurry.

CHAPTER 3

———◆◆◆———

Bertha Condemning Julli

Wiping her eyes and grabbing her hankie out of her pocket, she blew her nose and shrugged out of Freddie's arms. Still sniffling, she asked, "Freddie, what do I do now? I don't know anything about children or Julli for that matter." Bertha was nervous as she never associated with them.

"You'll learn. It'll be okay. It is only 'til Brionna and Colin come get her," replied Freddie, standing in front of her.

"How long?" came the question.

"Maybe a month or two," was all he could say, shrugging his shoulders. He knew that Bertha could not handle anything more than a challenge she had no idea of dealing with. She was tough, but when it was an emotional and personal nature, she was as weak as a newborn foal. He hoped that she would be able to handle what came her way; after all, he was there to help her if needed be.

"Are you sure?" Bertha asked, uncertain.

"No, madame," admitted Freddie, not sure himself.

"A month isn't that long. I still don't know," Bertha replied, avoiding looking at Freddie.

Looking at Bertha, Freddie asked again, "Did you finish the letter?"

"Yes, I read it," looking at Freddie. "Why else would I be crying?"

"Hormones, maybe." Freddie snickered, trying to get her to smile. He hated seeing her cry. There were two things he loved about Bertha, her smile and her temper. Her smile could make his world come crashing down on him gently, but her temper always made him fight her back. She would say and do things out of the ordinary, and he would end up laughing, only making her madder than a wet hen.

"How rude!" retorted Bertha, anger seeping into her voice.

"I know. I'm sorry, I couldn't resist," apologized Freddie, still smiling, liking it when she got mad and her face turned a light shade of red. She had spirit; he recalled how she could throw a temper and how long it would last before she cooled down.

"What exactly is going on out there with Brionna and Colin?" questioned Bertha, ignoring the man standing in front of her.

Walking over to the window, parting the curtains and glancing outside, he replied, "They refuse to give up the land that they have acquired. Seems someone wants to take away their claim. The land is valuable and Colin is determined to keep it. He put his sweat in that land and what money he had to get it."

"Why? It is just some forsaken land. A piece of land isn't always something to fight over," scoffed Bertha, remembering that her brothers had died fighting for their rights to the land in Ireland. They had not lived long enough to enjoy their victory or to get their spouses pregnant and preserve their seed. Her father had drank himself to death in the taverns after the deaths of his sons and wife. Bertha had been the one to take care of everything, including Brionna.

"Not your brother-in-law. He wants to keep it and if Brionna has another child and it's a boy, pass it down as his legacy," mentioned Freddie.

Widening her eyes at that remark, she couldn't help but ask the dreaded question: "Is Brionna pregnant again?"

Relief was evident on her face when she heard Freddie say, "Not as far as I know."

"She's too old for any more kids." An afterthought, she added, "What if Julli is the only child?"

Shrugging his shoulders, Freddie told Bertha, "Colin plans to put it in Julli's name anyway. When she is older and they pass away, it will be hers. Unless they have another child and it is a boy. Then the boy will get it."

"What if they have another girl?" Bertha couldn't resist asking.

"It will still be Julli's. That is the way Brionna wants it. She thought Colin was being prejudiced about a boy inheriting everything," Freddie said nonchalantly.

"Yes, most of the time boys inherit everything the parents have. The girls pretty much just get sold off with a dowry if they have one," uttered Bertha sarcastically.

"I take it you aren't fond of that rule?" queried Freddie, widening his eyes at that statement.

"Oh please! All girls should be given a fair chance," retorted Bertha, scrunching up her face, then quickly composing herself. Her father had tried to sell her dowry to the highest bidder for money he could spend at the tavern. If Brionna and Bertha's mother had survived childbirth, she would have kept her husband on the straight and narrow. Bertha had taken her dowry with her to America after Brionna left. She was supposed to give Brionna her share, but when Bertha found out they had married before leaving home, she swore to keep Brionna's dowry and use it for her own pleasure. When Brionna came asking for money, Bertha had extracted her revenge by turning her sister down.

"So should Julli," was his only remark, yanking her back to the conversation at hand.

Looking at Freddie, Bertha knew he believed in fairness, and oftentimes, it hurt his standing in the community. Bertha eyed Freddie before she commented, "Well, that remains to be seen."

Bertha wondered how she or anyone could have resisted his charms. He was as attractive as he was charming. She loved his strong face with his eagle-like nose and big brown eyes with their bushy eyebrows. She once had those eyes looking deeply into her soul. His long black hair was always braided into a ponytail, and one time she had run her fingers along the full length of his hair. His lips full and yet taut always managed to please her and had driven her out of her mind with wanting him closer to her. His broad shoulders and his thighs, as strong and muscled as they were, had felt so gentle against hers.

But that had been ages ago. She was over the infatuation she had for him, or was she? Remembering how he seduced her into his arms, she knew that the attraction didn't end there. He could be the most sensitive man while at the same time he could be cold and uncaring. He had earned his respect from the town years ago. Although he had come from a sheltered past, a colored one at that, it hadn't made its mark upon him. He lived life as he loved, free and without reservations. He only fought when he had to, but he could love whenever he wanted. He always said that was what attracted the women to him. She had seen him in action both in the workplace and out. He was the most endearing man she had ever been in love with.

For the life of her, she couldn't fathom why he never asked her to marry him even when they had slept together and she knew about his past. When she became damaged goods, he had still refused to marry her. Freddie had made it clear to her that he loved her but was not going to be controlled by a woman who cared more about her reputation than about herself or those she claimed to love.

He did support her in what she decided to do with her life. He had told her that her life was her risk to take, to do with as she pleased. She knew that their passion would never bind them into a life where they would have to live a complicated life as man and woman, married 'til death parted them. They both did what they wanted. They were free-spirited, independent, and stubborn. They both wanted to keep it that way. They were suited for each other; that much she knew. It was too bad that things had not worked out the way she wanted them to.

Shaking her head and noticing that Freddie was standing in front of her, looking up she saw how close they had become. All she had to do was lean up and she would have his lips on hers.

Freddie gazed at Bertha, seeing her feelings in her eyes. Clearing his throat, he moved a step back and asked her, "Want to get back to the business at hand?"

"Okay," came the hoarse reply. Politely clearing her throat and moving past him to the chair, she gingerly sat down and motioned for him to sit in the chair facing hers. "Okay," she repeated. "What are you not telling me?"

Sitting down across from her, he continued to look at her, taking in her features. He remembered when they had first met. It was the day she had run away from her first husband after finding out he had been cheating on her. Bertha had accidentally bumped into him in the alley, and they both toppled down. Freddie had landed on top of Bertha and thought she was the most beautiful woman he had ever seen when he managed to see. He noticed she had been crying; her eyes were red and puffy. She was still sniffling, and Freddie was drawn to her lips, red as a rose and very enticing. He felt her soft figure under him, and he was instantly turned on. She looked at him and did not say a word as he captured her lips in a kiss.

"Freddie, wake up!"

Jarred back to the present, Freddie shook his head, cleared his mind of the memories he held dear to him, and responded to the previous question.

"Fine. Julli's life was at stake. A threat almost became a tragedy as she almost died. Colin could not stand to see his daughter tortured so they decided to send her here to be out of danger. It was the only option and as hard as it was for them to send her away, it was the best decision for all concerned."

"How did Julli almost die?" came the shocked and quiet voice from Bertha. She leaned forward in her chair, enraged that a member of her family had been harmed.

He sighed deeply before he responded. "Someone put poison in Julli's drink a few months ago at a church picnic. There was a big panic and a lot of people were upset about it. Colin started accusing nearly everyone he could think of. Fortunately, the doctor was at the picnic and was able to flush the poison out of her body just in time. After that Brionna just kept Julli at home and pretty much kept her confined. They still hadn't found out who did it when we left on the carriage. I am hoping that they will have it all taken care of soon."

"Oh my grief!" She slammed her fan onto her lap and winced at the pain she inflicted on herself. "Who would do that to a child? I mean she is no threat to anyone," Bertha whispered in an outraged tone.

"Looks like you forgot that Colin is putting the land in Julli's name. So as long as the land is owned, they will go after whoever owns it," reasoned Freddie. "And the land has a lot to offer. The area has lots of grazing spots, good watering holes and is very fertile. They were able to have a good harvest and Brionna stocked up on canned goods. They also made a good profit selling their vegetables. The land itself could feed a family for generations. Also plenty of wood too, for warmth and cooking. Nothing there to lack for."

"So they were doing pretty good out there?" questioned Bertha, not sure if she believed that Brionna and them were doing as well as Freddie claimed they were.

"It was hard but they made it," he added smugly, patting down his vest and adjusting the small string tie he wore for this occasion.

"How did they do it?" Bertha asked, knowing that Brionna was a hard worker, but too much work would take too long, and it had only been almost five years. She remembered that it took her nearly fourteen years to get her plantation up and going the way it was now.

"Colin would work long hours, and Brionna helped as much as she could. Sometimes neighbors would come out and help. They always helped each other out there."

"What about Julli?" Gesturing to the kitchen door, Bertha was beginning to wonder if it was the fact Julli was treated badly, which would explain why they sent her to Bertha. Or they were too busy that they could not take care of her.

"Sometimes they had her with them and Brionna would have to take several breaks from working to care for her, while other times the neighbors had other kids to help watch. Most of the time it was the grandparents who took care of the kids so the parents could work and get stuff done that was needed."

"How was Julli treated?" Bertha smugly thought she was on the right track about Julli being mistreated.

"They all thought she was a good kid and didn't seem to mind that she couldn't hear." At what Freddie admitted, Bertha thought she had better stop with the wayward questions she was thinking because it was as if Freddie could read her mind.

"How much land does Colin have?" queried Bertha. She doubted Colin would have as much as she had accumulated the past few years.

"I don't rightly know. But what I can tell you is it is a lot." Freddie looked toward the kitchen door and sighed. "Like I said, they did not lack for much."

"So what did Brionna do?" Knowing the answer to the question, Bertha just wanted to hear what Freddie had to say. It had been years, and people could change.

"Brionna had two big gardens on the sides of the house," was all Freddie said.

"What about livestock?" with that, Bertha shuddered. She hated all sorts of animals. She didn't mind eating the meat now and then, but she refused to look at an animal and view it as a pet or something to eat after she saw it alive.

"Ha-ha, funny you should ask. Let's see." In deep thought, Freddie scratched his cheek. "I would say around a hundred or so cattle, not counting pigs, sheep, goats, chickens, and other animals as well."

"Yuck! That is quite a bit." Bertha shuddered.

"Colin is a busy guy. Brionna was also out feeding the men who came to help and get some food for their families as well."

"What about mining? Or is it all cattle?" She was not too overly concerned how they were getting their means; she just wanted to know what it was that kept Colin and Brionna afloat.

"There was no mention in the area about gold or any gems. Pretty much the talk was about cattle and growing food," Freddie stated to Bertha's disgust.

"I see, so they are pretty much set out there," stated Bertha, now knowing that her sister was provided for.

"Yes, pretty much," Freddie admitted, shrugging his shoulders in the way Bertha knew he would do when he was right.

"What if they don't have any more heirs? I mean Julli isn't capable of doing much." Bertha avoided Freddie's gaze as she went on. "People don't tend to handle it well when there is no man to be in charge of things. No one is going to believe that she can be the owner of some land and take care of it." Still avoiding him, she turned to look at the lamp on the table before replying with, "She is too young and with her being, well, a deaf and dumb female." Bertha glanced at Freddie, seeing his face twist in anger at what she had just said.

"You don't know Julli well enough to condemn her!" Freddie snapped, getting riled at Bertha's twisted thinking. It sure was not the way she was raised. That much Freddie knew.

"How dare you talk to me that way!" Bertha snapped back.

"I dare and you know it," muttered Freddie under his breath while giving Bertha a scowl. "I know your niece very well. She is an extremely bright girl. She is special. You would do well to hold your tongue."

Bertha eyed Freddie, as she decided whether or not to give in to his threat. "That remains to be seen. Brionna could have been exaggerating. Playing on my feelings to keep her pathetic little child. And you are not helping matters any."

Now enraged, Freddie got up and went over to Bertha. Grabbing her by the arms and hauling her to her feet, he snarled in her face.

"Watch your mouth, Bertha, I won't stand for that," he snapped, giving her a firm shake.

"Oh, always sticking up for the dumb and unfortunate. It is not that I am against her being a female, after all I am one too," Bertha hissed through her clenched teeth. "Why don't you just take her and be away from here? It is enough to know that society doesn't place well on the less fortunate."

Releasing his hold on her and turning away, he shook his head, and when he glanced back, he could see her rubbing her arms.

"Bertha, I am sorry." He swallowed, sighed, and rubbed his face in his hands. He needed to control himself around her. She made it easy for him to conduct himself improperly. "It is just that I have so much love for Julli and I don't like it when people, even you, put her down," replied Freddie. Then he added, "Brionna wants her here. You wouldn't turn your back on your own flesh and blood?"

Wanting to get back at him, she played on his sympathy. "Yes, I would."

Fighting back, Freddie accused her, "Like you did to Brionna and Colin when they got married?" Seeing Bertha's face glaze over, he knew he hit a sorry spot in her life. "When they asked for help and you were married to Timothy, you turned your back on them and they lost everything they owned." Not willing to give her the upper hand, he added, "Even when they moved to America before you?"

Not shocked that he would know about something like that, but just that he would bring it up. She sat down on the footstool and asked, "How did you know?" Then before he could answer her, she said, "Never mind. Brionna must have told you. What an idiot. But anyway, she wasn't dumb, just young and stupid. It's not like she is anything like her child who is deaf and dumb."

"You are the most infuriating and obnoxious woman I have ever met. At least Brionna isn't like you." Oddly enough, they were alike in so many ways, just not through looks or tempers. But definitely not in the way they judged people. Brionna was gentle and kept her opinions to herself 'til she got to know someone better, while Bertha would let the person know right at that moment, respectful or not.

"That is not fair," snapped Bertha through clenched teeth.

"Isn't it? Everything Brionna did you had to do better. Oh, you really gave her a run for her money years ago, didn't you?" commented Freddie.

"Well, I got myself here, didn't I?" Shrugging her shoulders, she stood up and kept her posture even though the heated glare from Freddie would have made men cower before it.

"And Brionna hasn't?"

"No, she ran off and decided to take the hard way," replied Bertha, not willing to put herself down beneath her sister.

"Which was what?" asked Freddie, incredulously piqued.

"Marrying Colin and letting him drag her all the way out there," stated Bertha, wanting to make herself seem better than her sister. At least Bertha had all she wanted and didn't have to work hard for what she got.

"At least she is happy," stated Freddie with conviction.

"Happy?" asked Bertha, wondering what that had to do with working hard, being dragged from your only family, and put to work to make provisions for a child.

"She has a wonderful husband, a beautiful child and she is well provided for."

"A deaf and dumb child," retorted Bertha.

"Maybe you should have been the deaf and dumb—!" Catching himself with that phrase, he admonished Bertha, "No, make that the dumb one."

"I made the right choices," replied Bertha, defending herself. Adding, "I married and here I am well-off."

"No wonder you are a widow thrice times," Freddie retorted angrily.

Flinching at the remark, she replied, "How rude!"

"Darn right," came the answer from Freddie.

Looking at him, Bertha came to a sudden realization that they were arguing about something that was a family situation, and Freddie was not family. He was just a good friend to both sisters.

She winced as she re-rubbed her arms where Freddie had previously grabbed her. "Okay. Please accept my apologies and continue," she suggested, hostilely glaring daggers at him.

Hearing Julli laughing in the kitchen, Freddie smiled before turning to face Bertha once again.

"Was that all that happened?" she asked when he looked at her. She too had heard Julli laughing in the next room. She liked it when Freddie smiled. Bertha hoped that the child would keep laughing, as it lightened up the tension that was between her and Freddie.

"No. Brionna nearly got killed too. Someone shot at her horse when she was out riding. The horse nearly threw Brionna off a cliff. It happened just three miles from the house. It was a good thing I was around when it happened," said Freddie.

"How awful!" Bertha, forgetting the past with her sister, jumped to her feet, knowing that no matter what happened, she would always be there to protect Brionna. "Then I think that they had better forget it all and come here. You'll need to go get them," stated Bertha, disturbed that there were people who wanted to kill her little sister.

"I can't." Freddie closed his eyes and shook his head.

"What do you mean you can't?" Bertha asked, confused.

"My duty is to stay with Julli and keep her safe. I cannot leave her to go to them and they will not leave. Colin may send Brionna here but I doubt she will leave her husband. I get this feeling that she will stay and fight, even if she or Colin dies." Freddie shrugged. "And I am needed here."

"Then you are a fool. I will get someone to go get them," taunted Bertha, upset that for once Freddie refused to do her bidding.

"Better to be a fool alive than a dead one," answered Freddie, undaunted by Bertha's remark.

"It's a stupid choice. I am sure that they will come when they find out I have no other choice than to put Julli into an orphanage," threatened Bertha, sure that she would get her way and Freddie wouldn't stand against her since Julli was her niece.

"It's their decision. As long as Julli is alive and well, they will not leave until this whole thing is over with." He grabbed

Bertha's arms and gave her a little shake. "Nothing will make them come here and nothing you do to me or Julli will make me go after them. I will stay and do my duty as I have been asked by them to do. Listen to me, I know that they are in danger. I was there with them and I know what is going on. Don't make a decision that you will end up regretting," stated Freddie, still standing his ground.

"Very irresponsible, if you ask me," retorted Bertha sarcastically.

"I didn't!" came out a biting remark, followed as sarcastically as she had been. "Ha-ha!" he had to add at the surprised yet angry look on her face.

"Stop it!" hissed Bertha, now riled that she could not get her way. "You are making me mad and I am tempted to have you thrown out of here." Shaking her head at him, she dared him, "Do not make me do that."

"Don't worry, Bertha, I know my way out of here," responded Freddie, still taunting her.

"And take that thing with you when you go." Bertha threw a bone using Julli as bait.

"What?" he thundered at Bertha. Going over to her and clenching his hands into fists, he thought better of how Julli would react knowing he hit a woman. Bertha was impossible. *Poor Julli having an aunt like her*, he thought to himself, wishing the situation would go better, or he could end up hitting Bertha.

"Okay, have it your way. I will let them know that you rejected their most prized possession. And I pity you. No, I pity any child that you would ever claim to have you for a mother." With that hurtful remark, Bertha came to the realization that he knew she had lost a baby, his and hers.

"Freddie, don't do this," begged Bertha, near tears.

Freddie took a look at Bertha and saw the tears. His anger at her about Julli lessened some to where he could focus on another matter.

"Why didn't you send word for me?" he asked, not giving in. Hurt seeped in his voice, and Bertha heard it.

"So you know?" was all she quietly said.

"Yes," answered Freddie. "I had hoped that you would have told me. I would have been here by your side."

Again came the giggling from Julli. They both turned to look at the hallway leading to the kitchen. Their conversation had been put on hold. Bertha was not used to the sound of a child giggling, especially in her own home. Bertha saw Freddie studying his hands, avoiding her gaze. She knew that she should have told him she was pregnant. But she was afraid that Freddie would have only assumed that she was trying to tie him to her. She never thought that maybe he actually wanted a child. Bertha had not been able to carry past her sixth month. She had woken up in the middle of the night, crying in pain.

The doctor had been sent for, and when he came, it was too late. The baby was stillborn. A little girl with dark skin, black hair, and huge eyelashes that framed blue eyes. She had not been able to hold her in her arms. There was a small service, and Bertha attended the funeral of her daughter. She had named her Freda Maire Mearse-Tahney. Bertha had regretted not letting Freddie know, but she was shamed that she lost a baby that they created. That was the sound they were never going to have on their own. Not even with each other.

Bertha realized that Freddie really loved her niece and would do anything for her. *If neither of us are going to have any kids, the next best thing would be to take care of my niece*, thought Bertha. Even though the thought of all the ridicule was a lot to bear, it would be something to think about. *Maybe not everyone is the same.* With that she looked at Freddie, hope glimmering in her eyes as she asked him, "What do you suggest I do about Julli?"

"I can't tell you what to do. I can only suggest you think about keeping your niece." Adding, "All I know is she is the only one in your family besides you, Brionna and Colin." Freddie was afraid Bertha would make the wrong choice again.

"But they are going to come and get her, right?" she stated, and with that, she got up and walked over to the window. Parting them, then closing them, changing her mind as the view was not pleasing at the moment.

"As far as I know or you send her back when they ask." Freddie walked over to her and put his hands on her shoulders, gently rubbing them.

"But it won't be forever?" Bertha asked, afraid.

"Not as far as I know," admitted Freddie with concern in his voice. He glanced down and took in the gentle curve of Bertha's shoulder.

Bertha, turning her head toward Freddie, admitted, "I am not sure I can do this."

"Why not? Consider it one of your hobbies," was the only reply to that.

"It won't be the same thing."

"I don't see how not." At that moment, Freddie removed his hands and wiped his eyes. "Gee, this woman will never change," he muttered under his breath.

Bertha sighed and responded with, "She will cost money. I only have a certain amount every month."

"Like I said that won't be a problem. I have stuff to take to the bank tomorrow and deposit into your account." At Bertha's nod, he added, only to rile some feathers, "Is it just the money or the fact that she is less fortunate than you and it will hurt your standing in society?"

"What do you mean?" Now riled, Bertha turned to face him.

"Can you see yourself going around parading a deaf little girl everywhere you go?" asked Freddie, trying to picture Bertha holding the hand of a child.

"Yes and no. It will be hard. I have high standards to keep. People will gossip and you know how I hate gossip."

"The same standards that cost us a baby?" quietly spoken by Freddie, still not over the news of their loss.

"That is not the same thing. This is my sister's baby."

She arched her shoulders and groaned when she felt the tension in her muscles. Freddie, hearing her groan, could not feel any anger, just compassion. This was a long day.

Bertha reached into her pocket and pulled out her hankie, which she then proceeded to blow her nose with. Freddie came over and put his hands on her back and gently began to massage it, all the while saying, "Why don't you take a deep breath and think about this later?"

Bertha, enjoying the massage, could only nod for within a minute or so there came a high, piercing laugh from the kitchen.

"What in the world?" Bertha fidgeted, not used to the sound. It had hurt her ears, and when she looked at Freddie, she saw that he was only smiling.

"Don't worry. That was only Julli having fun."

"But that was loud. Too loud," she said, covering her ears, worried that the neighbors would call the constable and she would have to deal with more rumors. She was not in the mood for it.

"Is she normally this loud?" asked Bertha, raising her eyebrow. She took her hands off of her ears when the noise subsided.

Guffawing, Freddie admitted, "No, she normally is louder than this."

Bertha's eyes widened at the mention of that, and all she could say was, "You're joking, right?"

Freddie shook his head, secretly laughing inside before adding, "Don't worry too much about it. Once she settles in you won't notice her." Was that an understatement. He didn't want Bertha to worry too much. In fact he did not want her to tell them they had to leave because she could not handle a noisy child in her home. And noisy Julli was.

"She is a good girl you say, so why would she be loud?" asked Bertha, trying to figure out why a child would be noisy like that, especially in another person's home.

"It has been a long day. So if you would ignore that for now and let me deal with her, I would appreciate it."

At Bertha's nod, he bowed to her and took a step back.

Trying to ease some worrying about Julli, he asked, changing the subject to one he had never talked to her about, "Is it so hard for you to remember how you used to be? The reason I fell in love with you?" At Bertha's stunned look, he shrugged his shoulders and said, "Thought so." Sighing, his shoulders slumped, and not looking at Bertha, he said, "Okay, well if madame has nothing else to speak with me about, I will go see to the child." Freddie bowed and with that turned to leave.

"Wait!" Bertha called out.

Turning to look at her, he saw that she was hurting as much as he was. The look on her face told all.

"Wait for what?" he asked. Adding, "I am tired of waiting." Knowing that he would not get a direct response to his question from her, as he could see it on her face.

"Freddie, you don't have to be this way," Bertha finally stated, not willing to admit defeat in any way. She hated the fact that Freddie knew her so well. But on the other hand she hated the fact that when he knew her, he knew what to do to help her. This was not one of those times.

With a look of amazement, Freddie just stared at her.

"Wow!" was all he choked out. He looked incredulously at Bertha, wondering why people say that the more time people were apart, the better they got along. It sure was not the case this time.

Bertha sighs and replies, "No, I haven't forgotten why you fell in love with me." Then she adds defensively, "But times have changed and so have I." Bertha did not want Freddie to know the whole truth. She did not mind saying a little white lie, but the timing was not right.

"You used to be fun. Now you are all businesslike, so prim and proper," admitted Freddie, revealing his feelings. "It is hard to have fun with you anymore."

Shocked, Bertha opened her mouth to defend herself, but the look of despair on Freddie's face stopped her.

"You are never around."

"Neither were you. It was always your call to serve society as the 'belle.' You did not have time for anyone, especially for us."

Bertha, not wanting Freddie to have the last say or to leave, walked over to him, not seeing anything but the man in front of her. Standing in front of him, she gently took his face in her hands. She raised on her tiptoes, and Freddie's arms made their way around her waist. Slowly they both leaned toward each other and kissed.

CHAPTER 4

―――――◆◆◆◆―――――

Screaming like Banshees

Just at that moment, Julli came sauntering into the room. Walking over to Freddie, she tugged on his pant for attention. When he kept ignoring her, she finally let out a wail, "Wah wah!" which caused Bertha to jump and pull away from Freddie's embrace.

Freddie looked down at Julli and noticed that she had a milk mustache. Pointing at her and laughing, he beckoned for Bertha to look. Bertha looked down at Julli, and when she saw what he was laughing at, she didn't think it was too funny, especially when Julli had a confused look on her face.

Still laughing at her, Freddie pointed to his lips, made the sign for a mustache by pointing to his face, and got into the process of milking a cow. Julli giggled and wiped her lips.

"She is kind of cute. She really does look like Brionna," came a quiet voice. The conversation that had happened just moments ago was forgotten.

"Yes, a beauty." Looking appraisingly at Bertha, he continued, "It runs in the family."

Bertha, blushing, shushed Freddie.

"Who is she?" came a small, squeaky voice, nasally but clear enough.

"She can talk," came the shocked voice of Bertha.

"Yes, she can talk," mimicked Freddie, taking comfort in Bertha's uneasiness. "Like Brionna wrote she could hear before she got sick, so yeah, she can talk, somewhat. Didn't Brionna refer to her as a chatterbox?"

"Yes, she did mention something of that sort," confirmed Bertha, now uneasy that she thought her family was playing a prank on her.

"Now she is a signing chatterbox." Freddie laughed, making the signs of a puppeteer talking. Julli giggled at that and nodded her head.

Looking at Julli, who was now hiding behind Freddie's leg, Bertha asked, "Can she hear at all?"

Narrowing his eyes and pondering the question, Freddie answered, "I seriously doubt it. She never flinched when we went shooting. She hardly ever moves at loud noises."

Confused, Bertha shook her head. "Then how does she know what you are saying?"

"We use signs. We pretty much use a lot of body language. Everyone has their own way of using their hands to communicate but we all have some of the same signs like 'eat' and 'time.' Some people blow kisses as a sign that they love someone. This is not that much different." Freddie made a show of giving Bertha an example by putting his hand up to his mouth and pretending to chew his food.

"Oh, I see," responded Bertha, intrigued at the idea. "You said 'eat,' right?"

"Very good," Freddie acknowledged Bertha. "She may not be able to hear but she is very smart. She uses her mind and can pretty much pick up what you are trying to say. She also looks at your mouth when you talk to her and it is one way she can get an idea of what you are saying. Ask me a question to ask her to see what she says. I won't use my voice or move my mouth," said Freddie, determined to show Bertha just how well Julli could understand him.

"You aren't making much sense," said Bertha, shrugging her shoulders. "I still don't see how she could possibly understand what you are saying to her by just signing."

"Ask me a question," encouraged Freddie, looking at her.

"Okay, umm, what is her favorite food?" asked Bertha, unconvinced.

"Watch." Freddie started signing to Julli as he said he would, without moving his mouth or making any noise.

"Julli, she wants to know what your favorite food is. Can you sign your favorite food to her?" asked Freddie without speaking, just moving his hands. He pointed to Bertha, then to Julli, and shrugged his shoulders, then proceeded to make the eating motion.

While Freddie was signing the question to Julli, Bertha watched as he moved his hands and noticed that some of it she could pick up on. Maybe it wouldn't be so bad after all.

Watching while Julli enthusiastically signed back to Freddie, she noticed that the little girl did indeed seem to understand what Freddie asked her.

"She says pancakes with blueberries is her favorite food and is sad that we couldn't find any in the kitchen," said Freddie with pride in his voice when Julli stopped signing. Bertha had picked up some subtle gestures from Julli, such as "kitchen" when Julli pointed to the room. She did catch the pancake motion, watching Julli pretend to flip and cook.

"Oh, I am sorry. I didn't know." Bertha was thrilled that Julli liked blueberries since it was her favorite fruit, but she did not care for pancakes. She had not caught or understood the picking of something and popping in the mouth that Julli had used for blueberries.

"Does any of this satisfy, madame?" came the question.

"Um, somewhat. Will she understand anyone besides you?" asked Bertha, uncertain of whether or not Freddie and Julli had set it up in a way.

"Well, only one way to find out. Care to give it a try?" asked Freddie.

"You mean I am to ask her something?" dumbfounded, Bertha asked.

"I thought you wanted to find out if she could understand you or not," said Freddie, shrugging.

Looking at Julli, who was staring at her with those blue eyes, Bertha thought that she had better keep asking and find out herself so that way she could have something to look forward to if she decided to keep Brionna's daughter for a while.

"Okay. Here goes. No voice and no moving my mouth," answered Bertha, now willing to give it a try.

Looking at Julli, she decided that the child might respond better if she was at the little girl's level, so kneeling down on her knees in front of the child, she got ready to ask her question. Taking a deep breath and thinking how to ask her. An idea came, and she thought that she would be able to thwart their plans of embarrassing her.

"What time does the clock tell?" Bertha asked, shrugging her shoulders at the word "what" and looking around, then pointed to the clock for the word "time."

Julli stared at her, not sure what to do first. Then to Bertha's amazement, the little girl seemed to get an idea of what Bertha asked her by looking around, and once she found the grandfather clock, she squinted her eyes at it as if in deep thought. Bertha saw her counting the numbers, and her eyes widened when Julli turned to her and signed at the same time she told Bertha, "Three o'clock on the big clock."

Bertha stared at Julli, taking in the proud look she had on her face, then at Freddie, who had some tears in his eyes. Bertha felt some tears forming in her eyes, and she rapidly blinked them away. She also got the feeling that this was something unusual even for Julli and Freddie by the way they acted. For a little girl not yet four years of age, that showed some maturity. Freddie got down on his knees next to Bertha and pulled Julli into a big hug.

"You wonderful little girl," she heard him say to Julli.

Bertha finally realized that she had judged her niece harshly. "But people who are deaf and dumb are not fit members of society. Everyone knows that."

"But what you saw right now, not all people are that way. Brionna and Colin accepted her for who she was, not the fact that she could not hear."

"Maybe. But will she always be deaf and dumb?" asked Bertha, not just worried about her reputation, but that of Freddie's as well. She had no knowledge of people who were considered to be like that. Most were locked in an institution or hidden from everyone's view.

"Probably, but stop with the dumb, it isn't fair to her," remarked Freddie, annoyed that Bertha kept thinking about herself and society. *Would she ever change and be who she used to be?*

"She knew the time, and she could talk," admitted Bertha quietly.

"Is that proof enough that she is smart?" asked Freddie, still hugging the little form.

"Yes," was the only audible reply from the still-amazed Bertha.

Freddie let Julli go only to stare into Bertha's eyes as he realized that she was a part of something special between the two of them, Freddie and Julli. Bertha knew that she had witnessed something that made Julli at her age very special as well as smart. She started shaking her head, then stopped when Freddie grabbed her hand and whispered, "It's okay."

Julli, upset at now getting ignored for a minute or two, tugged on Freddie's jacket and asked a question, "Who is she?" Julli had been taught to use her voice no matter if she could talk or not. She signed along with what she said. She looked at Bertha with wonder at how pretty she was and also how tall she could be. Julli thought Bertha was scary.

"This is your aunt. She is the lady we were talking about on the carriage. Do you remember?" signed Freddie, looking at Julli.

"Yes," was the only sign, along with a nod of her head. Julli glanced at Bertha, then back at Freddie, who was tapping her hand, still talking and signing to her.

"Her name is Aunt Bertha. Show me the *A* and the *B*," instructed Freddie. Watching as Julliannyia proceeded to show him the *A* and *B*, Bertha wondered just what else the little girl was capable of doing. After Julli showed him, he nodded his head and continued.

"Yes, always use the *A* on your chin and the *B* on your shoulder." Freddie demonstrated by pointing to Bertha.

"She looks mean," came an uneasy signing from the little girl.

"Yes, she is mean. She needs someone to warm up her heart." Freddie snickered while signing to Julli.

"I do not!" hissed Bertha, shocked that Freddie was encouraging Julli's belief that she was mean.

"Yes, Aunt Bertha is mean," came the small voice, with fast-moving hands.

Nodding his head in agreement, Freddie signed to her, "She may seem mean, and do you think she bites?"

"Freddie, stop it now!" thundered Bertha at Freddie when she saw the frightened look on her niece's face. She quickly calmed herself down and smiled stiffly.

"All right," said Freddie, laughing. Looking at Julli and seeing that she looked scared of her aunt. "Julli, let's show Aunt Bertha how banshees scream," suggested Freddie, trying to calm the frightened child.

At Julli's nod and huge grin, they started the game. Freddie started out by roaring at Julli and making Bertha scream, "Ahhh!"

Bertha's hands flew to her chest, knowing her heart was beating fast. Hearing Julli laugh, Freddie looked toward her aunt and charged after Julli instead, using his fingers on his head as horns, roaring the whole time. Bertha was yelling at Freddie to stop.

"Stop, Freddie!"

Roaring, Freddie told her, "Come on, you know this game."

Julli ran behind the chair, trying to put something between them. Freddie swerved around the chair, but not finding Julli as she had slid under. Bertha yelled at Freddie again to stop.

Freddie looked at Bertha and roared again, making her flinch. Julli got up from under the chair and ran to Bertha, only to hide behind the startled form of her aunt. Giggling, Julli peeks out, and seeing that Freddie could not find her, she takes off running toward him. As she got closer, she let out a bloodcurdling scream, making Freddie jump. Bertha groaned when she realized that once the banshee game started, it was hard to end it.

Freddie started to turn after her. Julli ran back toward her aunt, who sidestepped, and when Julli turned around to go back to her aunt, she ran into Freddie and knocked the breath out of him. He fell to the floor curled up in a ball, groaning and holding his midsection. Bertha yelled Freddie's name over the screaming of the child. She ran to him and knelt down in front of him. She started shaking him, then realized that he was not hurt at all.

Julli then decided that she was going to go after her aunt, so she started screaming again, making Bertha jump. Bertha screamed as she saw Julli coming at her and went into the arms of Freddie, who had gotten up and was laughing. The next thing Bertha knew was that she was lying under Freddie, who was pretending to protect her from the screaming child, who was now standing on the cushions. All three of them looked back and forth at each other.

Julli screamed at the same time Freddie roared, making Bertha join in by screaming her head off at them to stop it. Julli took off running, and Freddie was up and after her in a matter of seconds. Bertha lay there catching her breath.

"Freddie, stop her. We are in town and my neighbors are not used to this kind of noise," said Bertha loudly, which Freddie just ignored.

After Bertha got up to her feet, she realized that she was to see Freddie charging after Julli, who was running directly to her. Bertha decided that she could either run or stand her ground. After all, it was her home, not theirs. She was now remembering the game they had played so many years ago, so she pulled up her skirts and grabbed Julli's hand. They both ran toward the door, only to be blocked by Freddie, making them scream again. At the same time, Freddie ends up laughing hard that he starts coughing from lack of air. However, Freddie, and not even Bertha or Julli, was about to let the game end.

The now-determined woman got ready to stand her ground and get even somehow. Bertha keeps her eyes on Freddie while she nudges Julli to get behind her. Now caught up in the game, Bertha lets go of her skirts to stomp her feet and let out a feeble roar, until Julli does the same, and the volume of both of them increases. Ashes from the fireplace start flying with the motion of her full skirts swaying. Freddie watching them starts to laugh harder.

The four maids came running into the room, only to have a crazed man roar behind them, making them all scream and run over to Bertha with their hands fluttering in the air.

"Ahhh!" they screamed in unison.

Mauricia grabbed the vase by the bookshelf as Taylor grabbed her skirts and scrambled onto the small table in the corner. Paula and Nicole, both jumping on the love seat, were begging for their lives.

They were not aware that it was only a game. Panic filled them, and they watched Freddie scream. They were about to throw whatever they could to protect Bertha and themselves if need be. Bertha and Julli watch in amusement and start laughing at how funny things had gotten. Freddie, not being able to handle it anymore, doubled over in laughter.

Peters, the handyman, had watched the whole thing from the stairs and had an idea of what was going on. At the risk of being taken and resold as a slave for leaving his work, he put down his tools quietly and walked over to the doors. He snuck into the room behind Freddie. The women were silenced by Peters when he put his finger to his lips. Now with things being quieter somehow, Freddie stops laughing and slowly gets up, looking at the women. They had a hushed look on their faces. The hair on the back of his neck stood out, his eyes widened, and Freddie slowly turned around to see what had shushed them. Fearing the worst, he came face-to-face with nothing there.

Bertha laughs, and Freddie jerks around again to see what the problem was. After seeing her smile, Freddie sighs, thinking that they did that to get him to stop the game. Looking around quickly and not seeing anything, he mutters, "I've been duped."

He turns to sit in the chair, only to have someone tap him on the shoulder. When he turned around, Peters jumped up from his knees and roared into his face. Freddie let out a scream and toppled backward over the low-cut table, putting up his fists. Freddie stayed on his knees and, breathing heavily, saw it was only the handyman.

The maids stopped screaming when Freddie posed no threat, and Julli laughed out loud. Bertha laughs loudly, and Peters runs around Freddie to stand laughing in front of the women. Looking at each other, Bertha, Freddie, and Peters smiled between bouts of laughter.

Julli, wanting to get even with the tall stranger for scaring her friend, goes up to Peters, and when he looks down at her, she lets out a crazed wail and jerks her body every which way, making Peters scream. He takes several steps back, bumping the table and candles onto the floor. The women watching start screaming again; even Bertha got caught up in the screaming action.

"Peters, what are you doing?"

Freddie watching it all just sits there laughing. Bertha walking over to Julli takes her hand, and they walk over to Freddie. Freddie gets up and hoists Julli onto his back for a piggyback ride, but before he walks off with her, Bertha grabs his arm and shakes her head.

Julli got the idea that the game was over the way her aunt stopped Freddie, but Julli was too caught up in the moment to stop. She beckoned her aunt over, only to scream in her face.

"Rawr!"

Bertha screams and topples over backward, landing flat on her bottom. The maids scream again as they watch their mistress fall down. Freddie dumps Julli onto the couch and goes over to help Bertha.

Peters, now ticked off that someone had gotten the best of him, is determined to go after Julli. He slithered behind the couch over to the front, where Julli was, and jumped up out in front of her, roaring. Julli screams, swinging her arms out. Paula screams as well. Taylor grabs Nicole, and they topple over the chair. Bertha tries to get up but is brought back down onto her behind after Freddie, in his hurry, had stepped on her skirt, ripping the material. She screams at him, and Mauricia yells at Peters.

"Freddie, you ruined my dress!"

"Peters, you idiot of a man, stop it right now!"

Freddie now knowing his mistake runs over to Julli, only to be grabbed by Peters, who was hiding behind the couch, planning on getting the girl to scream again. Both men roar, Freddie out of being scared, and Peters slips and falls on his bottom, letting out a loud fart. The women distastefully yelled, "Ew!" and Julli could only laugh at the funny expressions they had on.

Bertha, finally getting up with the help of the maids, is soon back on her behind as Freddie accidentally bumps into one of the women who was trying to help her mistress up and sets them off all screaming again. No one dared to move.

After a few moments, they manage to calm themselves somewhat to take a few deep breaths and stifle an occasional giggle at how silly they must have been. Looking at each other, they all came to the realization that nothing serious had happened and that somehow the game that Freddie and Julli had started had gotten out of control.

"Madame, what in the world?" asked Mauricia, dumbstruck. Never in her life had she seen her mistress laugh out loud or run around. Bertha was always so calm and poised.

"Don't worry, it was just a game that Freddie and Julli were playing," admitted Bertha stoically. She looked at each of the servants and sighed gladly that they were all loyal servants and no one had gotten hurt.

Things take a turn for the worse when they hear a noise from the hall. All except Julli.

Julli watches as they froze up and glanced at the hallway. Curiosity got the better of her, and she walked over to the hall before anyone could stop her. Opening a door to look, she went out to see what could have made them stop playing the game.

A second later, she let out a scream, "Ahhh!" as she saw a black shadow go by her feet. Hearing the child scream, the maids started to scream themselves. Peters hid behind the curtains as best he could despite his bulky figure. Mauricia picked up the vase again, this time ready to throw it. The rest of them huddled together in the corner, not sure what to do. Bertha had no idea if someone was going to join in the game or if it was something different entirely. Freddie silenced them by putting up his hand and picking up the coat rack from the floor. He crept closer to the doors.

Just as he was about to open them, they were flung open by a huge walking cat. Bertha screamed at the sight, making the cat hiss and jump from Julli's arms onto Freddie, who threw down the weapon he had. Freddie's scream was muted with the cat on his head. He reached up and tried to get the vicious cat off his face. Finally getting it off of him, he tossed it when it hissed in his face.

The black fur ball went sailing into the air, only to land on the curtains where Peters was hiding. A roar came from him as he struggled to get the thing off of the curtains. The cat was clawing, hissing, and tearing into the material. Mauricia threw the vase at the cat, only to hit Peters in the face with it when the cat moved down.

Paula and Nicole just kept screaming repeatedly 'til Bertha went over and slapped them both. She did not know who could scream the loudest, the servants or Julli, but her ears were ringing already. Taylor grabbed as many books as she could and started throwing them as the cat let go of the curtains. At that moment, Freddie went over there to grab the cat the same time Taylor threw a book. One of them hit Freddie in the chest, and he howled in pain.

"Ouch!"

Everybody started yelling, and the commotion started all over again.

Julli, running back into the living room wanting to get to Freddie, slipped on the rug and went sailing in the air. Seeing the little child go up and then down set them all off screaming over again, and she landed on a big pile of ashes in the huge fireplace. The ashes went all over the room. It became quiet for a minute.

The cat finally went out of the doorway, and Taylor went after it. Peters started moaning, and Mauricia ran over to him, wiping his face with the hem of her apron. Nicole and Paula both sank down on the floor in a heap. Both Bertha and Freddie, out of breath, glanced around the room, now in a complete disarray.

The doors banged open as the constable came stomping into the house, waving his baton and his hand on his holster. Taking in the complete mess, his eyes widened as he surveyed what could have happened there.

"Are you folks all right? Madame?" he questioned, looking at Bertha.

"Yes, we are. Thank you, Officer, for coming," responded Bertha as authoritatively as she could sound.

Freddie started snickering, and the maids started to giggle. Peters kept moaning even with Mauricia cleaning up his wound.

"Were you folks attacked?" asked a neighbor, poking her head through the doorway.

"Uh um," was all Bertha could say before she was interrupted by Taylor.

"Oh yeah, we were. A big black cat," came the singsong voice from Taylor, who had managed to catch the cat. It was purring in her arms.

"Taylor, how did you—? Never mind!" Freddie shook his head, clearing his mind. He glanced at Taylor, confused. Paula and Nicole only shook their heads when Freddie glanced at them.

"Oh, isn't he a big fellow?" Taylor asked everyone.

"Is that your cat?" asked Freddie, curious as to why she went after it with the books and it later ended up being in her arms.

"If madame would be so kind as to let me keep it in the servants' quarters, then yes, it is my cat," responded Taylor, pleading to Bertha.

"Whatever! Let us get this room cleaned. Mauricia, go fetch some tea and, Paula, please quit biting your nails and help us get some order in this room. Taylor, put that thing into the servants' quarters and get back to help clean. Nicole, please go fetch some blueberries and whatever Cook is going to need to prepare dinner. If Constable would be kind enough to have a seat, I'll be able to explain it to you," ordered Bertha, sweetly offering the constable a seat.

"Good luck, madame." Freddie knowing that Bertha would think of something drastic to save face and the servants were loyal enough that they wouldn't go against the story that she was about to tell the constable.

"Mr. Tahney, please have a seat with us. It is good to see you again after so many years," politely came from Bertha.

Knowing that if he refused, it would give the constable the wrong impression, and rumors would start. He did not want that, especially with Julli being new there. He glared at Bertha and forced a stiff smile.

"Sure. Thank you, madame," he replied. Going over to the chair, turning it back over, he plopped down, worn out.

Peters got the broom and started sweeping up the ashes just as something moved in the fireplace.

"Madame," he interrupted Bertha, "something is in the fireplace."

All of them were brought to their feet as they heard a cough, and then a form began to come out of the ashes. Taylor began to scream, and the cat hissed. Bertha gasped as Freddie grabbed her arm and dragged her back. The constable got his baton ready again, and Peters started to whimper. Just then, they heard a child's voice say, "Have fun!"

Freddie let go of Bertha's arm and ran over to the little girl covered with ashes. He grabbed the towel from Paula, who had just grabbed stuff out of the cupboard, and wiped off Julli's face. Looking at her, he asked, "Are you okay?"

Seeing the little girl nod her head, relief went through the room. The constable put his baton back, waited for one of the maids to move the stuff off of the seat, and sat down on the cushions. While waiting for the reply to this strangeness that destroyed the room, he took in the disarray of the house and of the people there.

Bertha laughed at the look on the faces of the neighbors who were being shooed out by several of the handymen. Turning to see Julli all right, she made a beeline for her but was quickly pulled into someone's arms. Before the fact had registered, Freddie was kissing her with all the passion he had. The years of being lonely melted away, and Bertha returned the fervor with her own kisses. After a few minutes, they slowly pulled apart, glancing into each other's eyes. The next thing they knew was Julli had grabbed both their legs and was looking at them strangely. The look Julli had was priceless, and Bertha's heart melted.

Freddie cleared his throat and facing the Constable said, "I have a few questions to ask, madame. With your permission, Constable."

At the constable's nod, Freddie faced Bertha and slowly got down to his knee.

The maids gasped, and Julli's mouth was agape. Julli just stared at Freddie and wondered why he was down to her level when her aunt Bertha was taller. Bertha started breathing in short gasps.

"I, Freddie Tahney, would like to ask your hand in marriage," he asked quietly.

"Oh my," was all Bertha could say. Bertha looked quickly at Julli, then back at Freddie, to whom she nodded her head at.

Freddie reached into his pocket and pulled out a wooden box. Opening it, everyone could see the beautiful two-carat diamond ring. With shaking hands, Bertha put out her hand and said, "Yes!"

Freddie gets up and slowly places the ring on Bertha's now visibly shaking hand. He looked down and smiled at Julli.

"Madame, I have another question to ask," he said. Again, at the constable's nod, Freddie goes ahead and asks the question, ignoring the child pulling on his pant leg.

"Will madame consider keeping Julliannyia Maire Hamperston?" came the question.

Looking at her servants, she saw their eyes pleading with her. She knew now without a doubt that she was going to keep her sister's daughter with her. She would never have thought of it, but Julli had indeed brought some fun into the household, and everyone seemed to be in a good mood. It had to be the best day ever.

"On one condition."

"What is it?" asked Freddie, exasperated, wondering if asking a woman to marry him and accept her own niece was too much for a social, genteel woman to handle.

Looking at Julli, then at Freddie, she replied, "Freddie, you have to stay and help. All of you who want her here please promise that you will help too. I am not sure I can do this on my own, not yet anyways."

Mauricia came in with the tea at that point and said, "Madame, we want her here. We sure could use a little 'un to liven things up some. How about you, Mr. Tahney? You gonna stay with the child and madame?"

Knowing that they were waiting for him to decide, Freddie looked at Bertha, who secretly nodded her head. Smiling, he announced, "Gee, of course I will help! After all it seems Ms. Mearse and I will soon be wed," amid the cheers from the servants, and Julli was then given attention by Freddie, who pointed to Bertha clapping her hands, nudging Julli to copy with the clapping as well.

Quickly composing herself, she turned to face the constable and saw that he had a smile on his face. "Constable, this is my niece, Julli. She is my sister's little girl. And you know Freddie, my fiancée," stated Bertha proudly now that she had something to brag about.

Looking toward the ash-smeared little face, they all smiled at how a little girl could pull them together like never before. Seeing them smile at her, Julli broke out into a big grin, contrasting the whiteness of her teeth to the blackness of her ash-covered skin.

"Julli love Aunt Bertha and Freddie," came big signs from Julli.

CHAPTER 5

---◆◆◆---

The Night of the Party
June 8, 1816

After the tea with her aunt Bertha and Freddie as usual, Julli went back up to her room to get ready for her birthday party. Her dress and accessories were laid out on her bed. Julli donned her pink dress for the blue dress she had just received. Mauricia then sauntered into the room and proceeded to help Julli finish getting ready. Paula came in with a bustle and a corset, which Julli shook her head at, and both maids looked at each other and shrugged. *It is my party*, thought Julli.

Again shaking her head at the corset and the bustle, the maids quickly put them in the closet and helped Julli finish dressing.

Later as the evening sky dimmed and lanterns were being lit, Julli was at her best and ready to join the party. Julli walked down the stairs gracefully. The butler announced she was coming and asked the guests to greet her. Julli looked at him while he made the announcement and lip-read what he said. Nodding her thanks, the butler bowed and offered his arm, leading Julli down the steps.

The guests cheered to her, and Julli nodded to them as she walked past them to Freddie, who offered her his arm after bowing to her. Putting her hand on his arm, Julli looked around. Smiling at everyone, who bestowed a "happy birthday!" to her. Noticing that nearly everyone there was an associate of her aunt's, but at least she knew most of them. She did spot a few groups of her friends, but they were not close enough for her to want to associate with them. They waved, and Julli smiled as she waved back. The least she could do was be courteous and make her aunt happy enough.

The crowd parted in the middle of the floor, and the band started playing the waltz that Freddie loved. Julli tied the string that held up the hem of her dress to her wrist, and Freddie placed his hand on her waist. Smiling into each other's eyes, Freddie led her in the dance. Julli made it a point not to glance at her aunt, especially when she refused to don the corset and the bustle. Freddie mouthed, "You are beautiful."

Mouthing back, she said, "Thank You."

Tilting her head in the direction of her aunt, Julli rolled her eyes, which Freddie caught, and mouthed, "Mad!"

From that point on, both Julli and Freddie ignored everyone until the waltz ended, and the guests applauded. Curtsying to the guests while Freddie bowed, she blew a kiss to her aunt.

Her aunt stiffly smiled and curtsied to Julli amid the applause from the guests.

Walking over to the table laid out with presents of all shapes, Julli eyes the two-tier cake and arrays of appetizers.

Leave it to my aunt to make everyone feel like they are starving, thought Julli as she noticed the guests greedily stuffing their fingers into their mouths already filled full with appetizers.

Freddie leaves her standing at the table to get her a drink. Julli glances over all the presents and rests her eyes on a worn-out book. She eyes it and reads, "Holy Bible." Walking over to it, she opens it and sees the writing: "To a very beautiful lady. May He bless you this day and the rest of the days of your life."

There was no name. Julli picked it up and looked it over. Still no name. She eyed the presents again, but the book was the only thing not wrapped. Looking around, Julli didn't see the person responsible for the book. When the crowd parted ways, Julli looked over toward the balcony to see a man staring at her. Julli eyed his outfit: worn work boots, faded jeans, tan shirt, with blonde hair and seemingly blue eyes. Arms well used as muscles bulged through sleeves of his shirt. Intrigued, Julli started to walk toward him, only to be stopped by Bertha, who stepped in front of her.

"Time to cut the cake. Mauricia will take care of the presents," signed Bertha.

Freddie showed up, offered his arm to Julli, and walked her over to the cake. Paula held up a knife, and Bertha clapped her hands. Everyone stopped what they were doing and faced Julli.

"Today my niece turns sixteen. I have had so many wonderful years with her and wanted to wish her the best on this special day. We will start the 'Happy Birthday' song."

Everyone sang but Bertha and Freddie, who signed.

Waiting for them to finish, Julli kept her eyes on her aunt and Freddie. Finally, amid all the quietness, she took a deep breath and blew out all sixteen candles. Julli felt the thunderous round of applause. Smiling and waving to the guests, she picked up the knife and cut a small piece of cake. Paula scooped it up and put it on a plate for her. After that, the guests immersed themselves all over the room, and Julli was feeling claustrophobic and beckoned Freddie over to tell him she needed air. Freddie led Julli to the balcony, with her plate.

Pulling out a chair and helping seat her, Freddie got down on his knee and signed, "You did a good job. Actually your aunt got complimented on how beautiful your gown was without the bustle."

"Thank you! I am glad you warned me ahead of time what was to go on," she signed and, leaning forward, placed a kiss on his cheek. Signing she asked Freddie if she could eat alone. "Do you mind leaving me here alone to eat? I do not feel like going back in yet."

Nodding, Freddie gets up and bows to Julli as he leaves. Julli glances around, not finding anyone within a distance, so she grabs her fork and digs into the cake. Spice cake with purple and orange frosting. *Yummy!* thought Julli. After the second bite, Julli froze as she felt some eyes on her. Out of the corner of her eye, she sees the man again, tossing his smoke as he walks toward Julli.

Oh no! She hurriedly looks down at the cake and fidgets with it.

He approaches and stands in front of her. Julli looks up when she sees a hand waving to her out of the corner of her eye. She looks up to see him ask, "May I sit?" Julli was surprised that she did not have that much trouble lip-reading him even with his sideburns and the fact she had never lip-read him before.

Nodding her head, he sits across from her. Reaching into his jacket, he pulls out some paper and a container of ink. In his boots was a feather. Leaning over to get it, Julli notices up close how handsome he was. Sandy blonde hair, longish in the back and only short enough to frame his eyebrows. Julli looks at his arms when he rolls up his sleeves. They were hard-worked arms. His shirt was tight enough across his chest that she could see the muscles underneath.

Looking at Julli, he startles her when he asks, "Can you lip-read me?"

Shrugging her shoulders, she slowly nodded her head; then he starts to write. Julli notices he is left-handed, compared to her being right-handed.

She wondered how he could write wrong handed. The thought brought a smile to her lips, and she bowed her head to hide it.

"My name is Mark."

He then proceeds to hand the feather to Julli.

"I'm Julli," she writes and hands it back to him.

"I know. Happy birthday."

"Thanks. I am glad you came," wrote Julli.

"It is a privilege to come," he wrote as he spoke it out aloud to himself. Adding, he wrote, "I was not sure I would get the chance to meet you in person."

"Here I am."

"Yes. It is a pleasure to meet you." With that, he stuck out his hand and waited for Julli to offer hers, before bestowing a kiss on her gloved hand.

Julli watched, and when he leaned back into the chair, she wished that he had left his lips lingering longer.

"Hope you like the book," he wrote after Julli herself got comfortable. Julli had to reread that sentence before she was hit with the realization that he got her something. The book titled Holy Bible.

"That was from you?" Julli asked with her voice.

"Yes, it's a very good book," he answered. Looking into his eyes, she could see he was sincere.

"Okay, I'll read it. Thank you." And with that she handed the feather back to him. A smile playing at the corners of his lips, he nodded his head.

Julli flustered, then finished her cake. It was a good cake, but with the dryness of her mouth, it tasted like paper. How to ruin a good party, when nothing goes well.

When she was done, Mark picks up the feather and continues to write on the parchment. "Would you mind if we tried talking? I would like to keep the ink for when we don't understand each other."

"I think that would be okay."

"You have a beautiful voice. You should use it more often instead of having others talk for you."

Shocked but pleased with that compliment, Julli says, "Most people think I am from another country the way I say my words so I only talk when I am at home with my aunt, Freddie and the servants."

"It is a shame that they don't listen to you. I don't think I could ever get tired of hearing you talk," Mark complimented Julli.

"Well, thank you kindly. That helps to know at least I am not annoying you." She snickers at her own twisted joke, while Mark just looks at her, squinting his eyes.

"The French have a sign dictionary. It is for the deaf and only problem is it is in French, which I know nothing about."

"Yes, I know about it. I too have the dictionary. And I can read some French but the pronunciation is too hard for me."

"Wow, you are amazing." Mark beamed, impressed with Julli's education. "What else can you do?"

Laughing at that, she said, "Nearly anything but hear. I have done some gardening but hate cross-stitching."

"No, I mean like knowledge," encouraged Mark.

"Oh. I have taken courses in Spanish as well. I have studied Ireland and the languages. In addition, Latin as well. I can read and write pretty well. I guess you could say I was an overachiever."

Mark, impressed, only shook his head and said, "No, you are smart and that is good."

Picking up the feather, he writes something on it, shielding it from her view 'til he stood up and then showed her. "Would you dance with me?"

Not fully understanding, since she could not hear any music, but she sure could feel the band playing not too far from where she was sitting, especially with the balcony doors wide open.

Mark mimics dancing with his arms out and sways in tune with the music.

"Oh," says Julli.

She gets up when he moves her chair out from the table. Taking his hand when offered, she lets him lead her to the space where there were no tables or chairs. At that time, the band started playing a slow waltz called "A Love's Dream." Played mostly with the violin, only having the plucked guitar near the middle half. Julli puts her hand in his, and he gently places his left on her waist. Fortunately, they were close enough to the band that Julli could feel the music as they started slowly dancing. Looking up, he was watching her. With a smile at the corner of his mouth, he began leading her in tune to the waltz. Julli gazed at Mark, who started to lip-sync the tunes to the music, "A love's dream, you standing by me, it's my dream come true."

Julli felt so happy that Mark was the guy she had always dreamt about. Even though he could hear, he made sure, like Freddie did, that she could understand them. Eye contact was important to Julli as well as being able to see someone's face. Mark was one of the men who actually put a woman's needs above his own.

Time flew by. Julli felt like she was dancing on air. Never before had she felt like that around a man. And she had been around so many at her aunt's persistence. There was something about Mark that Julli found real interesting. Her interest was piqued more than before. She got the feeling that she could trust him. She found herself staring at his lips. Well-defined masculine lips. Her heart began racing, and Julli felt like she was in an oven. Even the chilly February night with snow still on the ground could not cool her down fast enough. Her stomach knotted up, and butterflies were present.

"Once more my love, come stand by my side. It was my dream come true."

Before either one could speak, the song was over. Mark bowed and waited for Julli to curtsy to him. Offering his arm again, he walked her back to the table. Julli felt like she was still walking on air and grabbed Mark's arm. Julli got flustered when he smiled at her.

Pulling out the chair for her, waiting for her to smooth her skirts, he sat next to her.

Again, he takes the feather and dips it in the ink before writing on the parchment.

"I would love to call on you. May I ask to come visit?"

"I would love that," wrote Julli, delighted that he wanted something to do with her, unlike others who only wanted to step up their reputation by associating with her and her aunt.

"I'll go ask your aunt." With that, he added, "Thank you, Julli, for the dance."

With that, he excused himself by getting up. Leaning over, he kissed Julli's gloved hand and left the balcony. Julli watches him disappear into the house and regrets not having more time with him. He made her think, and something happened with her heart when she was with him. She wrapped her shawl tighter around her. Now she was feeling the chill of the cold night.

Freddie comes out and escorts Julli back in. "Did you have fun being by yourself?" he asks as he leads her over to the table near the band. Freddie did not give a hint that he knew she had not been alone out on the balcony.

Julli decided that she was gonna tell Freddie in the privacy of her room later what had happened out on the balcony. He would understand better and remain calm, unlike her aunt. Julli nods her head, finally happy something went good on her day that had nothing to do with her aunt. At the insistence of the guests, Freddie bows to Julli, who curtsies back, not sure what was going on at that moment.

"May I have the honor of leading you in your birthday dance as your father?" he asked, using both his voice and signs. Julli, more than happy to oblige her uncle, role model father at that, happily nods her head yes and curtsies again.

They walked to the center of the room and got in the dance stance that they had practiced weeks on just for this night. The band started playing "Father's Lullaby in Standard D," which was just perfect for Julli's dance with her "father."

Swirling around with Freddie gave an elating feeling. He had been her father and uncle for so many years that it was the best dance she ever had with him. Guests stayed back from the center 'til Julli and Freddie completed the dance when the music ended. Amid thunderous applause, Julli and Freddie curtsied to each other, big smiles on their faces. Julli really loved Freddie. To Julli's dismay, Freddie moved away from her, leaving her alone on the dance floor.

The presents had been removed to her room, and guests were waiting for her to dance. The first dance, adult dance. Looking around but not finding Mark, she braves a smile and glides around the room, accepting well wishes from friends who greeted her. Noticing that her aunt was pointing to a group of men who was standing near the band. *Wow*, Julli thought, *my aunt is torturing those men in hopes that I will pick one of them.* Starting to giggle as they squirmed, being so close to the band. Ignoring them, she finally walks up to Neal, who is barely sixteen, and asks him, "How would you like to help me have some fun, liven the party some?"

"You know that we will get in trouble," he stated. She always managed somehow to get them both in trouble. She was the one who always started it.

"By who? It's my birthday party and I should be able to do whatever I want," demanded Julli. She was not going to be denied some fun.

"I guess, but you take the blame, right?" he asks. With his parents watching him like a hawk across the room, Neal did not feel like getting into too much trouble. His parents would not hesitate to make a big deal in front of all the guests.

Julli shrugs and says, "When do I not ever?"

Julli walks over to the men standing by the band; she nods to Neal, who bows. Julli looks them over and gets out her fan, but instead of opening it, she tossed it into the air. The guys were thinking whoever caught it were to dance with her. Unbeknown to them, Julli planned to scare them off by what she was going to do next. After one of them caught her fan, the others backed off, believing that he had won the opportunity to dance with the birthday girl. He bows and hands Julli the fan, which she tosses back into the air. To the men's amazement, that offered another opportunity, and they clamored over each other in an effort to get the fan.

Another guy grabbed it, walked over to Julli, and handed it to her, but to his shock, she tossed it again. This time it went farther across the room, and the guests grabbed people in their haste to move out of the way of the men. Julli started laughing when two of them started shoving, and one was knocked into a group of girls, who started to scream. "Ahhh!" Before the guy could do anything, the girls were hitting him with their fans. Julli could not help but laugh at that.

It was not 'til she saw Freddie shaking his head at her that she put an end to the chaos. Ignoring all the men, she walked over to where Neal was and curtsied to him.

"Hi, Neal. Would you do me the honor of being the first to dance with me?" asked Julli, using mostly her voice as she and Neal grew up together. Julli glanced at her aunt, who had a look of horror on her face. Snickering under her breath, she nodded to Neal, who eagerly bowed and offered her his arm. The guests gasp, but the band had started playing "Oh! Why Should the Girl of My Soul Be in Tears." Neal escorted Julli onto the dance floor and quickly swung her around into his arms. Both of them laughed. Now the guests had nothing better to do than to start rumors. Vicious gossip was sure to spread like wildfire by the morning of tomorrow.

In the center of the room, Neal bowed, while Julli curtsied. He offered his hand, and Julli gladly accepted it. She made sure the string was still tied to her wrist; then Neal placed his hand on her waist. Then with a flourish, the band played a faster rhythm, and Neal swirled Julli around the dance floor.

Giggling Julli told Neal, "You dance good."

Neal, blushing, mouths, "Thank you."

Neither gave a care to the onlookers, who were furiously chatting with each other. Julli and Neal gazed at each other and chuckled. They had been friends for too long to know not what the other was thinking. Looking at Neal, Julli wished that he had been older than his fifteen years, and then she would really have loved dancing her first adult dance with him. In a few years, he was going to have so many girls wanting him to call on them. He was that good-looking for a kid. There was no telling how his looks would change in the next few years, but Julli knew he was as cute as he was charming. Pending the fact that his parents were overweight and very obnoxious.

Poor guy, thought Julli. She loved being with Neal. He could make her laugh and calmed her down when she had an outing with her aunt. Like Freddie, Neal was her lifesaver too. He lived a few blocks down the street but was always willing to drop what he was doing to rush over to help Julli with what he could. He was lanky, with brown hair, pulled back from his face and tied with a black ribbon. Julli thought he looked dashing in his navy frock coat on top of his white shirt. He seemed uncomfortable with the cravat tucked in his shirt, but nonetheless, he was handsome. She only wanted what was best for him, and when he got older, she knew that the lady he picked was going to be by far the luckiest woman.

When the dance ended amid the applause of the guests, Neal bowed to Julli, and she curtsied back. Freddie came to escort Julli out to the foyer, where Bertha was.

"Happy birthday, Julli," says Aunt Bertha, bestowing a kiss on Julli's cheek.

Kissing her back on the other cheek, Julli signs, "Thank you. And thank you for a wonderful birthday. I had so much fun."

"Good, that is good. I see that you look ravishing with your style. However, for now, go enjoy yourself and mingle with the guests."

"Aunt Bertha," signed Julli, "I really appreciate this party, but do you think I may be excused early so I can go look at the presents that I received and start writing the thank-yous?"

Thinking that Julli had learned something, she said, "You may be excused after thanking the guests for coming."

"Thank you so much, Aunt," timidly signed Julli, relieved.

"So I'll see you in a bit." And with that her aunt went to greet other people and to thank those who were leaving. Always the perfect hostess. With that many people there watching, her aunt was calm and poised; but when they were gone, the mask was taken off, and the true Bertha was revealed. She was so good at disguising her emotions, feelings, and always made people feel like they could count on her. Julli swore she would never be like her aunt; in fact, she sure was not.

Freddie leads Julli back into the dance room, and the band stops when Freddie nods to the butler, who announces, "Ms. Hamperston wishes to make an announcement!"

Chairs were scraped back as men and women alike got to their feet.

Julli goes to the front of the room by Freddie and gazes at the crowd. Swallowing and wiping her sweaty hands on her skirt, she begins to sign, which Freddie translates.

"Thank you all for coming to my birthday party. I had so much fun. And oh, thank you all for the lovely gifts for my sixteenth bash. I hope you all enjoyed yourselves and please continue to do so. I am thankful for my aunt and Freddie, who have been there for me through the years. I owe all of this to them." Curtsying to her aunt and then to Freddie, who bowed to her, she continued, "I am so thankful for all of my friends who were able to come and enjoy themselves during this hard time. Thank you again."

Julli curtsied and saw that glasses from all had been raised and best wishes had been tossed her way. Thinking it was ridiculous, she curtsied again and left the room amid many well wishes waved to her. She made her grand exit by curtsying to everyone she walked by. A few of the women stopped her to bestow a kiss on her cheek, while some of the men took her hand kissed it.

Then finally, Julli was able to leave it all behind her by walking out of the room. She glanced back at the men she had disappointed and laughed to herself for they were embarrassed by their parents, who were chastising them for their improper behavior.

In the bedroom, Paula came to write down what gift and from whom after Julli opened them. Then mentally made a system where to put everything.

Picking up the book she got from Mark and placing it under her pillow, she finished opening the other gifts, and when done, she knew she had to get the thank-yous ready for her aunt to inspect. Julli hated that task, but since it made her aunt happy and there was no tension between them, she was going to do her best tonight. Paula put the presents away, and Julli thanked her by bestowing a kiss on her cheek.

An hour later, Julli finished the last thank-you note and got out her nightgown, preparing to don it, when Bertha came in.

"Well, you did great. I am proud of you," said Bertha, going over and placing a kiss on Julli's forehead.

"Thanks. And thank you for the party, Aunt Bertha. It was a real good night," admitted Julli, relieved that she made her aunt happy, but Julli ended up being happy as well.

"May I ask you a question?" At Julli's nod, Bertha continued. "Why Neal? He's too young," stated Bertha.

"Neal is my friend. And I'm glad we danced. He's been a good kid and I am just not ready to have you or anyone tell me who to dance with or what others expect from me. I know what I want better than anyone else," signed Julli, hoping they could keep the peace this night.

"But not as a suitor!" stated Bertha, shaking her head.

Julli sighs. "Okay, AB, I know. I grew up with him, remember?"

"Yes, I certainly do. But this is your night, not his," stated her aunt smugly.

"Fine, I'll accept callers." Shrugging her shoulders, she added as meekly as possible, "I think I'd like one in particular."

Bertha, beaming, asks enthusiastically, "Who, pray tell?"

"Mark." Julli spells his name, fidgeting.

"Who?" Dumbfounded, Bertha tries to recall the guests who were there.

"I danced with him out on the balcony. He is so nice and real good-looking," Julli told her aunt.

"You did what?" admonished Bertha.

"We danced and I was floating," signed Julli dreamily. She was not paying attention to her aunt, who was staring at her.

"Julli, who?" asked Bertha again, this time standing directly in front of Julli.

"Mark. I don't know his last name."

Bertha yells for Freddie, who comes quickly, walking into the room. It seemed like Freddie was never far behind Bertha, especially when there was going to be trouble.

"Yes, madame?" he asks, fearing the worst at the angry expression on Bertha's face.

"What? What's wrong?" signed Julli frantically, trying to find out what was going on.

"Do you know a man named Mark? Seems he was out on the balcony with Julli earlier," commented Bertha.

"Yes, madame," nodding his head, he admitted. "Mark. He does gardening."

"See, Aunt Bertha? Freddie knows him," begged Julli, knowing at that instant that nothing good was going to come out of anything the moment she told her aunt about dancing unchaperoned.

"Julli, he is beneath your status He is nothing but a commoner," stated Bertha smugly.

"No, he was here. Did you invite him, Freddie?" Julli asks Freddie, hoping he would be on her side.

"Yes, I did," stated Freddie uneasily, looking from Julli to Bertha and back. He knew that he was going to get Julli in hot water for what he set up without Bertha knowing. But the way she stood up to her aunt, in that dreamy, excited action, he was glad that he did what he did.

"Julli, stay away from him." Before Julli could do anything, Bertha was now checking Julli for any bruises. "Did he hurt you?" she asked.

"No, he didn't. He was so nice," signed Jull, pulling away from her aunt.

"Freddie, contact the constable. I don't want that man here ever." Still not satisfied, she glares at Freddie and adds, "Make sure you fire him."

"No, Aunt Bertha. No, please?" begs Julli, near tears. Lip-reading her aunt had\become easier over the years, so she didn't need her to sign the whole time.

"No, you'll have no more contact with him. Much less, have him call on you. The nerve of him."

"But, Aunt—," begged Julli again.

"No, that's enough. Do as I say," she added at the pitying look Julli gave. "I mean it," stated Bertha so firmly that Julli knew better than to argue with her aunt. Especially now.

"Freddie, make sure he is off the premises, please!" stated Bertha, not willing to give an inch.

"Yes, madame." Freddie bowed, looking at Julli apologetically. Julli then turned from him and glared at her aunt, who was just staring at her coolly.

"Good night, Julli," came the terse remark from Bertha.

Bertha, upon leaving the room, slammed the door and yelled for the maids to clean up and hurry. Now Bertha was going to ruin the night even more by being mean to everyone because Julli had disappointed her once again.

Freddie kisses Julli on the forehead and signs, "Happy birthday." Julli's smile leaves her face as the look on Freddie's loses its gleam when he hears Bertha calling for him.

"Good night, kiddo," winking at her before leaving the room.

Freddie runs to catch up with Bertha.

Sighing, Julli sits on the bed. Not in the mood to change her dress into a nightgown, she hits the pillow with such force that her hand hit something underneath it. Reaching under the pillow and pulling out the book, only to remember she hid it there while they were going through the presents. Seeing a piece of paper sticking out, Julli opens the book. Reading the note written on the piece of paper: "Meet me in the gazebo at midnight. We can write and dance some more!"

Without a doubt, Julli knew it was from Mark. The handwriting was the same she had seen him use earlier. With a squeal of delight, Julli bound up, ready to defy her aunt once more. Especially tonight, which was her birthday. No one, not even her aunt, was going to ruin another night. At the sound of the squeal, Mauricia and Paula came hastily in.

"Julli, do you need anything?" asked Mauricia, signing in her own way that she and Julli both knew.

"Oh, sorry. No, just happy I had a good time," answered Julli, signing, now feeling silly for the squeal.

To Julli's dismay, they came over to help her change into her nightgown. When Paula unbuttoned the dress and helped Julli slip out of it, she turned Julli to face her.

"You were beautiful," signed Paula. And without hesitation, she added, "Happy birthday you brat."

"Ha-ha! Thank you, Paula," signed Julli and with that gave Paula a kiss.

"Happy birthday, child," was from Mauricia, who told Paula that they had to hurry since Bertha needed them. After helping Julli don her nightgown, they both gave her a kiss on the forehead.

"Sleep well," came from Mauricia, and with that, both of them got ready to leave the room.

Only to stop when Julli sang out, "Thank you. Love you and Good night!"

Then they finally left Julli alone in the room.

Now thinking about how to get out to meet Mark, Julli noticed that she had less than twenty minutes to get to the gazebo. Opening her closet door, she got out her black hood and donned it while slipping her feet into the boots she wore for outdoors. Looking around, she snuck over to the small dresser, pulling out the hidden drawer. In her haste, she pushed stuff out of her way and reached for the bed sheet ladder that she made and used to climb out of the windows. Then proceeded to throw it out the window, watching as it unraveled itself to land on the ground. Julli, hoping that she was quiet enough and not about to be caught, blew out the candle. Poising herself on the sill, she looked down before she swung her legs out the window. She thought to herself, *It better be worth it. Ha-ha.*

She made it a point to be careful as there were icicles hanging around the window. If she broke any of them, she was afraid it would bring attention to her room. She did not see the hooded shape at the corner of the house, who was watching her, ready to help her if needed. Looking back and not seeing any candle lights under her door, she braved the cold night's breeze and got ready to sneak out, closing the window after she had a firm grip on the ladder. And with that went climbing down it to the snow-covered ground, where she then took off sprinting past the garden toward the gazebo.

CHAPTER 6

———◆◆◆———

Learning the Gospel
1816

Walking cautiously toward the gazebo door, Julli swallowed nervously. *Now was not the time to panic!* she said to herself.

What if it isn't him? What if—? She paused her thinking when the door opened, and Mark beckoned her in. Closing the door behind her, Julli stepped into the gazebo. There were two lanterns hanging up. On the bench, there was a candle, along with ink, parchments, and a couple of feathers. Next to the parchments was an open book. The wood stove in the corner gave off some heat for the small room.

Taking Julli by the arm, he led her over to the bench. There was a pillow on there, which Mark gestured to her to sit on.

After seating Julli, Mark sat down next to her, picked up the feather, and started writing.

"I'm glad you came." At Julli's nod, he continued, "It means a lot to me."

Smiling and taking the feather, she quickly scribbled, "You're welcome. I wasn't sure if you'd be here."

Handing him back the feather, Julli watched as he laid it down and picked up the book. Looking at him, she watched him point to his lips as he asked, "Can you lip-read me?"

Nodding her head, she replied, "Yes."

"I just wanted to show you something in the book that means a lot to me." Julli watched as Mark used the signs of pointing to the book and then to his heart, all the while using his voice.

Wow! thought Julli. *He sure knows how to make sure I understand him.*

Glancing at Mark, who smiled at her, Julli felt good about disobeying her aunt earlier, and she felt no regret in leaving the house to come out to be with him. He made her feel safe yet nervous, as she was alone with him at night. Unchaperoned was more like it.

Mark waited for her to look at him, then proceeded to ask her, "Have you ever read this book?"

Julli eyed the open book and wondered what it was. She watched as Mark gently closed the book to show her the title.

Julli's eyes widened when she looked at the name on the book. Holy Bible. It was the same book, yet more worn-out than the one she had received for her birthday from him. She shook her head and shrugged her shoulders. Looking at Mark, she saw that he had a disappointed look. Not just that; she could see it in his eyes.

"This book is very good. It is a book written by prophets of old. The stories are true. I believe in everything this book teaches." With an afterthought he added, "It is about the people before and after a man who became our Savior."

"Savior?" asked Julli, not fully understanding.

Mark got the parchment and wrote "Savior" on it. Showing Julli, who continued to shake her head.

"Jesus Christ."

"Who?" queried Julli.

"He was a Jew who was born of a virgin named Mary. His father was our Father in heaven."

"I am not sure I am following you," admitted Julli.

"Okay, Jesus Christ was born of a human female named Mary, who was impregnated by God, our Heavenly Father."

"Wait, are you talking about myth?" Julli grabbed the feather and wrote, "I know some myths. From Greece."

"No," wrote Mark. Then he continued, "It's not a myth. It's not from Greece. Most of the stories are from Jerusalem. The story is based on the teachings of the Lord. It was written long before Jesus Christ came and it goes on to tell the story of his ministry, teaching the people about the Gospel. Even after his death on the cross, his apostles kept preaching and the last chapter is Revelations."

"Did you say he died on a cross?" Still confused, not quite sure she understood him correctly.

"Yes. Have you ever been told about the Gospel?"

"Gospel?" Julli wrote, wondering now what they really were talking about. She had seen the church houses but never set foot in one.

"Yes, the story of Christ."

"Um. I have to say no, I do not know this story."

"One of my favorite parables is the 'Parable of the Ten Virgins.'"

"What is that?" asked Julli, interested. *If the book talked about women then maybe it would be worth reading*, she thought to herself.

"It is a parable told by Christ to the apostles and people who gathered to hear him preach. It is about ten virgins who go to meet the bridegroom and only five were prepared to be worthy to enter the house."

"Worthy?" wrote Julli, again confused.

"Yes. Worthy of Christ by having faith and preparing themselves for entrance to the house."

"Like marriage?"

"Something like that," he wrote. Then he added, "I especially love the story about the birth of Christ. Do you know why we have a star on the tree at Christmastime?"

"It makes the tree beautiful, that is all I know," answered Julli, not sure what he wanted her to answer.

"No." Swallowing and clearing his throat, he dipped the feather into more ink and continued his writing. "It symbolizes the star that was seen in the east over a stable where the Son of God was born. There were three wise men who studied stars and they were foretold about the star. They went out in search of it and when they found the star they knew that the newborn babe was indeed the Savior of the world."

At the mention of a newborn babe, Julli's interest was piqued.

"You said 'newborn babe,'" she said, making sure Mark understood her by signing "baby" by placing her arms out as if she was holding a baby in them.

"Yes." Mark nodded. He continued to write for Julli to read. "The babe is the man who died on the cross. The babe was born on what we consider to be Christmas."

"Where was he born?" wrote Julli, intrigued. She was going to have to check her books and verify what Mark was telling her.

"He was born in Jerusalem in a stable."

"A stable? Why?"

"There was no room in the inn that night as many travelers were told to go to their birth town and pay a census. It was a proclamation that they had to follow," wrote Mark, watching Julli read each word he wrote.

"What about women?" Now fascinated by the story, Julli had to find out more.

"Along with the Virgin Mary, there is a story about a woman who became queen and saved her people, the Jews, from being killed." Dipping in more ink and getting out another parchment, Mark continued telling Julli more. "Also there is a woman named Ruth who stayed with her mother-in-law Naomi, and became one of the people who believed."

"Believed in what?"

"In the Gospel of Jesus Christ and our Heavenly Father," wrote Mark, scrunching up his face in deep thought.

Julli could not resist giggling at the look Mark made.

Looking at her, Mark asked, "Something find your fancy?"

Nodding her head, Julli replied, "You look so serious."

"I am serious when it comes to the Gospel," replied Mark.

"I can see that," said Julli, looking at him. She noticed that his eyes were a deeper blue than she had thought. His eyes were framed by long eyelashes, nearly golden.

"Are you going to pay attention to what I am telling you?" he asked, noticing that Julli was paying more attention to his face than to what he was writing.

"Oh, I am sorry," she said, flustered.

Laughing, he said, "Nothing to be sorry about."

Smiling at that, Julli decided that she had better pay attention to what he was writing, or he would probably get up and leave. Just after she had found a guy she was interested in.

"Okay, back to the subject at hand," she told Mark, gesturing to the parchment.

"Thank you." He continued his writing "There are so many different apostles, and there are stories about Jesus's disciples. There also was a woman who devoted her life to Jesus's ministry and gave up all she owned just to help out."

"That sounds interesting. I think I will like reading the book."

"It is not just the book you should be interested in. It is in the blessings our Heavenly Father will bestow upon you for your faith in Him."

"Do you know him?" At Mark's nod, Julli pondered another question. "Where does he live?"

Julli watched as Mark reread her question and shrugged his shoulders before trying to sign "heaven" by pointing to the sky.

"In the sky?" asked Julli, dumbfounded.

"No, in heaven. Past the sky."

Confused, Julli shook her head, but willing to go along with Mark.

"Do you know who the Almighty Father in heaven is?" he asked her, then reached over to the floor by her and unfolded the blanket that he put on her lap.

"Thank you," said Julli, surprised that he actually put the blanket on her instead of asking if she was cold. Her legs had gotten somewhat chilled, but she was having too much fun writing with Mark that she had not given it much thought.

"Welcome," gestured Mark, saluting her like a king.

"I am sorry, what was the question?" asked Julli, flustered by the action, having lost track of what they were talking about. She had too much fun being taken care of by a man other than Freddie or Neal.

"Oh, it was, umm . . ." Mark paused, lost himself, and he had to look at the parchment to see where they left off. Julli smiled when she realized that, not only was she losing her mind, Mark was too. Then he found the spot and showed it to Julli.

"I guess so. He is someone people pray to in church," she wrote, glad that she knew something related to what Mark seemed real knowledgeable about.

"Yes." Nodding his head, he continued to write and talk out aloud. "He created the world and everything in it. He is our God. He had a son born of a virgin. His son died on the cross to atone for the sins of all mankind."

"That is not good. This is just a story, right?"

"No. It is true. I promise you this. I would not be sitting here writing these things to you if I didn't have a belief in it myself."

Swallowing, she took a minute to look deeply into Mark's eyes. Sighing, Julli wondered what was going on with him. She had never known a man who loved to write as much as she did. It was surprising that he did not make any effort to lower his eyes below her chin. *Maybe he is not interested in the same things other men are*, thought Julli.

"Please read the part I marked," signed Mark, pointing to Julli, then the book. Nodding her head to go along with him, Mark picked up the book, and Julli looked at where he pointed.

Clearing her throat and grabbing the book, she reads, "Saint Matthew chapter 11 verse 5: The blind receive their sight, and the lame walk, the lepers are cleansed, and the deaf hear, the dead are raised up, and the poor have the Gospel preached to them."

Julli, not understanding what she had just read, looks questioningly at Mark and shrugs her shoulders. She picks up the feather and draws a big question mark on the parchment.

Looking back at the book, she taps the page and shakes her head.

"No, I do not hear," Julli said, pointing to her ears and shaking her head. Looking back at the book, she reread the last sentence. "'The poor have the Gospel preached to them.' I think you are mistaken," Julli signs. Then she adds smugly, "I am not poor either."

Julli looks at Mark, who sits there, eyeing her with a shocked expression. Before Julli could react in any way, Mark bursts out laughing.

"No, you're not poor. Of course not!" he said between breaths.

Julli, not understanding him, just glares at him, not even one ounce remotely amused. Her feelings now hurt, she gathers her skirts and gets up. Before she could stomp off, Mark lays his hand on her arm, stopping her. Glancing at the hand, then at the face of the man who was standing in front of her, Julli doesn't know whether or not to remain angry. Looking at Mark, who was gazing at her, his face serious, Julli resolves not to remain angry. *Maybe he wasn't trying to be insulting*, she thought.

"It doesn't mean you won't hear or that you are poor," Mark replied. Grabbing the pen, he wrote, "It just means that you have never heard the Gospel and that you were poor as you didn't have it in your life."

"I am not sure I understand you," she scribbled.

She watched as Mark squinted his eyes and scratched his forehead in his way of trying to think of how to get Julli to understand him.

Tilting his head to the side, he paused to look at the section of the book they were discussing, before he picked up the feather and continued the lesson.

"Are you sure you want to learn this?"

Nodding her head, she motioned for him to continue.

"How about Noah and the ark?" he wrote, and shock was evidence on his face when Julli shook her head.

"God had instructed Noah to build an ark and gather two of every kind of animal. God flooded the earth and Noah and the animals inside survived," wrote Mark, who looked at Julli.

"Two of every animal? That is silly," she wrote, wondering why they were talking about animals.

"No, one male and female of each species."

"That makes for a breeding situation, doesn't it?" wrote, Julli thinking it was silly that someone would go to all the trouble to get one male and one female of each unless they were to breed them.

Laughing aloud at what she wrote, Mark doubled over, hiding his face from Julli, who was not able to lip-read him at that time.

Staring at him bowled over laughing, Julli wondered what was so funny. *Was it something I wrote or was there something else that I missed?* she wondered. She sat there waiting for him to quit, and when he did, she kept her face expressionless.

"Did I insult you?" he wrote.

"Well," Julli writes, "when you laughed, I didn't know what was so funny. If I can not read your lips and you don't write it down, I take that as an insult."

"I am sorry," was the sincere apology.

"Oh. Guess I can forgive you, if you try not to do that again."

"Do you still have the book?" he asked, pointing to the one he had.

"Yes. You gave me the same book. I guess I will read it after all." Julli took pleasure in the delight that Mark showed.

"Please do. If you have any questions or want to talk with me about it, please let Freddie know and he will set up a meeting," advised Mark.

"Freddie?" Julli, shocked, could not believe that. "He knows about this?"

"Yes. Freddie has his own belief."

"No, I mean, Freddie knows about this meeting?" At Mark's nod, she asked more. "The book, the dance, and all?" Julli pointed to the book, the room, and pointed to both her and Mark.

"Yes, he does. He also will be here to escort you back to the house soon," wrote Mark.

"Oh. I didn't know. Aunt Bertha will be furious when she finds out," stated Julli, well aware how fast her aunt could blow her top.

"Don't tell her. Not yet." begged Mark.

"Okay," agreed Julli, not wanting to let her aunt know, especially now after what happened earlier.

"I have known Freddie for a while now. He and I have talked and I feel like I have known you forever."

"Wow! I didn't know that."

"Freddie helped set the meeting tonight. He hoped you were going to make it," Mark told Julli. Then he added, "Freddie snuck the note in the book for me."

"What do you mean?"

"Freddie and I sort of planned this last week. It would help keep your aunt off your back if she knew you had a friend or rather a suitor."

Julli was not happy with that but was glad that it was Freddie who set it up rather than her aunt. Freddie was more in tune with what interested Julli.

"I know what happened earlier tonight, how your aunt blew a fuse," he admitted. "Julli, when I first saw you a few weeks ago, I knew that I had to meet you."

At Julli's stunned look, he added, "I know that it seems sudden but I really want to get to know you."

"So Freddie hid this from me!" stated Julli, not happy at all finding out. Especially knowing that her beloved Freddie had set her up again, but this time looked more promising.

"I am sorry that Freddie didn't tell you. He told me that he had one failed try with Lieutenant Megston and I was glad it didn't work out," admitted Mark, trying not to rile Julli.

"Are you and Freddie now in charge of my life?" furious now, Julli was scrambling her words together as well as her signs.

Upset that he had riled her, he could only say, "No, we aren't. Freddie only wants the best for you and your aunt would not have your best interests at heart. So please forgive us if we offended you." With that, he bowed his head.

Not finding a guy who would take her interests to heart besides Freddie and Neal, Julli was inclined to forgive him for now. It would not hurt; besides, she had found that she really liked Mark, who made her feel important.

Nodding her head after he looked at her, he surprised her by asking, "Please join me in a prayer?"

"Prayer? You mean the 'kneel down and fold arms' thing?" Julli now wondered what she was doing.

"Yes. A prayer to thank Him for this chance to share the Gospel with you and to be here at this time."

"Oh." As an afterthought, she added, "Umm, okay." She was willing to go along with it to see if she could figure out what the guy was really into.

He took her hand and placed a pillow on the ground, motioning for her to kneel with him. Julli pulled her skirts up, and together they kneeled facing each other. Mark made it a point to keep his face up so Julli could see his lips moving.

He looks so calm yet so worked up about this subject, thought Julli to herself. *I for the life of me can not fathom why Aunt Bertha is so set against me finding a guy so down-to-earth like Mark,* she added before she tilted her head down, but high enough still so she could read Mark's lips.

"Almighty Father, kind and generous, thank Thee for this night. I thank Thee for the chance I have with Julli to be with her and to share the Gospel with her. Please watch over us as this night goes by. Please help Julli to read the Holy Bible and to understand Thy will. In the name of Christ, amen."

Flustered, Julli adds a small, silent "amen" and gets up.

"Thank you, Mark. I will read the book."

"And pray," he added, putting his hands together and bowing his head.

"Pray? Alone?" Julli asked, not sure what she was to do. And added, "How?"

"Yes. You put your hands together after you kneel and bow your head. The Bible tells you how. All you have to do is read it. It will answer any questions you have."

"Okay, I will try," Julli said, willing to please Mark since he seemed to be sincere in what he was talking about.

Julli watched Mark grab the ink and put it away with the feathers in his jacket. He then handed her a parchment wrapped with a ribbon.

"Read these too please?" he begged her.

Julli nods. *Another gift from him,* she acknowledges. Taking them and putting them in her hood pocket, she decided she was going to read them as soon as she got to her room.

"You have made me happy tonight. Thank you." Bowing to Julli, Mark then asks her by swaying as if he was dancing to music. "Would you like to dance with me?"

Nodding, Julli put her hand in his, and he led her to the middle of the gazebo. Placing her hand in his, they made the same motion as before on the balcony. When Mark brought Julli closer to him, they gazed deeply into each other's eyes. Mark led them by gently motioning to Julli to follow his lead. Swaying as if there was music, they danced for what seemed like eternity. Suddenly there was music coming from the balcony, not far from where they were.

Mark slowed the pace while telling Julli that they were playing a ballad called "Meet Me by Midnight." He signed, pointing to her, then tapping his pocket watch and putting up his finger first as a one, then adding the two.

"They are playing a song. I believe Freddie got them to agree to one more request before they left. It is called 'Meet me by Midnight,'" acknowledged Mark to Julli, making sure she could see his face as he told her that. Julli could feel the faint rhythm of the violin and plucked guitar. It felt like they were playing right outside the doors of the gazebo. It added more romance to the dance. Since it was a ballad, the moves were those of a one-step waltz. Julli followed Mark's example as he led her in the dance.

Julli felt as if the song was meant for them. Julli felt Mark's gaze on her as she smiled to herself. It felt so right, so peaceful, yet exhilarating. Not once taking their eyes off each other, they slowed down 'til they were just standing there. Julli had butterflies in her stomach as her breathing became shallow. They got closer 'til Mark gently cupped Julli's chin in his hand and leaned down to kiss her on the lips.

Sweet bliss! thought Julli, closing her eyes and savoring the moment.

The kiss lingered softly at first; then Mark drew her closer in his arms, at which moment his lips began searing hers in a fevered motion that made Julli gasp. She slid her arms around his neck as he tightened his hold on her waist. She felt a powerful wave of passion, hunger, and longing. *Man, he can kiss good*, she thought quietly. Julli's heart beat faster, and she felt herself getting warm in the cold night. She wanted the night to go on forever so she could be in this state of euphoria. She wanted to remain in the arms of Mark. Never before had she felt like this.

All of a sudden, Mark stiffens and pulls away, breaking the kiss, when there was a knock at the door. Flustered, Julli steps back and licks her lips, which were quivering. They look each other in the eyes before Mark gracefully relinquishes his hold on her. Mark nods to the door and says, "Freddie is here."

Julli willed her heart to slow down; after all, she had not run a race. The feeling was amazing. She pulled her coat closer around her as Mark left to go open the door for Freddie. She smoothed back strands of hair from her face and felt that she seemed to be blushing.

Next thing to happen was Freddie came in, and hence, the moment was gone. It was not that Freddie was not special to her, it was just that he was more of a father to her, while Mark was, as Bertha would put it, a suitor.

Mark and Freddie both come over to Julli, and bowing to her, Mark hands her over to Freddie, who offers his arm. Mark turns to get a lantern, which he hands to Freddie, who takes it. Julli sees him mouth the words, "Thank you, sir."

Freddie nods and beckons Julli to go with him. Mark raises his hand and winks at Julli, who waves her hand as well before they walk out the door into the dark night. Freddie, guiding her back to the house through the garden, exclaimed when he felt a snowflake land on his face, "Look, Julli, it is snowing!" He turned her face to his while he spoke that.

Julli, looking up toward the sky, could feel the snowflakes landing on her face as well. She started giggling and told Freddie, "I love this time of the year. The snow is cold but it feels so good when you get a snowflake on your face."

Freddie laughs and pats Julli's hand. "Did you have the time of your life?"

"Oh yes, I did. Thank you, Dad!"

Freddie stood there dumbfounded. That was the first time Julli had ever called him "dad" other than Freddie, which she normally said. He sniffled his tears back and stood up prouder than he had ever been for years. He finally did something right by Julli. Colin would have been proud of the way Freddie raised his daughter.

"Race you to the house!" With that, Julli left him in the garden with the lantern, shocked but mildly amused that she was having fun.

CHAPTER 7

❖━━━━◆◆◆━━━━

Death of Freddie
Five Months Later, November 10, 1816

"Well, about time you came home," stated Bertha as Julli walked into the house. Looking at the grandfather clock, Julli noticed it was barely ten o'clock.

Taking off her coat and giving it to Mauricia to put away, Julli grabbed her duffel bag and eyed her aunt.

Signing, she said, "Well, I am home safe and sound. It's not even curfew."

Julli paused in her steps as her aunt came storming to stand in front of her. Her eyes widened at the expression on her aunt's face.

"Julli, this has got to stop," signed Bertha.

"What has to stop?" asked Julli. Then she added, "What am I doing to displease you?" Julli flared at her aunt, signing rapidly.

"Julli, you've got to calm down. I can't understand you when you're like this," snapped Bertha.

Standing her ground, Julli waited for her aunt to continue. Exhaling slowly, she calmed herself.

"I've gotten word you've been to the church. You also go to as many meetings as you can," stated Bertha, waiting for Julli to deny them.

"True. I go as often as possible." Julli relented. "There is nothing wrong with that, is there?"

"No, but every week and especially on Sundays?"

"Yes. That is the most they have. But thinking about going every Wednesday night for Bible study, if that would be okay as well?" sarcastically Julli admitted.

"Oh," was all Bertha could say.

Pacing the floor, trying to get more out of Julli, Bertha finally asked, "Who chaperones you at the night meetings?"

"What? Don't you trust me?" Julli questioned, shocked after trying the past few months to do so well and keep her aunt from getting disappointed. It seemed no matter what she did, her aunt always found something wrong with it.

"Well?" snapped Bertha, not ready to give in.

"Okay, fine. Freddie goes with me," Julli gave in to Bertha.

Just staring at Julli, Bertha was not sure she believed Julli just yet. Freddie had been well-known to stick up for Julli, more times than Bertha could count. Therefore, it wouldn't be anything new.

"Ask Freddie," was all Julli could say. She eyed her aunt and narrowed her eyes at her aunt's remark.

"All right. I'll ask him." Glancing around, Bertha asked, "Where is he then?"

At that moment, Freddie came sauntering into the room. Seeing the women facing each other, he instantly knew there was trouble brewing. *Not again!* he thought. Already knowing what it was about, he volunteered, "I took Julli to church." Before either of the women could say or sign anything, he added, "There was a meeting about three churches and which one Julli should join. You can even ask Pastor Keshmet."

At the mention of Pastor Keshmet, Bertha knew that Freddie and Julli had nothing to hide. She had been friends with the pastor for years, and he would never lie, especially to Bertha, who donated so much every year. She knew then she could count on the pastor to tell her what had been going on and whom Julli was associating with before, during, and after the meetings.

"Okay," she said, giving in for now. "Which one does Pastor Keshmet recommend?"

"Well, not sure yet," replied Freddie.

"He will let me know on Sunday," replied Julli, signing.

"Please keep me informed. I would like to make a contribution to whichever church you join so you can have some help with what you need," signed Bertha to both Julli's and Freddie's surprise. She added, "What? Is there something wrong with that?"

Both quickly shaking their heads, Julli went over and gave her aunt a hug. Looking at Freddie, Julli signed, "Well, Aunt Bertha approves of this."

Freddie goes to Bertha and says, "Thank you."

Nodding her head, she then replied, "You both are excused." And with that she gathered up her skirts and quietly walked out of the room.

Freddie and Julli glanced at each other, and Julli mouthed, "Wow!" Then both smiled, and Julli gathered her skirts and proceeded to walk up the stairs to her room. Looking back at Freddie, she blew him a kiss, which he grabbed in the air and put over his heart. She waited 'til Freddie did the same, for which she copied his actions to his kiss. Only then did she go up the stairs to her room, followed by the maid.

Freddie went to the lanterns and turned the wicks down before blowing them out. He made sure the bolts were on the doors, all windows closed, and drapes pulled. It was the maid's job, but Freddie had done it for years, and at least he knew everybody was safe in the house. Satisfied, he smiled, knowing that tomorrow was going to be a long day. Then he scolded himself to get to bed so he could deal with what was to come.

Done, he slowly went up the stairs himself to his room, only to stop in midair and grab his chest. It hurt. He couldn't have done anything to make him suffer as he did now. Not even dealing with two stubborn women could make him hurt. Crying out, he sprawled onto the bottom of the stairs.

"Bertha!"

Upon hearing Freddie cry out, the maids and Bertha came running into the room to see him lying there. He was not moving. Bertha kneeled down by him, and with the candle in her hand, she could see that Freddie looked pale.

Yelling for the butler to go get the constable and the doctor, she leaned over Freddie, not finding any breath. She told Nicole to go get Julli.

Julli had barely donned her nightgown when Nicole barged into the room, telling Julli to come quick. The look on Nicole's face told Julli to go with her. Nicole grabbed Julli's hand, and together they made their way down the stairs, being guided down by the candle Nicole was holding.

Several lanterns and even more candles illuminated the bottom of the stairs. Julli saw her aunt Bertha huddled over a form on the floor. Straining to see but couldn't. When Julli saw the boots of whoever was lying there, she let out a loud scream.

"No. Freddie, no!"

Julli nearly knocked Nicole down the stairs in her haste to get to Freddie. Bertha sat there sobbing. The maids and butler were huddled en masse, just standing there. When Julli finally reached Bertha and Freddie, she kept screaming his name.

"Freddie, no. It's me, Julli," shaking Freddie and pounding on his chest, but he still wouldn't respond. "Get up!" she yelled.

Bertha placed her hand on Julli's shoulder, only to have her flick it off, and Julli continued to scream. "Freddie!"

Bertha tried to get Julli's attention, but Julli would not have any of it. Mauricia came to kneel by Julli but was knocked down as Julli grabbed Freddie's body and cradled it, all the while sobbing hysterically. Julli looked at Freddie motionless in her arms and let out another scream. Several of the maids came closer to help, but Bertha shook them away. Julli would be impossible to deal with at this time.

Bertha, sobbing herself, was soon led away from them as the constable had come and was holding her. Julli sat there cradling Freddie and wailing. No one dared to get close to Julli as they knew by her actions that she would fight them. Finally, after a while the doctor made his way through the now-huge crowd outside the doors. Julli could see huddled forms illuminated by lanterns outside. The group of men and women outside the doors could be seen and heard, all asking, "What happened?" and "Who is it?"

When the doctor reached the group huddled around Julli, he motioned for the maids to get Julli back so he could examine Freddie, but they all shook their heads. It was only Mauricia who had the nerves to try. But as soon as Mauricia touched Julli, she saw red. A deep, dark red of anger, rage, and fear. Julli started lashing out at everyone who was within range of her fury.

"No!" was all she screamed repeatedly.

Trying to gather Freddie back into her arms, she was stopped when the constable and Mauricia grabbed her and held her back. Julli saw the doctor make his way over to the body, and fearing the worst, she let out an ear-piercing scream. The doctor flinched and told the constable, "Get her out of here."

But even when they dragged her out of the room, her screams were so loud that not one person could hear another. The crowd flinched, looking at one another, wondering how anyone was going to quiet the noise. Many of them had lived nearby and heard her scream when she was growing up, so it was nothing new, but these screams were worse than any they had ever heard coming from Julli. Looking at his helper, the doctor only mouthed the words, "Quiet her."

Julli could not see the form of Freddie anymore and went crazy screaming like a bloodcurdling banshee. She saw the helper coming toward her, blocking her view. Even Mauricia and the constable were at their wits trying to keep Julli out of the room. Still writhing in their arms, Julli frantically tried to break free. She had to get to Freddie. Freddie needed her. She stomped on the constable's foot and boxed Mauricia on the head. When she was free, she turned to run back to Freddie but fell down as she was tripped. The constable was not going to be outsmarted by a girl, so he did his best in holding Julli down.

Writhing to her side, she was able to knock him off of her and got up, only to be grabbed by Mauricia, who decided that enough was enough. The constable came over, grabbed Julli's other arm, and between the two of them, they struggled to hold her back. An arm went around her neck, and a rag soaked with chloroform was put on her face over her nose and mouth.

No, thought Julli. *Don't,* eyeing Mauricia and the constable. Not willing to give in, Julli took a big breath, planning to scream once more.

Julli struggled again before the whole world was blackened out, and she sagged into the arms of Mauricia and Nicole when the constable let go. The rag was removed, and fingers were put on her neck, checking for her pulse. Her wrist was felt for a pulse as well. Not finding anything, the helper leaned his head onto her chest, listening for her heartbeat. Upon hearing it, he sighed in relief and nodded to the servants to take her to her room. He followed them and checked Julli again before he left to go back to the doctor.

When Julli awoke the next morning, she groaned as her head felt like a ton of bricks had crashed on her, and her throat was parched. Looking around, she realized she was in her own bed. Groaning again, she laid back down; only then did she see her aunt in the chair next to her bed. Upon hearing Julli move about, Bertha woke up with a start.

Signing to her aunt, she said, "I had the worst nightmare of all," closing her eyes. Then when she opened them, she took in her aunt's ragged look. She saw her aunt had been crying. Squinting, Julli saw her aunt did look haggard and worn out. She actually looked old.

Her aunt still not saying, or rather still not signing, anything, Julli decides to break the ice.

"Did I keep you up all night?"

Bertha, sighing and trying to compose herself, avoided Julli's glare. She smoothed back her hair from her face and grabbed the glass of water near her. After taking a sip, she said, "No, you actually slept pretty good. I couldn't sleep. How are you feeling?"

Yawning, she signed, "I feel gross. I don't ever want to feel like that again." Wiping the sleep from her eyes, she smoothed back her hair and grimaced at how gritty she felt.

Nodding, Bertha agreed with her. She picked up a glass, and after pouring water, she handed it to Julli, who greedily gulped it down. Sighing, she lay back on the bed.

"What do you remember?" asked Bertha, scooting closer to the bed.

"Um, I think I would rather tell Freddie. He'll understand more."

At the mention of Freddie's name, Bertha broke all composure and started sobbing. Julli stared at her aunt in shock. She wondered what had gotten her aunt to lose it. She waited for her aunt to regain some sort of control and watched Bertha as she picked up the hankie to wipe her eyes and blow her nose.

Bertha looked at Julli amid the tears and signed, "If only. If only he could."

Julli's eyes widened, and fear gripped her once again.

Freddie. He had lain on the floor, not moving, not breathing. Ice-cold fear struck in the pit of Julli's stomach. Her hands got cold, and she felt empty.

With that, Julli bound out of bed before Bertha could stop her and was out of the door, running across the hall to Freddie's room. Banging on his door for what seemed like eternity, Julli finally threw open the doors, only to see a now-empty room. No trace of clothing or decorations, let alone the fact that the bed is stripped. Dazed, she stumbled into the room, looking frantically for Freddie or anything of his. He could not have packed up and left; that much Julli knew. Gone were his bows and arrows, his Winchester, his books, and his chest, which Julli used to hide in when she was younger. Dread filled her, and she let out a whimper.

Someone reached out and grabbed Julli, startling her so badly that she screamed and started struggling. She was hauled into the arms of a man who held her through her struggles 'til she finally stopped and looked up to see who it was. Her jaw dropped when she saw it was Mark, not Freddie. *How?* was all she could think of.

"It is okay." Mark tilted her face up toward his as he spoke.

"Wha—?" Not able to finish her question.

"It is okay," repeated Mark. He then embraced her into his arms, holding her. Julli, still not comprehending what was going on, pushed herself away from him.

"What do you mean?" she was finally able to choke out. "Where is Freddie?"

Mark looked at Julli, and she saw sadness mingled with tears in his eyes.

No! thought Julli. *No!*

Then came the realization that her nightmare had not been just a bad dream. It had actually happened. Tears formed in her eyes as she asked the dreaded question, "Is Freddie—?"

Mark could only shake his head; his lips did not contain a smile. It was not a joke. Julli did not ask how or why Mark was there; she could only shake her head at the flashback of memories of what happened last night. Freddie had lain on the floor, and everyone was crying. Freddie would not move, and Julli knew that he was dead, but how?

"How did it happen?" signed Julli sadly.

"The doctor said that his heart just stopped working," was all Mark could tell her. At the mention of "heart," Julli felt hers beating, and it hurt. The news that Freddie died because his heart stopped shocked Julli, and she placed her hands over her heart, feeling it beating.

Shaking her head while Mark nodded, Julli emitted a sob, and tears formed in her eyes.

Then both of them started sobbing, Mark not being able to control himself either.

"No," wailed Julli. Sinking to the floor, Mark kept his hold on Julli. She reached up and put her arm around his neck. Laying her cheek against his chest, she let out the flood of tears. Wailing loudly Freddie's name.

Another round of arms went onto the sobbing form of Julli. Julli realized it was her aunt Bertha. Letting go of Mark, Julli then clung to her aunt, who held her as both of them sobbed.

They both had lost someone who meant everything to them. Bertha lost her companion, and Julli had lost her "father." They clung to each other and shared their grief. Julli felt Mark's arms around them, giving support as well as sympathy.

When Julli was cried out, she fell asleep. She was carried to her room and placed on the bed. A quilt had been tucked on her. Julli stayed in her bed for the next day, refusing to eat. She only drank a little water. She was devoid of emotion. Nothing existed anymore. She stared blankly at the wall and ignored everyone who came into her room. Even when Mark came to visit, she just turned away and closed her eyes. Not even Neal or Pastor Keshmet could rouse her from her bed. She refused to look at Bertha, who came to check on her frequently. She completely ignored the maids when they came to clean her room.

After all of that, her aunt could not handle it anymore and finally confronted Julli. Bertha sat on the bed, pulling the covers off of Julli, who got angry at that.

"It is time for you to get up," said her aunt, hoping Julli for once would obey.

"Why? There's nothing," replied Julli glumly. Sitting up, she pulled the covers back onto her. Her aunt, not giving in to pity, pulled them off of Julli's face.

"Get up for me?" her aunt asked, rather begged, signing "please" over and over.

"No, I don't feel like it," stated Julli, still not willing to do anything but stay in bed.

"Then get up for Freddie," her aunt snuck in. She eyed Julli's hair, which was uncombed and in disarray. Julli had not even bothered to change her clothes or anything.

"What?" asked Julli, now sitting up in the bed. She eyed her aunt quizzically.

"His funeral is at two o'clock. You have two hours to get ready," her aunt mentioned as quietly as if she was afraid of Julli's reaction. "Besides, Mark is here to take you."

"Why? He left me," was all she said. Julli glanced around the room, blinking back tears. All the stuff she had gotten from or made for Freddie had been put in her room.

The bows and arrows, the chest, which had been put at the foot of her bed, and more stuff.

Julli could not believe the nerve of her aunt. She had lost Freddie, who meant everything to her. Her aunt was just being her old self, the one smug and obnoxious. Waving her hand in front of Julli's face, her aunt beckoned Julli to look at her.

"Mark has been here for the last couple of days. He has been a big help," stated Bertha, giving herself the benefit of the doubt for Julli. "He left me as well. Do it for him. Come on," begged Bertha, signing, knowing well that Julli was talking about Freddie, not Mark. Desperate that Julli not regret her rash decisions, she tugged on Julli's hand. Julli only pulled her hand back and shook her head.

Julli ignored her aunt, who after that just left the room. Julli did not dare glance at her when she felt the door shut with enough force she could feel it through her bed.

Julli fluffed her pillow, only to find the Holy Bible under it. Enraged, she threw the book across the room and pounced on her bed all her frustration at God for taking Freddie from her. Screaming and ripping her quilts to shreds. Tearing her pillows apart and screeching at the feathers floating in the air. Venting all her hurt and anger at Freddie for leaving and at God for taking him from her. Her face distorted in rage and her hair flying all over her face.

"I hate you!" screamed Julli, looking up at the ceiling. She couldn't decide whom she hated more, Freddie or God. With a sob, she threw herself onto the bed again and pulled what was left of the covers over her shaking body.

After a few minutes, Julli finally stopped the hysterics and started to be rational again.

"He can't do that to me!" hiccuped Julli, wiping her eyes with the hem of her nightgown.

She threw herself onto the now-destroyed bed several times, watching as the feathers floated into the air. She was determined not to be happy anymore. She had lost the person who meant the world to her. She did not care what happened thereon. Julli felt betrayed, left alone by Freddie. Not just him but by all who were near to her.

Wanting now to get out of the house, *Maybe go for a ride?* she suggested to herself.

Getting out of bed, she stomps to the closet, flinging it open, and sees a black dress. Grimacing, she thinks, *Ugh, just what Aunt Bertha would wear.* Reaching in, she takes it out, tosses it onto the floor, then looks back into the closet where she had just removed the dress.

There was a bear claw necklace hanging in there. White claw tied with brown rawhide strips and tied on a beaded black strip of rope. Julli looked at it for a moment before she decided what to do about it being in her closet. "Why was it behind the dress?" she mumbled to herself. Now determined to see if it was real, Julli reached in and unhooked the chain with shaking hands and stood there, staring at it. Seeing Freddie, she smiled, before reality kicked in. Freddie was there no more.

No more smiling, Julli mentally scolded herself, wiping the smile off of her face. *What do I do now?* scratching her head. Giving in for an unknown reason, Julli decides to get dressed and go to the funeral. After all, Freddie would want her to. Maybe the necklace was a clue. Maybe she was supposed to do something. Maybe Freddie had gotten her the necklace before that night. Was it a necklace of Freddie's that she had never seen before? Who knew?

Putting on the black dress, again as usual without a bustle or a corset, she quickly brushed her hair back into a braid. "Just like Freddie would have his," she muttered.

Sighing deeply, she sat down on the chair and waited, staring at the clock on the dresser next to her bed. Mentally she willed the time to go by fast.

Right before it was time, Julli was ready to go. Wearing the black cashmere dress with the necklace, Julli went down the stairs. The butler did not say a word as he opened the doors for Julli, who walked past him in a daze. By the carriage stood Mark, wearing black pants and a black suit. He came bounding up the rest of the stairs, and Julli just looked at him. Without a word, Julli offered him her hand, and he led her down to the carriage. One of the coachmen opened the doors, and Julli saw her aunt.

Bertha was sitting alone, wearing black as well. Julli had not donned the black veil as her aunt had. Taking the seat across from her aunt, Bertha took in the necklace Julli was wearing and didn't say a word. Julli picked up the claw and planted a kiss on the tip of it before letting it fall back onto her chest. She was sure her aunt was going to start crying, but miraculously Bertha didn't. Beckoning to the driver to proceed, they went on their way. Slowly.

Julli made it a point not to look at anyone. Especially her aunt, who kept glancing at her. Many of the townsfolk showed up, walking behind the wagon that carried the coffin. Freddie had so many friends that they were like a swarm of black ants creeping toward a picnic basket. She could not distinguish man from woman or child from dog. She didn't even acknowledge her friends, Neal, Mark, or any of the household servants she had known for so long. She did not see anything; everything was a blur. It was all in black-and-white.

The funeral went as well as could be expected as her aunt had been in charge of it. Pastor Keshmet officiated. It was all a blank; the whole thing seemed to last only minutes. When her aunt nudged her, she caught the words "ashes to ashes, dust to dust." She and Bertha got up from their seats and walked over to the pastor, who handed them a rose each. Julli took it with shaking hands and followed her aunt over to the frozen ground, where they both kneeled. They each placed a rose onto the coffin before taking a handful of dirt and sprinkled it as well.

Her aunt had brought a band that played the "Alknomook," which was the Cherokee Indian death song. There were several different tribes there for the chanting. Julli had never seen any Indians chant like they did at the funeral. They were dressed in skins with elaborate beading designs on their outfits. Julli did not know or recognize any of them or which tribes they belonged to. Freddie had been friends with nearly every tribe and had respect from Indians and whites alike.

She tried to lip-read the chanting, but their language was unknown to her, and they moved and stomped around the coffin, making it harder to see their lips. They also waved their arms up and down and bobbed as well. There were several women who sat by the men who were banging on the drums. It seemed like the whole mass of tribes were in their own way chanting and dancing to show respect for Freddie.

Julli wished she had known more about Freddie and his tribe. He always came back with a souvenir of some sort for Julli. Once it was an arrow, which Bertha made him put in his room, stating that Julli could get hurt from it. Another time he gave her a beaded necklace of multi-colors, and all Bertha could say about that was to wear it when no one was around.

Julli could not look at the coffin without seeing Freddie. She could not see anything or anyone but the coffin, which lay in front of her. She did not even flinch when the wind gushed and chills went through her body.

She wondered what he was thinking if he could think while dead. Was he smiling? Did they dress him in his favorite suit? Did they know who he really was? Was his stuff with him as he had always said he wanted when he died? Where was his tribe located? Who was the next of kin? So many questions unanswered.

Freddie had put his life around Julli's. She was his everything. He was the one she went to when she was hurt, sad, or upset. He was closer to her than her aunt was. She realized that everything was about her, and she didn't know much about Freddie but the way he took care of her. He would rather talk about Julli's family than his own. He really had loved her like she was his own blood and flesh.

Julli was not too aware of what had been said; she stood there numb to it all. She didn't look or acknowledge any of the sympathies coming from the friends who had shown up. She was immune to all the crying going on. She didn't even move when Mark came to lead her to the carriage. She didn't want to leave. She kept shaking her head at everyone and everything. She would not budge from the spot she was at. She shrugged and flicked at every hand she saw or felt. Mark and Neal both agreed they'd stay and bring her home when she was ready. Julli didn't even see her aunt leave.

She kept staring at the coffin, expecting Freddie to jump up and make her scream like a banshee as he had years ago. Julli stared blankly when the men shoveled dirt on the coffin, forever hiding Freddie from her. Time went by, and still Julli stood there. Her face expressionless. Her mind a blank. There was no more love.

CHAPTER 8

———◆◆◆———

Going West for Love
January 6, 1817
Two Months Later

I t had been two months since Freddie's untimely death. Mark had left three weeks after the funeral. He wrote her weekly, but Julli had not replied to any of his letters. Except for the last one. Mark wrote telling Julli that he had acquired some land and wanted to know if she would like to go out there to be with him. He had written that he had built a house, a small one, but nonetheless a home. He said the neighbors were helpful out there. He had begged Julli over and over to consider his request. Without her aunt knowing about it, she had finally replied that she would come out. Just not when.

Since that fateful day, Julli stopped going to church and reading the Holy Bible, whereas her aunt began to frequently attend the meetings and read the book. She was always trying to involve Julli, but she refused to pay any heed. Her grief was too deep. Even with Aunt Bertha going to the services and meetings, it wasn't the same. Aunt Bertha was without Freddie. So was Julli. Nothing was the same. The house was so quiet that the neighbors wondered if anyone was still alive there or still living in the home.

Until the day her aunt Bertha received a telegram from Mark for Julli about the trip she was planning on taking.

Storming into her room, she slammed the doors open. Shocked at the bang, Julli jumped up from her table, where she was writing, spilling the ink and knocking the stack of papers onto the spill. Frantically Julli grabbed her apron and tried to clean up the mess as her aunt came into the room, confronting Julli.

Stopping what she was doing, Julli turned to face her aunt. Exhaling and trying to remain calm, she looked at her aunt.

Hurt, Bertha handed Julli the telegram. Watching as Julli unfolded it and read what it said. When Julli closed the note and laid it down, she turned to face her aunt.

"When were you going to talk to me?" Bertha gestured to the note.

"I wasn't. And I am of age and have my own means," Julli sighed, signing slowly.

Bertha shrugged, putting out her hands. "So you were planning on leaving me without a word?"

"No," said Julli. "Actually I was going to tell you I would be gone for a while but I was going to just leave," admitted Julli, trying to avoid her aunt's look.

"Leave for where?" asked Bertha, shocked, never dreaming that Julli would one day leave her.

"To go be with Mark and help him set his claim," signed Julli, avoiding looking at her aunt.

Bertha grabbed Julli's face and turned her to face her. "Where?"

"Three thousand miles from here. No, make that the other side of the world." Julli was angry and upset that her aunt was questioning her about where she was planning on going. "Any place would be better than here," retorted Julli angrily. She was not happy that her aunt had found out.

"Why?" Bertha pushed for more information, still turning Julli to look at her when she was talking to her.

"There is nothing for me here. Freddie is gone and you are always at the meetings. Neal is in boarding school and I just don't want to be here anymore," snapped Julli, tired and not wanting to talk.

"I am still here." Grabbing Julli by the arm, Bertha forced her to look at her.

"It is not the same, Aunt Bertha," came from Julli facetiously.

"I don't see how it isn't." Bertha, not wanting to, still asked Julli, hoping that Julli was jesting with her, "When were you planning on leaving?"

"This Thursday," was all Julli would offer. A sudden emptiness hit her in the pit of her stomach. She knew what she was doing to her aunt. She hated the hurt look, the tears, and the pain she was causing her aunt. She dreaded the thought of leaving her aunt, but she really needed to get out of the house. In addition, away from the memories she carried with her daily.

Bertha winced at the soonest of the date, barely the day after tomorrow. That was not much time. Bertha removed her hand from Julli's arm, took a step back, and sniffled at the harshness of the situation.

Not willing to give in to her aunt, Julli turns from her aunt, only to have her aunt block her path.

"But how will you get to where you are going?" Bertha demands. She wanted to know what was going on with Julli, why she was being so evasive to the questions she was asking. "Are you really planning to leave?" Asking that, Bertha walked over to the table and started looking through the papers. Julli goes over there, gingerly takes them away from her aunt, and places them in the drawer. Turning to her aunt, she shrugs.

"Don't worry, it is all taken care of."

"Please tell me." Frustrated at the lack of information offered, her aunt pleaded her cause, "I am your aunt, I need to know."

"Carriage and then wagon the rest of the way," signed Julli, making the sign for carriage and adding wagon.

Grimacing at her selection of travel, her aunt then asked another question, fearing worse news than what was just told.

"Who is going with you?"

"I have already hired a driver and there will be a woman traveling with us. They are married and they have a claim on a homestead not far from where Mark staked his. I have already paid them and they are getting stuff ready for the trip. Everything is taken care of, Aunt," signed Julli, not about to reveal too much information. She didn't want her aunt keeping tabs on her through someone. She really needed her space. She was so tired of being treated with kid gloves.

"Julli, but I need to know. Please?" begged Bertha, crying as she both asked and signed. Julli only shook her head, refusing to give out any more information. "How long will you be gone?" sniffled Bertha.

"That is the thing I am not sure about. Mark was talking about me moving out there permanently. He said I could have the run of the house and my own bedroom," admitted Julli, glad that she was going to have something of her own, even though it was Mark's property.

Going over to her aunt, she grabs the handkerchief and gently wipes her aunt's eyes.

"I will write you every week. Don't worry, I will be fine." Looking at her aunt, Julli swallows and blinks back the tears.

"That is not what I mean. Do you want me to go with you? We can take a trip, make it you and me?" begged Bertha, anything to keep Julli close.

"No," smiling to soften the blow. "But thank you for offering." With that, she gives Bertha a hug. Adding, "You have your stuff to do and I need to find my way." Pacing a few steps, then turning to face her aunt, she signs more. "I can't live here like this anymore. I can't go anywhere around here without knowing someone is buried there. I just can't. I need to get out and have my own life. I need to see if I have what it takes to be my own person like Freddie taught me. You taught me to be independent and strong and to think for myself. I need to do that. I just can't do that here."

Walking away from Bertha to look out the window, Julli does not see her aunt praying. She only sees the trees and the grass. Bricks leading a pathway beyond to the gazebo, where she had secretly met with Mark. Smiling at the memory of her and Mark dancing. Remembering how they gazed into each other's eyes as Mark led her into a waltz. Her left hand in his right and the gentle pressure of his left hand on her waist. Her heart had soared with feelings she had never experienced with a man before.

Oh, and the kiss. Julli put her hand to her lips and closed her eyes, savoring the past. Her blue dress, her navy slippers, and the sapphire stone necklace.

Opening her eyes, jarred to the present when she felt a hand on her arm. Turning to Bertha, she finally saw how sad her aunt was.

Taking in the redness of Bertha's eyes, the hurt look, and the dejected posture, Julli could not help but get teary eyed. Pulling her aunt into her arms with a sob. The women clung to each other. Both crying, with Bertha rubbing Julli's back.

Closing her eyes, she breathed in deeply her aunt's perfume. Violets and hibiscus. She was going to miss her aunt. She had been there for her all these years, and Bertha was like a mother to her. Just like Freddie had been like a father.

Reaching into her pocket, Julli pulled out her hankie before stepping out of the embrace to wipe her aunt's eyes. Smoothing back strands of hair that escaped from her aunt's coiffure Julli placed a kiss on Bertha's cheek.

"I'm going to miss you more than you know." She cried while signing, "I love you."

"As will I. You mean everything to me and I am sorry that it has to be this way," came from Bertha, signing as well. She took the hankie from Julli and wiped the tears from Julli's face. "Well, since I cannot change your mind about leaving, would you spend the day with me tomorrow? We can go about the town and get whatever else you need," begged Bertha, wanting a chance not only to help Julli but also a chance to get Julli to change her mind.

"Aunt, you do not need to worry about that, I only need a few things. Mark wrote me that he has nearly everything needed for the house and all that."

"Who will help you out there?" asked Bertha, still not convinced she should let Julli go. Julli had never done much in the house as she had maids that did the job.

"What do you mean?" asked Julli, not understanding what her aunt was saying.

"You won't have any servants, right?" She cocked her head at the maids, who were lingering outside the door.

Julli, glancing at them, acknowledged what her aunt was trying to tell her. "That is true, I can always learn."

"Maybe you should consider getting a dog. They are good at protection and I know that a lot of people have one or two." At Julli's shock at the mention of a dog for protection, her aunt hastily added, "I am just worried about you." Bertha stated this sighing.

"Please don't fret, Aunt. I am sure everything will be okay. As long as you will come out and visit. You will come out, right?"

"I guess so. Just promise me that you will be careful and let me know if you need anything." Signing and drawing Julli into a hug, her aunt could no longer control what Julli had going for her. It was all Julli's decisions, her choices, and Bertha knew she could not stop Julli from making her own mistakes. Bertha knew the world was going to be harder for Julli, who had little knowledge of what could really go on out in the real world.

"I promise, Aunt, I really will," said Julli, giving in to her aunt's embrace.

Julli had spent the next day with her aunt. They did have some fun despite the fact her aunt kept coming up with little things to try dissuading Julli's mind about leaving. Bertha had taken Julli out to eat; they munched on appetizers and talked about exotic foods that they had tried. Bertha also tried persuading Julli to consider taking up a styling job at the warehouse where they made clothing. Julli turned her aunt down, even when she reminded Julli that she wanted her own style. Nothing was going to dissuade Julli from going. Her mind was set on it.

Julli spent that night visiting with her aunt. Since it was Wednesday night and there was a meeting at the church house, her aunt had canceled going, so Julli felt that she owed it to Bertha to spend time with her. It was the least Julli could do since she was leaving in the morning.

She had boarded the carriage before her aunt was up the morning after. She did not want any drama coming from Bertha and was already uneasy about leaving the home she had grown up in. They had ridden the carriage 'til they passed three towns before she finally got in the wagon with the scoutmaster and his wife.

The trip West was going to be a fun one at it, or so Julli thought as this was her first trip alone. Peace and personal space she hoped for. They were going to be on the road for weeks but were told there were stops along the way where they could stock up on supplies. Julli was not sure how long it was going to take them to get to where Mark was. She was very eager to have the journey start but was anxious to have it over. She did not know that it would be harder without Freddie, her aunt, or one of the maids with her. It was worth the risk learning to fend for herself and not having to depend on anyone. Or so she thought.

"How are you doing?" the scoutmaster's wife asked her after a few days. She shrugged, putting out her hands, and pointed to Julli.

Laughing, Julli replied, "I am doing okay. Just tired." Julli signed and said at the same time. But instead of signing like she did with her family and close friends, she gave the woman the thumbs-up and sighed dramatically.

With that, the wife turned to talk to her husband, who glanced back and chuckled. They were a nice-enough couple, but Julli feared that they sometimes only wanted her company as she paid for everything. They either didn't want to make friends or they were just not the talkative type of people.

Julli wondered what was said but knew the driver had things on his mind, so she did not want to interrupt him. She wanted to get to Mark as soon as possible.

The trip had started out exciting, but as the days went on, it had been lonely for Julli. The scoutmaster and his wife were kind enough to make an effort to talk to Julli, but they only checked with her when they made a stop and camped every night. She went everywhere the woman did and had not really talked to anyone since she left her aunt's a couple of weeks ago.

She did learn how to make a campfire by observing them night after night, and Julli noticed that a lot of the food was made by the wife, and occasionally, they were allowed to sleep in and bathe while the driver went hunting for some meat. She was now getting the hang of the outdoorsy stuff. She had not yet gotten over the sight of Zeke plucking the birds he shot for their meal. She did find it fascinating how Mindy tied the birds on the stick and put them over the fire to cook them. Julli would forget the gory sight of the plucking and cutting up at the smell of the food cooking. She wondered why she had never bothered to learn to cook besides pancakes.

She only wished that she had studied the books more before she decided to make the trek out West. She had found out that the layers of petticoats even without the bustle were not exactly helpful. She had bought some clothes similar to what the other pioneers were wearing. It was simpler and more comfortable, but the weather made her wish she had brought her heavier dresses and coats as her aunt had suggested. She did leave her fan and parasol with her aunt, not sure she was going to use it amongst the simple folks.

Julli looked at her hands; they used to be smooth and well taken care of. Now to her horror, she had scratches on them, and her nails had chipped. Her hands and face were darker than the rest of her body. Julli had never been out in the sun so long or dealt with a sunburn. It hurt. Her nose was peeling, and her lips were chapped. She needed to talk to the woman about getting some balm. Julli made it a mental point to offer to take them out to dinner the next town they got to. Maybe she and the woman could actually get cleaned up and wear something new for once.

Julli eyed the dress she had worn for two days straight. The hem was ripped, and she had sweat stains. Julli groaned when she saw how ragged she looked. Her hair was only brushed back into a braid, and she was too tired most nights to brush it the full hundred strokes. The bonnet she wore did nothing to shield her face from the sun. Neither did the wagon cover when they took it off and used the cover as a blanket to hide their belongings. *Ugh, why didn't I set it up where I had more accommodations?* she scolded herself for not knowing things would be drastically different.

Julli and the woman would walk behind or by the wagon, giving the horses a chance not to pull a heavy load. It also took their mind off of boredom and kept their bums from getting raw sitting for hours. Julli enjoyed the walks, especially when dusk fell. It was cooler, and the only problem was Julli absolutely hated the bugs and the lack of cool air.

Before long the woman turned and told Julli, "We are approaching a town. Should be there in around an hour or so." She made the sign for town, as Julli had shown her the past few places they had gotten to and left. Then pointed to her wrist for time and put up one finger, showing "one."

"Okay," said Julli, then tapped the woman on the shoulder when she started to turn back to the front. "Do you think the town has a bath and restaurant?" asked Julli, who had to use more body language than anything when she talked. Pretending to bathe and then making the motion of eating, then adding the shape of a house.

The lady asked her husband, who shrugged and nodded his head. Turning back to face Julli, she nodded her head along with a thumbs-up. Julli beamed at that gesture and clapped her hands, which they laughed about.

When they approached the town a little over an hour, Julli was so glad when they stopped at a boardinghouse. *Now, I can clean up and get presentable again.* She tapped the woman on the shoulder and told her, "I would like to take you guys out to eat, will that be okay?" pointing to both the wife and husband and making the signs of eating.

At their nod and smile, Julli grabbed a few of her belongings and headed into the house with the scoutmaster's wife. They were sent to a room, and Julli waited for the woman to lead her to the room where they could bathe and change.

Julli smiled when she removed her clothing and sank wearily into the tub, which the maid poured hot water into. She was not used to the place so took a quick bath, scrubbing everywhere she could and rinsing her hair several times before getting out.

Before she could get the towel wrapped around her, the maid again came in and drained the tub. She did not spare Julli a glance as she went about her job. Walking over to her room, she accidentally bumped into the scoutmaster's wife. "I am so sorry."

Julli quickly moved out of the way, but not before her arm was grabbed and the woman said, "That is okay." Smiling at Julli, she then added, "We are going to go downstairs to eat. The owner has offered us a meal," speaking slowly to make sure Julli could understand her.

"I want to pay for it," offered Julli, wanting to keep her spirits up by being generous.

When the woman shook her head, Julli added, "You guys have helped me and treated me good. I just want to take you out to eat," signing while pointing to the woman and giving the thumbs-up before adding the eating sign. At the woman's questioning look, Julli made the signs of her paying for the three of them. Pointing at herself, she pretended to get her bag and pay.

"Okay, I will let my husband know." Smiling at finally understanding Julli, she nodded her head, before she went into the room for her bath.

Julli went into her room and dried her hair before putting on a purple chemise dress with a lighter purple blouse. She put on her spencer jacket and donned black boots. Looking at herself in the mirror, she decreed, *Not bad for a green foot. Ha-ha.*

She hastily donned her bloomers, and like before, she refused again to wear the bustle. She had seen so many out here not wearing one. Mostly the upper class wore them, but the lower-class folks didn't.

Julli felt she had more in common with the lower class than with the upper class. Even though she was raised to be more refined, she had always seemed to prefer being simple.

When she went downstairs, she spotted the driver and his wife, who waved her over to sit with them. Julli ignored the appreciating looks and whistles from the scrawny men who were up at the counter drinking their ale. Before she could sit down in the chair that the scoutmaster pulled out for her, she was spun around to face a different man. This time he was bigger and burlier than the others she ignored.

"What the matta, missy? Too good to sit with us folks?" slurred the burly man, gesturing to himself and his partners, who leered at that.

Julli stared at the man with shock. *Who did he think he was to treat her like that?* With that the scoutmaster moved over to Julli and stated, "Excuse me. Let go of her."

The wife got up and grabbed Julli, making her stay behind her, as her husband faced the stranger.

"She too good for the likes of me, huh?" again came the slurred words from the intruder.

"Leave her alone," stated Julli's friend. He stood in front of the man's view, and both stared at each other.

Glaring at the man defending Julli, the stranger faced him and retorted, "You wanna a piece of me huh?" With that, he poked the scoutmaster on the chest with his finger. Julli grimaced at how filthy his hands were.

Julli, getting upset that her friend was being harassed, started signing and using her voice as well. "Leave him alone, you brute!" she snapped angrily.

"Huh?" came the shocked voice of the man. He paused to look at Julli. She shuddered at the look he gave her. It gave her a bad feeling. Something was wrong with that man.

"You heard me, you brute," stated Julli, not going to give an inch. *Maybe he will listen to me*, she added to herself. If push came to shove, she was going to shove with all her might.

"Whadda the matta, honey? Can't talk right?" he replied, trying to see Julli behind the man protecting her. Julli saw the other men snickering and slamming their mugs on the table. She looked at the man who was insulting them directly, and fear consumed her. She willed herself to remain calm.

The burly man finally got to look at Julli when he leaned to the side. She was darn right pretty. He was not going to let the opportunity pass him by. When he saw Julli just glaring at him, in her way of standing up to him, it riled him. No prissy girl was going to treat him that way.

He shoved the scoutmaster and lounged for Julli. The wife was shoved out of the way by Julli as she got her strength fueled by fear, and she overcame it by boxing the man on the ears. No one was going to harass her friends because of her. She was so sick and tired of people acting like she was dumb or just a trinket for their amusement. She had seen Freddie knock men on their feet, and he showed her how to defend herself. If worse came, she was going to fight the best she could.

"Ow!" he howled in pain. "You hit me, you little wretch!" he yelled at Julli. He stood up to his full height and faced Julli, who was standing her ground, anger in her eyes. Her stance defensive. Her hands bunched into fists, ready to use them again if necessary.

Before he could do anything, he was grabbed back by the owner of the franchise, who pointed a gun at his head. Julli watched in amazement as the guys stared each other down, and finally after muttering something she couldn't catch, the man she had boxed gave her one final glance, then stomped out of the room. He shoved anyone in his way, and the men who were with him took a look at the owner with his gun and decided they had better leave as well.

Everybody stared at Julli, and several bystanders started applauding. It took guts for a woman to box a man twice her size.

Julli looked around and saw the wife getting up, helped by her husband, and rushed over to apologize. "I am so sorry!" she signed by putting her fist over her heart.

The scoutmaster helped his wife up and looked at her before he responded to Julli by saying, "You saved my wife," sighing as he looked at his wife. Then he muttered a "thank you."

Julli only nodded her head. When several people came over to congratulate her and make sure everything was okay, they could not figure out why she would not answer them. One lady patted Julli on the arm, and another curtsied to her. Several of the men tipped their hats to her.

"Excuse me, folks. Please leave Julli alone," asked the scoutmaster.

The franchise owner came over, and since he had one of those bushy mustaches, Julli could not lip-read him. Julli just stared at him, not understanding him at all. To her relief, the scoutmaster's wife spoke for her, "Thank you." The added, "Yes, we would like to eat in in the privacy of our room."

Julli noticed that the maid was gathering up the mugs and dirty dishes that the men had left. She saw the sad face on the lady and figured that they probably left without paying. Wanting to smooth things over as the problem was because of her, she went over to the owner and said, "I am going to pay for their meal and drinks."

The owner just stared at Julli, not understanding her way of speaking nasally. One of the women there understood enough, walked over to Julli and the owner, and told him, "She is going to pay for their meals and drinks."

"Why?" the man asked, confused.

"If it was not for me, they would not have caused any problems. I am sorry for the damage they caused," signed Julli, using her voice as well as signing. It seemed the one lady could understand her enough for she spoke to the owner again in Julli's behalf.

"She feels responsible for what happened. So she wants to pay," stated the woman.

"Okay." The owner nodded. He gestured to the maid, who came over and told him how much it was for the men. Julli lip-read the girl for the amount, pulled out her money pouch, and handed the owner the amount due.

Julli felt good that she did clean up the mess, even though it was not her fault. When her friend grabbed her arm and nodded to the stairs, she nodded along with her. But before they grabbed their stuff off the table, Julli saw that the men were talking about something. How right she was in assuming it was about her.

"What the matter with her?" asked the franchise owner to the man in charge of the women, pointing to Julli.

"She is deaf," replied the scoutmaster. Julli saw him glance at her and smiled. *Now I have a friend I can trust*, Julli said to herself.

Julli saw the muddled mass of bystanders back away and chat between themselves. Pointing at her, Julli could only assume that they were talking about her. Either her bravery or the fact that she could not hear. *What was new?* she thought to herself. She had that happen to her way too often when new people came into the town. Looking at the wife, she nodded her head, and they were led out of the room by one of the servants.

They left the next morning at sunrise. They did not want to linger any longer in that town for fear there would be another confrontation with the guy and his gang.

That was not the only reason. After the townspeople found out Julli was deaf, the folks who had nothing better to do than to gossip about her had swarmed the streets. When she looked out of the window, she saw several men placing their hands on their shotguns, and women grabbed their children back out of her sight. *Wow*, thought Julli. *They are the ones who are dumb.* Julli decided that she was going to have some fun. She stood at the window half the night and kept peeking out and jerking forward. She couldn't stop laughing every time someone would scamper as fast as they could. She saw the sheriff coming out on the street, talking to some of the folks, and when Julli saw him staring at her through the window, she repeated her actions and laughed even harder when he scurried out of her sight. Mindy came into the room and walked over to see what was making Julli laugh. She snickered when she saw several more folks scamper at Julli's face in the window. Looking at Julli, Mindy said, "Wow, some folks sure are scared of nothing."

Julli thought it would be funny to test Mindy. She took a step forward, putting out her hands and scrunching up her face. Mindy just looked at Julli and asked, "Trying to make me deaf like you?"

Both women cracked up laughing. Zeke came in and told them, "The sheriff wants us to leave before someone gets hurt. We have 'til morning to be gone."

Julli looked at Mindy, who raised her eyebrow, and they both stepped forward up to Zeke and made the scariest faces they could. Zeke, looking scared, took a step back, only to go forward and scare the girls back. They all started laughing so hard that Mindy had to stop to say, "I have to go to the bathroom." Julli and Zeke continued laughing after Mindy left.

Julli had finally found out what her friends' names were. Zeke and Miranda, Mindy for short. They were like the best folks Julli had come across. Zeke had told Julli that they would be neighbors as he had set up a claim only a few miles from where she would be with Mark.

"Anytime you need anything, just come up to our place and we will help you as much as we can," Zeke told Julli, trying to sign as much as he could, Julli all the while having a hard time communicating with him as he had no teeth. After a few tries, he had given up and had his wife relay his messages to Julli. It gave Miranda and Julli a chance to get to know each other better. Julli lip-reading Mindy while teaching her some signs.

CHAPTER 9

———◆◆◆———

Reunited with Mark, Getting a Job, Homestead
February 13, 1817

The next few days went by fast to Julli's delight. She and Miranda were making progress in their communication skills, as was Zeke, much to his chagrin. Before Julli knew it, they were heading to the town called Johnsville.

It would not be much longer 'til Julli was reunited with Mark, whom she had not seen for nearly a year. The butterflies fluttered in Julli's stomach at the prospect of seeing Mark again. *What if he doesn't like me?* she asked herself, worried that she had changed too much. She was not the bubbly sixteen-year-old he had kissed; she was now seventeen, nearly eighteen.

Looking at her hands and face in the mirror, she hoped she had not changed too much for him not to recognize her. In less than two hours, she would be at the boardinghouse, and Zeke was going to send word to Mark through the sheriff. The women were to go in and clean up. Julli thought it was very generous of Zeke to want the women to freshen up while he still toiled after the long drive. She was pretty sure that once Zeke's head hit the pillows tonight, he would be sound asleep 'til midday tomorrow. Julli had to laugh at that sight. The poor man earned it.

They got to Johnsville and headed into the boardinghouse named Tillie's. Both Mindy and Julli glanced at each other and smiled. Julli could smell the food cooking in the evening air, and her stomach growled. Mindy went up to the counter to talk to the clerk, while Julli wandered around the room. There were all sorts of decorations on the walls, from bear hides to dried flowers framed. The sight was rustic but feminine as well.

A hand touched her on the shoulder, and Julli turned to face Mindy, who gestured to the stairs. *Where is Mark?* Julli wondered. And they went up the stairs into the rooms, opened by a male servant. Bowing to the women after making sure, they entered the room, and Mindy nodded to him. "Wow!" gushed Julli, full of excitement. She ran over to the window and parted the curtains, letting in some sun. She wanted to take in all she could of this new town that Mark had brought her to by his letters. She was glad that there was a fire going in the hearth in the room as it had gotten real chilly out.

Mindy came to stand by her at the window, and they both looked out, taking in the view 'til the door reopened and the servants brought in a tub, which they put in the corner and proceeded to fill with hot water fresh from the stove. Mindy gestured to the tub and told Julli, "I am going to go find out about the food. I will be back in ten minutes."

With that, Julli replied, "Okay." Then she got busy getting ready for her bath. Mindy shut the door and left Julli to the tub.

Julli hurried in cleaning herself even though she wanted to soak her aching body. She knew that Mindy needed to bath also and didn't want to slow her friend down by making her wait. Getting out of the water, wrapping a towel around herself, she hurriedly grabbed her clothes and went behind the changing curtain and donned her clothes. She decided that she could only wear the simple dress that she and Mindy picked out a few towns back and hadn't worn yet. It was of a deep purple hue, which made Julli's skin seem even darker and her eyes more blue.

Just as she was starting to brush and braid her hair, she felt a pounding on the door. Before she could go over there to answer it, Mark opened it and came into the room. Julli stared at him. He had only changed a little as his skin was darker from the sun and his muscles were bigger. Julli dropped the brush and gave a squeal of joy when Mark quickly grabbed her into his arms. She could feel him laughing. She wrapped her arms around his neck as he picked her off her feet and swung her around a couple times before placing her back on the floor. Her hair whipped about them, still damp. She looked into his eyes and saw that he was pleased with her. He smiled at her, and Julli found out she couldn't stop herself from being so giddy with happiness.

Unable to stop smiling, they pulled apart to look each other up and down, before Mark grabbed her again. The hug was fiercely possessive yet gentle enough that Julli could breathe. Finally, Mark let her go enough that she was able to stand on her own feet, but still held on to her. Julli watched as Mark leaned down, and she met his lips with her own, hungering for the taste and feel of him again.

To Julli's dismay, Mark ended the kiss when Mindy came and knocked at the door. Still looking at Julli, he mouthed the words, "Always interrupted." Julli had to laugh at that. Then Mark looked at Mindy and said, "I know." Shrugging his shoulders at Julli, he added, "Let's get out of here so she can have the room." With that, Julli glanced at Mindy, who only shrugged and nodded her head but who was smiling also.

With a squeal of delight, Julli tore herself out of Mark's arms, ran over to Mindy to grab her into a bear hug, and kissed her on the cheek. Dragging Mindy over to Mark, not knowing for sure if they had met each other or not, she introduced Mark to Mindy, "This is Mark I was telling you about. This is my good friend Miranda. She likes to be called Mindy."

Mark turns and says, "Hi, thanks for bringing Julli to me safe and sound. For that I am in your debt." Mark bows his head to Mindy. Then he looks at Julli and asks, "Julli, are you ready to go?"

Julli looks at Mark, smiling, and says, "Yes, Mark, I am."

Then they both say their good-byes and walk out of the room holding hands. Halfway down the hall, Mark stops, turns to Julli, and looks at her. Julli wondered if he was going to remember how they used to communicate. She hoped that she did not disappoint him.

Mark then asked her, "Julli, are you hungry?"

He made sure he looked right at her. Julli was relieved to know he had not forgotten.

Julli said, "Yes, I am! But where do we go to eat?"

"Do not worry. I know a place that we can go to, if that is all right with you?"

With that question from Mark, Julli nods and says, "Yes, Mark, I would love to." Then signs, "But where are we going?"

Mark says, "We are going to Gunpoint Inn, I know the owner."

With that said, they both started to walk. They walked over to Gunpoint Inn. Mark leads her in and takes her over to meet the owner.

"Kathrin, I would like you to meet Julli. Julli, this is my friend Kathrin. She has helped me out a lot since I moved out here about a year ago. I knew her husband back East."

Kathrin smiles and then says, "Hello, Julli, you are lucky to have Mark. He has been a great help." She kept pointing to Mark and giving the thumbs-up. Mark had told her that Julli was deaf but not dumb. Kathrin also learned a little body language to pass for sign language.

Julli says, signing along with using her voice, "Hi, I am very glad to meet you. I did not know that you could be a woman running a place like this."

Kathrin looked at Julli, and sadness was in her voice when she replied, "Oh, Julli, this place was my husband's. But now that he is gone, I needed the income so I took over. It helps me to keep the memories of my dead but loving husband."

"Oh, Kathrin! I am sorry for your loss," said Julli, remembering her own a year ago. She had to fight back tears and sniffled. "I too lost someone very close to me a little over a year ago but it seems like it was only yesterday."

"Thank you and I am sorry for yours as well. Word of Freddie's death had reached a lot of the folks here and those who knew him or of him mourned as well," replied Kathrin, hoping that she had not offended Julli. Mark had told them all that Julli had lost it when her guardian had died.

Accepting the consolations from Kathrin, she looked at Mark, then back to Kathrin, who wiped her hands on her apron.

"I would have never thought that your husband was dead. You seem to enjoy running the place." With that, Julli patted Kathrin on the arm.

Then Mark interrupted, "Okay, I think that it is time for food, before all the sadness ruins my appetite." Mildly frustrated that Julli and Kathrin were chatting about their losses when he had only plans to take Julli out to eat and woo her.

Both women laughed when Mark got done signing to Julli and also used his voice so Kathrin knew what he signed.

Kathrin led them to a table and said, "I will have Cook prepare what you requested for when Julli came here."

Mark pulled out the chair and waited for Julli to sit before helping scoot the chair back up to the table. Then he went to the corner and pulled out his chair and sat down.

Julli placed her hands on the table, only to have them grabbed by Mark, who was gazing at her.

"I am so glad that you decided to come. I was not sure if you wanted anything to do with me after I left. But then I got your telegram saying you were coming," admitted Mark, feigning uncertainty. But he was beaming when he added, "I was so happy to know that you were going to come, but you never said exactly when." Mark made sure she could see what he was saying.

Julli felt a little remorse for putting Mark through a period of worrying, but she had not known where to go or had the time while she was traveling with Zeke and Miranda.

All Julli could do was shrug her shoulders and put on her best pouting face. Mark laughed at that, and Julli smiled. She had not thought too much about letting anyone know where she was; she was afraid something would happen and she would miss the rendezvous with Mark.

Mark looked at Julli and asked, "Why did you not send word where you were?"

"I had no idea where to go and we were always in a hurry to get somewhere else. Zeke and his wife had stuff they had to do and I tagged along with Mindy so I would not be left alone."

"I really wanted to know what was going on and if you were okay. I thought that something might have happened to you."

"I am so sorry I did not send word," signed Julli, afraid that she upset Mark.

"Did you want to surprise me, Julli?" was all Mark signed, to Julli's relief.

"Yes, I did. I was not sure if you wanted to see me after these past few months though," admitted Julli, both signing and talking.

"Why would you think that?" astounded, Mark asked, putting his hands out.

"I was not so sane when Freddie died. I practically ignored everyone, especially you. I did read all the letters you sent but I just could not get the feeling of doing anything for a long time." Shaking her head, she signed, "I am sorry."

When she was done signing, Mark grabbed her hands and said, "Nothing matters anymore. You are here and we are going to have a lot of fun together."

Looking at Julli, he added, "I really missed you."

"And I, you as well," admitted Julli with downcast eyes.

Picking up her hand, he laid a kiss on the palm of it before Kathrin came in with the food. Julli smiled at that gesture, her heart bursting with love.

Putting the plates on the table, Julli noticed that she had blueberry pancakes with fresh blueberries on top, and cinnamon sugar was sprinkled on it as well. Kathrin set down a small pitcher of maple syrup next to it. Julli's eyes widened at the food in front of her.

"Something the matter?" asked Mark, gesturing to her plate.

"No, it looks really good. Mark, you remembered my favorite food." Looking at Kathrin, she said, "Thank you!" Julli looks at the plate that Kathrin set in front of Mark and notices that he has fried potatoes with slices of ham and a biscuit. Julli makes it a mental note to learn how to make that. Watching Mark place his napkin on his lap, she does the same and picks up her fork. But before she can dig in, he stops her by placing his hand over hers.

"Do you mind if we pray first?"

"No." She shakes her head. Nodding at her, Mark takes her hand, and they proceed to bow their heads in prayer.

"Our Father, thank you for this day. Thank you for Julli who is with me out here. Thank you for the food that you have humbly graced the table with. In Jesus's name, Amen."

Julli adds, "Amen."

And Mark leans over the table to plant a kiss on her cheek. They go ahead and dig in. Julli savored her first bite, then ate with gusto. She did not care about manners; she was famished. Kathrin put a glass of milk on the table, and Julli grabbed and drank it greedily. She did not notice that other guests were staring at her. Not until Mark tapped her on the shoulder and asked, "So how is the food?" Glancing at the other guests, she felt herself blush before she replied to Mark's question.

"It is really good. I have to thank the cook before we leave." She signed the whole sentence as she had her mouth stuffed still with blueberries.

"Would you like to thank him now?"

"Oh yes," nodding her head. Then it dawned on her that they were being watched. *Oh great!* she thought to herself. *Mark must be ashamed of me.* Julli looked around the room real quick, only to catch the people turning their heads from her. Not one person looked her squarely in the eye.

Mark just looked at her with a smile on his face, his plate half eaten. He gestured for the servant to come over and whispered something in the maid's ear. Julli watched as she nodded to Mark and left the room in a hurry.

"What was that about?" Julli signed, scrunching up her face.

"You said you wanted to thank the cook?"

"Yes, I did."

"Look," pointing to the door as a burly man came out, wiping his hands on the apron. The cook was none other than Zeke.

"Wha—?"

Laughing, Zeke came over and pulled Julli out of her chair to squish her in a bear hug. Julli could not help but laugh out loud. Her friend was the cook. And he was a real darn good one at that. Julli started to wonder why Zeke never cooked on the drive, besides the fact he was driving and taking care of the ox.

"Glad you like the food. This is something I'll have to take up with Mindy when she comes here later to eat," came cheerfully from Zeke. Julli wondered how his wife was going to react when he told her. *I hope he breaks it to her gently.* She snickered to herself.

With wonder at how their friendship was, Julli watched as Mark and Zeke shook hands. It seemed like everywhere she went, Mark was well-known. She got a little upset that the men were standing there chatting and Julli could not lip-read either man.

Then with a bow to Julli, Zeke hurried back into the kitchen to finish his orders.

"I did not know. That was a surprise."

"Zeke has been the cook for a few years. His wife Mindy has never been out here 'til now. That is why it was so easy to have you travel with them as he had gone back East to get Mindy to bring her out here."

"Nobody told me anything." Julli wondered at how much more she was going to find out that she had not been told.

"You do miss out a lot. I am sorry," apologized Mark.

Picking up her fork and laying it back down when she realized that she did not have any crumbs on her plate to pick at. She was somewhat upset that she missed out on a lot of events because no one thought to tell her. Now with Mark not telling her what they talked about, Julli felt out of place. It would not be the first time, and it was not going to be the last either.

Mark mimicked Julli in picking up his fork, only to lay it back down the same way Julli did.

"I take it you must not have ate much on your trip," he stated. Julli felt self-conscious about having eaten like she was uncivilized. Julli looked down at herself and noticed that her dress did seem to be somewhat too large on her. She had not focused that much on her body while she was on the trip out there.

Signing, she admitted, "I did eat but there was not much to pick from. Mindy is a good cook but it was long and hot during the day and cold at night so we did not take much time to fix anything fancy like this." Shrugging her shoulders, she continued with her signing, "There were a few times that I felt like I was overdressed or plain just not wearing clothes."

"What do you mean?" asked Mark, frowning at the statement from Julli.

"Well, a few days ago, we were at this town, Zeke had to get some more feed for the oxen and we rested up a little. When I went downstairs to eat with them, some disgustingly rude man grabbed me and he scared me." Swallowing, she went on with the story, watching Mark's face go from disbelief to anger. "Zeke told the man to leave me alone but he kept glaring at me like I was something he had to have to play with." Julli sighed and finished her story. "When he would not leave Zeke alone, I got so mad and boxed him on the ear!" stated Julli, putting up her fists and pretending to punch the man. All the while, the guests were staring at her, wondering what in the world a well-bred lady was doing acting like that.

"You did what?" Mark burst out laughing in disbelief. The guests looked at them in horror.

Julli nervously repeated, "I boxed him on the ear." Watching Mark looking at her between fits of laughter. Julli glanced around and saw that several of the customers were talking about them the way they were pointing and chattering with each other. *Here we go again!* Julli muttered.

"You boxed him?" questioned Mark, picking up the napkin and wiping his eyes.

"Yes, I did," stated Julli as confidently as she could.

"How big of a guy was he?" came the questions from Mark, who kept looking at her with laughter in his eyes. Mark glanced around and ignored the other guests, whom he could hear murmuring amongst themselves.

"Taller than you and real fat," admitted Julli, showing Mark how tall and fat the guy was by getting up.

"What did he do about that?" edged Mark on after Julli sat back down. He wanted to know the end result to the story.

"He just yelled at me. Then the storekeeper had a gun pointed at his head. I guess they had some words and then he stomped off," was all Julli was going to say. She stopped signing when she noticed that a few kids were mimicking her.

"I wish I had been there for you," stated Mark, not happy at all. Julli watched as he grabbed the napkin off his lap and bunched it into a ball before tossing it onto the table. Anger evident on his face.

"It is okay. All in all, the trip was not so bad," admitted Julli, hoping that she had not upset Mark too much by the little details she told him.

He grabbed Julli's hand and kissed her on the wrist. Sighing, he looked at her, and his face softened at the look of bewilderment on Julli's. "I really have missed being around you."

Flustered, Julli smoothed her skirts; she did not want to talk about the trip anymore. She only wanted Mark's attention.

"What did you learn?"

"Well," putting down her napkin after wiping the corners of her mouth, "basically I learned how to make do out there. I watched Mindy prepare the food and helped with the dishes." Adding, "Then they taught me how to identify tracks. Well, some of them.

"Zeke told me that there were lots of wild animals and it would do me good to have a dog by my side. They bark a lot when someone comes or at noises. And since I cannot hear, it does make sense to have one." At Mark's raised eyebrow, she added, "Only if you think I should have one."

"That is something to consider. What kind of dog did you have in mind?"

"I am not sure. Probably something large like a Labrador or a German shepherd." Julli made the signs of how big she wanted a dog to be by showing Mark where her thigh was.

"Okay, I will see what we can do," suggested Mark, looking appreciatively at the skirt that hid her thigh from his sight. Julli, noticing where his eyes strayed, hurriedly put her hand back up.

Mark finished his food. Julli noticed that he had some things on his mind by the way he stared intensely at his plate. She took that moment to take in everything. He was wearing a navy shirt under a black vest, black canvas field trousers, and black boots. Luckily, he was not wearing a cravat. His sideburns had gotten darker and longer since she last saw him. His hands had a few cuts on them. She made it a point to ask him later how he hurt them.

Seeing Julli looking at him, he smiled and reached over the table to grab her hand.

"Do you miss your aunt?"

Julli signed and said, "I had to keep it a secret as long as I could, so my aunt would stay off my back. She found out when you sent the telegram with the information. She did everything she could to stop me from coming out here. I do miss my aunt. I have not had much thought of her while I was traveling." When done, she placed her hands on the table, noticing the stains on the tablecloth. Julli also noticed that the plates and glasses were not like the fine china dishware her aunt used. There were chips on them. At the mention of her aunt, Julli wondered how Bertha was faring with Julli being gone.

155

"I know that she misses you. We will send word to her tomorrow after I come back into town to get you and take you out to the homestead."

Disappointment showed on her face at that. "I was hoping to go out as soon as I got here," she admitted. She had been looking forward to seeing the place Mark called home.

Smiling at that, Mark told her, "Don't worry, you will see it before long. I still have to put the bed in the room for you and I thought that you would like to stay at the boardinghouse with your friends, just for tonight."

"Oh," signed Julli, glad that she could sleep in a bed and be close to her friends but sad that Mark was putting off having her out there. "That would work. I will have to let them know."

"Already told them and they agreed to accommodate you tonight," gestured Mark. Julli found out that he seemed to know her well enough to make decisions for her. She was in a strange land away from everything that she had known.

Glad that Mark thought of her, she smiled and mouthed, "Thank you."

Waving Kathrin over, he told her, "Thank you. The meal was delicious as always."

Kathrin beamed at that. Julli noticed that Kathrin gave Mark a special treatment. *Well*, thought Julli, *they had known each other for a while so it isn't that big of a deal.*

"How is everything going for you?" Julli saw Mark asking Kathrin. He kept glancing at Julli, making sure she knew what he said.

"It is going okay. Could use more help," replied Kathrin, looking around. Julli saw that Kathrin was wearing a printed dress with a white apron. The sleeves were short and buttoned in the back. Her golden hair was wrapped in a bun at the back of her head. Julli noticed that there were no curls in the womenfolk's hair. Some of the women did wear bonnets, but most had them off while in the restaurant.

Looking at Julli, she asked, "How would you feel about helping out here?"

Shocked at the outright question, Julli's mouth dropped open before she could stop it. Closing her mouth, she looked Kathrin squarely in the eye.

"What do you mean?" Looking around, Julli saw a few servants busily running around the place. "Don't you have servants?"

Laughing at that, Kathrin replied, "I do not believe in slavery and when someone works for me, I pay them. Unlike some others but mostly us folks fend for ourselves on our own."

Glancing at Mark, who nods his head, Julli ponders how she could be of help to Kathrin. She had barely learned to make pancakes, or flapjacks as they were normally called. It was going to be different, just like moving to a different place. Looking at both Mark, who kept nodding, and Kathrin, who pleaded with her eyes.

Julli told Kathrin, "I would love to help you," signing uncertainly. Not quite sure if it was a joke or not, but the looks on Mark's and Kathrin's faces were ones not bordering on a joke.

"Oh, that is great!" cheered Kathrin. She went over to Julli and pulled her up off her feet to give her a hug. Julli hugged Kathrin back, all the while smiling.

"We are going to do so good with you here," stated Kathrin after she let go of Julli, who quickly sat back down dumbfounded. "Mark, make sure you bring Julli back in two days so she can get started." Again, to Julli she said, "That is great!" With that, she walked off out of the room.

"What just happened?" asked Julli, not sure she could believe her own eyes at what had just transpired there. She glanced at her hands fidgeting with the napkin.

Mark only looked at her and shrugged. "You got a job and now you can earn your own money." Then as an afterthought, he added a question, "What do you really know how to do?"

"What would I have to do?"

"Umm, I am not sure. I guess you clean off tables, set them, wash dishes and maybe cook. I believe that you would have to clean the rooms as well."

"Are you serious?" Shocked, Julli was not sure she really was to do that. Her aunt had always made the servants do the housework, and Julli went along with it as it gave her more time to herself.

"Yes. Or you could stay at the homestead and make do with what we have," suggested Mark.

"I do know how to clean and set a table." She added when Mark looked quizzically at her, "I have done dishes before. I am sure I can clean the rooms." She widened her eyes at the look Mark gave her. It was one where he was not sure she was a working girl.

"And cook?" signed Mark, showing Julli the cutting, paring, and chopping signs, along with the frying, cutting, and wiping the table off.

"Cook?" Swallowing, Julli fidgeted with the napkin again. "Umm, I am not so sure I would be qualified to do that," signed Julli, nervous about that one thing she had never had to learn, not even on the trip, as Mindy was in charge of the food.

"You can learn. Kathrin is a patient woman," encouraged Mark, nodding his head.

"I hope so," signed Julli, still not sure she would measure up as a cook.

"Well, congratulations to getting yourself a job and becoming even more independent. I am proud of you." With that, he grabbed her hands and planted several kisses on both of them. Julli was then glad that she took the job. It seemed to make Mark happy, and it would give her something to do 'til she got used to the new place.

Getting up, reaching into his vest pocket for some money, which he put on the table for the meal, he turned to Julli and asked, "Are you ready to go?"

Nodding her head, she gave Mark her hand when he offered, and he pulled the chair back when she got up.

"I will walk you to the door. Then I am going to head home," signed Mark, not caring that they were still in the public's eye.

All Julli could do was agree with him and let him lead her out of the room amid the stares coming from the customers still sitting at their tables.

Mark still had hold of her arm when they went up the stairs to the doors of the room that Julli was going to stay the night in. Mindy and her husband, Zeke, were to stay in the room next to Julli's. As they neared the door, Mark loosened his hold on her arm and turned her to face him.

"I am so glad you came," he signed happily.

"Me too," signed Julli, not wanting the night to end.

Then Mark quickly grabs Julli into a hug that seemed to take forever.

Julli smiles as Mark starts to let her out of the hug, but before he could say his good-byes, Julli takes his hand and asks for a kiss. "Can I have a kiss?" she asked nervously. It was not common for a woman to ask a man for a kiss; usually it happened the other way around.

Mark smiles at that request, and when he started to lean down to give Julli a kiss, she wraps her arms around his neck. Marks pulls Julli closer to him. His lips gently touch hers. Julli moved closer to deepen the kiss. She felt Mark make a noise deep in his chest. She also felt his heart beating fast like hers was.

Just before Mark broke the kiss, his hand went onto her cheek, and he gently rubbed his fingers along the side of her face. The kiss deepened and became more passionate. Julli could feel the heat scorching her whole body, and she never wanted that feeling to end.

I think I am falling in love with him, she thought to herself.

Mark broke off the kiss to place another kiss on her forehead. Pulling back, they could feel the mutual feeling that they both had for each other. It was a lover's feeling. He removed his hand from her face and pulled out of the embrace.

Gazing into each other's eyes, taking in their features, Julli says, "Mark, I think that I have fallen in love with you."

That made Mark smile, and then he said, "Julli, I love you too."

After Mark left her at the door, Julli hurried to bed, not bothering to brush her hair or change her undergarments. She was so wound up after the time she spent with Mark that she could not sleep very well.

She woke up the next morning groggily, when Mindy came in and gave her a gentle shake.

"Mark is here," she said, hoping Julli would get up.

"What? Already?" At Mindy's nod, Julli yawned and signed, "Okay, thank you."

After Mindy left the room, Julli jumped out of bed and began the preparations to get ready to leave. She was going to see the homestead. Julli wondered if it was what she expected, or would it be less than what she was used to and be disappointed? Shrugging her shoulders, she grabbed her bag and pulled out her dresses, looking at them and not sure which one to put on. She held up the light red Empire-style gown and the less formal plain green Western dress she had bought and decided since she wanted to impress Mark the red dress would show her confidence.

Julli hurriedly removed her nightgown for the dress. She grabbed her brush out of the bag as well and brushed her hair, putting it in a high bun and wrapping the ends into hairpins. She glanced at the mirror on the dresser and was satisfied. She could get herself presentable without help. Mark should be impressed that she did not need a servant to do nearly everything for her.

Grabbing all of her stuff into the bag, glancing around the room, she then picked up the bag and walked out of the room.

She walked down and saw Mark look up. She nearly stumbled coming down the stairs at the appreciative look on Mark's face. She noticed that he had changed shirts but was wearing the trousers he had on last night. The only difference was he added a Western duster and a black hat.

Julli noticed that it was chillier in the mornings out West. She had brought her spencer jacket but was not sure if it was going to be warm enough as she could see her breath in the room. The chilly air sent chills down her body, and she rubbed her arms.

Mark walked over to Julli, grabbed her bag, and placed a kiss on her forehead. He looked at Julli, and she felt nervous. She had never been around Mark that early in the morning.

"Do you have everything?"

"No, I do have some stuff in the wagon," Julli told him, looking around for Mindy or Zeke. Not finding them, she focused on what Mark had to say to her. She was a little worried that Mark would think she had too much stuff or not the right stuff for the homestead.

"Not anymore. I loaded what was yours last night before I left so they are in the house."

"Then this is all I have with me right now."

"Okay, we are to stop by Zeke's on the way to the homestead. Something about Mindy cooking breakfast." Julli grimacing at the mention of Mindy's quick and not-so-flavorful breakfasts, Mark had to laugh. "It isn't so bad. From what I know about Mindy, when she takes the time, it is actually pretty good."

"You think? She hardly ever took time to flavor the foods."

"Well, she is at her home now, so let's see."

Mark took her arm and led her out of the boardinghouse to a carriage waiting outside the doors. The air was nippy, and Julli was shivering even with all the clothes she had on. Mark helped Julli up the carriage and placed her bag next to her before he got up himself. Grabbing a blanket he had on the front, he shook it open and placed it on Julli's lap. And clicking to the horse, off they went.

Julli watched as Mark expertly handled the horse leading the carriage. She looked at the small town as they rode out, leaving it for a couple of days. It was smaller than where she grew up in. There was a general store, a barbershop, two boardinghouses, sheriff's office, a saloon called the Rust Bucket, and a post office. Julli made a mental note to check out every store and office and get to know her way around. Remembering that she agreed to help Kathrin out in a couple of days, that would give her a chance to come to town nearly every day. With Mark's permission, look for a puppy to train to help her. Her aunt gave her some ideas in making her own life easier out West. Especially since she did not have any servants to help her.

They went to Zeke and Miranda's for breakfast. For once Miranda's food had flavor, which Julli acknowledge by smiling at Mindy. Then they said their good-byes and went on to Mark's place. Julli tried hard to memorize how to get where they were going and how to get back to town. The ride was nearly eleven miles, and they got there around one o' clock.

Julli looked at the homestead with awe. It was small compared to her aunt's place, but it was going to be hers and Mark's place. Mark stopped the carriage right in front of the house. She could see the windows were closed as it was chilly. Mark tied off the reins, got down, and walked over to Julli's side to help her out. She picked up her skirts and took the hand he offered. Gingerly she got down and breathed a sigh of relief. She was home, if she could call it that.

Still holding on to her hand, Mark led her to the door and opened it. Julli walked inside and took in the surroundings. It was sparsely decorated; a small square table with three wooden chairs was placed not too far from the brick fireplace. There was a pile of wood, and the fire was going, just barely. There was a potted plant on one of the side tables. Dishes were stacked on the shelf by the pantry, which was open. Mark led her to one of the doors on the right, which Julli assumed was her room.

Opening it for her, she stepped in to see a bed with a feather quilt and pillow. That was her quilt. She saw there was a folding changing screen in the corner not far from another fireplace. On the basin were a washing bowl and a pitcher. She saw another door, a smaller one, which she suspected was the closet. Walking over to the screen, she took a peek behind it to see there was a potty bowl. The window across from her bed was closed and was adorned with the flowered curtains her aunt had sent with her. She looked at Mark with approval on her face. She caught the smile he quickly hid.

"Come out and I will show you the rest."

Putting her hand in his again, they walked out in the nippy weather, heading out to the barn. Mark opened it, and Julli saw that he had bales of hay, bins of feed, and some farming equipment.

"What do you think?"

"I love it. It is so nice and homely."

"Homely?" asked Mark, his mouth open in shock.

"Yes, I mean it has the feel of a home," admitted Julli, signing quietly.

"Oh, I see."

Julli could see the disappointment on his face from the term 'homely' she used because he thought she meant plain. She punched him on the arm and smiling shook her head, signing, "Gotcha!"

Laughing, she hurried into Mark's arms and gave him a hug. Mark was not about to let Julli go as he cupped her chin in his hand and leaned down. The kiss went on for several minutes 'til Mark released her and took her hand again, leading her back to the house. He only let go of her hand to close the barn doors.

Walking back to the house, holding hands, Mark turned to face her and asked, "What would you like to do?"

Flustered at that question, she wondered what was there to do.

"I do not know. Are there any chores we need to do?"

Mark gestured to the ox and carriage. "I need to get the ox off the yoke and put him out to pasture. If you want to go ahead and go in, I'll be in shortly."

Julli nodded her head, but before she could walk away, Mark grabbed her in a hug in which they ended up kissing each other passionately. Julli pulled away to tell him, "Go put the ox out and I'll see you when you come in." with that Mark nodded and swatted her on the bum when she left. The look of shock on Julli's face made Mark burst out laughing. Julli felt her face go red.

"Something the matter?" he asked when he caught his breath.

"No," was all she could say. It was somewhat embarrassing, but it was Mark who hit her, so it was not too upsetting. Julli envisioned them being together and wondered if this was one of Mark's ways of hinting toward that. She turned and walked into the house, catching Mark in the corner of her eye laughing at her.

She got herself busy in preparing the house. She took off her spencer jacket as it was warm enough in there. She hung it on a peg and walked into the bedroom. Seeing the bed, Julli wanted to lie down on it and feel how soft it would be for her to sleep on. Seeing only one bed, Julli wondered if Mark was going to sleep on the floor or out in the barn. Shrugging the nagging thought out of her mind, she turned her attention to her own needs.

First things first, she went over to the screen and eyed it. "Well, I gotta go and Mark is outside," she said, so she went about her business relieving herself. Julli had watched the servants enough to know that she would have to dump the contents in a bowl somewhere, so she hurried outside to the side of the house and dumped it.

On her way back, she spied Mark pulling the carriage into the barn.

"I better get some coffee going for him," she muttered to herself.

In the pantry, she found the coffee beans and the grinder, which she proceeded to set on the table and grind. She went over to the pump, got some water into the coffeepot, and placed it on the fireplace wire for cooking. Julli grabbed the poker and stoked the fire. Soon she had the water going and put in the grind.

She in her hurry forgot that the grind should be placed in the water, then on the stove. Julli was in a situation where she was to serve the man, and she had never done that before.

"Oh well!" she said aloud, not aware that Mark had snuck into the room, until she felt his arms around her midsection. He placed a kiss on her neck, and Julli tilted her head to receive more. Instead, he spun her around, kissing her fervently that Julli forgot all about the coffee. Before she knew what was going on, they were in the bedroom, and Mark was undressing her with his eyes.

"Julli, I want to be with you," Mark said, lowering his mouth back to hers as he shut the door with his foot.

CHAPTER 10

———◆◆◆———

Pregnancy, Dog, and Death of Mark

Two months later, Julli noticed that she had not had her period. She had been feeling queasy around food and tired often. She thought it was because of taking care of the homestead and Mark plus working at the boardinghouse with Kathrin. She decided she needed to talk to Mark and let him know what was going on.

"Mark, I need to talk to you," signed Julli that night.

Looking at her, Mark noticed she looked tired. "Okay, what is it?" he signed back.

Not sure how to tell him, she wiped her sweaty hands on the apron she was wearing. "I have not had my monthly. I am around two months late."

"What?" asked Mark, not sure he was understanding her.

"I am late for my monthly," she repeated, this time signing with what she said.

"Are you sure?" asked Mark, exasperated.

Julli nodded her head and signed, "Yes, I am." Pausing to take a calming breath, she added, "I think I need to go see the doctor."

Mark stared at Julli. She could feel the heat of his gaze. It was not one of love that she got to know real well. "Okay, we both are off tomorrow, so I can take you if you want me to?" he suggested.

"I would like it if you went with me." Julli smiled, glad that she finally told him.

The next day, they picked up Mindy, whom Mark the other night had told was needed for Julli at the doctor's office. He did not tell Mindy the reason why Julli was seeing the doctor. Mindy thought it best to wait and have Julli tell her what was going on.

Mark helped Julli and Mindy out of the wagon, when Julli ran to the side and heaved the meal she just had previously eaten. She grabbed the post and straightened up, wiping her mouth with the back of her hand. Mindy stood there staring at Julli, and Mark turned his face. Julli stood there 'til her stomach stopped with the vomiting and calmed down enough that she could then breathe deeply. As far as she could remember, Julli had not felt that sick her whole life. She swallowed several times before walking back shakily to Mark and Miranda. Mark looked at her but did not say a word. Mindy took it as a time to be silent as well.

Mindy took Julli's arm and led her into the doctor's office; then Mark took off to the general store. Julli was going to wait for Mark, but Mindy nudged her into the room, where the doctor was sitting at his desk. He put up his finger and signaled for them to wait a minute while he finished some paperwork he was doing. Julli glanced at Mindy, who was looking at her intently.

Then when he was done, he smiled at them and asked, "What can I do for you, misses?"

Julli looked at Mindy, stricken, who told the doctor that Julli was sick.

"My name is Miranda and this is Julli. She just threw up outside," nodding to Julli, who rolled her eyes. He got up from the chair and started talking with his head down. Mindy interrupted him, saying, "I am sorry, Julli is deaf. I am here to help make sure that she understands you and vice versa."

"I see. Does the throwing up have anything to do with her hearing loss?" he asked, going back to his desk and picking up his pen to write down something. He had on his apron, and it was smudged with all colors of stuff smeared on it.

"Oh no, she has been deaf since she was a baby." Mindy looked at Julli, who moved her hands, suggesting she sign as well. "She has been throwing up." Pausing, she couldn't finish 'til Julli put up her fingers, showing two of them, and said, "Weeks." Then she finished, adding, "For two weeks now."

The doctor nodded his head and said, "Oh, I see. Okay, well, let's get started." Julli could not see his lips, and therefore she could not understand what he was saying.

Shaking her head no at Mindy, who caught on and stopped him. "Julli needs you to look at her when you talk. She can read lips real good. I am only here to make sure that things are understood." Mindy signed to Julli as she spoke with the doctor.

"Oh. So I look at her when I talk?" He pushed his glasses on top of his forehead and looked intensely at Julli.

"Yes, that is how it goes." Both women nodded. Mindy was doing well at signing to Julli, interpreting for Julli as well as talking to the doctor.

Turning to Julli, he asked her, enunciating his words as he spoke, "Can . . . you . . . lip . . . read . . . me?"

Bursting out laughing, Julli forgot about the queasiness in her stomach and how the doctor was overdoing with his mouth. Looking at Mindy, she signed, "Sorry but he is making it harder to lip-read him like that."

Mindy smiled and snickered, while the doctor kept his straight-faced expression.

"No, sir, what I mean is that you talk like you are to me but make sure Julli can see your lips."

He kept looking at Julli, then, squinting his eyes at her, asked normally, "Can you lip-read me?"

Julli giggled and nodded her head. For once someone actually listened to them when they tried explaining how to communicate with Julli. Maybe the doctor wasn't as stupid as he looked.

"Okay. Here is what we will do. You will sit on the table in the other room. Then I will check you out and see what the problem is." When Julli nodded, he looked at both women and asked, "Are both of you in need of being checked out?"

"No, sir. It is only Julli," confirmed Mindy, hoping she was not going to have to make a visit to the doctor anytime soon. "He gives me the creeps," Mindy signed to Julli, who giggled.

"Okay, very well. If you would follow me," he suggested.

Both of them followed him, with Mindy tagging behind. She was led to a curtained room, and Mindy looked at Julli and said, "The doctor said he will be with you in a minute. If you need me just call for me, okay?" At Julli's nod, Mindy then left the room. Sitting on the table, Julli wonders what could be wrong with her. The doctor comes in, pulls up a chair, and starts asking her questions.

"So what is the problem?" he asked, making sure Julli could lip-read him.

Swallowing before answering with her voice, she said, "I have not had my monthly for a couple of months."

At that reply, the doctor scratched his head, before asking, "Any pain?"

"No, just like before a monthly," stated Julli. "And I am real tired." She sighed deeply.

The doctor ponders what she told him, then tells Julli to lie down on the table and pull up her skirt. He stands over her and keeps his face toward her as he did the checkup. After that he nods his head at her, helping her to sit up.

"Give me a minute." And with that, he pulls back the curtain and calls for Mindy.

"Miss, you can come in." Mindy comes in, but Julli is not sure what the doctor's diagnostic is, so she shrugs and shakes her head.

The doctor comes in and tells Julli, "You are in good health. The only thing is you are pregnant."

"Pregnant?" Julli questioned, shocked. She shakes her head and frowns at the doctor.

"Yes, I would say a couple months. You will have a baby around or before Christmas." He shrugged. Then he smiled when Julli's eyes widened and her mouth dropped open.

"Wow!" was all she could sign. She was in shock. She was pregnant with Mark's baby. She looked at Mindy, who smiled, with her eyes wide. Julli could tell that Mindy was happy for her.

"I take it you are married?" the doctor inquired, looking at Julli, then to Mindy, who was about to repeat the question to Julli in case she did not understand him.

"Um, uh, no. We talked about it but we have not set a date," Julli stumbled on, answering the question. She could lip-read him well enough; it was just the shock that gave her the dazed look.

"I would suggest you get married. Not too many folks here support an unwed mother," he stated, eyeing both Julli and Mindy. Mindy held up her ringed finger, and the doctor nodded at her. When he looked at Julli, she hid her hands behind her and shrugged.

"I will talk to Mark," was all she could say.

"Okay." He looked at Mindy and back at Julli. "That explains why you are sick. You have what is called morning sickness. It can stop or you could be sick the rest of your pregnancy. Do you understand what I am saying?"

Julli looks at Mindy, who signed some of what the doctor said. "Yes, I get what you said."

"Do you have any more questions or symptoms?" When Julli shakes her head, he suggests, looking at her and to her belly, "If I was you, I would look into getting a midwife. I do not normally deal with pregnancies but I can give you the name of the woman who is a midwife and a good one at it."

Julli agrees, and she tells him, "Thank you."

With that, he said, "When you go out front, pay my helper and she will give you the name."

Mindy nodded to Julli and signed, "Well, that you can use."

"You are done," he said and tilted his head to the door. Julli grabbed her stuff and followed Mindy out to the front, where she paid for her doctor's appointment. She followed Mindy out of the doctor's office. Julli felt pretty happy about the news as they walked toward the general store, where they found Mark lingering against a wall.

"Julli has some news to tell you," stated Mindy; then she walked off toward the boardinghouse to see her husband, Zeke, while he was working. Julli watched her walk off and then turned to Mark. He only looked at Julli as though he was not seeing her.

"What did the doctor say?" was about all he asked.

"He said I am pregnant," signed Julli, not aware that Mark was going to be nervous. Julli expected him to be as happy as she was. She was not prepared for what came next.

"No way," retorted Mark sarcastically. He threw out the straw he had been nibbling on.

"Yes, and I should have the baby before Christmas," said Julli, giddy, grabbing his arm. She placed her other hand on her midriff and smiled. *A baby! That for sure was good news*, she thought.

Julli watched as Mark shrugged off her hand and rolled up his sleeves, before he turned to look at her. "That is not good. We did not plan on this."

Dumbfounded, Julli asked him, signing, "What do you mean?"

"What I mean is, it was not supposed to happen. We are not ready to have a baby, especially now," stated Mark angrily. He put his hand in his pocket and pulled out some change. Counting it, he said, "We do not have much money for extra food and all."

"What do we do?" Julli asked nervously. She was starting to feel nauseated again. All she wanted was for them to be happy; at least they were together.

"I am going to have to find some more work," replied Mark, avoiding Julli's gaze. He kept his face turned toward her while he asked, "Do you think you can work a while longer?"

Julli could not believe that Mark did not share her excitement. She was upset that he was not happy. And she resented the way he was acting. After all, it was him who seduced her before they got married. Just because Julli let him have his way with her did not mean that he had the right to treat her like that. "No, I cannot stand the smell of the food at the boardinghouse. Kathrin told me not to come back 'til I was feeling better."

"That is not good," was all he said, shaking his head. Then he added, "We cannot be together anymore. I will sleep in the front room."

"What do you mean?" Julli fought to keep the tears at bay. She pulled out her hankie and blew her nose after she wiped at her eyes. *Let him think I had dust in my eyes.*

"We can't sleep together anymore. You are pregnant," admitted Mark.

"But, what about getting married?" she had to ask as she told the doctor that she would talk to him about it before people had more gossip to spread. She knew how rumors could hurt a person's reputation. Mark had a good one, and she didn't need it ruined because of her.

"We cannot afford it right now. Maybe later," said Mark rudely.

Crying, Julli says, "But I don't want to be unwed and pregnant." She could not bear the thought of being alone through something like this. What she had learned from church popped in her head. "The Lord commands that we be married before we have a child. You helped teach me that," she added.

"I am sorry, but we cannot do that right now." With that, he turns to face her and takes her arm, leading her to the carriage across the street. Mark helps her in and gets in, then grabs the reins. They leave the town in silence.

Later that night, Zeke came by to talk to Mark. Julli stayed in the house while the men chatted. Zeke came in the open doorway, and when Julli nodded at him, he pulled out the chair and sat down. Sighing dejectedly, he looked at Julli.

"I offered to pay for the ceremony but Mark told me no and said that it was you guys' problem. I told him that it would be the right thing to do, but for some reason he doesn't want to do it."

"That is okay. Thank you for trying," signed Julli, near tears.

She watched as Zeke got up, gave her a kiss on the forehead, and walked out. That night Julli cried herself to sleep. Mark had picked up his blankets and went out to the barn.

Julli stayed at home alone during the day for the next few days. Mark rarely came into the house. When he came home one night after a long day working, he went into the barn to clean, then came in to eat. Julli had prepared a simple meal of biscuits and gravy, one food that she could handle. Julli was glad that Mark had come home and was in the house with her. It had gotten lonely the past few nights.

Mark only looked at Julli when she gave him his plate and sat down next to him. He bowed his head, and Julli knew instantly that he was praying. He did not look at Julli like he used to, so she could see what he was saying. When he got done, he still would not look at Julli. Mark picked up his fork and ignored her the remainder of the meal. After Julli picked up his plate to wash it, he walked out to the barn to sleep with the animals. Julli looked around for him, then realized she was alone again.

She broke down, crying uncontrollably. Julli ran into her room, slammed the door, and threw herself onto her bed. She stayed in bed long after Mark had left the barn. She was not aware that he had come in to check on her when he couldn't hear her crying anymore. He had taken the quilt and covered Julli. She had no recollection of feeling the kiss on her cheek.

She kept herself busy with taking walks down the river and keeping the house clean. She only cooked for herself, which was easy as she only made what she could handle. A few days later, Mark came in to talk to her. She wore a simple skirt and blouse, which were getting tighter on her. She was getting bigger, and the telltale sign of being pregnant was there plain as day. She hoped that he would notice, and maybe his attitude toward her would change.

"I have a job." At Julli's questioning look, he continued, "I will be gone a few months. The Wristletons ranch is hiring hands to help with the cattle roundup and I signed up for work. It will give us some extra income."

Looking at Mark, she blinked several times, before asking, "Are you sure that is what you want?"

"No, but we need the extra money," he stated. He made it a point not to look at Julli's belly, which was swollen.

Trying to keep Mark's attention and show him that all was okay, she placed her hand on her belly and said, "We will miss you."

"You will be fine," replied Mark, completely ignoring the motion Julli made and the comment she said. "I will have Zeke and Mindy come check on you and help with what you need. I have put money in the bank and will let them know to give you so much a week for what you need."

"What about getting married?" begged Julli. She grabbed Mark's hand and put it to her chest.

"We can do that after I get back," he said stonily, pulling his hand away from Julli.

"But—," Julli begged again, in tears. That was all she had done the past few weeks, cried.

"No, you will have to make do," admonished Mark.

Julli tried again to have Mark pay some heed to her. She said, "Mark, I love you."

"Yeah." And with that, he walked over to the sink. Julli watched as he grabbed some matches out of the container and went into the pantry to come out with another lantern.

"Well, going to get some sleep," was all he said as he walked out of the house, once again leaving Julli in tears and alone.

"Wait, Mark—," yelled Julli, then stopped. She had felt something weird in her tummy. It felt like a flutter of butterfly wings. A real light yet subtle movement, which was the telltale that she had a baby growing inside of her. Her mouth dropped in surprise. She could feel the baby! It was alive and moving inside her.

"Good night," was all Mark flung at her.

Julli placed her hand on her belly, hoping to feel the slight movement again. Smiling through her tears, she decided to focus on the baby and herself. *Someday Mark will wake up and see what he is missing out on.* She got ready for bed, and while lying there, she placed her hand on her belly, patting it while whispering, "Momma loves you."

Mindy came over the day Mark left for the cattle roundup. She helped Julli with simple tasks and gave her a ride into town ten days later.

"Wow, you are getting bigger!" giggled Mindy.

"I know. I have already felt the baby moving," signed Julli happily.

"Wow, that is great. What did Mark say?" asked Mindy, gazing at Julli's tummy. Julli had tied her apron up higher as her belly was sticking out more as every day went by.

"Nothing. I didn't get the chance to tell him," she signed. Lately she had been mentally talking to herself, since there was no one there to sign back to, or rather chat with, her.

Julli smiled and gave Mindy a hug. Even though Zeke and Mark had been friends for a while, Zeke had not approved of what Mark was doing. Especially to Julli and the baby that they were going to have.

"Zeke wanted me to tell you that a friend's dog had pups. He said he remembered that you wanted a puppy to help you out," came from Mindy. Julli noticed that Mindy kept looking at Julli's belly. Either it was sticking out way more than she thought or there was something else as to why Mindy would stare at Julli.

"Yes, I still want a puppy," exclaimed Julli, signing. She was going to have to stop by the boardinghouse and thank Zeke for remembering.

Mindy took Julli to the house where the puppies were. While the lady and Mindy chatted, Julli sat down and played with the four puppies that were left over. Julli petted each of them but noticed that one kept climbing onto her lap and nibbling on her finger. It was a black male Labrador.

Julli jumps when she feels a hand on her arm. It was Mindy, who asked, "Did you find the one you wanted?" At Julli's nod, she turns to the lady and says, "Yes, she has."

Julli gets up and picks up the puppy. Signing, she says, "This one. I'll name him Luke."

Both the lady and Mindy nod their approval. Julli brushes off her skirts, and when she puts the puppy close to her belly, she feels the baby moving. *Even the baby approves*, she thought.

On their way back to the homestead, Mindy drops Julli off, promising to come check on her in a couple of days. "I am glad you found your puppy." Ruffling his fur, she adds, "I wish Zeke would let me have one as well, but you need him more than anyone else."

"You can come over anytime and play with him if you want," signed Julli, feeling elated that she was getting things set for her peace of mind. It did not help with Mark being gone so much.

July 16, 1817

As promised, Mindy came over every two days for the next three weeks. But the week after, she came bringing the sheriff with her.

Julli was outside playing with the pup when she saw them pull up. Mindy did not seem happy, and the sheriff had a somber look on his face. Julli wondered what was going on.

"Julli, we need to talk," was pretty much all Mindy could say. She gestured that Julli lead them into the house.

Picking up the puppy, she led them inside the house and asked, "Would you like some lemonade?"

"No thank you, miss." The sheriff shook his head.

Sitting down and placing the pup in the basket she got for him, she turned to Mindy and the sheriff, signing, "What is it?"

"It is about Mark," stated Mindy, signing the sign Julli had taught was for Mark.

"What about him?" signed Julli. She had hoped Mark would have been home, but that was just a dream she had.

Julli watched as the sheriff looked from her to Mindy, then back. He swallowed and took off his hat before saying, "I am sorry to inform you, miss, but Mark was killed on the roundup."

"What? How?" Shocked, Julli dropped the glass she was holding. The pup jumped, started whining, and Mindy went over to him and shushed him. "It is okay, Luke." She glanced at Julli sitting there and went ahead to clean up the mess of broken glass.

"Rustlers," stated the sheriff.

"What?" Julli looked at Mindy, who paused what she was doing and made the sign of "cattle stealers."

"No, not again." Julli sighed, closing her eyes while tears poured out slowly down her cheeks. The puppy had gotten out of his basket and was pawing at Julli's skirts, wanting her to pick him up. When she obliged him, he lathered her face with kisses.

"What does she mean?" questioned Sheriff Moore.

"She lost her dad only a few months ago," whispered Mindy.

"I see, well, my apologies, miss." When Julli looked at him, she caught that statement. He nodded his head, put his hat back on, and walked out of the house.

"Why?" Julli shrugged with her hands outward. "Every time I love someone he takes him or her from me. I hate him," signed Julli furiously.

"Who?" questioned Mindy, scrunching her face.

"God!" yelled Julli angrily. She slammed her fists onto the table, making Luke yelp and jump off her lap.

"It was not God, it was rustlers that killed Mark," defended Mindy, placing her hands on Julli's shoulders.

"Still God took him from me!" snapped Julli at Mindy. She shrugged Mindy's hands off of her and glared at her.

"Julli, what can I do to help?" asked Mindy, helpless.

"Get out and leave me alone." Enraged, Julli got up and pointed to the door. "Just leave me alone!"

Mindy gets up, tears streaming down her face, and leaves. Julli sits back down and picks up Luke, petting him. She breaks down and sobs, holding on to Luke, who whines. She had lost Freddie, moved away from her aunt, and now lost her boyfriend. God had forsaken her. Everything she loved, he had taken from her. He was not going to take her baby or her dog, she vowed. No one was going to hurt her ever again.

Zeke came over that night. Julli jumped when Luke got up barking his head off. Julli quickly went to the window to peek out and saw Zeke getting down from his horse. She opened the door, which let Luke out, yapping at Zeke and giving Zeke permission to enter.

Zeke nodded to Julli and pulled out a chair. He gave her a hard look before he said slowly, "Mindy is hurting for you. She only wants to help you as much as she can." When Julli just stared at him, he added, "The town has reserved tomorrow for the funeral. Everybody will be there to pay their respects."

"I am not going!" snapped Julli.

"But—," Zeke said but was interrupted by Julli.

"No, I am not going. We were not married and I want to be left alone."

"You were his woman, everybody knows that you are having his baby. No one is against you." Zeke, who could not sign every word like Mindy or Julli, used more body language.

"It doesn't matter. Mark left us and there is no point in going," signed Julli. She got up, picked up Luke, and carried him with her to the sink. She got a glass out of the cupboard and went back to the table. She put Luke down before she sat in the chair. As she was about to reach for the pitcher of water, it was taken by Zeke.

"Dang blast it, Julli, I had not taken you for a quitter!" yelled Zeke, angry that Julli chose the safest way out of her responsibilities.

"I am not, it just is not the time for me," she signed, then sighed when she saw the look on Zeke's face.

"Time for you?" snapped Zeke. "Not only did you lose the man you love, but the baby lost its father." With that he banged on the table.

"I know that!" Julli snapped back. She took a deep, calming breath. She had learned that Zeke would not give up easily. Only when the odds were against him, but he always found a reason.

"Then go for the baby. That is the least you can do." There it was, the reason.

Placing her hands on the table, she rubbed her palms together before she asked, "What will that accomplish?"

"Gee, I don't know," stated Zeke, looking her squarely in the eye. "Give you peace of mind?"

"No, it was over for us when he left." Shaking her head, she gestured the giving-up sign.

"No, it wasn't. Did you bother to check with the bank?"

"No, why should I?" asked Julli, wondering what Zeke was getting at. Day by day she had gotten used to his way of speaking. It was easier to lip-read him now than it was before. He used to enounce his words, making it harder for Julli. Now he talked to her slowly but normally.

"He left you guys enough money to tide youse over for a few years." When he said that, Julli's eyes widened, and she stared at him questioningly.

"What? He was always going on and on about money," signed Julli, making the sign for money.

"I know. Mark was proud, I'll admit that." Julli watched as Zeke tried his best to sign the words he knew so she would understand what he had to say next. "He wanted your aunt to be out here when you guys got married, when you did." At Julli's surprised look, he nodded and added, "Yeah, he loved you enough to want the best for you."

Luke, hating being ignored, pawed Julli's skirt, and when she patted her lap, he jumped up gingerly. Julli petted him and said, "Good boy."

Tears forming in her eyes, she took a quavering breath before she signed dejectedly, "I have failed every person who ever loved me."

"No, you haven't," reprimanded Zeke. He reached over and patted Julli's hand. "You still got me and Mindy. Kathrin has said she would help you, and besides, you have two others that are going to depend on you."

"What? Who?" signed Julli, wiping her eyes with the napkin from the table, wondering who would need to depend on her. It was more that she depended on others.

"Your baby and Luke," admitted Zeke, pointing to her belly and the puppy.

With what Zeke just said, Julli hit herself on the side of the head. How could she not think about that at a time like this? Was the shock too great that she wasn't thinking clearly? Rubbing her belly and Luke, who was now lying on her lap, she gazed at both of them. He was getting bigger, as was her belly. Soon there would be only room for the baby. The image of her baby and Luke arguing over who would sit on her lap made her smile.

She put Luke down before getting up and went over to Zeke and placed a kiss on his forehead. "Please tell Mindy to come in the morning. I owe her an apology," she begged him.

"So you'll go?" he asked, begging, putting his palms together and intertwining his fingers.

Nodding her head, she signed, "Yes, I will. I really owe it to the baby, don't I?" She batted her eyes at him after she signed.

Laughing at her, he said, "Not just the baby but Mark did love you a lot, so you owe him as well."

"Zeke, tell me, how did Mark die?" Julli asked quietly. Zeke had to lean closer to her to hear.

"Don't rightly know. All the sheriff could say was that there were some rustlers. Probably six or seven. Either Mark was trying to stop them and got shot or he was in the wrong place at the wrong time. The Wristletons have had problems with rustlers before. But they never had any shooting which took the life of a hand. A few others were wounded." With that, he pretended to put his gun in his holster, and Julli got the idea basically from a few words she was able to understand, along with lots of body language.

Julli was worried that Mark had died for nothing. "What is the point? I mean, why take someone else's cattle?" She had never learned about this kind of thing and could not fathom taking from another person their livelihood.

"My guess is, they can cover the brands and sell them off, probably for more money," Zeke told her using body language, by getting up, putting a brand in the fire, and using it on an imaginary cow. Then reaching into his pocket and pulling out some change, which he pretended to barter. Zeke could be the most animated person when it came to trying to communicate with Julli.

"Where did they go?" Julli asked, pointing to the north, south, east, and west.

"No one knows. The other guy went tracking them and he hasn't shown up. The town is worried about him. Some say that he was a part of it while others think he too got killed." Julli looked at Zeke, and when he pulled out his pretend gun, she flinched.

"Oh no." She shuddered. She wrapped her arms around her and rubbed them, trying to get rid of the chills she felt.

"Yeah, so anything I can do for you?" he asked, concern evident on his face.

"No, not at the moment," signed Julli sadly. If only he could bring Mark back. That was an impossible job, Julli knew, but that was the only thing she could wish for that would help.

"Kathrin says if you need anything just let us know." Zeke was not going to give up. He was going to make sure Julli was taken care of and only wanted her to be happy and to have her baby. Maybe the baby would take her mind off her loss. Only time would tell.

At that moment, Julli felt her tummy squelch, and before she knew what she was doing, she shoved herself from the table and barely made it to the sink, where she threw up. Zeke had gotten up and went over to her, wiping her face when she stopped heaving.

"Wow, dang it, woman, I thought you were pregnant, not sick." He reeled back from Julli, afraid that he was going to get sick from her. Julli looked at him in horror, only to see him laughing. Just for that, Julli punched him on the arm and shook her finger at him.

Helping her back to the chair, Julli looked at Zeke and signed, "The doctor said it would stop or it would go the whole pregnancy. I am thinking it will go the rest of the time I am pregnant."

He gets up and gives Julli a quick hug. Then pats her tummy. Before he leaves, he tells Luke, "Watch over your mommy and baby."

CHAPTER 11

Funeral, Baby, and Stranger

The next morning, Julli woke up when Luke jumped and barked on her bed. She groggily got up, grabbed her robe, and opened her door, only to see Mindy coming in. *Drats, I forgot to lock the door again,* Julli scolded herself.

Julli took in the black dress that Mindy was wearing. It accentuated her pale skin and wavy brown hair. Mindy's eyes were about as bloodshot and puffy as Julli's were.

"Good morning, Julli," said Mindy, looking directly at Julli.

"Oh, Mindy. I am so sorry I yelled at you. I did not mean what I said," admitted Julli, begging for forgiveness. She had hurt her best friend, and yet she came back.

"I know. Forget it okay?" With that, Mindy walked over and patted Julli on the arm. She turned to Luke and gave him a kiss on the head before he bound outside. "Let's get you dressed and ready. Zeke is not very patient when it comes to something he wants to be on time for." Nodding at Julli, who just stood there, she put out her hands and shooed her. "Go get dressed."

Julli stood her ground. "I don't have anything black."

"Yes, you do," stated Mindy. Julli raised her eyebrows at that statement, wanting to debate with Mindy on which dress would be suitable and appropriate considering she only had dresses for not being pregnant and for dress-up days, not including a funeral. Mindy goes outside and comes back in with a paper-wrapped package. She hands it to Julli and says, "Now go get dressed."

"But—!" Julli argued. She was not in the mood for being treated like a kid. She was a woman pregnant and mourning a loss.

"No, now shoo."

Julli grabs the package, tucks it under her arm, and walks over to Mindy. "I am sorry."

Mindy just pulls Julli into a hug, then tells her, "Go do what I said. Get dressed."

Julli walked into her room and was about to call for Luke, when she saw that Mindy was already playing tug-of-war with him.

Smiling, she closed the door, walked over to her bed, and laid down the package. She gasped when she saw that it was a black cashmere dress, not much different from the one she wore months ago to Freddie's funeral. The skirt had the tie-back strings that could be adjusted especially for pregnant women. The blouse was loose in the front and longer than what she normally wore.

Julli stifled a sob when she realized that she had friends who really cared about her. There was no price mark on the dress, so Julli wondered just how much Mindy, or rather Zeke, had paid for it. Swallowing, she removed her nightgown to put on the outfit. If she knew Zeke, he would send his wife in to make sure Julli was okay. She had to hurry, and once it was on, she got her brush and started brushing her hair so she could easily tie it back into a bun.

Julli was putting on the final touches to her hair when Mindy came in with Luke.

"Wow, you look good. I am glad it fits," admitted Mindy appreciatively.

Julli, smoothing down the skirt and fidgeting with the sleeves of her blouse, replied, "Thank you."

"Well, are you about ready to go?" At Julli's nod, she added, "Zeke has been hollering at me the last few minutes."

Laughing at the impatience of Zeke, she nodded her head yes. She then called for Luke, "Luke!"

Julli wondered why he was not coming when she called him, 'til Mindy signed, "Zeke has him in the carriage."

"But it is a funeral, not a picnic," Julli remarked.

"Go talk to Zeke." Mindy shrugged indifferently.

Walking outside, she sees Luke sitting regally on the seat by Zeke. She looks at Mindy and signs, "Never mind." Both women smile and walk to the carriage, and Mindy helps Julli in, while Zeke grabs her arm to help her as well. It did not make matters easier when Luke decided that he was going to help too, by jumping in front of Julli and lathering her face with kisses.

"Okay, boy, thank you," said Julli to the pup, and Mindy, laughing, shoved him over. Luke decided since Julli was now in, he would take his place by Zeke again, leaving Mindy to ride in the back with Julli. Laughter, it was all anyone could do as Zeke clicked the reins at the ox and Luke decided to tell the ox to move by barking at it in his own commanding way.

On the way to town for the funeral, they passed several families who were going to attend. Julli tried to ignore them, but Mindy gestured to them as they waved somberly. Nearly everyone they passed wore black. Like Freddie, Mark was well-known and respected. Julli sighed as she recalled how she missed most of Freddie's funeral. They had told her she was in a deep shock, so that was accepted for her. But it was her aunt who suffered the most. Freddie was her soul mate, and they had been together for years.

Julli felt queasy when they rode into town. The streets were swarmed with folks dressed in their Sunday clothes. Julli could not decide whether or not to nod back to the men who tipped their hats at her or the women who bowed their heads. It was all so confusing. Julli had no feelings, except that she was feeling empty.

Julli was not the little least surprised when she saw that they were heading to the boardinghouse or the fact that Kathrin was in a carriage as well. Julli took in the black veil and dress that Kathrin had on and wondered why it was her wearing the veil.

"Why is Kathrin wearing the veil?" signed Julli to Mindy

"He was her cousin," admitted Mindy, uneasy where the questions were leading.

"What? Nobody told me about that," signed Julli, upset.

"Oh! She was always telling Mark to tell you. She had him stay at the boardinghouse before you came out and even after he stopped living at the homestead. She was always arguing with him that he had to go home and start a family." After a few moments, Mindy added to Julli's surprise, "Yes, she pushed him to have the wedding at the homestead and she would pay for most of it, if only he would have agreed to it."

"Wow, and I did not know that," Julli signed dismissively. It seemed that everyone knew what was going on but her. Either they assumed Mark told her, which he hadn't, or they didn't think it was their place to say anything.

"I don't know why Mark or Kathrin did not tell you. I guess we just assumed you knew." With that, Julli got the acknowledgment that what she had thought was true.

"Well, I didn't 'til now. It all makes sense," signed Julli, making the giving-up sign.

Mindy scrunched up her face and squinted her eyes at Julli. "What does?"

"The special treatment she always gave to him," Julli signed. She recalled at the boardinghouse the first night she was reunited with Mark, how well Kathrin treated him.

"Mark was the one who introduced Michael to Kathrin. He was the reason they got married. Mark set it all up." At Julli's raised eyebrows, Mindy nodded.

"Wow," Julli signed. With that, she added, subduedly, "Again I didn't know that."

"Whoa, here we are, ladies," interrupted Zeke, pulling on the reins to stop the carriage.

Luke barks and jumps down, greeting people as they walked by. "Luke, stop it!" admonishes Julli. She wanted her dog to greet people cordially, but not when he was jumping onto them.

"Don't worry, I'll keep the mutt with me," Zeke said, patting his leg for Luke's attention.

The sheriff came over and told them, "We have loaded the coffin. I will lead the funeral train to the cemetery."

Mindy looked at Julli and made sure she understood him. At her nod, Mindy said, "Okay."

"My condolences to you, miss" The sheriff looked at Julli, then tipped his hat and left to get on his horse.

Mindy grabs Julli's hand and says, "Here we go."

Zeke clicks to the ox, and Luke jumps back in to sit again in the front next to Zeke. Julli watched as they drove past Kathrin's carriage, then noticed Kathrin was right behind them, with the coffin behind her. The townsfolk all started walking the mile to the graveyard.

"Kathrin hired someone to play Mark's favorite song at the burial," Mindy whispered to Julli, nodding her head when Julli signed a violin playing.

"Oh, I didn't know." Julli was getting very irritated with having to admit she knew nothing.

"Okay, I'll shut up," mumbled Mindy, but not before Julli caught that.

Sighing, Julli signed, "No, it is just that it isn't fair that everyone knows stuff and I don't know a thing." Tears formed and threatened to pour at that neglect of communication. It was not fair that people shared information with each other but just not her. She was only deaf, nothing else.

"I am sorry," signed Mindy, regretting her big mouth. She looked at Julli, and an idea popped into her head. "You can read well, right?" she signed, pretending to write.

"Yes, why?" asked Julli, wondering why Mindy would ask that when she had seen Julli writing in her journal.

"How about every time I come to town or talk with people, I write down what I hear and let you read the day after I get home?" suggested Mindy, wanting to do something as she knew there were times that Julli could not understand her. "Would that help keep you up with what is going on?" she asked, brightening up at her idea.

"Are you serious?" Julli asked. At Mindy's nod, Julli added thankfully, "That would help so much."

"Here we are, ladies," again Zeke interrupted, who apparently had not paid any attention to what the womenfolk were talking about. Julli knew that Mindy would tell him later.

Zeke ties the reins and gets down to help Julli out. Mindy slips a rope loosely tied around Luke's neck and gives it to Zeke to hang on to. Zeke put it in his other hand and helped his wife out of the carriage. His refusal to give the rope back to Mindy made Julli laugh. They really did make a good couple. Julli only wished she and Mark had been able to have something like that. It was special, and Julli was afraid she would never have that kind of bond.

Mindy leads Julli over to where Kathrin was sitting, near the coffin. Not sure what to do now that she knew the reason of Mark's special treatment. Julli almost balked at walking over there, but Kathrin put out her gloved hand and beckoned Julli over.

"I am so glad you came." In addition, with that Kathrin got up and gave Julli a hug.

"Well, there was nothing else really for me to do," admitted Julli, signing with a shrug.

"You know, Mark really did love you a lot." At that, Julli could only nod her head.

"He had a bad way of showing it," signed Julli dejectedly.

Kathrin nodded her head and admitted, "You got to see a side of him I had wished you never did."

"What do you mean?" Julli had to ask, signing by putting a question mark in the air. Some of what Kathrin said made sense, but she wanted to know exactly what Kathrin was getting at.

"How he was there for you before Freddie died, and how he treated you on his own territory."

"He sure changed," signed Julli miserably.

"That was the kind of person Mark really was," stated Kathrin, not exactly siding with Mark, but not totally being against him.

"So, you were cousins?" Julli signed. She hoped that was all there was to it.

"Yes. His dad was brothers with mine and we hardly saw each other growing up."

"Oh, I see." Julli was sort of relieved. She added, "I am glad that you were there for him."

Kathrin nodded her head and patted Julli's hand. "I only wish he had grown up faster."

"Grown up?" Julli was losing the direction of the conversation. Either Kathrin was against him or for him, Julli was sure getting confused.

"Mark knew that having you in his home alone was not a good idea. When he found out you were pregnant, he freaked out," Kathrin said. "He was so scared that he messed up. After he tried helping to bring the Gospel to others, he went against all he preached and believed in."

"I know, it was my fault," Julli affirmed whose fault it was.

"No, it wasn't. Do not apologize. He knew what he was doing more than you were. I am sorry for that. Please keep it in mind that I would like to be around the baby." Julli staggered at that request. She had never dreamt that Mark had family and that Kathrin would be a second cousin to her baby. "After all it is part of my family too."

"Oh, I would not take the baby from you." Julli was astounded that Kathrin would think that of her. She had worked for her a little over three months 'til she could not handle it anymore. They had gotten along so well.

"Thank you, Julli. That was one thing Mark was right about," said Kathrin, with gladness evident on her face. She leaned sideways to give Julli a hug.

"What thing?" Julli asked, flabbergasted.

"You have a stubborn streak to you but you can be loving and considerate of others," Kathrin declared to Julli. She pulled her veil up a little so Julli could lip-read better.

"Oh, yeah, that," acknowledged Julli to that one little thing.

"Julli, I know this is a hard time. Please keep in mind that Mark would like you to keep reading the book he gave you." Julli's eyes glazed over, and Kathrin saw that. "It will help you so much," she promised Julli.

"You really mean that?" Julli cheered up a little after Kathrin nodded her head.

"Yes. That was one thing Mark and I believed in." At Julli's stunned look, Kathrin nodded her head again and stressed, "Really believed in."

The pastor came over and shook hands with Kathrin, and when Julli was introduced to the pastor for the first time, she just stared at him, not able to lip-read. He talked slowly but enunciating his words, which made it even harder.

"I will help Julli." Mindy comes over and looks at her, rolling her eyes as she knew exactly why Julli was having trouble with the pastor.

Mindy says, "He is sorry for your loss and wants you to know that Mark is with his Heavenly Father." Julli nods to that and makes it a point to ignore the pastor afterward.

Zeke, with Luke tied to his pants loop, puts a blanket on the ground by Julli's feet for Mindy to sit on. "My wife will help you," he declared a statement, which received no arguments from anyone, especially Julli, who was really appreciating their help.

One of her hands taking Mindy's and patting Luke with the other, she nods at them thankfully.

The pastor begins officiating, and Julli tried hard to keep up with Mindy, who was doing her darnedest to make sure Julli could lip-read her as fast as the pastor was talking.

Pretty much most of what was said did not register with Julli. She was going to have to talk with Mindy and have her repeat as much as she could remember. Julli only hoped Mindy's memory was good as Zeke's cooking. Julli sat there staring at Mindy and was flustered that she could not keep up fast enough.

Julli got up when the band started playing "A Love's Dream." Kathrin grabbed Julli's hand and held on to it 'til the song was done. Julli glanced at Kathrin and saw that she had taken her veil off and tears were streaming down her face. Swallowing, Julli did her best not to cry, but seeing Kathrin's tears, she began her own torrent of sorrow.

Kathrin tugged at Julli's hand when the song ended and mouthed, "That was for both of you." Julli let the flood of tears go. The dam broke, and there was nothing anyone could do to stop it. Not even Luke, whining and licking her hand, could get her to cease. Not even feeling the baby move put a damper on the torrent that had broken through.

The rest of the funeral went by, and like with Freddie's, it was a blur. Julli was led by Mindy and Zeke back to the carriage. The ride home was in silence. Julli did not see Luke lying down on the floor by her feet. She did not feel nauseated as normal. She did not remember getting home or Mindy helping her remove her dress and slip the flannel nightgown over her head.

All she could remember was the coffin being laid in the ground and the fact that Luke would not leave her side on the bed. She could feel the baby move and was reminded she was pregnant, but Julli refused to eat afterward. She was so tired of death following her and claiming the lives of those she loved.

December 14, 1817

Julli went the next five months refusing to see anyone or go into town. Her nausea subsided, and she felt better the further along she got. She stayed home and played with Luke as well as taught him to come to her when there was noise in or outside the house. Her belly was bigger, as was Luke. Julli found solace in the two things that meant the world to her, her unborn baby and her dog, Luke. Mindy came to check on Julli often, as did Kathrin, but Julli was not in a welcoming mood. She did not talk to them or sign in any way when they were around her. Mindy stocked her pantry for her, and Kathrin made sure Julli had food, as well as Luke.

Julli spent her days rocking in the chair out on the porch. When it got colder out and before the first snow came, Julli went out to the woods and started gathering branches. Luke, as always, was her only faithful companion. Julli would spend the cold days in her room with the fire going. Luke would play with his toys, which she got for him, or gnaw on a bone that Zeke had brought over for him.

Julli refused to celebrate any of the holidays. She stayed home alone wrapped up in her misery. Her only comfort was her unborn baby moving more as each day went by. The hits and kicks to her belly were visible now. Julli went about the house in her bloomers and blouse as she did not have much that actually fit her. Her housecoat was one thing she put on when she was alerted by Luke's barking that someone was there. When it was Mindy, Zeke, or Kathrin, Luke would bark and paw at the door. Julli could tell when someone was there and who it was just by the way Luke acted. Kathrin brought turkey and stuffing for thanksgiving, which Julli only ate a few bites of and gave the rest to Luke, who happily obliged her, cleaning up every morsel.

Finally, Zeke came over and told Julli, "Enough is enough. You are starving the baby."

"No, I am just not hungry," she glumly admitted. She had been so tired and did not have much energy to do much, let alone get wood and play with Luke. Food had only been when she was actually hungry or when they came and left platters loaded with food for Julli. She hated wasting the food, but nothing really initiated her stomach to be hungry. So Luke got fat off the courses Julli set in front of him.

"Well, most women are fat when they are with child. You are nothing but bones with a big belly," stated Zeke, poking her with his finger. Pointing at Luke, he added, "That dog is not just fat, he is big."

Laughing at that, Julli poked him back and said, "I am fine."

"No, you are not. We are going to go see the midwife today," he threatened. He was worried about her. She hardly ate, but he had seen her chopping wood and playing with Luke. Too much work and not enough food made for a bad pregnancy given the fact that Julli was the slender yet smallish type.

"What for?" she signed.

"To make sure everything is okay," Zeke snapped at her.

"Everything is okay," she snapped back, willing to fight with him just for the sake of amusement.

"Julli, don't make me pick you up and take you," threatened Zeke, coming closer to her. Julli knew Zeke was a man of his word, but she wanted to have some fun with him.

"You wouldn't dare!" challenged Julli.

Zeke gave her that look he had when he was going to get his way. "Really?"

"Zeke, come on. You would not pick up a pregnant woman, would you?" Now Julli knew that she had pushed him a little too far.

"Oh, dang right I would." He stood up to his dare. "Still dare me?"

"No, give me a minute," signed Julli hurriedly. She went to her room, grabbed her coat, and made sure Luke was in the house before she left with Zeke.

Mindy was working at the boardinghouse, so she was not able to come to the checkup. Zeke stayed behind the curtain and heard everything the midwife said.

Julli noticed that Zeke was nervous. Since he was the one who brought her, Julli wanted to have some fun with him to get back for threatening her. The midwife checked Julli and said, "Everything sounds good."

She saw Zeke through the curtain wipe his hand with his bandana. It was chilly in the room even with the fire going. "But you need to eat more."

"I eat enough raw meat," stated Julli, putting on her coat.

"No, you don't!" admonished the midwife. Julli saw Zeke sit up suddenly. Julli had to fight down the urge to laugh. She desperately wanted and needed to laugh but figured she would wait 'til she got home and let it spill out.

"What else do I need to do?" Julli asked obediently. She glanced at the curtain and saw the silhouette of Zeke relax as he leaned back on the back of the seat. The midwife put an end to the joke when she cleared her throat and added for emphasis, "If you want a healthy baby, you will eat more and stop wallowing. Mourning for the father is not helping either one of you."

At the mention of the father, Julli got upset and stormed out. Zeke was knocked back into the chair he had just gotten up from.

Zeke caught up with her and asked, "Do you want Mindy to come stay with you?"

"No, I will be fine," stated Julli cynically. She wrapped her coat tighter around her as they headed out to the homestead. She made it a point to stare ahead and ignore Zeke, which upset him.

Zeke gave up trying to talk some sense into Julli on the ride back to the homestead. Julli did not want to sit there in the cold and have Zeke chat with her, so she hurriedly got herself down from the carriage. Her big belly made it harder for her to do things on her own, and she wished her pride was not bigger than her belly as she really could have used Mindy's help. Especially now. She had felt some pains on the way home but did not want to worry Zeke, so she did not say anything.

"Zeke, can you send Mindy over tomorrow?" Julli wanted to break the ice. She loved Zeke and Mindy dearly but just was not in the mood to be Julli. Looking at Zeke, she gave in to a request. "That is if she is not busy."

"You betcha. Need any help?" asked Zeke, wanting to know before he headed home.

"Not right now, but thank you." With that, she blew Zeke a kiss and waved.

"Okay. Take care." Zeke clicked the reins, and the horse shook his head before he took a step.

"You too," Julli called out to Zeke.

Julli walked into the house. She let Luke out and threw some snowballs at him to chase. The air was a little nippy for an early-December day. Julli glanced at the woodpile and noticed that there was more wood freshly chopped. "It couldn't have been Zeke because he was with me," muttered Julli. She walked over to the pile and grabbed a handful, which she carried into her bedroom. Not satisfied, she went out for another load.

Brushing off her coat, she called for Luke to come in. She took off her coat, hung it on the back of the chair, and hollered, "Luke!" At that, he finally came bounding toward her from the fields.

Before she could close the door, Luke came leaping in, knocking it wide open. The force of the door hitting her in the tummy made Julli bowl over in pain. Luke, sensing something was wrong, went over to her and licked her face. Julli, gasping for air and from the pains coursing through her body, walked weakly to her bedroom. There was excruciating pain, and she let out a scream. "Ahhh!"

"Zeke!" Julli screamed his name, but he had long gone out of hearing range. Luke started barking, and Julli managed to tell him, "Help! Go get Zeke!" With that, Luke bound out of the house across the fields covered with snow.

Julli went to her bed and lay down. Sweat beaded on her forehead, and she grunted and ground her teeth with every contraction she was having. The pain was bad, and Julli felt like she was not going to make it through the night. She hoped that Luke remembered the commands she taught him when Zeke was around. It sure would help if he actually paid attention to her instead of running off chasing stray animals.

Julli swallowed and tried taking calming breaths. She felt so weak, and every muscle in her stomach hurt. She turned to her side, which seemed to help some in helping her breathe but not with the pains. She clenched and unclenched her fists with every contraction. She writhed on the bed, trying to ease the pain. *Oh, why does it have to hurt so badly?* she asked herself.

In the distance, she felt heavy footsteps hurrying toward her. Julli fervently prayed that it was Zeke and not Luke who came back with something he had picked up. She felt the cold air suddenly stop as the outside door had been shut.

"Zeke, I knew that you would come back," Julli said, trying to look through the pain. She felt a hand on her forehead. When Julli looked again, it was not Zeke, but it was a stranger whom Luke had brought back to her. The man looked at Julli and said, "Miss, I am not Zeke but I am Keith. And I am looking for Mark."

"I need Zeke."

"Well, I, don't think that I can leave you here without helping," the stranger named Keith admitted. He then asked her, "What is the matter?" When she did not answer that question, he asked a few more, hoping then she would answer the next ones. He asked, "Where can I find Mark and who is Zeke?"

Julli was not able to focus on what the man was saying, partly because of the pain and because the guy was not looking at her.

Julli starts screaming as more pain rocked her core being. She looks at the man, saying, "I need a midwife. Though I don't think that I will make it there to town without my baby coming."

"What?" he asked, not sure he understood at all what Julli was saying. Then looking down, he saw that her belly was protruded, and it dawned on him that she was having a baby. "Oh crap!"

Luke started whining, and Keith stood there knowing that if the lady did not get her baby out of her, she would die.

"Okay, this should be as easy as helping a mare foal a colt," he muttered to himself, not aware that Julli was deaf.

Julli, screaming, yells at the man, "Help me, you idiot!"

Keith looked at her for a minute. He was not sure he heard her correctly. Then he says, "Well, miss, I am not an idiot. And I am trying to!"

Julli yells, "No, you are looking at me like you have never seen a lady have a baby. The man you are looking for is dead. He had died some time ago. He was working to bring in money for me and him, when he was killed."

"What?" Keith wonders what is going on with the woman besides being in pain. He was trying real hard to keep up with her, and her rambling was getting him nowhere.

"Mark is dead?" he asked Julli, not caring if she was in pain at the moment. He needed to know what happened to his cousin and why there was a lady giving birth in Mark's bed. "No, I have not, but I have helped my mare give birth to her colt." With that he added, "Do you know how he died?"

"No, I do not. The sheriff said that Mark was killed on the roundup and really, it is not the same thing." Taking a deep breath between contractions, she glared at Keith. "I am not a mare, mister!" Julli told Keith.

Keith shakes his head and says, "Well, miss, I am sorry if you thought I called you a mare." He adds, "But you must know that Mark and I are family, and my name is Keith."

"Fine. Did you say Keith?"

"Yes. We'll see what I can do to help you and your baby."

Julli screamed, "Fine! Then if you are going to help me, then help me!"

"Okay, you do not have to ask me twice, miss," Keith said as calmly as he could muster. Keith's show of confidence was lacking as he started to run around the room looking for what he could use to help the lady with her labor.

Julli screamed at Keith, "What are you looking for?" Julli lay there taking deep breaths. Her sides started to hurt even more, and she was having a harder time breathing. She managed to turn onto her back and watched him quickly go through the stuff in her room. She had to ask, "Why are you running around like a chicken that lost its head?"

Keith stops and looks at Julli, wondering what was up with the name-calling and all. Then he started to laugh when it dawned to him what she had said. He started to laugh harder at Julli, who was lying there giving him the evil eye.

"Miss, I'm trying to find some towels and something for you to bite on." Then he paused and asked, with his eyes wide, "Do I really look like a chicken without its head?"

"Yes, sadly, Mr. Keith, you do! Though I do not like the looks of it." Taking another deep breath, she wondered what the heck the man was doing in her room, especially when she had instructed Luke to go get Zeke. "Why are you looking for those things?" Julli asked.

Julli wondered how she was to have the baby if Mindy, Zeke, and the midwife were not there. She had seen the man say something about a mare, which riled her, not helping with her breathing. She was having a baby, not some surgery thing she needed something to bite on; besides, she sure as heck was not hungry.

Amid all the confusion, neither one had noticed Luke going over by the corner and lifting his leg, relieving himself. Luke got tired of whining, and all the bickering between his mistress and the man he managed to bring to the house was not helping him hold it in.

Finally looking in her closet, Keith found some towels that he placed on the bed next to her legs. Julli watched him through eyes squinted from pain as he walked over to the fireplace and rekindled the fire. He walked out of the room to grab a pan and a pitcher that he filled with water.

Walking back to the room, he stepped on some liquid. "Ew!" was his mutter when he noticed that the dog had done his deed in the house. He made it a mental point to let the dog out as soon as he could. That did not help, and if the dog made any more accidents, he was going to have a woman on his bum for a while.

He set the cauldron on the rack and poured the water into it. Not quite sure if he was on the right track or not, he filled it as full as he could. Turning to grab some rags out of the pile of towels he had put on the bed, he noticed that Julli had lifted up her legs and was trying to get comfortable.

Julli watched as Keith put the water on to warm it up and grabbed the towels. She was not sure she could speak now and figured that the man would not know sign language, so she just beckoned him over when he looked her way.

"Help me sit up, please," she asked hoarsely. It was real hot in the room, and nothing was helping her feel better. She just wanted the pain to go away.

Julli took the arm he offered, and they both dragged her upward so she could sit a little more up. He fluffed her pillows and grabbed her quilt, which he folded sloppily into a square and put behind her back.

"Didn't your mother teach you how to fold?" Julli snapped at him before she realized what she was doing. She just didn't feel so good, and it did not help that she did not know the man.

"Didn't your mother teach you how to be nice?" he snapped back, looking at Julli defensively. He was not going to put up with a woman sassing him even if she was in labor.

"I am in pain, what do you expect?" growled Julli, trying but failing to be nice. Her contractions were closer together, and she writhed on the bed, gripping the sheets.

"Oh, my mistake. I thought you were a nun," retorted Keith, turning his face away from Julli as he said that, which caused Julli to get upset with him.

Therefore she told him, "Shut up!"

"Okay, madame," he offered, backing down. He got the rag and put cool water on it and was going to wipe her forehead, when she told him something he didn't expect to hear.

"I need your help. I can't take my skirt off."

"Um, okay," he said before he snickered. "What woman can?"

"What did you say?" Julli wheezed, straining to get comfortable.

"I expect you want me to undress you all the way to your bare bum?" he suggested. Keith was having fun where the conversation was going, but it would be the first time with a woman who was in hard labor. The fact she was having a baby took some of the joy out of it.

"What for?" hissed Julli, trying to focus through her pain.

"To have your baby." He took off his coat and tossed it onto the chair next to the fireplace in her room. Julli wasn't sure, but she thought she saw some scars on his arms after he rolled up his sleeves.

"Don't you dare undress me all the way!" she begged. Julli was trying to keep her modesty, but it was hard with all the pain. She snapped at Keith when he came over to lift her back up to untie the strings to her skirt.

"Why? You plan to have the baby wrapped in your bloomers?"

"No, I just don't want you to see me naked," she snapped when he pulled her skirt out from underneath her. He untied the strings that held her bloomers above her belly and looked at her. Julli could not stop him even if she wanted to; she needed the undergarments off so she could have her baby. But when she saw his hands pulling up her shirt, she hit his hand and said, "Leave my shirt alone!"

"Like I haven't seen women before."

"Ahhh!" Wheezing, she clenches the sheets in her fists and grunts at the next contraction. She tells Keith, "Ow, please get it off of me."

"With pleasure, madame," he muttered. He glanced over to the edge of the bed, reached down, pulled up the sheet, and placed it over Julli's semi nakedness before he unbuttoned her shirt. "The best part of getting a woman naked and I can't enjoy it," he grunted in frustration. He loved undressing women, but he sure as heck did not enjoy this one. She was as mean as a polecat.

"Shut up and keep yourself from me, you hear me?"

"Now, why would I wanna do that?" When she gave him an evil look, he added hastily, "You are not my type anyways."

"Ahhh!" screamed Julli as the contraction reached the breaking point. "Hurry up!"

"I didn't know you liked it quick," he sassed her after tossing her clothes onto the floor in the corner.

"Shut up!"

Keith realizes he is the stupidest man in the whole world. Her boots were still on, and it was no wonder that it was hard to take off her clothes. Smacking himself on the side of the head hard, he mutters, "And I consider myself to be a ladies' man?" He gets off the bed to remove her boots, and when he gets one off, Julli kicks him in the stomach with the other foot. Julli groans an apology when he pops back up holding his midsection, "I am sorry."

Keith eyed Julli and wondered how she managed to do that. He got his breath back and sighed. "How are you doing?"

Not being able to answer him as she suffered a real painful contraction, which had her writhing on the bed, and she tried bending her legs back to ease some of the pressure. Arching her back to ease some of the tension caused her leg to fling out and kick Keith squarely in the jaw.

Down went Keith, holding his jaw, wondering if every woman was like that when in labor. She had quite a kick. He tasted blood in his mouth. He got up slowly and edged around the bed to the other side. Maybe it was safer there.

How wrong was he? Julli was having another spasm, and instead of gripping the sheet, she grabbed a chunk of hair from Keith's head.

"What is your problem?" he snapped at her, grabbing the hand that was stuck on his head, gripping his hair by the roots.

Not hearing or seeing him clearly, Julli did not answer the question. She finally let go of his hair, not realizing that she had grabbed Keith instead of the sheet.

"Don't you know how babies are made?" asked Julli, not fully aware of what she said.

"Umm, yeah I do," admitted Keith. Then changing the subject, he asked, "Where are you from?"

"How would I know? It will come when it does."

Keith gets the towels, dips them in warm water, and cracks up laughing. Either the woman is very delusional or something was really wrong with her. He proceeds to lift up the sheet, only to be stopped when Julli yells, "What do you think you are doing?"

"I have to check and see if the baby is coming."

"Can't you check without using your hands or eyes?" snapped Julli, avoiding his gaze.

She saw his hands reach the edge of the sheet and stop when he replied, shocked, "Wow, you want me to use my feet?" Keith was shocked when Julli refused to let him check her to see how far along she was. He decided he had to go along with it. After all, she was in hard labor.

"It hurts. Make it stop," Julli whined, flinging herself back onto the mattress. She hurt so bad.

He grabbed a rag, dipped it in the cold water, and wrung it out before wiping Julli's forehead with it. He did not know if women needed a drink or not, but he was raised to be a gentleman, so he asked, "Would you like a drink?"

She was taken aback by that. "You are dumber than you look. Can't you see I am busy having a baby?"

Not believing his ears, he burst out laughing and stopped when Julli grabbed his hand and squeezed with all her might, groaning through the contraction. He winced as the pressure got harder and harder. Then before he knew it, he too was groaning through the pain.

Julli slowly let go of his hand when the contraction subsided. She sighed deeply for a minute or so, then looked at the man, whose hand she had grabbed. She quickly let it go when she saw him grimace at the hold she had on him. "I am sorry."

"It is okay, I think you need to let me check and see if the baby is coming."

"Make it quick."

Julli watched as Keith went over and lifted up the sheet on her stomach, and she grimaced again when he saw her grunting.

"I see the baby's head! Push with everything you got!" he yelled at Julli, not realizing she could not hear him. He yelled at her again, "Push!"

"Push? What?"

She let out a scream as she felt the urge to push the baby. Julli gripped the sheets, leaned forward, and lifted her legs, straining with her might. Luke jumped on the bed by her and lay down with his head on her chest. Julli felt some comfort in that and promised that she would reward Luke for being there for her.

"Keep pushing!" Finally after one long push, Keith grabbed the towels and cradled the baby's head. He turned the shoulders and mumbled what Julli could not hear; then another contraction came, and the baby was out of her and into Keith's hands. Julli leaned back and breathed a sigh of relief. Luke, upon sensing that Julli was done, turned his head and watched Keith wrap the baby in the towels.

"You have a baby girl." Julli caught "girl." Keith was laughing as he cradled the baby. He crooned some words to the baby, who was fussing. Julli watched Keith handle her baby with the utmost care. It felt so right, some stranger helping her during her labor and cradling her wee babe. Too bad it was not the father standing there proud; that would have been a sight Julli would have cherished forever.

Keith got his knife out of his bootstrap and laid the baby on Julli's abdomen, while he went over to the fire and washed it in the hot water. He came over and took care of what Julli needed done.

Julli gazed at her baby and smiled. Button nose and small head, hands, and body. Julli thought she was the most beautiful little baby she had ever seen. "Mark, see what we made," she whispered.

At the mention of Mark's name, Keith paused and looked at Julli. It dawned on him that this woman was Mark's and the baby was his. "Wow, so Mark finally got a family." He looked at the baby with pride; he helped bring the child into the world, and both mother and baby were doing okay. Keith gave a silent prayer of thanks.

Now that the hard part was done and over for Julli, she glanced at Keith and said wearily, "I am sorry I was rude. I am Julli."

"I am Keith." With that, he came to sit on the bed by her, took her hand in his, and kissed the top. "So this is your and Mark's baby girl?" At Julli's nod, he added, "When did you and Mark get hitched?'

"We did not. He got killed in the roundup a few months ago."

The baby started to get fussy, and Julli wondered what to do. She had seen women leaving the room with a fussy baby and returning with it calmed down or asleep. "What do I do?"

"Try feeding her." At Julli's scrunched-up face, he added, "Put her to your breast and feed her the milk you have."

Julli's face got red, and she bit her lip. "Well, you are here."

"Okay, okay!" Keith got up and stepped back a few paces. "Who is Zeke?"

"My neighbor. He lives just down that way about a couple miles." Julli pointed over her head and looked at him before she asked, "Can you go get him and his wife, Mindy?"

"You got it, madame."

Julli watched as Keith left with Luke. She hoped this time Luke would get Zeke. She was glad that Keith had come when he did, or she would have feared the worst, a bad labor and a baby not born properly. She looked at the baby, who was fussing, and pulled herself into an upright sitting position, careful as she could still feel the pains. Julli unbuttoned her blouse and put the baby up to her breasts.

"I'll name you Pamela Maire Hamperston."

Julli looks at the little face with long curly brown hair and tiny hands. She felt pride, so much pride in herself that she started to sing the lullaby Freddie used to sign to her. It was an Irish lullaby.

> Too-ra-loo-ra-loo-ral, over in Killarney many years ago, me mither sang a song to me in tones so sweet and low.
> Just a simple little ditty, in her good ould Irish way. And I'd give the world if she could sing that song to me this day.

Too-ra-loo-ra-loo-ral, too-ra-loo-ra-li, too-ra-loo-ra-
loo-ral, hush now, don't you cry!

Too-ra-loo-ra-loo-ral, too-ra-loo-ra-li, too-ra-loo-ra-
loo-ral, that's an Irish lul-la-by!

Oft, in dreams I wander to that cot again.

I feel her arms a-hugging me as when she held me
then.

And I hear a her voice a-hummin' to me as in days
of yore.

When she used to rock me fast asleep outside the
cabin door.

Julli took Pamela off her bosom and placed her on her shoulder, burping her, rubbing her little back, and continued,

Too-ra-loo-ra-loo-ral, too-ra-loo-ra-li, Too-ra-loo-ra-
loo-ral, hush now don't you cry!

Too-ra-loo-ra-loo-ral, too-ra-loo-ra-li, Too-ra-loo-ra-
loo-ral, that's an Irish lul-la-by.

Oh, I can hear that music, I can hear that song,
filling me with memories of a mother's love, so
strong its melody still haunts me, these many
years gone by.

Too-ra-loo-ra-loo-ral, until the day I die.

Julli felt a small but an evident burp from her baby and gingerly turned her facing the other way so she could nurse on the other breast. Julli giggled and smiled at the newborn baby in her arms. She had become a mother, and she was a woman now. Life seemed to brighten right that moment. Love shining in Julli's face as she said a silent prayer, "Thank you, Father, for this beautiful gift. She is the most amazing present I could have ever received. Thank you, Mark, for giving me the chance to have something of you. Thank you. Amen."

Soon after Pamela had got done feeding from her mother, Julli looked at her daughter, smiling, thanking Mark that she had a beautiful baby girl. Even though Mark was dead, Julli had a feeling as if he were with them in the room. Julli started to cry, not just for the loss she and the baby suffered, but that Pamela was there to be with her. All the memories of the times Julli had with Mark would be passed on to Pamela.

Then before she could wipe her eyes, she felt a cold air rush toward her as the doors were flung open. Then Luke, Zeke, Mindy, and Keith had come into the room.

Mindy hurried to Julli's side and gave her a kiss on the forehead. Luke jumped on the bed and lay at Julli's feet. He sniffed the bed and was not sure what to make of it. When Pamela fussed, his ears were cocked up, and he slowly got up on all fours, tilting his head toward the baby Julli was holding. Julli saw that stance he had and encouraged him to come see the baby. "Come on, Luke, it's okay."

Luke eyed Julli, then slowly walked over to sniff at the baby. A small fist flung out and hit him square on the nose. Julli, not sure what to do, could only gasp in shock when Luke came closer and licked the baby on the forehead. Then he lay down on Julli's legs. When Mindy tried to shove him over, he would not budge. He lay there watching the baby.

Mindy started to sign to Julli, when Keith asked her, "Why are you moving your hands when you talk to her?"

Zeke turns and tells Keith, "Mister, our friend Julli is deaf, that is why my wife is signing to her,"

"Oh, I did not know. I thought it was the pain that made her sound different to me," he admitted, feeling guilty for yelling at her. She looked as normal as any other person. "So Mark got her pregnant and died?" he asked Zeke.

"Yes. He died in a cattle roundup few months ago," stated Zeke, ignoring Keith. The new mother and baby were more interesting to look at.

"Sorry but are you sure she is deaf?" When Keith asked that question, Zeke looked at him quickly and clenched his hands into fists. Keith took a step back and asked, "She's not from another country? I am asking because she has this, uh, um, accent if you will." Shrugging his shoulders at the look Zeke gave him, he added, "She told me that my cousin was dead and that the child was Mark's." When Zeke agreed to that, Keith added, "I thought they were wed." Seeing Zeke shake his head, Keith added somberly, "It is sad that he had died before meeting his daughter."

"Yes, it is. But even though Mark is not alive, he is still with us. A piece of Mark still lives though his daughter," said Mindy, signing to Julli though tears of happiness. Zeke came up to his wife and gently put his hand on her shoulder.

CHAPTER 12

Party Changes to Death of Four

After Julli gave birth to Pamela, she and Keith became good friends. Julli went to Zeke's for Christmas and celebrated the New Year with Kathrin at the boardinghouse. Mindy and Zeke came often to visit and help Julli with the baby. Kathrin also made her twice-a-week visits out to see Julli and Pamela. Julli's attitude changed. She was loving, social, and, more importantly, happy. Luke kept Julli company and watched over Pamela. He obeyed Julli when she signed or said a command to him. He was a big dog now. Julli never had any worries about him being that big 'til Pamela started to sit up and his tail got the better of her. But she did not keep them separated. They were nearly the same age; only he was older and bigger. Luke was more loyal to Pamela than he was to Julli. All Julli could do was laugh about that.

Keith had given Julli a yellow rose for Valentine's Day in February. In return, she had cooked him a meal that he ate with gusto. After that, he was over nearly every day just to get a sample of her cooking, or so he said.

"Do you believe in reincarnation?" Julli asked Mindy one day. She signed the signs of "dead" and "rising."

Shaking her head, Mindy replied, glancing at Julli, "No, why do you ask that?"

"Sometimes it feels like Luke is really Mark, the way he dotes on Pamela. Every night when she wakes up for her feeding, he is there pawing at me to wake up. Even when I leave her in the bassinet, he lets me know when she is awake or makes a sound," signed Julli. She had to wonder herself if it was true or if she just got a very protective dog.

"Do not let anyone hear you say that," admonished Mindy, making the sign for hanging.

"I am just saying. You are my friend and I was just expressing my feelings," Julli admitted, bewildered, signing "friend."

"Julli, you know that I will always be your friend." Adding, she snuck in, "You can always tell me anything."

Julli goes over to the bassinet and picks up Pamela. As she told Mindy, Luke was there checking to make sure things were okay.

"Now I see what you mean," stated Mindy, baffled. She was going to talk to Zeke about that.

Mindy goes over and places a kiss on Pamela's cheek. She gives Julli a brief hug and signs, "I will be over the day after tomorrow."

"Okay. See you then." She watches Mindy leave and how Luke only acknowledges her for a brief moment; then he lies back down, watching Julli take care of Pamela.

Julli had gained a few pounds and was jubilant. She felt renewed, and she owed it to Mark's cousin Keith. If it was not for him, she would have had a lot more problems during the labor. Luke obeyed more commands from Julli, and when Mindy and Kathrin came over, they signed more.

Julli was teaching Pamela to sign. She was told that the baby was too young to learn, but Julli wanted to be able to understand her little one as soon as was possible. Julli knew that even though she had lost her hearing at an early age, she could have a chance of having a child who inherited the deafness. No one she knew talked about whether or not her baby could hear. They were more focused on how cute and chubby she was.

Pamela was growing up into a beauty. Her long eyelashes adorned big blue eyes that gazed into a person's soul. Even though she had been born three weeks early, everyone who saw her said she was as healthy as a newborn colt. Keith kept calling her his li'l mare. Pamela had gained weight and filled out more into a chubby little girl. She had Julli's button nose, sensuously shaped lips, and the two things she had of Mark's were her hair and ears.

Keith pounded on the door even though it was open, letting in some early spring breeze. Luke barked once and went over to Keith, wagging his tail. Julli looked at Pamela, who only yawned at the noise. Pamela slept through the dog's deep bark. She was so used to it.

"Hello, Keith. What brings you out here?" Julli asked, not the least bit surprised to see him.

"Kathrin asked me to make sure things were going good. She has extra customers right now, so she said to tell you she would be out when she could," alleged Keith. His cousin seemed to have an obsession in sending him out there. Keith knew well enough he wanted to come out and see Julli.

"Oh, okay, thanks for letting me know," signed Julli, making sure she dragged out a long thank-you sign, which Keith didn't pay attention to.

"And I also wanted to see my li'l mare." He walks over to Pamela and gives her a kiss on the head. "And wanted to see you," he signed to Julli, giving her the sign for "see you."

"What for?" Julli asked, peeping at him. She hoped he did not notice that she liked looking at him. He was easy on the eyes, and Julli felt calm when he was around.

Pretending not to notice the peek, he waited for her to look at him before he signed, "Did Mindy tell you about the barn raising party the Holsters are hosting this weekend?"

"Yes, she did. She already signed me up to bring some food. I was made aware it was a potluck, right?" Julli signed hesitantly.

"Yep," Keith concurred. "Gonna be lots of food for hungry men like me."

Julli laughed at that. She had seen Keith eat, and somehow he managed to keep his figure. He always said that he worked it off by thinking how to have fun.

"Oh, speaking of which, are you hungry?" offered Julli. She did the same thing every night except for when she went into town and ate.

"Well, I don't want you to go to the extra trouble."

"Oh, come on. I am not that bad of a cook or you would have been dead long ago." At that Keith burst out laughing. He always found something funny with what Julli said. "I can fry up some potatoes and I have chopped steak."

At the mention of steak and potatoes, Keith beamed and said, "I will go wash up." He whistled for Luke to go with him, but the dog just stayed at the same spot, by Pamela. Keith, shaking his head at the dog, told Julli, "You got one very spoiled dog."

Julli laughed at that. Keith could not get Luke to leave Pamela's side. She felt good that she had picked out Luke from the litter and kept him.

Julli laid Pamela in the bassinet, and of course, Luke came over and stood protectively by the sleeping baby.

Julli got out the potatoes and kindled the fire to fry up the meat first. She was going to add the potatoes after the meat was done so the grease would give added flavor to the spuds.

Keith came in, and Luke left his spot for a second to get his ears scratched. Julli swore that the dog and Keith were like best friends. Aside from Pamela, that is.

"Need any help?" Keith asked.

"Oh, no thanks. Everything is fine. Food should be done soon," signed Julli, wiping her hands on her apron after putting up a thumbs-up.

Keith goes over and sits in the rocking chair next to Pamela. Luke only looked at Keith, then lay back down. Keith looks at the sleeping baby and whistles a tune. Luke cocks his head, lifting up his ears, and when the whistling stops, he lays his head back on the floor.

Julli gets the feeling that Keith was watching her. She turns and sees him whistling at her intensely. For a few moments, she ignored him; then it bothered her, so she turned to face him.

"Something on your mind?" she gestured, putting out her hands and cocking her head.

"Uh, um, yeah, but it can wait 'til after we eat," Keith decided, signing "eat."

Julli then completely ignores Keith. She only stops what she is doing to glance over at Pamela, who is still sleeping.

Keith, seeing that the food was done, gets up to grab a couple of plates off the counter and puts them on the table, while Julli gets out the forks and mugs. Keith went over to the sink, grabbed the pitcher, and pumped the faucet for water. Julli, watching him, realizes that it seemed so normal, so right, having Keith there. He pretty much fit into everything except . . .

Julli grabbed the back of the chair, only to have Keith stop her. He went over, pulled it out for her, and helped scoot it up to the table. He grabbed the rags, went over to the fireplace, and brought over the food that she had cooked. Setting it down on the table, Luke bound over to them to sit on the floor. She watched as Keith sat down across from her.

Keith reached over for Julli's hand. Keith nodded to her, and they bowed for a prayer.

"Our Father, please bless the food that you have graced us with. We ask that thou watch over us as we go through this night. Please keep us full of thy grace. In the name of Jesus, amen."

Whenever Keith would come over for a meal, he always led the mealtime with a prayer. Julli had gotten used to it. It seemed like Keith was trying to keep a tradition. She had seen him pray when he was stressed out and sometimes when he was happy about something. He never repeated his prayers to Julli. Once, Julli had asked him why he would not let her see his prayers. He only replied with, "That is between our Father and me."

Julli wondered what was up with the quiet, somber like Keith. He was usually bubbly and playing pranks on Julli, but not today.

"Would you go with me to the party?" he gushed out so hurriedly that Julli could not read his lips very well.

"What?" asked Julli, taken aback by the sudden speech.

"You saw what I said." When Julli shakes her head, disorientated, he sighs and asks again, "Would you go with me?"

"Is that what you wanted to ask me?" Julli asked, baffled, signing by pointing to him and her and adding a big question mark in the air.

"Yeah, so will you?"

"Do I have a choice?"

"Umm, no. Luke and Pamela want you to," he said, gesturing to the dog and the baby. Julli glances at Pamela, who was asleep, and Luke, who just cocked his head.

Laughing at that, she said, "Do not twist my arm." At the solemn look he gave her, she added, puzzled, "I would love to. Since Luke and Pamela both agreed I should."

"I thought so." Keith nods to Luke, who just looks at him. Then says, "She has been trained good by you and the baby." Julli grabs the napkin and tosses it at Keith for that. He catches it and snickers out loud, while Julli pretends to act wounded.

"Oh and uh, you have to wear only your bloomers and, I don't know, your corset," stated Keith, guffawing at the disturbed look on Julli's face. "No, I was just jesting. You do need to be dressed but, no black."

"Why no black?" Julli signed, concern in her signing.

"Black at a barn raising is bad luck." With that, Keith shudders his head in dread.

"What do you mean?" asked Julli, dismayed.

"What I mean is you gotta lighten up more." Keith laughs, amused at the look on Julli's face.

Sighing, she eyes him, and not able to keep a straight face, she laughingly says, "Oh, you imbecile."

"Can't be still," said Keith, exasperated that she told him to be still. He loved playing lip-reading games with Julli, just to watch her get upset and realize he was joking with her. He knew Julli could not stay mad at him for long. It was just his charm.

"Oh, shut up," Julli signed crossly, but her eyes gave her away, and they both cracked up laughing.

Keith calmed himself down and put on his most strict face as he told Julli, "Since Zeke smashed his hand, he cannot help out and Mindy gets the day off. She goes in the morning to get stuff going, then said she would come back and get you in the afternoon for your shift. They told me that they would watch Pamela for a couple hours that night. I hope you do not mind."

"Oh, that would be fine."

"Good, I was afraid I lost my touch."

They laugh. Julli starts eating and misses the thoughtfully loving look on Keith's face.

When the day of the barn raising came, Mindy came to get Julli and Pamela. They helped serve the men food and water. Keith was there as well. Julli sat there in a rocking chair, nursing Pamela, with a blanket over her to shield her from prying eyes. She looked and watched Keith.

Keith had rolled up his sleeves, and luckily the day was warm, but the exertion of building a barn took its toll on him and the other men as they were sweating. Julli saw his muscles strain beneath his shirt as he helped the men raise the foundation. Julli was glad it was not her working out there.

"What is going on?" asked Mindy, who brought some lemonade for Julli.

Glancing at Keith, Julli said, "What do you know, really know about Keith?"

"Besides being cousins with Kathrin, not too much." She paused and saw Julli watching Keith working. "He is a hard worker and everybody likes him."

"There is something about him that piques my curiosity," admitted Julli, not quite sure she could put her finger on it.

"What do you mean?" asked Mindy, signing a question mark.

"Did you notice the scars on his arms?" Julli points to her own arm and made the sign of cuts.

"Yeah, I have." Mindy nodded.

"Got any idea what they are from?" Julli asked, looking at Mindy.

"No. he does not talk about himself or his past much for the matter. No one that I know of asks about his past or anything. Zeke only says that Keith is very up-front and honest," Mindy only says, shaking her head when she stopped at every sentence.

"Yes, that he is," admitted Julli, mystified about Keith's past.

Julli sat there rocking Pamela, with Luke sitting next to the chair. She watched Keith working and did not see the knowing look Mindy gave her.

"Well, ready?"

"Yes, I am just not looking forward to leaving Pamela for even a few hours." Panicked, Julli is having second thoughts, not about the date, but leaving Pamela with their neighbors.

"Do not worry, she will be fine," Mindy signed. Sighing and adding, "You need to have some time for yourself. You deserve it."

"Okay," agreed Julli for now.

They got in the wagon, Julli holding on to Pamela, and when Mindy clicked the reins at the horse, Luke came bounding and jumped into the wagon as it was moving. Mindy burst out laughing when the wagon jerked at the force of Luke's weight. Julli glanced back and rolled her eyes. The Labrador had to jar the wagon, waking up Pamela, whom Julli quickly started nursing.

Julli had barely finished nursing Pamela when they arrived home. Mindy tied the reins and went over to help Julli out, when Pamela started fussing again.

"Looks like you have to attend to her again. But I will see you in a few hours," admonished Mindy, not going to let Julli pass up the opportunity to get out and have some fun. More importantly, she was going to watch Pamela, whom she adored dearly.

After taking care of Pamela and laying her down for a nap, Julli donned her purple chemise dress, with her darker purple spencer jacket. She eyed herself in the mirror as she braided her hair and deftly swirled it into several loops at the back of her head. *Not too bad.*

She looked at Luke, who was ignoring her as Pamela had woken up. Peeking at the bassinet, she noticed with relief that her baby was not fussing; she was just looking around. She turned to look at Pamela, then at Luke, who was watching her. "What do you think?" Pamela babbled and cooed, while Luke got up and barked several times. "Okay, you win!" she told the dog.

Julli rarely wore any rouge, and this night gave exception to her rule. She was going to a party, and she was excited about going. There was something about tonight, and Julli wanted to know what was in store for her. Looking at the clock, Julli saw that she had about twenty minutes before Keith was to come and take them to Zeke's, where Pamela and Luke were to stay for a few hours.

Pamela started crying, and Luke jumped up. Julli, seeing the dog move, knew that Pamela was ready for her feeding. Smiling, she walked over to the baby, now four months old, and gingerly picked her up out of the bassinet. Luke followed, and Julli sat down in the rocking chair, with Luke lathering Pamela's cheeks with kisses.

"Okay, boy, let me feed her." She unbuttoned her blouse, tossed the blanket over her shoulder, and put Pamela in the nursing position. She looked at Luke, who was gazing at them. Julli put her hand out, and Luke went under so she could rub his head. She scratched behind his ears and laughed when his tail thumped on the floor. He was a big dog. Luke had learned so much, and Julli relied on him so much. Wherever Julli and Pamela went, Luke was there as well. He was well mannered and ignored other dogs when he accompanied Julli, or rather Pamela. "Luke, you are a great dog. I am so happy that you are here with us," Julli told him.

"So am I," replied Keith, standing in the doorway.

Luke looked up, and Julli then saw Keith standing there.

"So am I," he repeated.

"How long have you been there?"

"Give or take a few minutes." Seeing that Pamela was nursing still, his only comment was, ""I'll wait outside 'til you guys are ready to go."

Julli watched Keith walk out. He was wearing tan trousers, with a cream-colored shirt. He had a brown vest on, and his black hair was damp. Julli had always thought he was very handsome in his own cocky, rustic way. He always ran his hand thru his hair, saying that he couldn't figure out why women had to brush when they could just use their fingers. Keith was so much fun to be with. Even when there was nothing to laugh about, he always came up with some comment or did something that broke the hold of boredom and put fun in its stead.

Pamela, done getting her fill, yawned and pulled the blanket down. Julli hastily buttoned her blouse back up and was getting ready to get up when a hand went under her elbow and lifted her. Julli looked at Keith, who only shrugged and said, "I am impatient."

Laughing, Julli let him lead her out to the carriage. Keith helped her get in and went back into the house. Came out with Julli's coat, which he placed on her lap, under Pamela. Luke, not going to be left behind, got in the back, panting, with his broad tongue hanging out. Keith laughed and got in on the other side.

"Giddap," called Keith, and when the horse did not move on command, Luke started barking frantically at it. The horse snorted and bobbed its head, and they were off. Julli could only look at Keith, who shrugged, laughing. "Dog rules."

They dropped Pamela and Luke off with Zeke and Miranda. Julli was about to cry. She had never left her baby alone that long. Zeke and Mindy told her, "Go have fun. We will watch her."

"Are you sure? What if she cries and wants to be fed?" Julli was worried.

"Julli, I have taken care of babies back East, so rest assured she is in the most capable hands." When Julli looked at her, she added, "Besides yours, I mean. Come on, let me play aunt for once."

"See, Luke will stay with us and watch over her. Come on, let Mindy play aunt."

"Okay." The she goes over and gives Pamela a kiss, sniffles, and asks again, "Are you sure?"

"Go. Have some fun." Zeke rolls his eyes at Julli.

With that, Julli sighs and looks at Luke, telling him, "Watch Pamela." Luke sits there obediently, wagging his tail.

"Even the dog wants you to leave," signed Keith impatiently.

"Okay," said Julli. "Be good, baby. Momma will be back soon," giving Pamela a kiss on the cheek.

On the way to the party, Julli sniffled and sighed, rubbing her arms. She missed her baby already and contemplated telling Keith to turn back. Julli looked at Keith, who only shook his head and said, "Everything will be fine."

When they got to the party, it had gotten a little nippy. Keith grabbed Julli's coat off the seat and helped her into it before he got out. He put out his hand, which Julli took, using his strength to get her out of the carriage. Julli felt weird touching Keith's hand. She gasped at the shock of the realization that there was something going on between her and Keith. Julli was not sure if Keith noticed it yet or not, so she thought she had better keep it to herself for a while. That had never happened before. She always considered Keith to be Mark and Kathrin's cousin.

All thoughts Julli had were dashed away when Kathrin came running out to greet them. Giving Julli a hug and a peck on Keith's cheek, she said, "The party is starting."

Julli was glad when Kathrin took her hand and dragged her away from Keith. At least she didn't have to deal with touching him again. Her feelings were shook up. It was almost a year since Mark died, and Julli was confused. Keith made her feel so alive, vibrant, and willing to enjoy life. Mark had made her feel that way but differently. Mark wanted her to be grown-up and respectful like her aunt had been but without the snobbishness.

Julli did not know that she could have fun. Everyone who was there was polite and courteous. Kathrin made sure that Julli understood what was going on and what people were saying. The more people she got to know, the easier lip-reading them became. Many of the folks used their own body language to communicate with her. When Kathrin left to help with something, a woman came up and was blabbing her mouth, which Julli could not understand. It was depressing when she shook her head and the woman stomped off, muttering whatevers.

Keith came over to her, bringing her some hot lemonade.

"Thank you." She curtsied to him.

"You're welcome, madame." With that, he bowed from the waist all the way down 'til he looked like he was broken in half. Julli had to cover her mouth as she giggled at that sight.

Keith, seeing that she was laughing, smiled at her and clinked his mug against hers.

They stood there for a few minutes, savoring the hot, sweetened drink. Then Keith nudged her with his elbow and said, "Come with me." When Julli paused, he said, "I have a surprise for you." With that, he grabbed her elbow and guided her over to the small wagon perched not far from the barn. Julli glanced at the small campfire that was going and willingly walked over to it to warm herself. Keith placed a footstool by the fire and told her to sit. She scrutinized him as he grabbed another footstool, placing it across from her, and then he picked up his plucked guitar.

"What are you doing?" asked Julli, uneasy.

"Just showing you something. I just hope you like it." He sat down and strummed a few notes. Satisfied, he asked Julli, "Can you see my lips?"

Nodding her head, she took a sip of her drink.

"Okay, here goes." Clearing his throat, he began plucking the strings.

"My beautiful rose, mine and mine only, my beautiful rose," he started off slowly.

"Springtime comes and you bloom, your scent fills my heart. One whiff of your scent and you're mine forever." He strummed faster, glancing at Julli, whose eyes widened.

"My beautiful rose, mine and mine only, my beautiful rose. Summertime arrives along with you in full bloom, your scent still fills my heart." He then slowed down, giving Julli a chance to look at him. He winked at her, and she felt herself blushing. It was a good thing it was dark enough, so he couldn't see her feelings on her face. Julli felt uneasy at the wave of emotions that hit her.

"My beautiful rose, mine and mine only, my beautiful rose."

Julli sat there watching Keith sing the song to her. It was slow, and she could lip-read every word he sang. At the end of the verses of "My Beautiful Rose," he strummed the strings a little faster, then slowed the tempo down.

"Fall comes and you're withering away, your scent fills my heart one last time. In my memories you'll be, your scent always with me," he sang faster, then slowed down again.

"My beautiful rose, mine and mine only my beautiful rose. One last whiff of your scent and you're still mine forever. My beautiful rose, mine and mine only, my beautiful rose," he sang and strummed slower.

"You'll always be my beautiful rose. My beautiful rose, mine and mine only, my beautiful rose. Winter's here and you're in my heart, remembering your scent." He sped up, only to slow again after a few words. Julli could not tear her eyes from him. His face was displaying his feelings for her through his song. He closed his eyes, only to glance at her when he opened them. After strumming a few notes, he finished singing.

"My beautiful rose, mine and mine only, my beautiful rose." He slowed down even more.

"My beautiful rose, one whiff of your scent and you were mine forever." He slowed to a few words with each strum, then to one word each. The last word, he strummed a fast tempo, then stopped. The song ended with him looking intensely at Julli.

Julli looked at Keith, speechless. Her mouth gaped open, and she was very much so perplexed at what was going on at this moment. Keith got off the footstool, walked over to where Julli sat, and placed his footstool next to her. He laid his guitar down up against the wagon.

"That's a beautiful song, Keith"

"It's for a beautiful lady. Do you have any idea who she may be?" A smile crinkled at the corners of his sensuous mouth.

"Oh, Keith, tell me who she is," Julli signed and whispered at the same time, as he leaned down to look into her eyes.

"I don't need to tell you who she is, you already know," he replied with one hand as he gently captured her lips in a kiss so thoroughly gentle that all she could think of was Keith and the sweet caress of his lips against hers. He took advantage of that moment to pull her closer to him, and the kiss deepened.

Breaking the moment, Keith keeps his hold on Julli as he says, "I am so sorry, Julli, I did not know this would happen."

Julli stares at him with eyes widened in guilt. Keith looks at her and says, "If there was anything that I could say to make it easier for you I would. Julli, I think I am falling in love with you and I know that you have feelings for me too."

Julli looks at Keith and feels shaken that he had told her how he felt. There was no way she could lie to him and tell him that she did not return his feelings. Therefore, taking a deep breath, she then looks back at Keith and says, "Keith, I do think I love you but with Mark passing only a year ago I am a bit confused. I thought that I would never find someone that loves me and who I love besides my baby and Luke."

"I would do anything for you, I hope you realize that," Keith told Julli adoringly.

"I know, but you, Mark, and Kathrin all being my friends and the fact that you are related, makes it harder," signed Julli, perplexed that nothing was going right.

"How?" asked Keith, demanding an answer.

"I guess it is just everybody is sort of weaved into a lineage somehow, and I have no knowledge of my parents and their families. You have what I don't have," Julli signed, sighing when she signed "parents and families."

"Julli, you have me and Kathrin out here. We will be the family you need," said Keith passionately.

"Thank you, Keith."

He pulled Julli into a hug. Julli felt so safe there. She hugged him back. The hug went on forever and forever.

Until somebody shouted, and Keith pulled away.

Looking over her head, he strained to hear what the commotion was all about.

Signing, he said, "Zeke's homestead is ablaze!"

Julli's face paled even in the darkness of the night. Keith grabbed Julli by the hand, leading Julli back to the carriage to take her to her baby and friends, who were in need of help. Keith hurried all the way there. Other townsfolk were hurrying out there as well. Everyone was clamoring, grabbing pails of water and burlap sacks. Horses were neighing and shaking their manes. Several of the cattle were lowing, and dogs were barking, whining, and running all over. Julli saw some chickens going into the paths of wagons, carriages, and horses, being trampled in the process. Nobody cared. In the confusion they hardly paid any heed to where they were going.

Julli sat by Keith, wondering, *Is Pamela and them okay? What happened? What is going on? Why did it happen to everyone I cared about?*

Why was Keith not talking to her? Before they got halfway there, Keith looks at her and says, "They said there was a fire at Zeke's. Nobody has said anything about Pamela or anybody yet. We will find out more when we get there." At Julli's worried look, he added, "I am sure they are okay."

Julli fervently wanted to pray. She was so worried that she started bawling. Keith was busy handling the reins, so he did not comfort her. Not that she would have accepted it anyways.

There was fire everywhere. The house, the stable, and the barn were all burning. There were neighbors trying to catch the animals. In Julli's haste to get out to find her baby, she fell out of the carriage before Keith could stop. She did not care. She wanted her baby. Frantically looking around, Julli could see people running all over but did not find Mindy, Zeke, or Luke.

Screaming for Luke, Keith grabbed her arm and pulled her over to where the neighbors were gathering in a circle over a form on the ground. "No, not again!" shrieked Julli, remembering when she had seen Freddie lying at the bottom of the stairs barely two years ago. "Luke!" shouted Julli. "Mindy, Zeke, where are you?"

Keith grabbed her arms and turned her to face him. "Zeke is on the ground. I will go find Mindy and the baby."

"Luke?" Julli reminded Keith.

"And that mutt of yours as well," added Keith, agreeing to finding Luke as well.

Julli shoved her way through the crowd to where Zeke lay on the ground. He was badly burnt. Julli awkwardly walked over and kneeled by him. Sobbing her fears out about him being hurt badly and possibly dying. When Zeke saw that Julli was there, he raised his burnt hand to her. Julli took his hand in hers, cradling it. She had to take several deep breaths to calm herself.

"I am so sorry," he gasped, wheezing as he looked at Julli through burnt skin.

Leaning over him, she asked, "What do you mean?"

"I tried to stop them but there were too many." He gasped with every breath he took.

"Who?" demanded Julli; she needed to know who would hurt her friends by burning their home with them in it.

"I don't know. They somehow killed Luke." With that, he started sobbing. His chest heaving with every sob.

"What?" Glancing around, not seeing whom she was looking for, she wiped her eyes on the back of her hand and asked, "Where is Pamela?"

Not hearing her over the burning blaze and people yelling, he looked at her and told her, "The dog is over by the field."

Upon hearing that, one man took off looking for the dog. A couple more followed with lanterns.

"Julli, forgive me," begged Zeke, clenching her hand in his.

Not understanding him, she asked, "For what"

"Not protecting Pamela," Zeke admitted. He looked at Julli, tears streaming down his face.

"What do you mean?" yelled Julli. She looked at the closest person and asked, "Did he say he could not protect my Pamela?" At the nod confirming what she thought he said, fear gripped her in the pit of her stomach, and she wanted to throw up.

There was a commotion when one of the men brought over the dog. Julli looked and saw that it was Luke. He lay limply in the arms of the man. Julli choked back a moan as they gently laid him by Zeke. There was blood; Julli could see it and smell it. Her puppy, her big dog and faithful companion, had been killed.

Julli looked back at Zeke, who coughed and spoke, "I tried, but—." Zeke stopped what he was saying and stared blankly at Julli. His hand that Julli was holding went limp. A man presumably the doctor came over and leaned over Zeke, listening for a heartbeat. Finding none, he shook his head, and the crowd gasped.

"No, Zeke!" screamed Julli. Not again. She did not want her friend to die. "Zeke, wake up."

Keith pulled Julli to her feet and held her tightly while she sobbed.

"Keith, where is Pamela?" she asked. However, the look on his face told all. Keith had been told that there was a good chance that Zeke's wife and the child were in the house. A neighbor had just pulled Zeke out when the house collapsed, burning embers everywhere. No one had seen Mindy or the baby.

"Keith, listen to me, where is my baby?" screamed Julli. She grabbed his face and turned it to her; there she saw the pain etched on it.

He held her tightly as he said, "I am sorry." Julli fainted when he told her that.

CHAPTER 13

———◆◆◆———

Missing Her Baby and Aunt Comes Out

Julli was carried to the carriage, lain down, and taken home. Keith laid her on the bed, removed her boots, unbuttoned her blouse, and untied her skirt. He covered her with a quilt and placed a kiss on her soot-smeared cheek. He then sat down on the chair near the bed, placed his elbows on his knees, and sighed in his hands. Julli had lost everything, including her baby, dog, and her friends. That was a lot for someone to take in one night. To top it off, he had sung her the song he worked on the past few weeks. His attempts to impress her with his love worked 'til the fire had destroyed everything Julli held dear to her. Keith worried what the next few hours were going to be like.

He rubbed his palms on his face and grimaced. There was going to be a lot to do. He was not sure where to start.

Julli whimpered in her sleep. She had the dream where Keith sang a song to her and kissed her; then there was a fire, and she could not find her baby. Someone had killed her dog, and her friend Zeke died from burns all over his body. With a start, Julli woke up, sweat pouring all over her. She looked around her and saw Keith sleeping on the chair with his head on the bed.

Dazed, Keith wakes up, looks up at Julli, who is staring at him, and sits up, stretching, and groans when he feels the aches in his body. Julli looks at Keith with a glazed expression on her face. She looks to the bassinet and doesn't see her baby. She looked around the room and doesn't see her dog either. Julli looks at Keith and sees a man who told her everything would be okay, only to find out nothing was okay. Julli did not know what she was supposed to feel.

She had gone through shock when Freddie died, and the feeling was the same now as it was before. The only thing that bothered her physically was the fact that she had not nursed her baby since before the party. Julli hated the feeling of not being able to do something about it.

Keith comes over, sits on the bed by Julli, and asks, "Are you okay?"

"Okay?" Julli asked tonelessly; pulling the sheet up over her chest up to her chin, trying to hide the telltale signs of not having nursed her baby.

"Yes, are you okay?" he repeats, signing this time.

"No, I am not okay." Julli shook her head abruptly, then snapped at Keith, "I want my baby. Where is she?"

"I think you had better change and come with me." He had noticed that her blouse was soaked but did not want to rile her by saying anything. He knew for a fact that she was going to suffer for several weeks. It had to be hard on her, and his heart bled for the loss she was going to have to deal with.

He gets up, looks at Julli, sighs, and walks out of the room, shutting the door. Julli looks around the room in a daze. Her mind blank, her heart cold and empty. She got up from the bed, walked over to the closet, and opened it. She knew what she had to do. She had lost too many people not to know the routine. She swore that she would be strong for her baby. She grabbed a bag and stuffed hankies in it. Not sure, but she knew there was a big whopping chance she was going to use them. But she could not cry. She could yell, scream, gnash her teeth, but no crying. She pulled out the black cashmere dress she wore to Mark's funeral. Julli went over to the dresser and looked at her jewelry box. She opened it and picked up the necklace that she found in her closet when she got ready to go to Freddie's funeral.

Two things to wear to remind her of the loss she suffered. The black cashmere dress and the bear claw necklace. The two reminders of the two she loved dearly and lost. She went over to the screen and changed her clothes. She was in a trance, where she knew she had to do what she had to do and hating it. Walking out from behind the screen, putting on the necklace, Julli stopped to look at herself in the mirror. Her hair was in disarray. There were streaks of black on her face. Her eyes were bloodshot and puffy. Julli grimaced at the reflection and ignored it as she went over to pick up her boots.

She put them on and grabbed her coat. It smelled of smoke. Julli put her coat on and opened the door to see Keith sitting at the table with the book Mark had given to her. Swallowing, she entered the main room, and Keith looked at her somberly. He closed the book, pushed the chair back, and got up. He went over to the door, opened it, and grabbed his coat, following Julli to the carriage.

Julli pulled herself onto the seat and stared blankly ahead as Keith went around and got in himself. He clicked to the horse, and they went onto the road to Zeke and Miranda's place. Keith kept glancing at Julli, who was completely devoid of any emotion. She sat there in icy silence 'til they arrived at the burnt-down homestead.

There were neighbors walking around trying to make some sense of what happened and to look for any remains. Julli sat there 'til Keith grabbed her elbow and helped her down from the carriage. He kept his hand on her arm as he led her past the debris over to where the men were digging a couple of graves. The sheriff came by and tipped his hat at Julli, who completely ignored him. She kept on walking to the graves and did not falter when she saw there were four, two large and a smaller one. There was a fourth hole, smaller than any of the three.

She stepped back when they brought over the body of Zeke wrapped in skins. She stood there watching emotionlessly when they took off their hats and bowed their heads. Julli did not shed a tear when they put dirt on the body of Zeke. She saw a few men going to the debris where the house was, and they scooped up some of the ashes and carried it over to the grave next to Zeke's. They scattered the ashes, got their shovels, and dumped dirt back into the grave.

She did not flinch when she saw the body of Luke carried over to the third grave. Keith took her elbow again and led her over to where they were going to bury her dog, Luke. Julli reached out and ruffled the fur behind his head and let her hand drop when he did not respond to her touch. Keith nodded to the men, who gingerly placed Luke into the grave. Keith stepped up and said a prayer. Julli watched as they sprinkled dirt onto Luke's body, hiding him from her sight forever.

Looking at the fourth grave, Julli could not bear the sight of her baby being placed in a dark, damp prison. She finally looked at Keith and asked, "Where is Pamela?"

Keith turned her to the debris and tipped his head in the direction of the house. Julli pulled her arm free from Keith, stumbling over the debris in her attempt to get to the burnt house. Some of the men came to help her, and she swatted their efforts by shaking her head and knocking down their hands.

Julli finally got to the area where the chairs were scorched and looked for any sign that was Pamela's. She at last came upon an item she knew was her baby's. It was the silver rattle that Kathrin had given to Pamela for Christmas. It was not as burnt as the rest of the stuff that were scorched. Julli looked around for anything else that was Pamela's.

Not finding anything remotely like a scrap of material, a strand of hair, or something, Julli sank to her knees. She placed the rattle on her chest and moaned when she felt it jingle. Julli, not wanting to give up, kept poring over every inch of the ground. She could not find anything. Nothing.

Keith walks over to Julli. She feels his hand on her arm. She turns to Keith, gets up with support from him, and goes into his open arms. Julli sighs as she nestles her head on his chest. She feels his heart beating. They stood there holding on to each other. Julli steps out of the embrace to look at Keith and wipe away the tears that were running down her face. Keith copies her action by wiping his own with the back of his hand. Julli took Keith's face in her hands and says, "I cannot find anything. Are you sure they were in the house?"

Keith sighs and dejectedly says, "There would have been no way they got out and we didn't find them." Looking at Julli, he added somberly, "The man who pulled Zeke out swore he heard him yell for Mindy. It was too late for him to go back in when the roof caved."

She looks at the ground where she saw the rattle. Keith, knowing what she was looking for, tells her that that was the likely spot. "The sheriff said that how bad the fire was going, it was like someone poured kerosene everywhere. The whole place was soaked with it."

Julli stares dismissively at Keith when he said that. She glanced around the area and sighed. She was so tired. She could not cry anymore. She totally hated death, which kept following her and taking those she loved.

Closing her eyes, she pointed to the ground where she had found the rattle. Keith bent down on one knee, and using his hat, he scooped up the ashes around the area where the toy was found. Then, gingerly holding his hat, he whistled. The pastor and other workers stopped what they were doing and came over. The pastor and Keith chatted a few minutes, and Keith placed his hat in her hands. The pastor beckoned her to follow him.

She felt Keith supporting her as he led her to the grave for Pamela. Slowly she fell to her knees, still holding the hat. In a daze, she waited for the pastor to start the ceremony. Several workers and their wives crowded around, sorrow on their faces. Julli knew that the pastor was praying for Pamela's spirit to go home to the Heavenly Father. She did not care what he said; she only knew what she felt. Emptiness, hatred, and pain. Julli felt Keith place his hand on hers and gently push down. Julli laid the hat in the grave, and a hand grabbed some dirt, placing it on the ashes. Looking at the hand, Julli recognized it as belonging to Kathrin. Julli swallowed back tears and laid her baby's ashes to rest.

Julli stood up on wobbly legs, felt Kathrin give her a hug, and Julli ignored her. She felt Keith giving her a kiss on the forehead. He cups her face gently and lifts it up. Julli kept her eyes closed for a little while, and when she opened them, Keith tried to talk. He swallowed several times before he was able to have the strength to say what he needed to say. "Julli, I am so sorry." Shaking his head, he adds sincerely, "Please forgive me?"

Julli wonders why Keith would ask her to forgive him when he was there with her when Zeke, Mindy, Pamela, and Luke were killed. She said sadly, "Keith, you didn't know that this was going to happen. Therefore I do not have to forgive you. You were there with me when I lost my baby," shaking her head angrily. "The being that you worship and pray to has taken too much from me. He has earned my hatred."

"Julli, don't take your anger out at him. He is merciful and loving," corrected Keith, upset that Julli was taking her anger out on something he devoted his life to.

"Loving?" she snapped at Keith. "How can you say that when you can see here that there is death? What god would let good, innocent people and pets be killed?" She was sure that there was no god, that it was just a myth. Every time she drew closer to him, something bad in her life happened.

Keith swallowed and admitted, "Everything happens for a reason."

"Oh, I see. So it was just for a reason people that I love are taken from me?" Julli asked him, offended. What right did he have to tell her that it was for a reason she lost her baby?

"Yes and no," Keith admitted. "He does not take them from you."

Julli was riled at that. "Really? What would you know?" she snapped.

"I lost my family as well," Keith told her miserably. He wiped the back of his hand across his face, wiping the tears Julli had not seen 'til now.

"Mark was one of them, as well as Pamela!" acknowledged Julli to Keith.

"Yes, but I too lost my child." With that, Julli stared at him, not understanding where he was coming from. She could not fathom he would understand what she was going through.

"What?" she asked. "I did not know you had a child." Julli looked at Keith and saw how wretched he looked. He seemed to have shrunk into a tiny man. Gone was the joking face she knew so well.

"My wife died in childbirth along with my baby." His eyes were bright with unshed tears. Julli could see him with a baby in his arms; actually, she did when Pamela was born.

Julli realized sorrowfully that Keith did indeed know her loss. "I did not know that," she said, reaching out to hold his hand. She tried to say something, but nothing came to mind.

"It happened years ago but the pain is still as fresh as if it happened yesterday," Keith told her, squeezing and cradling her hand. "So losing your baby is like I lost mine. I was there when Pamela was born just like I was there when my wife had our baby."

"I am sorry," Julli signed with one hand. She was so choked up that she could not speak.

"Do not be." Keith looked squarely at Julli and replied optimistically, "Their deaths only brought me closer to the Lord."

"Oh, good for you," came from Julli sarcastically. She was not so sure that it was a good thing. Replace loved ones with something they could not see or feel.

"Julli, stop and think," begged Keith desperately. "Mark left, replacing his absence with Pamela."

Keith tried to soothe the pain with what he said, but it backfired when Julli asked, "And who replaces Pamela?" She pulled her hand out of his and stomped her foot. Ashes rose and slowly settled around them.

"No one. I do not know." Keith was at a loss what to say about that.

"See? I have nothing!" Seeing him shrug and ponder her question, she knew she had him at the moment. He could not always be right.

Keith tried hard to think, but all he could admit to was this, "No, it does not always happen that way."

"Well, go tell it to the god you worship. I sure do not believe that he is a good god."

With that, she clutched the rattle closer to her chest and stumbled out of the debris. She walked off the property toward her home. Julli refused to peek back. That chapter of her life was over, and she had become an emotionless human being.

Julli walked into her home, not glancing at anything. Not touching anything, she went right into her bedroom. Lying down on the bed, she sank wearily onto the pillow and looked at the rattle.

She could see Pamela holding the rattle, shaking it. She wished to hear the jingling and then the laughing in her little baby way. Julli looked over to the bassinet, and she could see Luke lying there, his head cocked with his ears up, listening to Pamela cooing. Julli pulled the quilt over her, closed her eyes, and went to sleep. She willed herself not to feel anything.

Nothing could take away her pain. Maybe if she slept, she would come to the realization it was just a nightmare.

Keith snuck in to check on Julli and found her sleeping on the bed. He went over to her, smoothed back her hair, and placed a kiss on her forehead. He did not know what he could do to make things better for her. He himself could not believe that the baby he helped bring into the world was gone. Just like with his child, born one minute, then taken the next. Keith looked at Julli sleeping; he knew he had to do something. Anything at all to help her.

Bertha looked at the telegram in disbelief. She could not believe what had happened the last two years Julli had been gone. She also could not believe that her niece had lost Mark, then her baby, along with a dog. Bertha reread the telegram before she yelled for the butler to come do her biddings. She did not have much time. Her niece needed her.

Julli struggled to make each day count. She cleaned up the house, put Pamela's stuff in her closet, and vowed never to open it. Along with Pamela's stuff, she put in her dress and the necklace. She contemplated putting in the book as well. She glanced at it and finally came to the decision that it belonged in there as well. Therefore, into the closet it went.

She also took the long way into town, not going past the homestead she used to love going to. Too many memories lay there. When Julli would be in town, she ignored every dog, woman, and baby. She did not need another reminder of what she had lost. She did her business and left to go back home as quickly as she could. She did not even go to the boardinghouse to see Kathrin, who came out begging Julli to come see her. She could not bear to see what others had that she lost.

Sadly enough, she also ignored Keith. He came out daily to check on her, but she made it a point to shut the bedroom door when he was there, not granting him permission to see her. It was not that she blamed him; she just could not deal with life at that time. She willed herself to forget him. It hurt her since he had been a part of her life up 'til now.

Until that day her aunt came out to see her. Julli was washing the dishes when she saw a carriage pull up. She wondered who it was.

The driver stepped down, opened the carriage door, and Julli gasped when she saw her aunt step out. Julli dropped the dishes, wiped her hands on her apron, and dazedly walked out the door to greet her aunt.

"Julli, my dear!" came cheerfully from Bertha. She looked as she did two years ago. Poised and of course proper. Julli could not believe her eyes.

Bertha grabbed Julli in a hug, not caring for once what Julli was wearing or the fact she was not clean. Julli stood there for what seemed like eternity before her arms went around her aunt, hugging her back. She breathed in deeply the scent of her aunt. How she had missed her aunt Bertha. The smell of violets and hibiscus. They stood there in the hot sun, holding on to each other. The time spent apart brought them closer together than ever before.

"Come on, let us go in," suggested Bertha, not liking being out in the sun.

Julli nodded and led the way into the house. Bertha removed her bonnet and got out her fan, which she proceeded to open and fan herself with.

"It is sure hot out here," she said, stating the obvious.

"Yes, it is," signed Julli nonchalantly.

"Julli, I missed you so much," Bertha told Julli. She made it a point to make sure Julli got what she said. She looked around the house. It was clean and lacked a lot of stuff, which made it very simple. It could be fixed in a matter of days.

"And I, you," Julli answered. She saw her aunt take in the surroundings. She was not ashamed of how she lived. She liked it simple.

Bertha went over to the faucet and asked, "Can I have a drink? My throat is parched."

"Oh yes." Julli walks over there and pumps the water, puts a mug under it, filling it up, and hands to her aunt.

"Well, I see you have a nice quaint home," came saucily from Bertha, which Julli knew was not what she meant.

"It is Mark's." Julli then corrected herself, "I mean was."

Bertha did not miss the correction Julli added. She wondered what Julli was feeling, or rather thinking. "I know."

"How did you get here, I mean what are you doing here?" stuttered Julli. Now with her aunt there, she was starting to feel as though everything was beneath her. She shook her head when she asked the question.

"I came to see you," responded Bertha gaily. Julli knew her aunt was happy to see her, but she had to wonder why her aunt came out, especially now.

"Why?" Julli asked, puzzled. She needed her aunt to tell her the reason for the visit.

Bertha took another sip of water and placed it down on the table before she answered the question. "Because I wanted to and also 'cause I got this telegram."

Julli closed her eyes; she did not need people telling her aunt everything. When was she going to have peace? "Who sent it?"

"A man named Keith, said he was a cousin of Mark's," replied Bertha, looking at Julli for any clue what she was thinking.

Nothing, even when Julli said, "Oh!"

Bertha sits up straight, sighs, and looks at Julli, wondering how she was going to talk to her without her getting upset with her. Deciding to take the direct approach she always took with Julli, she straightened up more and looked Julli in the eye squarely. "Julli, I was so sorry to hear about your baby."

Julli only looked at her aunt and asked, "Pamela?"

"Yes. I was told you had a little girl." Watching Julli, Bertha noticed that Julli was devoid of any emotion. She did not flinch, cry, or show signs of getting upset. Now Bertha was getting real worried. She was right to come out at this time.

"I see," was all Julli said monotonously.

"Julli, this is hard on you I am sure." With that, Bertha reached out and placed her hand on Julli's.

"What would you know?" came from Julli unthinkingly. No one could ever know her loss, her pain, and her regrets.

"I too lost a baby." When Julli's eyes widened, Bertha continued, "Well, I did not exactly give birth. I lost it before it was born."

"How?" Julli grabbed her aunt's hand and squeezed. She did not know that her aunt had lost a baby as well. Julli realized that there was so much she did not know about her aunt. Maybe she needed to get to know her before anything else happened.

"Came too early." Bertha sighed.

"Why did it come too early?"

"I do not know," replied Bertha, sitting down. She nodded to the chair by her for Julli to sit upon.

"Why does everybody I love die?" asked Julli bluntly, coming to the point.

Bertha blinked several times. She looked at Julli and saw the hurt evident in her eyes. "I do not know, my dear. Sometimes it is meant to help us. Things just happen, I guess."

"Well, I hate it!" snapped Julli angrily. She did not want to accept what her aunt had to say. She knew that her aunt was going to say what was on her mind, and Julli knew she obviously came out for a reason. Was it to cajole Julli to move back East?

"I know you do," Bertha agreed with Julli. She too hated that fact that she lost the ones she loved as well. Seemed like tragedy was meant to follow them no matter what.

"I lost my ma and pa," she added apathetically "Not to forget to mention Freddie, Mark, Luke, and Pamela." She slammed her hands on the table, not caring that she hurt herself. Her anger was manifested in her whole being. She felt tears coming and swallowed them back, saying, "It hurts a lot!"

"I know!" crooned Bertha, getting up, going to Julli, and hugging her.

Julli hugged her aunt around the waist. She felt her aunt patting her on the head. It was almost like when she was growing up and her aunt had tried being there for Julli. There were times Julli was glad her aunt had helped her through her childhood, but she had wished her aunt could have reverted to the aunt she was when she first came to see her years ago.

Her aunt pulled out of the embrace, went back to sit down, and looked squarely at Julli.

"I am here and I will stay as long as you need me to," she avowed to Julli.

Julli nods her head, not wanting to be alone. Anything was better; even putting up with her aunt made the day seem less bleak.

Turning to the driver, who brought in her bags, she said, "You may put the carriage in the barn and take care of the horses. You do not mind staying out in the barn, do you?"

The driver politely replied, "No, madame." He bowed and gladly walked out to the barn, away from the women's chattering.

"Well, Julli, let's unpack my stuff and then you can show me around." Decided, Bertha did not want to deal too much on Julli on the first day she was visiting. She did not want Julli to tell her to leave before she could explain the true nature of her visit.

"Around?"

"Yes, I want to go to town later on," she confirmed by going over to pick up her bags and take them into the bedroom. "But right now we have some catching up to do."

Julli talked with her aunt as the day passed. She found out that Neal had left for boarding school, vowing never to return to his parents' place. Mauricia stopped working, and Paula ran away with another servant. Lieutenant Megston was killed by pirates. There were so many things to catch up on with her aunt, but she hoped that they would take a while and not bring up the subject Julli wanted desperately to avoid.

Julli came to the realization that if she would have stayed with Bertha, the things Bertha told her would still have happened, but her part wouldn't have. She would not have moved out West, gotten pregnant, lost Mark, and had to bury her child. Desperately Julli wished she could reverse time and take back what she lost.

Bertha, looking at the time, exclaimed, "Let's get ready to go to town to eat. I want to see more of the place."

Bertha wore a long-sleeved blouse that Julli thought was still too low cut, although she did like the sea blue skirt her aunt had on. She looked prim and proper as usual. Julli sighed when she realized that she did not have any clothes for going out to eat with her aunt. The least she could do was brush her hair and put it up in a neat bun like her aunt's.

"Julli, this is for you," said Bertha, handing her a package.

"Not again, Aunt Bertha," groaned Julli, not wanting to put up with any more theatrics on how she should dress. When Julli opened the package, she saw that her aunt had not only brought her blue dress but the sapphire necklace as well. Looking at her aunt, she saw that she was holding up the blue slippers Julli wore two years ago.

"Now you should get dressed," her aunt stated, then closed the door.

Julli got dressed, almost feeling like she was sixteen again. She smoothed down her skirts and took a peek in the mirror. "Wow!" she signed to herself. "I look almost like I did."

Bertha comes into the room, telling her, "Wow, you look beautiful."

"Thank you," Julli signed as she slipped on her shoes. Both women looked appreciatively at each other, and Bertha nodded in approval when they looked in the mirror.

"Let's go. I am anxious to see the town and meet your friends."

Julli and Bertha got in the carriage and went into town. Julli chatted with her aunt, telling her about the town of Johnsville. Julli also talked about the townsfolk and how they treated her. She stayed away from the subject of Zeke, Mindy, Pamela, and Luke as well as Mark and Keith. Bertha had questions to ask that Julli did not really want to answer.

"What is your relationship with this man named Keith?" Bertha asked, looking at Julli. This man she asked about was the one that sent her the message that Julli needed her help. If he sent it to Bertha, then he must have cared for her niece.

"Oh, he is a cousin of Mark and Kathrin's," Julli admitted, trying hard to keep her face emotionless. She knew her aunt would notice the vibes Julli was giving out, so she had to try hard. "He is a good man." Julli shrugged, trying to act disinterested.

"I see." Not willing to change the subject much, her aunt asked again, "Why did you not send word to me about your pregnancy?" Watching Julli's face, she caught a view of pain in her eyes before she blinked and waved to a peddler walking on the side of the road.

"Aunt, I don't know." Julli closed her eyes for a moment, signing, "I just felt ashamed I guess." She opened them to finish signing, "Having a baby without being wed was not exactly something I thought you would want to know."

"I wanted to know," pushed Bertha. She did not need Julli to ask for her forgiveness; she just wanted Julli to realize that she was there for her if needed.

"I am sorry," whispered Julli, signing the "sorry" sign. "I wish you could have seen her." Julli took a chance and looked at her aunt.

"Me too, Julli," replied Bertha, hurt. She had a great-niece and had not gotten to meet her. If the baby was anything like Julli, Bertha knew she would have been in love. Julli had not been so bad, and she loved her niece so much that she would have welcomed the baby into the family and her home regardless of rumors.

Bertha asked, wondering how much of her past Julli knew about. It had seemed that everything evolved around Julli's interests that she was not sure if Julli really knew about their family lineage and all.

"Did you know that when I found out your ma was pregnant, I made a blanket for you?" Bertha shocked Julli with that question.

"No. Where is it?" asked Julli, whose interest was piqued in the sort of change of subject.

"Probably at the homestead they left to you," suggested Bertha.

"What? I have a homestead?" Julli signed, dumbfounded. She was shocked beyond measure. All these years and her aunt had not said a word.

"Yes. Your pa put it in your name years ago," Bertha declared, willing Julli to believe her. She did not like the look that Julli gave her. She did not want to distance her niece after all this time.

Julli sat up, tapped her fingers on the side of the carriage, and, looking at her aunt, asked, "Where is it?"

Not quite so sure, Bertha herself did not know. She thought Julli could use some space from every place where she left a loved one. She brightened as an idea came to her, a way of keeping Julli with her for a while. "I am not quite sure. We can go there sometime."

"Why didn't you tell me long ago?" Julli signed, dismayed that she had never put it past her aunt to be so secretive. She always thought her aunt was just one of those snobby rich people who worried more about themselves than anyone else.

"I was afraid you were going to leave me." Bertha picked up her hankie and wiped at the corners of her eyes. The gesture made Julli look at her quizzically. Her aunt seemed more human and emotional than ever before. "You left me anyway," Bertha added to Julli's shock.

"But—?"

"I know. I had hoped that things would be different. I was afraid that you would think I withheld information from you with the purpose of hurting you more. In fact, I only wanted to make sure that the homestead was worth what your pa paid for."

"So is it?" Julli's eyes brightened at that. Maybe if it was still good, she could go see for herself.

"Yes. It was the source of your income. I am very sorry I kept that from you," Bertha signed dishearteningly. She had not meant to tell her at this time. Not since Julli lost her baby.

"What about my ma and pa?" Julli signed, putting her hands to her chin and then to her forehead.

"From what I know, your pa, Colin, died from some illness. All I know is your ma, Brionna, was killed. They said it was more or less her going insane when Colin died."

"Colin? That was his name?" Julli leaned forward, looking at her aunt.

"Yes. Your mother's name was Brionna. She was my younger sister. You look so much like her. I was pretty sure Freddie told you about them," stated Bertha, not liking the look Julli gave her. It was the same look she used to give when she found out Bertha had done something Julli had not wanted her to. The look was of distrust. Even the compliment did not earn her Julli's benefit of the doubt.

"Really? I see." Julli peeked at Bertha through her watery eyes and asked, "What do you think? I mean about what happened to my parents?"

Bertha looked away at the passing land before she sighed and turned to Julli, saying, "I am sure she was killed. It was not the first time they were threatened."

"Threatened? How?" Julli grabbed her aunt's arm and cocked her head.

"I have your mother's letter to me. I kept it over the years. And the telegram I got when your mother and father were found dead," Bertha signed. She made sure that Julli got the words "letter," "telegram," and "dead" since she did not know the signs to them. Bertha glanced at Julli, whom she noticed was silently crying. She saw Julli sigh and blink back tears. What a day to tell her niece.

"Who sent the telegram?" Julli signed, swallowing the bitterness she felt.

"I do not know. I am guessing the sheriff." Her aunt shrugged her shoulders and continued to gaze at Julli as they neared their destination in the town. Julli was deep in thought the rest of the way, and Bertha knew it was a lot for Julli to digest.

They arrived at the boardinghouse and went in. The driver nodded and clicked the reins to the horses, and he headed over to the stables. Julli glanced at him, and he averted his gaze onto the horses.

"Isn't he going to come in to eat?" she could not resist asking her aunt.

"No, not today. It is just you and me," stated Bertha, uneasy. She straightened her bonnet and smoothed down her skirts. She looked at Julli and couldn't help the impulse to smooth back a curl that had blown onto Julli's face. Instead of getting upset with her aunt, Julli for once relished the gesture. It brought back memories, and Julli again wondered why she was so mean and inconsiderate toward her aunt.

When they entered the restaurant, Kathrin came gleefully over to Julli, grabbing her in a big hug. Julli could not help but smile at the loving gesture Kathrin showed.

Julli turned to her aunt, still holding on to Kathrin, and said, "This is Kathrin, my friend and, Kathrin, this is my aunt, Bertha."

"It is a pleasure to meet you. Julli talked about you often." Kathrin smiled at Bertha.

"I am so pleased to make your acquaintance," Bertha said stoically. Actually Julli hardly mentioned the woman, except to say she was related to Mark. Bertha took in the simple long-sleeved, printed dress the woman wore. She had a white apron on, and Bertha grimaced when she saw the stains from the food on it. Kathrin was not bad to look at. She had stress lines around her eyes, and when she smiled, they crinkled, belying her age.

Kathrin leads them to a table near the corner of the room. She looks at Julli and gushes, "You look marvelously wonderful."

"Thank you. My aunt brought my dress out," Julli told her, signing to her meekly.

"Julli wore the dress when she turned sixteen," avowed Bertha, making Julli uncomfortable. So like her aunt to say things still that popped in her head.

"Was that the time you met Mark?" Kathrin asked, taking a risk in asking that question.

Pausing, giving her aunt darts, Julli admitted, "Yes." The way Julli signed to Kathrin while glaring at her aunt gave Kathrin warning bells. She decided to stay on the safe path and remain quiet. The questions could come at a later time, when Julli was up to it.

"Would you like the specials? It is roast beef with spuds and a salad. Biscuits come with it," Kathrin asked instead, playing hostess once again.

"Yes, please. That will be two of them," Julli ordered without looking at her aunt for confirmation.

Giving Julli a quick squeeze on the shoulder, Kathrin took off, placing their orders. Both Julli and Bertha watched her walk to the kitchen. Then Bertha broke the silence by tapping Julli on the hand, signing, "She seems wonderful."

Nodding, Julli agreed with her aunt. Avoiding her aunt's gaze, she admitted, signing, "She is Mark and Keith's cousin."

Bertha had to wait for Julli to look at her before she casually asked, "Oh, family?"

"Yes," Julli signed. Now she was with her aunt, she reverted back to signing without her voice, not caring what others would think. Julli was so tired of using her voice; it was nice for a change to sign. She loved the way people stared at them when they did not move their mouths and the way they wondered if something was terribly wrong with them.

"I would love to meet the Keith you mentioned." Surprised, Julli took in what her aunt said.

"Well, I don't know where he is at the moment. I haven't really talked to him since a few weeks ago," she admitted, fidgeting with her hands when she got done signing.

"Why not?" came carefully from Bertha, who noticed Julli's fidgeting. How it used to irritate Bertha years ago, but not today. Today she was to be the understanding, supportive, and loving aunt that Julli needed her to be.

"The night of the party when the fire was started, Keith sang a song to me that he wrote." Julli sighed as she signed, "It was beautiful."

Bertha tilted her head to the side, studying Julli's face. There was a little glimmer of emotion when Julli signed that. "That was so sweet of him," signed Bertha.

Nodding her head, Julli signed, "I know." Julli wanted to feel the way she did several weeks ago when Keith sang that "beautiful rose" song to her. It had made her feel special and unique.

"How do you feel about him?" her aunt asked while Julli was in a faraway daze.

"I am not sure," Julli stated. She finally affirmed what her aunt had a feeling about when Julli talked about Keith and the song. "Sometimes I think I love him and other times I am afraid to be around him."

"Why?" pushed Bertha, wanting to know what Julli was feeling.

"Every time I love someone, they die," Julli signed slowly. Bertha had no trouble reading the signs. She just had trouble with the fact that Julli thought everyone died after she loved them. Bertha remembered that she had once felt that way about her family and checked herself in what she was saying to Julli.

"Not necessarily. I am still here," she volunteered, trying to cheer Julli up. She did not want Julli angry with her.

"I know. But still, I am afraid," signed Julli, scared that she was going to lose more.

"I see." Bertha could only pat Julli's hand at that.

Kathrin brings in the food and sets it in front of Bertha and Julli. Bertha gasps at the size of the portions. Julli snickers and says, "They eat heartily out here."

"I can see that." Bertha glances at the other customers and watches a skinny woman eat with gusto.

"What does that woman do? Work in a mine?" asked Bertha, amazed that someone as skinny as that woman could stuff her mouth full of food.

Laughing, Julli replied, "No, she sews at the general store."

"Oh, I see," replied Bertha, who did not see.

"Come on, it's good. Kathrin is a good cook."

Bertha takes a bite and says, surprised, daintily wiping the corners of her mouth, "The food is pretty good."

Julli and her aunt ate the meal, all the while chatting about things that had changed since Julli's move out West.

When they were done, Julli could not find Kathrin and asked the servant to let her know that they appreciated the food and that it was good to see Kathrin.

Julli paid for the meal, and they put on their bonnets as they went outside to wait for the carriage. Julli looked around without seeing the town; she did not pay any heed to the gossip that had already started. She only cared that her aunt was with her and they looked regal compared to the townspeople.

When the carriage finally came, Julli waited 'til the driver had helped her aunt in before refusing the help offered to her next. After getting in herself, she expected them to be on their way. She was not in the mood to have the past brought up again. With a will, she crossed her fingers mentally in the hopes her aunt would be quiet for once.

Bertha tells Julli out of the blue, "I want to see where the graves are." Dashing all hopes Julli had for a nice quiet evening. Sighing, she looked at her aunt, saw the pleading in her eyes, and sighed desolately. Julli then nodded and pointed out the directions to the driver, who only nodded.

The driver drove them to the town's cemetery, down past Main Street. Julli pointed out where to go, and when they got to the destined place, she showed Bertha where Mark's grave was. Julli got out before the driver could get down and walked over to the grave. Bertha finally caught up with her, and they read out loud the writing on the stone together:

Mark Lee Dwitten
Best Friend, Family Man
8 Feb 1790 to 17 July 1817

Bertha cried silently. Julli stood there looking at the grave. She gave her aunt the benefit of the doubt. Moreover, was she right in doing so?

"I know I was against him. I hated him for taking you from me. All in all he was a good man. He helped me during our loss of Freddie. And being Pamela's father, I owe him my gratitude. He gave you something very precious."

Julli was quiet. Not saying much. Fighting to hold back tears. Julli walked stiffly back to the carriage, climbed in, and waited for her aunt to come back. She kept staring out at the land before her, willing herself not to show any emotion. She couldn't.

Next they go to Zeke's homestead. Bertha held Julli's hand on the way there. Julli ignored her aunt, pretending to focus on the directions on how to get there. As they neared the site, Julli gasps and grabs her aunt's hand. It was so desolated, barren, and maliciously destroyed. They had removed most of the debris and cleaned up what they could. Julli could still see the house, the barn, and the stable. When the driver passed what used to be the doorway, Julli gasped and looked back, seeing Zeke standing there, smiling and waving to her. Julli looked at her aunt with a confused expression on her face. Bertha turns and looks back, not finding anything, and shakes her head questioningly at Julli.

Julli starts crying. She missed her friends Zeke and Mindy. They came upon a grave site with a little white picket fence around it. If Julli had not known the area well, she would have said they were on the wrong property. The driver pulls on the reins, and the horses stop right in front of the four graves. Her aunt takes her hand, places a kiss on it, and gets down from the carriage. This time Bertha refused the help from either the driver or Julli.

Together they walk over to the graves. Julli sees that there are headstones already put at the head. She gasped and wondered who would have had the money for them. Kathrin came to mind. She would have to have a talk with her about it. Or rather thank her.

The first two were titled Cathelroan. The first one was Zeke's. Then Mindy's was next. Julli sank to the ground on her knees when she saw the markings on the next two stones. Beautifully etched onto the stone, she read aloud:

> Pamela Maire Hamperston-Dwitten
> Daughter and beloved child
> 14-Dec 1817 to 21-April 1818

Julli looked toward Luke's grave and saw that there was also a headstone. On it was written

> Luke
> Faithful dog, Companion
> 2-April 1817 to 21-April 1818

With a sob, Julli started wailing. She clutched her hands together at her chest. Her heart was broken. She missed her baby and her dog so much. The emptiness was too much to bear. She could see Pamela smiling, with Luke standing guard over her. Julli cries harder, realizing that it was only her memories that were going to have to satisfy her. She cried for her loss, for their loss of life with her, and never getting to see each other again.

Bertha cradles Julli in her arms, all the while sobbing herself. Julli wailed out in pain, "Pamela! Luke!" and Bertha sobbed even more at the sound of the anguish coming from her niece. She wished she could take away the pain that Julli was suffering from. Bertha knew some of what Julli was going through. It was a different kind of pain. Bertha wished that Julli would forgive herself and give the Heavenly Father a chance to heal her wounds. That is what Julli needed to heal properly. Bertha held on to Julli, as she sank down to the ground on her knees and gathered Julli closer to her.

Bertha sat there holding her while she sang the childhood lullaby that her mother sang to her when they were little, "Seoithin, Seo Ho."

"Seoithin, seo hó, mo stór é mo leanbh, Mo sheoid gan cealg, mo chuid gan tsaoil mhór, Seoithin seo ho, nach mór é an taitneamh, Mo stóirin na leaba, na chodladh gan brón."

Julli's sobs quieted down; she could feel her aunt singing a song. Nestling her head upon her aunt's chest, she felt her aunt continue.

"A leanbh mo chléibh go n-eiri do chodhladh leat, Séan is sonas gach oiche do chóir, Tá mise le do thaobh ag guidhe ort na mbeannacht, Seothin a leanbh is codail go foill."

"Ar mhullach an ti tá siodha, geala faol chaoin re an Earra ag imirt is spoirt.

"Seo iad aniar iad le glaoch ar mo leanbh, Le mian é tharraingt isteach san lios mór."

Holding on to Julli, Bertha continues her singing, patting down Julli's wayward curls.

"A leanbh mo chléibh go n-eiri do chodhladh leat, Séan is sonas gach oiche do chóir, Tá mise le do thaobh ag guidhe ort na mbeannacht, Seothin a leanbh is codail go foill."

Julli felt her aunt slow down and stop. Not wanting it to stop, she sighed and snuggled closer to her aunt, who welcomed it. Julli and her aunt sat there sharing their grief with each other. Julli felt as if her burdens were lifted from her heart, replaced with compassion, understanding, and love.

"Hello, Keith." Julli felt her aunt say something.

Strong arms help Julli up. Gasping, she notices that they belong to Keith. She would know those hands anywhere. Julli wipes her tears and grabs the hands. Holding them, she puts them up to her cheek. Julli looks at Keith, seeing tears in his eyes as well. He pulls her into a hug, holding her, while Bertha wipes her eyes and smiles.

She could tell that Keith and Julli belonged together. They were destined to be soul mates. Bertha silently prayed, thanking the Heavenly Father for the blessing that Julli was receiving. Asked him to watch over the loved ones they had lost and to bless them with a new beginning. Not forgetting the past but living the future with it.

Julli pulled out of the embrace to tell Keith, "This is my aunt Bertha."

"It is a pleasure to finally meet you. I am glad you came out to be with Julli." With that, he places a kiss on Julli's head and turns to take Bertha's hand, placing a kiss on it. Julli smiled at them both through her tears.

"Are you sure you have to go?" Julli asked him after he walked her and her aunt to the carriage.

"Yes, for now. But I'll be over tomorrow, if you and your aunt wouldn't mind my company," he replied, getting consent from Bertha as well as from Julli.

Julli rode the carriage home with her aunt. Keith had left to go do some work for a friend but promised he would come over the next day to visit with them.

When they got home, Julli went into the room with her aunt, waiting for her to get out the papers that she told Julli about. Then Bertha excused herself to go to bed, leaving Julli alone with the letters.

The next day, Julli went for a walk alone to ponder what she had read in the letters last night. Her aunt had wanted to stay in and rest, which Julli did not mind.

When Keith came over, Julli surprised him. "Keith, I want to leave. I want to go to where I was born. My parents died there. And there are too many memories back East and out here." She caught the understanding look he gave her about the pain of staying there or going back East. "I read the letter from my ma that Aunt Bertha gave to me. I want to know what I have and see what I can do."

"Would you like me to go with you?" asked Keith, signing. He tilted his head and looked at Julli.

"You have family here." She had figured there was a chance he would say that. Julli looked at him endearingly and saw that he returned the look as well.

"You are my family. I have the memories. That is all I need to remember them," was all he said, gathering her into his arms. Julli rested her head on his shoulder and sighed. She was thankful for Keith and the understanding he showed to her.

Not saying another word, they held hands and walked back to the house. Julli was not sure how her aunt would respond to her decision after she told her.

"Okay, then I guess we should go," was all she said, signing, and they sat down at the kitchen table, talking and planning what they should do.

They left the next morning. Julli felt guilty for not visiting the graves again, but she had comfort that she still had her aunt and Keith. Someday she would get over the past and move on to a brighter future. She had to believe that.

This was Julli's second trip out West, but this time she had her aunt and Keith with her. Surprisingly, her aunt did not complain about much, to which Julli was grateful. They did make a few stops at the outposts and had a few overnighters in the boardinghouses they came across, just because her aunt begged them to get a good night's sleep and relax some. Julli could not relax enough. She wanted to see what her parents had left to her.

They went to the claims center and found out the information they needed. Julli was happy that Keith and her aunt could hear as they were able to do the inquiring as quickly as possible. Her aunt made it a point to tell Julli what had transpired and what she learned. Julli could not believe her luck as she held the paper that listed her as the beneficiary to the claim that was in her pa's name. She was having good luck now.

Keith pulled the wagon into a homestead not far out of town. Julli jumped out of the wagon as soon as Keith pulled on the reins when they stopped in front of the house. It was big, bigger than the one she lived in with Mark. However, not as humongous as her aunt's.

Bertha gave Julli the keys to the door, and Julli squealed in delight. She ran up the few steps and unlocked the door, flinging it open. There was dust everywhere. All the windows were closed, and curtains were shut. Keith caught up with her and walked over to the windows, coughing as he clung them open, shattering dust everywhere. Julli could not contain her excitement as she flung open every curtain and opened every door that was closed.

She came into a room and pulled open the curtains to find a trunk next to the bed. Opening it, Julli pulled out a pink and purple baby blanket.

"Aunt Bertha, come quick!" hollered Julli.

Julli looked through the trunk for more stuff and came upon a book. Opening it, Julli saw that it was a journal. She flipped through it to find out it was her ma's by the writing clearly legible still. The writing was not recognized by Julli, but when she read the name, she gasped. It said, "Journal of Brionna Maire Mearse Hamperston." Julli opened it to the next page but was interrupted by her aunt Bertha, who had then come up the stairs to the room where Julli was in.

Bertha took one look at the blanket Julli held in one hand and the journal in the other and said gleefully, "Welcome home!"

Julli looks at her and signs, "This is the land that my parents had." At Bertha's nod, she continued asking by way of sign language, "Why did they stay here and not come with me to your place?"

Bertha looked sad and said, "My dear, it is better not to think back and ask why, just remember that they loved you and wanted the best for you."

CHAPTER 14

———◆◆◆———

New Start

J ulli put the journal back in the trunk along with the blanket. She had so much to do. She glanced around the room and took in the bed and dresser. Whoever had come had cleaned it up, then covered everything with sheets and left. The house had not been disturbed since then. Julli walked around a few more minutes before she went to help her aunt. She stopped at the room that had a baby bassinet in it and wondered if that had been hers. There was nothing to hint it was the room she was living in before she went to her aunt's. Just the bassinet, with a sheet over it. Wanting to know more about her history there at the house, she knew that she would have to wait 'til someone came forward, like neighbors and people from the town who knew her and her folks years ago. Hopefully there was someone who could give some information.

Julli knew that between her and her aunt, it would only take a few days to clean down everything and get things going. Keith and the driver were put to work outside and only came in when the women called for them. They helped clean up the outside by moving branches, dead trees, and debris that had accumulated over the years.

Julli went outside and saw some flowers growing not far from the house. The area where her ma had the garden was overrun by weeds. There were shrubs growing, and Julli sighed; it was going to take a while to get the place looking nearly as good as she imagined it used to be. Bertha had gone into town and ordered some potted plants and seeds for flowers and vegetables. They were told it was too late to start planting, but they could keep the seeds and plant next year, Julli reasoned. All they could do was make the best of the rest of the year left. Julli put herself into the task of making the house as clean as possible with the help of her aunt. There was a lot missing that Julli could have used, and without her knowing, her aunt had already ordered stuff to make the house pleasant and livable. As well as for their comfort and well-being.

It was a few days before Julli found out what was really in store for her.

There were four riders fast approaching when Julli was outside beating the rugs on the clothesline a few days later. Bertha came out as she heard the horses neighing and the riders shouting. She went over to where Julli was and stood by her. Both women stood there, wondering what was going on. They had no idea who the riders were or what they wanted. They had only been at the homestead for a couple of days.

The men reined the horses; one got off and sauntered over to Bertha and Julli. Julli noticed that he was the oldest of the rest of the men. White hair adorned a face that had seen better times, icy brown eyes set in a stern weathered face, and he was taller than Julli when he came to stand in front of the women.

"Howdy, madames," he acknowledged by taking off his hat and tilting his head to them.

"How do, sir," replied her aunt. Julli could not take her eyes off the face of the man standing in front of her. Somehow the eyes seemed familiar. She was pretty sure she had never met the man. Then she remembered that she was born here on this homestead. Maybe the man would know who she was, but she couldn't put her finger on why she seemed to know him.

"What you folks doing here?" he asked, businesslike. He took a long glance at Julli curiously before turning to look at the woman who answered the question. Julli was shocked that she could lip-read him as soon as he spoke. There was something about him; Julli just did not know what yet.

"We live here. This is my niece's property." Her aunt drew herself up to her full height as she said that. She knew how to deal with men who were forthright in their inquiries.

"I was not made aware of that," he said passively. Dusting his hat with his hand, he turned and glanced at the men behind him on the horses and told them, "Hang on, guys."

"Well, I am sorry. But this is my niece, Julli." At the mention of Julli's name, his eyes flickered something akin to recognition. Julli swore he knew who she was the way his face registered delight, which he quickly covered with a stern, businesslike face.

"Who does that make you?" came the question Bertha was prepared to answer. Bertha had dealt with men like him before, so it was easy for her to give the information without revealing too much.

"I am her aunt. My name is Bertha Mearse," she stated, folding her arms in a defiant way.

"No young 'un has claim to this here property. I do not recognize either one of ya. Or youse names," he stated back, holding his ground, ready to fight. He did not know that Bertha had a weapon to use, the names of her sister and brother-in-law.

"Maybe you will recognize these, Colin and Brionna Hamperston?"

Surprise was etched on his face at the mention of the names of Julli's parents. Julli watched him intently as he spoke with her aunt. "Yes, I do with those."

"This is their daughter, Julli." Julli knew she was staring at the man, but she could not take her eyes off him. She saw a memory showing that the man was younger and was holding Julli on his knees, bouncing her up and down. Those were the same eyes, only older.

"Aw geeze crap." Looking at Julli, he chuckles, swatting his leg with his hat. "Dang, you look just like ya ma," he signed. Julli was struck dumb; the man knew how to sign to her.

"You know my ma?" signed Julli back. She peeked at the other men and saw them just looking slightly confused. Maybe they had never seen their boss sign, or they just did not know what was being said as Paul's back was to them.

"Did." His face glazed over at the mention of Julli's ma. "She was downright purty." He smiled and touched Julli's nose. Julli had not been touched by any man but Freddie on the nose, but she did not seem to mind; in fact, she enjoyed the tap.

Julli smiled at the tap and wished she could remember more. "And my pa?" She wanted to know. She had to know what Paul had to say about her parents.

"Good man he was, Colin his name was." The lanky old stranger nodded his head and placed one hand on his belt as he said that. He had missed his friend Colin, Julli's father. His wife, Brionna, had been a great woman, kind and caring. There had not come any friends for Paul as good as Colin and Brionna had been to him.

"Yes."

"My apologies, madames. I am Paul. These galoots behind me are my hired hands, Tom, Jerry, and Aaron."

Julli nodded and curtsied to the men, who took off their hats and greeted Julli and her aunt by saying, "Miss."

"We have been running this place since youse folks' death." Looks at Julli and walks up to her, grabbing her in a hug. When he set her back down, he takes her hand, bestowing a kiss on it, and says, "Welcome home, Ms. Julli."

Looking around, he asks, looking for someone in particular, "Where be the dang redskin?"

"Who?" Bertha and Julli asked in unison. Since Paul was signing along with talking, both women could understand him. He scrunched his face, pretending to be hurt by their question following his own. Julli had to smile at his attempt in faking hurt.

"Freddie the old coot," Paul admonished. He laughed at the coot part but sobered at what he heard next.

"He died a couple years ago," Bertha spoke for her and Julli. She did not want Julli having another emotional breakdown. They had moved to her birthplace, and she wanted to keep Julli happy, busy and happy as long as she could to help deal with the pain.

"Dang. He was a good man. Even though he was a blasted redskin. Always going on about herbs and whatnots." Paul cracked up laughing, and Bertha joined in. Julli did not see the punch line behind the joke. She had loved Freddie and thought he was the most awesome man she had ever had the pleasure of calling her father.

"Yes, he was," Julli signed, not too happy with Freddie's memory being tarnished with being called a blasted redskin. Julli had thought he was more of a brown man than red and wondered why the white folks called them redskins.

"Me and the boys come back tonight, if that is okay with you women," asked Paul, anxious. He wanted the chance to visit with Colin and Brionna's daughter and see if she could stand up to what life out here had in store for her. If she could handle it, he would know she was truly their daughter, the little girl he remembered.

"Please do. We have a lot to talk about." Both she and Bertha agreed. They could use some company as well as some answers to the questions they had. Julli felt energized in the fact that she would find out who she really was. That was provided Paul could tell her what she needed to know.

"Yes, mum, we sure do."

Paul tilted his head and slammed his hat back on his head. He nodded to the women, and he turned and sauntered back to his horse. Julli could not make out what the men said to him or what his reply was. He sat upon the horse, belonging there, and whispered something. The men looked at Julli with amazement, and they all tipped their hats off to her before Paul said something again, and with that, they reined their horses around and took off to the west. Paul turned to look back and waved to Julli. She put up her hand as he pulled on the reins, making his horse rear up. Julli gasped, afraid he was going to fall off. He only let out a "whoop!" With that, Paul and his hands left in a trail of dust.

Julli wondered why they had stopped by after a few days. She was made aware by Keith and her aunt that the sheriff was to have told them. Apparently by the way Paul acted, the news of her moving back home had not reached him. Julli had the feeling that no one really had been notified about the new people who came out to claim what was Julli's.

"Aunt Bertha, I am a little confused." Julli turned to look at her aunt; she could see that Bertha was not totally paying attention to her. Nothing new about that.

"Why?"

"I seem to have these memories or flashbacks. They happened when I saw Paul's eyes. Is there a chance I knew him when I was little?" Julli pondered what she said. She had a deep feeling in the pit of her stomach that she was soon to connect some dots in her life. The only memories she had were growing up at Bertha's town house in the city back East. The only people she remembered were her aunt, Freddie, and the servants. A few of her friends like Neal whom she grew up with. It was a pity she had no recollection of being out here or remembering any of the people.

"Yes, there could be a connection. We will have to find out when they come back over later. I need to go prepare food. If I am right we will be feeding seven people instead of the three of us," Bertha started going on and on, and then she realized that Julli was staring at her but not really paying attention to her. It seemed they both were in their own world at this moment. Bertha tapped Julli on the arm, and Julli flinched; she was having little flashbacks that she was not sure what to make do with.

Shrugging out of the daze, she turned to her aunt and asked her, signing, "Okay. What do I need to do?"

"I don't know. Let me see, maybe have Keith help you put the beds in the rooms so if they do stay, they will have a place to lie down instead of out in the barn."

"Well, Keith went into town but I could ask Teagrans if he would not mind helping me."

Bertha said, exasperated, "Julli, he is my servant, that is what he is for."

"No, he is not under my command and this is my place," she signed, standing up to her aunt. "Moreover, I will not allow you to treat him as such. How long has he been with you anyways?"

"About two years," admitted Bertha, putting up two fingers, wondering how she had missed the fact that Julli and the servants always got along. Julli never treated them beneath her. Bertha had always stood by society's demands on how slaves and servants should be treated. It never occurred to her to treat one above their rank.

"I think since he has been loyal to you, you should treat him as if he was your family." At Bertha's stunned look, Julli changed it to "friend." "Treat him as if he was your friend."

"You have to be jesting," Bertha exclaimed. She put her hand on her chest and breathed faster. She was not sure how the town was going to react to her treating Teagrans as if he was one of them. If she got stoned, it would be Julli's fault.

"No, I am not. Don't you see why I had so many friends back East with you?" At Bertha's confirmation to that by nodding her head, she added, "Yeah, because I treated them as if they were my friends, not slaves or servants." Julli reprimanded her aunt.

"It is not within society's standards that they be treated equal." Bertha was getting upset with Julli, but she did not dare make Julli mad. It was her home, and she had the right to impose rules.

Julli was not going to give her aunt an inch to move. She told her flat out straight, "Treat him equal or you can move your stuff to the lower rooms."

"Surely you wouldn't," gasped Bertha, not sure if Julli would keep her dare.

Julli folded her arms and took up a defensive stance as she signed, "Wouldn't I, Aunt?"

Bertha had nothing to say to that, so Julli turned and went in search of Teagrans to ask for his help. She hoped that her aunt would stop with the society crap and see her servant for what he really was, a big black man who had respect for Bertha even in his situation of being her slave. She knew her aunt treated them good, but they were still slaves to her. Her aunt called them her servants as she didn't really like the word "slave," much to Julli's relief, but she wished her aunt would give them their freedom and let them live life the way she should, free and their own masters.

Julli did not have to go far to find Teagrans, who was coming into the house. When he saw Julli, he quickly bowed to her. That was the final straw. Julli walked over to him, and when he kept his posture bent and eyes averted, Julli reached down and tilted his head up toward her.

"Teagrans, can you understand me well enough?"

"Yes, mum." He kept his face to Julli but averted his eyes. He was brought up not to look a woman, or rather a white person, in the eyes or stand up to their full height. If they did, they were severely whipped, tortured, or sold.

"Okay, here is the rule of the house." At his nod and averting of his eyes, Julli shook his head a little. "No, you will stand up straight, no bowing to me, and look me in the eye."

"But, mum—?"

"No, this is my house and you are not my servant. You are my friend. And my friends don't bow to me."

"Okay, mum." He straightened up, sighed, and looked questioningly in Julli's eyes.

"That is better. As long as you are here, you will sleep in the spare bedroom. You will eat at the table with us and what you need, let me know."

"Yes, mum."

He saw Bertha and quickly assumed his former position of bowing and aversion of his eyes.

"No." She tapped Teagrans on the shoulder. "Get up."

Bertha slowly came to stand by Julli; she swallowed at the icy glare Julli directed her way. This one time, Bertha knew she was not in her proper place. It was Julli's place, so that meant following her rules, not society's or Bertha's own set of rules.

"Teagrans?" Bertha looked at him still bowing and got an elbow from Julli, who gave her the silent dare, *Treat Teagrans equally or sleep in the smaller room.* Bertha had a lot of stuff and loved having the space to move around in. She was not about to give up the bedroom she had claimed upon their arrival there.

"Yes, mum?"

"Do as Julli says." When he straightened up, he was smiling, his eyes crinkled, and he showed his full smile with white teeth. Bertha had never realized how tall Teagrans was or how nice his face was when his eyes sparkled and he smiled. Julli had been right all along.

"Thank you, Teagrans. Julli is right, out here from now on, you are our friend and will have our respect."

"Thank you, mum." For once he gratefully bowed his thanks to Bertha and Julli. Knowing what he was gesturing for, Julli accepted his thanks.

"Oh, ain't that nice?" Came clapping from someone in the doorway. When Bertha jumped and Teagrans quickly put his head down and moved back a few paces toward the door, Julli looked and took in the stockiness of the man standing in the hall. He was impeccably dressed. Brown leather boots, black pin-striped trousers tucked in the boots, white shirt with a black vest on top, and a black cravat was round his neck. On top of his head was a top hat of black material. Julli noticed he wore a holster, with a flint revolver tucked in it. His hair was salt-and-pepper and his green eyes bloodshot and shrunken in a weathered face that Julli instantly distrusted.

"Who are you?"

"My apologies for intruding on your little moment there. My name is Timothy Jackson."

He offered his hand to Bertha, who gave him hers. Then laughed when he only got the tips of her fingers. Turning to Julli, he offered again, but Julli refused to shake the hand of a man she instinctively did not trust.

"Something the matter, miss?"

"No." She looked at Bertha and gave a quick shake of her head. Then added, signing, "What are you doing here?"

He noticed the refusal to shake hands with him. He did not seem the least bit surprised when Julli signed to him. She did not use her voice. He just looked at Julli long and hard, as he saucily said," So you are Brionna's little girl." Julli gasped when he pointed to her and then signed "little" by pointing near his knees.

He raised his eyebrow at Julli's gasp. The look he gave to Julli was one of curiosity, but something else was in it; Julli was not sure what. He put his hat back on his head before he replied with, "Just came out to meet the new neighbors. I own the ranch over there." He pointed south, which Julli knew was several miles past her property.

"Well, it was nice meeting you." Bertha curtsied, always the respected hostess.

Turning to Julli, he said, eying her, "I have a daughter about your age. Her name is Melissa."

"Oh, that is nice." Julli did not like the way his eyes checked her out. They gave her the goose bumps. She knew she had to at least be nice or, her house or not, her aunt would chastise her. She gave a stiff smile, which suddenly disappeared when he raised his eyebrow.

"She is the apple of my eye. I should send her over one of these days." Timothy knew Julli had an instant distrust for him the way she acted. He was going to have to change the way he was going to treat her.

"It would be nice for Julli to have a friend. How old is your daughter?" inquired Bertha. She gave him one of her winning smiles and put her hand on his arm. Bertha could charm the skin off a snake if it suited her purpose.

"About twenty," he said, ignoring Bertha's hand, and kept looking at Julli. She swallowed the bile that rose to her throat. She hoped that his daughter was nothing like her father, and if she was, there was going to be trouble.

"Julli is eighteen," stated Bertha, trying to make conversation with Timothy and find out all she could about their neighbors.

"Ain't that right?" He eyed Julli with aversion and distaste. The telltale look was not lost on Julli, who was a good judge of people by how they looked at her. She could pretty much tell what kind of person they were by reading their eyes, their behavior, and Timothy did not give Julli a good vibe from him, especially with him eyeing her like that.

"Well, I will leave you two to go about your day. It was a pleasure meeting ya." With that, he tipped his hat at them, watching Bertha curtsy to him, but Julli turned from him. He stiffly walked out of the door, which Teagrans quickly closed behind him.

"Phew!" admitted Julli. "It sure stunk in here." Teagrans laughs and stops at the glare from Bertha. At least Teagrans agreed with her; she could tell in the way his eyes kept the humor in them.

"Julli, you need to be more courteous to our neighbors. Seems they are the only ones close to us," snapped Bertha, riled that Julli showed a lack of respect to their new neighbor. It was good to save face by being friendly rather than to have them angry and cause problems behind a person's back.

"Didn't you get a bad vibe from him?" asked Julli, worried. She did not want her aunt to be taken with that vile snake. That is how she pictured him, with his shrunken eyes and the cocky way he held himself.

"No, I did not. He seemed quite respectable. And wealthy," she added, beaming.

Julli grimaced and made a horror face. "Ugh, if you want him go for him. He made my skin crawl."

"Who made your skin crawl?" asked Keith, who had come in through the back door. Teagrans and Bertha brightened when they saw Keith coming in as well as heard what he asked. He strode over to Julli and tapped her on the shoulder before spinning her around, grabbing her into a big hug. "Do I make your skin crawl?" he asked.

"Ha-ha. Nope. You will have to try harder next time," she said laughing. She returned the hug and was relieved that it was Keith, not the stranger, touching her.

"Shoots, I have to try harder next time?" he asked, with eyes wide and his mouth dropped. Laughing, Julli shut his mouth with her finger under his chin, pushing 'til it closed. She nodded her head yes and started laughing again when Keith feigned a wounded heart.

"So what were you guys talking about that made your skin crawl?" asked Keith again. This time he signed since Julli was looking at him.

Looking at her, he saw her pretend to gag as she signed, "The new neighbor. A Timothy something."

"Timothy Jackson," replied Bertha, upset that Julli had a lack of respect for the man. It did not help matters any when Teagrans agreed with her by rolling his eyes along with Julli.

Julli glanced at Teagrans, who rolled his eyes. It took all of Julli's will not to laugh with her aunt's face so stern. Right then and there, Julli knew that she and Teagrans were going to be best friends.

"Oh, I missed him?" Keith asked. He had tried hurrying home to help Julli and to tell her the news he got from the mayor.

"Yeah, and the hands who came and are coming for supper."

"Hands?" At that, Keith did not act surprised. He had met them on his way home, and they were going out to check on some cattle a few miles away down near the river.

"Yes, Paul and three others," Julli signs to him. She was glad that her aunt let her sign the good part. She wanted to tell Keith about Paul and how she believed that he could fill in the missing gaps of her life before she went to her aunt Bertha's. He was a ticket Julli was not going to let go of.

Keith looked at Teagrans and Bertha, who nodded, before he asked, "Old man?"

"Yes," signed Julli. She turned his head to look at her when she was talking and vice versa. He would keep forgetting to look directly at her when there were other people present.

"Oh, already met him. He told me that you look and act so much like ya ma that it was remarkable," Keith mimicked Paul's words. He took off his pretend hat and pretended to slam it back on his head and yelled out a fake "whoop."

Julli, noticing that, decided to mimic what she could. "He did say she was purty."

"Ha-ha. I bet." Keith laughs. "And he is not far off." reasons Keith, gazing appreciatively at Julli. Julli blushes when she sees the intensity of Keith's gaze. Bertha too noticed it, and she decided it was time to put her foot down on the romantic moment and get everyone busy for company.

"Okay, well, I am going to go get the food going. Who knows when they will come?"

"For supper or for your attention?" suggested Keith, snickering. He could not pass up on making Bertha flustered. It was like a prank he could not get enough of.

Laughing, Bertha swats him on the arm, scolding him, "Oh, stop it!"

Julli laughs at the bantering between her aunt and Keith.

Teagrans snickered and walked out to the kitchen. He knew that Bertha was going to need his help in cooking, and he wanted to see if she was going to treat him differently now that Julli demanded her aunt to treat him equally. He also had an idea of a meal, provided they had the ingredients to what he needed to make it.

"Well, seems like you have neighbors and ranch hands so, what more do you need?" asked Keith saucily.

"A hug would help," replies Julli, opening her arms. There was something about being held by Keith that made her feel safer than she had ever felt. His strong arms gave her strength, the beating of his heart told her he felt for her, and the looks he gave turned her legs into putty.

Keith goes over and hugs Julli. She sighs and breathes in the musky scent of him and wraps her arms around his waist tighter. Keith returns the favor with tightening his arms around her back.

"I don't ever want to let you go," he says sadly.

"Then don't let me go," Julli replies. Then she adds, "But when I have to go to the bathroom you will have to let go."

"Oh, do you have to go?" He lets go of her so fast that she could not believe he fell for the sarcasm. They were always playing games with each other, and it was one bond Julli never wanted to stop. They had so much fun; it was almost as if Keith had grown up with her.

"I need to talk to you."

"Okay," and she looks at him sadly, pouts, and sighs dejectedly.

"I did not mean now." He resumes the hug and pulls back, only to say snidely, "Well, okay fine, have it your way."

"Fine, shut up and give me a hug." She laughingly pulled him back into the embrace. With Keith, she could never really remain serious. He was like a ray of sunshine in her life. The only time he could not make her smile was when she was suffering and ignored him. Julli did not want to go back to that time when she treated him badly.

Keith leads her to the living room, still hugging her, and watches her as she sits down on the love seat when he finally broke the embrace.

"I've been to the office of the mayor of Johnsville. You do have the property registered in your name under your parents. Seems you owe thirteen years of taxes that the property did not provide." At Julli's shocked look, he added, "The money went to the hands and the care of the house but most of the money is not accounted for. I have to check with the bank tomorrow to find out what is going on."

"Well, Aunt told me that my upbringing was the source of where the money went to," Julli told him, unsure what he was leading to. She started to wonder if something was wrong and they did not have any money. She was sure that her pa had paid the land off, and he owned it lock, stock, and barrel. Which would mean Julli owned it. She did not want to be told that she could not own the land unless she was married and it was in the man's name.

"Then I guess your aunt will have to come with me tomorrow to the bank to verify that," Keith offered.

"Okay, you can tell her," Julli told him, straight-faced. She waited for him to push for more information as to what she meant.

"Tell her what?" Keith asked quizzically. He wanted to know what Julli was implying at.

"That she needs to go with you. I am pretty sure she will be willing." Julli struggled so hard to keep her face expressionless. She just had to goad him into another word-bantering game.

"Willing or not, she has to," reprimanded Keith.

He was not catching on to the joke, 'til Julli admitted, "No one can force her."

Keith finally picked up on the game. He heard Bertha coming into the room and pointed over to the side. Julli caught it and saw her aunt out of the corner of her eye.

"Fine, then I guess I better get some rope," he stated angrily.

"Rope?" Julli asked, feigning innocence.

"Yeah, tie her down and take her into town," Keith snarled at Julli, hoping Bertha had not picked up the game yet. She was one keen old lady.

"Are you serious?" came thundering from Bertha. Julli took in the angry look and could not resist laughing. She bowled over, nearly sprawling onto the floor, as Keith cracked up watching her. The laughter was contagious, as Bertha, too, giggled; then when she saw Julli nearly lying on the floor, holding her midsection, tears streaming down her face, it was her turn to arch forward over in laughter. Teagrans comes in to snicker at the women sprawled on the floor and looks at Keith guffawing at them. That was a sight for sore eyes. Teagrans had never seen or heard Bertha act or laugh like that in the two years he had been her servant. It was a memory he was going to keep.

Supper went well. Paul and the three hands showed up, freshly shaven and donning clean clothes. They washed up at the basin near the kitchen door. Julli took pride in the knowledge that those four ranch hands kept this ranch going. It was a lot of land and cattle for only four men, but they did an excellent job, and Julli wanted to thank them.

Aaron was by far the youngest of them. He was tall and lanky, with a head full of blonde hair. He had a nice-enough face that flaunted green eyes. He seemed shy but had excellent manners, so she knew that he had to be her aunt's favorite.

Jerry came next into her view. Compared to Aaron, he was taller and had a belly. Julli thought his eyes were blue; then when she looked closer, they were green. She found out that they were what was called hazel. He refused to take off his holster, with his flint revolver in it, and when he and Paul got into an argument about it, Julli told them, "It is okay. You can leave them on if you choose." Jerry looked at Julli as she walked away and unbuckled his holster and tossed it at Paul.

Tom came into view when he sat at the table, near the doorway. He was shorter than the four of them but was tall and lanky as well. He was nearly bald and had to tie a bandana around his forehead to hold the hat up. Julli thought he looked more like a pirate minus the black rag on the head and sword. Add an eye patch and tie his bandana on his head, oh, he sure would have passed for one, even frightened Julli with a sneer.

Paul sat by Keith, and they were engaged in a friendly conversation. Julli peeked at Paul every now and then. The feeling of familiarity remained with her. She was so glad that he remembered her and probably had the kindest eyes she had seen in a man. They were brown, the shade of wet leather, contrasting with his head of white hair. He kept peeking around the doorway and saw Julli watching him. He would not get insulted; in fact he would laugh and sign something like "little girl" or "time for bed."

Her aunt and Teagrans had made a spicy dish called jambalaya. There were biscuits fresh from the oven, made by Teagrans as well. He had also prepared a deep-fried thing he said was corn mush. It was made out of corn; that was all Julli could tell. Julli thought it was all delicious. Teagrans should cook for them from now on. He seemed to have grown two inches when Bertha praised him. Julli noticed that he still kept his duties as a servant/butler, but he seemed to enjoy it more now that Bertha had started treating him as a friend.

Her aunt had made some lemonade, which the hands said was refreshing after a long day of work. Julli had to agree with them; her throat was parched from nervousness. She had a lot to ask Paul but was afraid he would give her blank answers too.

Julli felt pride in knowing that she did something good with Teagrans and her aunt. She only hoped that her aunt would remember the rule and not revert back to being a high-class snob.

The men retired into the main room, while Julli and Bertha cleared off the table and put the food away. Teagrans was shooed out, but he insisted that he help as he cooked most of the food.

Teagrans then shooed the women out of the kitchen. Julli and Bertha obliged him that job without any complaints. After all, he wanted to cook and clean up, and since Bertha treated him better, he wanted to use a skill that he had, which was cooking. And cook he could.

CHAPTER 15

---◆-◆-◆---

Neighbors, Ranch Hands, and Rustlers

J ulli and her aunt went in the main room, where the men were. Paul saw them coming, and he got up quickly and hissed at the hands to get up as well. Julli thought he was well mannered with what he told the hands to do. He also made her feel unique. With the warm looks he gave her and the kind way he treated her when she was around him, she thought her pa had chosen a good friend.

"When a lady enters the room, you get off your feet and stay standing 'til she has been seated." Julli knew she liked Paul. He was sort of like Freddie but different in a somber way. How Freddie used to scurry to Bertha's whims. This man made it a point to let a woman know he was the man but she was his queen and should be treated as such.

"Excuse me, gentlemen," Julli spoke after she sat down, and the men quickly sat as well. "I do have some questions I would like to ask whether or not Keith talked to you about it."

"Anything, Ms. Julli," exclaimed Paul, eager to hear and watch Julli sign. It had been so long since she was a little girl, when he used to bounce on his knee. He had learned a few signs, but Julli always wanted to look in his eyes. He remembered her when she was born and how proud they all had been. He also remembered when she had the fever and the doctor thought she would die.

"I just wanted to know a little about each of you and what stories you could tell me about the last few years. As you know, I am Colin and Brionna's daughter. I read in my ma's letter to my aunt Bertha how I lost my hearing. In addition to that," Julli added, "my ma had been threatened. Not to forget the fact that I was nearly killed by some poison and there were rustlers." Julli signed and spoke so fast that when she was done, not only was she out of breath, but everyone was looking at her in a funny way. Even her aunt Bertha was staring at her.

"Whoa, slow down, little girl. One thing at a time," came from Paul, who was laughing his head off at her excitement. He only understood a few words of what she said or signed. Most of it was a blah-blah.

Aaron stood up, bowed to Julli, and said, "I am Aaron. I have been here going on seven years. I do not have a wife or woman yet. I am pleased that you are back, Ms. Julli. With that, he sat down, red in the face. He wiped the perspiration off his forehead with the back of his hand, getting a look from Bertha, which caused him to reach into his back pocket for his bandana.

Because Julli was sitting there watching Aaron, Keith had to tap her on the arm, asking, "Did you understand him?"

"Perfectly." Julli nodded her head affirmatively. She was glad that Aaron stood up and spoke slowly. Paul had taught them good in the short time since she met them earlier. "Thank you, Aaron, for sharing with me. It is a pleasure to meet you too," she signed and accepted the tilted-head gesture directed her way.

Looking at another man, this one did not get up or tip his head. He just flat out stated, "My name is Jerry. I have been here ten years. I was married but my wife took off and left me for some rich drunkard. I am a good shot. It is Aaron that can track. Miss." Like her, he wanted to get it over with.

Julli caught some of it but had to ask, "Well, I am glad that you are still here working with Paul and Aaron. Did you say your wife left you for a rich drunkard?"

Bertha gasped when Julli picked up those words. She did not dare to hope Julli would understand that much coming from a man whose lips were covered by a long droopy mustache.

"Yes, miss." He only nodded his head and turned his gaze away to look at Paul.

"Then you are better off without her. I pity her," Julli signed slowly as she enunciated her words to compensate for the quickness that Jerry spoke with. "Welcome to the ranch," she signed.

Jerry swerved his head to Julli and muttered, "Thank you, miss."

Paul waved for her attention and said, "That there old coot has been with me since you left. He ain't married nor has a woman waiting for him. No brats like him around," guffawing, and the others joined in. Julli thought it was funny but did not laugh. She did not like it when children were called brats. She was going to have to have a talk with Paul and ask him to refrain from calling kids that name.

"He is right. I ain't got any brats like meself. Don't rightly know what I would do having to tend to snot-nosed brats." At the look of anger from Julli, he quickly swallowed and commented, "I used to be rich. Left my family and money to come West and never looked back. My name's Tom."

Julli was glad that she was able to lip-read enough from the men to understand what they said without the help of Keith or her aunt. It was a pity they did not sign as well. She would have to remedy that in the near future if they were going to continue working on the ranch.

"Well, I am glad that you have been here all these years. You must have driven Paul crazy." With that, she laughed; only she did not laugh alone. Julli found a way to put a joke to the hard, weathered men without insulting them.

"Ain't me that is crazy, it is Paul." Amid the laughter, he added, "Paul there is a good cattleman, he knows them cattle like he knows his way to the taverns." More laughter. Julli was not so sure she liked the word "tavern" but smiled anyway. She was going to have to get some balm for her eyes; they were hurting from squinting to read their lips.

"Oh, shut ya mouth ya old goat," came from Paul. They continued laughing. Even Keith was laughing with them. Of course, Keith would; he found a joke in nearly everything.

Tom looked at Julli apologetically. "You asked me and I told ya."

"Okay, thank you, gentlemen. I am glad to know something about you men. I would like you all to stay on helping Paul if he would stay." She looked at Paul and was dismayed when he retorted defensively. His eyes flashed fire, and she could see the passion he had for the place.

"I will stay! Nothing can get me to leave this place." Paul sat up straighter and looked at Julli troubled. "Besides, I promised ya pa I would make sure things went good."

"What promise?" asked Bertha, finally getting in a word. It was not normal for her aunt to remain quiet that long. She loved to make her presence known by going up to people and talking with them. Julli looked from Paul to Bertha and back when Paul waved for her attention.

"Promised to make good for his baby girl." He took a good long look at Julli and signed, "My goddaughter."

Bertha gasped, putting her hand over her mouth, as Keith sat there in shock, and Julli stumbled over her signs, asking, "I am your goddaughter?"

"Yessum. Freddie and I were there when ya ma had you," Paul replied, ecstatic. He remembered it like it was yesterday. Brionna had squeezed Colin's hand 'til it was past the color of purple. He and Freddie were getting rags, hot water, and they were not too sure if should they have placed a piece of wood in her hands, she might have broken it and gotten splinters. She had one heck of a grip. Neither Paul nor Freddie was about to loan her their hands, so it was Colin who suffered the pain of labor hand squeeze.

"Please tell me more," Julli signed subduedly. She was mesmerized with Paul's eyes. They showed his emotions, and she knew she could trust him.

"Colin and me got together few years before ya ma got pregnant with ya. She was mighty fine." Bertha cleared her throat at the compliment to her sister, not sure she liked another man saying nice things while he was a friend of the husband. "They loved each other lots. Colin got the claim and I came to help him and ya ma as well. Ya were born in the room upstairs with the baby bed." Paul pointed to the room above the main room. Julli knew that room well enough to know which one.

"I knew it when I saw it!" She was delighted that she had been on the right track.

"Yessum. When ya pa sent you from here, Freddie went to keep you safe. That was Freddie's promise to ya pa." Paul's eyes dimmed at that memory. Julli wished so much that she had the power to jump into Paul's memories. It would save time but would also take away the charming conversation she was having with him.

Julli looked at her aunt when she signed, "I know that Freddie took care of me. And so did you." Bertha smiled at Julli, enamored with the fact her niece acknowledged her being a part of her life. She closed her eyes, keeping the confession from Julli close to her. She was glad that she was able to take care of Julli; that much she realized years ago.

Paul waited a few moments 'til Julli looked back at him, and he continued, "Well, anyways, been here since. No woman for me, them cattle are my life. This land is my woman." He put out his hands and pointed to the window.

"What do you mean?" Bertha asked, not sure she understood the Western slang that Paul was talking about. She remembered to sign so Julli could keep up with the direction the talk was going.

"I am married to the land. I will not leave it for anything," Paul stated. Julli saw the determination on his face, and she knew that if she ever fired Paul, it would kill him.

"Oh, I see," came affirmatively from Bertha, and Julli knew well that her aunt was jealous. Bertha liked to have it said that if someone could not have her, he would die. Well, Paul made it clear to Bertha that the land meant more than she did.

"Julli, gotsa be frank with ya. Ranch ain't doing as well as it was before ya pa died. Rustlers take them cattle and use the north side of the land to hide them and change the brands." Paul swallowed and wiped the back of his hand across his lips. The other men nodded. Then Paul continued, "Never been able to catch one of them cow bandits. Even our—I mean youse—cattle have been stolen and brands changed. Have already sent for sheriff to come out and check but he is either chicken or paid for with rustler's money."

"Who is the rustler?" Keith asked with slit eyes. He was not happy upon hearing that someone had been stealing cattle from Julli. He knew the dangers of tangling with a rustler, especially when they got spooked. He rubbed his wrists and arms at the memory of the torture he suffered at the hands of a leader of rustlers. He did not want to go through that again. Not if he could help it.

"I dunno. Nobody has seen or caught him," Jerry spoke up. Julli missed that part of the conversation, but luckily, Bertha had been watching her and saw her scrunch up her face trying to put the words together to make sense of what had been said, and she signed to Julli when she glanced at her.

Keith, not liking where the conversation was going, looked at Julli, signing as he asked, "How many cattle have been stolen?" Julli could see the anger evident on his face. She had hardly ever seen him like that, and it kind of scared her.

"Over a hundred nearly every year," came from Aaron. Julli remembered he was said to be the best tracker, so he would know the numbers.

"Wow, which means I still have a lot of cattle, right?" Julli asked, putting out her hands and pointing to each of her fingers.

At the look on Paul's face, she could not believe it when he glumly said, "Sorta. I would say near about three hundred head."

Julli was depressed. After that comment about only having three hundred or so head of cattle, she had asked to be excused from the room. The men had stood up, even her aunt. She had hurried up the stairs to the room where she was born. Earlier when cleaning the house up, she had told Keith to put the baby bed somewhere she would not have to see it for a long time. It was not that she did not want the memory that she was born there but that she had lost her own baby and could not use it.

What got her so upset was the fact she had her hopes dashed. She had looked forward to seeing where she was born, where her parents died, and had hoped to make something of the land she was given. She just thought that once she came out, nothing else could go wrong. Rustlers had stolen cattle from her parents, and Mark had been killed by rustlers. The word "rustlers" brought hatred in her. She hated them, whoever they were.

Keith and Bertha visited with the ranch hands for a while longer; then they excused themselves to go sleep out at their camp by the cattle. They were afraid if they stayed too long, the numbers would dwindle, and Julli would be left with nothing, and they would be without jobs.

Julli did not know what was said after she left the room; she was too discouraged to find out for fear that she would have more bad news. It was not what she needed.

Julli grabbed the brush and flung it onto the floor. She groaned and put her head in her arms and muttered intangibly. Sitting there for several minutes, then with a gloomy look on her face, she got up, walked to the window, and opened the curtains. She could see acres of land from there. There were mountains past where her boundary line ended. Even in the darkness of the night, she knew that she was on the best portion of land in the county. The moon shone over the mountains, illuminating the shapes of the bushes, trees, and dips in the land. Julli had to admit that it was beautiful out here. No wonder her pa had not wanted to leave. She was going to do everything it took to make sure that her ma and pa's dream came true. She was going to stay and make the ranch as it used to be in its former glory.

The next morning found Julli sleeping on top of her covers, fully dressed, and she groggily got up, looked toward the window, and noticed it was past morning. She had been tired; she had to deal with so much that it consumed her energy, leaving her drained. She was not sure where the day was going to take her, but it was not going to leave without her making her mark upon it.

Julli hurriedly changed and put her hair hastily up in a bun. She did not care what her aunt was going to say; she had other things to do.

Walking down the stairs, she noticed that it seemed eerily quiet. The stillness of the room gave her the knowledge that she was alone. Julli was not used to being in a house that big after living in a small home for over a year. She had gotten used to the confining space that she had considered her home. The one Mark had built.

Nobody being in the main rooms or the kitchen, Julli ventured outside to see where they were. The carriage and wagon were still in the barn, and the horses were still in the stable. Julli looked out toward the mountains and sighed; they were beautiful. The land leading from them flattened itself out, and Julli knew that the river lay on the other side. That was one thing she did not get to see lately.

Only about fifty more steps 'til she got to the river, Julli was going to take the time to relax and enjoy the sunshine. She might even take a dip in the river if she was in the mood for it. Her plans changed abruptly as she felt the thunderous thudding of horses galloping. Julli looked around her to see where it was coming from.

She saw herds of cattle running near the direction she was walking in. She saw the dust floating in the air on top of the other cows that were following the leader of the herd. They were moving fast, and Julli froze there. She could feel the hooves pounding on the ground as they galloped toward the river. Not far behind them were several riders shooting and waving their guns in the air. Julli ran over to a rock and perched on it, wanting to see more of this sight, which she had never seen before. She was not prepared for anything when the ground by the rock she was on sprayed dust into the air. Julli looked down and saw that it was chipped, and she saw the ball that had just been fired at her. Julli glanced up in time to see a rider pointing at her amid the dust from the cattle.

She ducked as quickly as she could and slid behind the rock. Julli felt herself perspiring; she was breathing heavily. Something was wrong with the picture. As far as she knew, this was still within the boundary of her claim. She could not fathom why anyone would point a gun at her or shoot even. Breathing shakily, wiping her hands on her skirts, she glanced around her and saw that she was pretty much stranded behind a rock. It was over a mile to the house, and Julli did not think she was up to the run. She felt an object hit the rock next to her. She sat back down and knew instinctively that they were shooting at her. She was not going to get up at all.

Soon there was no more plodding of hooves upon the ground or dust flying at being shot at. Julli took the chance to get up slowly and peer over the rock. She saw the small outline of the cattle and riders heading toward the mountains. Getting up, she peered at the house and scrambled to get there. In her haste, she stepped on a rock and went down. Scraping her knees and the palms of her hands.

"Ow!" she yelled, looking at the blood running down the meaty section of her palm. Pulling up her skirt, she saw that both of her knees were bleeding as well. They were scraped good. She needed to get them looked at, and she also did not want to get shot at again, so she took off running toward the house. She tripped over some weeds and fell down. Getting back up, she hurried the remainder of the way, watching for the plants so she would not trip over them.

Keith came running toward Julli about fifty feet from the house. She saw him coming and grimaced at the sharp, burning sensation she felt on her hands and knees.

"Are you all right?" he asked when he got to her. She barely had time to nod at him, when he grabbed her arm and half dragged and half carried her into the house.

"Are you out of your mind?" he thundered at her. Julli could see the anger along with worry on his face, in the way he was fuming around her. Julli watched as he flung his arms out several times, forgetting to keep his face to her so she could lip-read. Pacing back and forth in quick, stomping strides, he finally turned to her, and that was when he saw the blood.

"Are you okay?" he asked, grabbing her hands and wincing at the deep gashes. He grabbed the sheet off the corner table and ripped it, making bandages for her hands.

"Anywhere else?" Not being able to lip-read him, Julli took his behavior as a question and nodded, reaching down and pulling up her skirts. She saw her bloomers had been torn at the knees and soaked with blood.

Keith took one look and swore under his breath. She had never seen him this angry or worried about her. She watched as he got more rags from the sheet and used several to clean her knees before binding them with the rags. Julli winced and groaned when the burning intensified.

"It hurts," she said. She tried to sign, but the bandages were covering nearly all of her hand, and she had trouble moving her fingers.

Keith heard her and looked at her, worry in his eyes and face. He leaned over to her and pulled her into his embrace, running his hands up and down her back and shoulders before he leaned back and placed a kiss on her forehead. Julli could feel the wetness of his tears as she felt the kiss. She closed her eyes and felt a pang of remorse as she had slept in and then this happened. What was Keith thinking? She could tell he was concerned about her.

She felt the thudding of boots stomping in the house. She did not have to see or hear to know it was the men who decided to stay and help with the ranch.

Keith pulled away from her and went to the doorway, where he hollered something. Before she knew it, the men came stomping over to the room they were in. When they came in, they quickly pulled off their hats from their heads. Julli did not see any greetings but knew that something had happened. Their faces were grim; they were swatting the dust off them with their hats. Followed by Bertha and Teagrans hurriedly. They took no heed of Julli.

For once Julli wished that she could hear. No one spoke to her; she was kept in silence. She could only fathom what they were saying. Words she caught were "rustlers," "cattle," and "U.S. marshal." Nobody, not Keith nor her aunt, was telling her what they were saying. Julli was sure that this was her parents' place and they should report to Julli whatever happened on it. After all, she was their daughter.

"Stop!" yelled Julli. Finally, they looked at her and saw her for the first time.

Bertha came over to her, and when she saw the bandaged hands and knees, she started crying. She took Julli's bandaged hands in hers and said, "Are you okay?"

Finally! Someone had noticed her. Her aunt, not remembering to sign or look at Julli, only gestured to the room upstairs. Julli shook her head, and at her aunt's frustrated grunt, the men turned to them.

"Are you all right, miss?" came from Aaron.

"Yes, and you want to tell me what happened?" asked Julli, upset that no one had bothered to remember she was there. She needed to know what was going on. She was getting frustrated, and it hurt worse than her scrapes.

Paul came over to her and angrily took in the fact that Julli had been hurt. He looked at her and remarked, "Seems you got the worst of us all."

That riled Julli so much that she stood up, ignoring the pain in her knees. "Yes, and you guys are completely ignoring me. I need to know what happened."

"Like we said, rustlers took the cattle. They shot at us and when we tried to head them off, they too were shooting at ya aunt." Jerry stood up when he told Julli that. Julli caught the words that he was saying. She gave him a hurt look. After all, she had not heard a word they said, so that comment was not fair.

"Well, you all have forgotten that I can't hear. It isn't fair if you come in and just talk without letting me see your faces." With that, she walked over to the door and added, "When you all are ready to tell me what is going on, I will be outside looking at where they went."

Keith grabs her arm, spins her around to face him, and says angrily, "They took your cattle!"

"My cattle?"

"Yes, and they shot at your aunt when we came upon them."

"I know, I got that much from Jerry. I was out there near the rocks when I looked around and saw them herding the cattle towards the mountains." It hurt that Keith too was not focusing on the fact that they were all talking and Julli could not see what they were saying. It was not fair. If they did not pay attention to her and take the time, she was going to do something regrettably.

"I am sorry, miss. We got caught up in the moment," replied Paul, finally taking in what Julli must have been feeling, being left out of the conversation. It was her place, and they had to let her know what was going on. He nodded to the ranch hands, said something, and they tilted their heads to Julli as they walked out of the room.

"My apologies, Ms. Julli," he said, signing to her. He had taken in the fact that her hands and knees were wrapped in rags and deducted the fact that she had gotten hurt. It did not help that they were busily trying to figure out what to do that they did not include her. Colin and Brionna would be upset with him at this time, but he was sure Colin would have understood where he was coming from.

Julli sighed. She knew that what they had gone through was just as important as what she had also. She signed, letting him know by speaking as well, "It is okay. I am sorry I was a spoiled brat. I just wanted to know what was going on and be a part of it."

"No apologies, miss. It was our fault not letting you know." He glanced at Bertha and beckoned her over to help.

"Seems the rustlers took the rest of the cattle. We could not stop them and now you do not have any cattle for the market or for calves next year."

Julli looked at her aunt, then at Paul. Getting what they were saying and signing. Julli sighed, wiped her forehead with the back of her bandaged hand, and spoke using as much signs as she could, "I see. We will have to get them back." She was determined that nothing stand in her way. Not rustlers and not God.

Keith came over, put his hands on her shoulders, and looked her deeply in the eyes. He had been so worried about her that he allowed his frustrations at the rustlers and situation to keep from doing what he knew he was supposed to do. Tell Julli what was going on.

"Julli, the time was not at the moment to stop and take the chance, something could happen while trying to tell you." Letting go of her shoulders, he raked his hands through his hair and flung his arms out in apology. "I am sorry. I just got caught up in the situation."

Julli smiled. She accepted his apology with her smile. It did not stop her from wanting to know more.

"Who were they and why were they shooting?" she asked. She had to speak slowly so that she pronounced her words correctly so Keith, Bertha, and Paul could understand her. She wished Keith had not bandaged her hands, but she could see his need to take care of her. She appreciated the gesture however rough it had been.

"Don't rightly know. There were too many of them, and with them shooting, we didn't stop to check to see who they were, the guys and I were too busy trying to stay alive," Paul admonished Julli, then felt bad at what he said and how he said it, remembering Julli had not grown up here and it was not fair of him to treat her like that.

Julli stared at Paul in shock. The way he just spoke and treated her injured her feelings. She did not stop to think that he was the man who kept the ranch going for years and he knew what was going on. She just thought the kind and loving treatment she had received from him would never stop.

"I am sorry, Ms. Julli. I didn't mean to snap at you."

"No, it is my fault. I know that you have a lot on your mind and I can't expect you to just drop what you are doing and treat me with kid gloves." She goes over to Paul and gives him a hug.

"We will figure out what to do to get the cattle back. I am not going to let those rustlers get away with taking what is mine and harming my family." She turned to Keith and Bertha while she said that to Paul. "I might not have grown up here but I was raised to be strong and independent. I am not about to tuck my tail and run away."

"Now that is ya pa talking. The strength you are talking about is ya ma. That means you are definitely my goddaughter," rebuked Paul to Julli, flicking her on the nose.

Keith smiled at Julli, amazed at how strong she had become through her trials. This thing with the rustlers was not going to get her down, he could tell.

Bertha only peeked at Julli before she walked over to her and signed, "I am here for you. I, too, will fight for what is rightfully yours." Giving her a hug, Julli knew that she did not need to hear to get the understanding of what was going on there and then.

She had her family and friends, who had her back, and she owed them respect. From the looks of it, Paul deserved a little more than normal; after all, he had been there for her since birth by keeping the ranch going the best he could.

They were going to find a way to beat the rustlers; they just had to figure out how to do it. Julli vowed to make each day count in getting to the bottom of the whole mess they were in, no matter how long or what measures they had to take. Nothing was going to stand in her way. She was going to make sure of that.

"We just gotta get busy and figure out what to do. Paul, check in with me about the cattle and the records that you have. Keith, see what you can find out in town. Aunt Bertha, you have the social graces of a butterfly, think the job for you would be for you to go into town, talk to your friends, and see what you can find out as well. Anyone who has extra cattle to sell, we will buy and we will keep going 'til we have nothing left. I am not going to give up."

Julli felt as if her parents were standing by her, hugging her for sticking up and showing what she was made of. If they were still alive, Julli was sure they would be proud to call her their baby.

CHAPTER 16

Keith, Picnic, and Aunt Kidnapped

Julli refused to allow the rustlers to dampen her spirits the next few days. The ranch hands went about their business minus the cattle for the sheriff had come out and only took Aaron with him to scour the mountainside. Julli got tired of waiting for news and put everybody to work. Teagrans kept track of the food supplies that they had, and he had kept the house clean. Jerry took Tom with him to town to do odd jobs for some people 'til Julli called him home for work. Paul stayed to help Keith work on the ranch; after all, they still had goats, sheep, horses, chickens, and geese to take care of. Bertha went into town and made inquiries. She also hired a lawyer for Julli in the matters of finances and deed to the ranch.

Julli and Keith rekindle their romance.

It was Keith's idea to take a horse ride to the hillsides and find a good picnic area. When Keith had found the spot he liked, he hurried to get the stuff going, only telling Teagrans what he needed him to make. Bertha had not wanted to stay in the hot house, so she had Paul saddle her horse so she could go into town. She had planned to go by herself, but Paul, being the gentleman he was, told her he had to go or he was going to hog-tie her in the house. Appalled at that image, Bertha begged him to tag along.

Keith went into the house and encouraged Julli to go with him. He had to promise that he would get her home before dark so she could do some reading. "Only if you promise to get me back before dark. I wanted to finish reading the papers the lawyer sent over."

Keith saddled the two horses, and they went off for a ride. Keith watched Julli sitting astride hers and wondered if maybe she had been an Indian in her past life. She sat there so regal and knew the movements of the horse. She flowed with the horse. Julli seemed so at home there on top of the mare that Keith took the longer route just so he could watch her.

When they reached the secluded area Keith had picked, he reins his horse, and Julli, seeing that, does the same. He gets down and walks over to Julli, holding the reins of both horses, and Julli gets down before he could help her, making him groan in frustration. She was so independent that he was afraid that she would stop him from being a gentleman. He offered his arm and walked her safely over to the blanket, mindful that her knees were still sore. Julli gasped when she saw that Keith had put a blanket on the ground, with rose petals on it. It was beautiful. Since the day was hot, there were no candles around the picnic area, which Julli was thankful for. She gave Keith a smile as he helped her sit down.

Keith signs to Julli, "Julli, you look so beautiful today. I am glad that you came out for a ride with me. You make me happy and I want to be a little more than just friends. I love you a lot,

Julli, and want you to be happy. Although watching you the past few weeks, you have seemed to change and I wonder if you still have any feelings for me. I know that you did before but I really want to know if it is still the same feeling or not."

Julli looked down at her hands, wanting to tell Keith how she felt, but she did not know how to word them out to where he could understand where she was coming from. Keith looked at her and said, "Julli, if you do not know yet, it's okay. You just need time to think about how you feel."

Julli looked at Keith and responded by placing her hand on his arm, saying, "Keith, you have been there for me. We have been through a lot. You were the man who held Pamela when she was born, you sang her to sleep a few times when she was cranky." Julli saw his eyes mist over at the mention of her baby. She swallowed and continued on, speaking slowly, "It was you who always spoiled Luke at the table and when you went fishing, you always had him with you.

"Keith, you have been the steadfast man in my life the past few months. You manage to always make me smile and forget my worries. You have been the best friend a woman could ask for." Julli felt her heart shrink as he turned from her. Julli quickly pulled Keith's arm toward her; she was not done. She had seen how hurt he looked, but if only he would wait 'til she was done talking, then he would see how she felt.

She said, "Keith, I know that it hurts you not knowing if someone loves you or not. But I can tell you that I do love you." Stopping there, Julli turned his face to hers, leaned forward, and kissed Keith. The shock of Julli kissing him wore off quickly as he gathered her closer to him. Julli wrapped her arms around his neck and leaned onto him.

Julli broke the kiss with a smile. Still holding on to her, Keith said very sweetly and softly, "Julli, my beautiful rose, I love you with all of my heart. There is nothing that could take your place."

Julli watched as Keith leaned back, pointed to his heart, then to his lips. "You make my heart skip a beat and my lips are at your service whether it is for lip-reading or kissing." However, it all seemed to be part of a fairy tale, but if it was, it was hers for the taking. Julli kissed Keith once more; the feel of his lips against hers made her breathless. Julli wonders how he can make her feel like flying. Keith starts to let go of Julli, when she stops him.

Julli looks at Keith and asks, "Keith, would you keep holding me? I feel so safe when I am in your arms." She nestled her head on the curve of his shoulder and felt his heart beating. It was the most awesome feeling, to put her hand on his chest, and he covered it with his own.

Keith holds her closer and then pulls back to tell her, "If you want me to I will not let you go. Julli, I always want you safe."

Julli smiles, but after a few more moments, they start to let go of each other. Keith looks at Julli with a deep love in his eyes.

Keith kissed Julli once more, then asked, "Julli, my love, I had brought food, and if you are ready, I will say a prayer." Again with the prayer stuff still. Keith would not give up his obsession to pray. He was always telling Julli to mind her own business; it was between him and his Father in heaven. Since she did not believe in him, mildly put, she had no right to try depriving him of something his ma had instilled.

Julli nods her head and then says, "Yes, Keith dear, I am." She felt so good that she was nearly willing to do anything, even put off her resentment toward God. Her heart was soaring, and she felt loved, truly and deeply.

Keith started to say the payer. "Dear Lord, thanks for sending us out here on this beautiful day as we give our thanks for all the food we have here with us, and, Lord, thanks for bringing Julli and me together. Amen." With the prayer said, Keith handed Julli her plate.

"Keith, who did all this cooking?" Julli asked, signing grandly. She ignored the pain when she moved her hands. The skin was healing, and she took care, but she wanted to do what she did best, signing to the man who made her heart soar. She was happy as well as shocked at the way the day was going.

"Teagrans did, my love. I wanted to do something for you," signed Keith. Julli looked at the courses. There was sliced, fried ham, baked potato, and strawberries and blueberries, with cream for dipping. Along with the meal was some fresh apricot juice that she knew was Teagrans's specially made apricot juice. He sure was a great cook. It was one of his better talents.

Julli waited 'til Keith was done serving them, and with gusto she ate every scrap, morsel, and crumb, leaving nothing for the ants that were scurrying not far from them.

After they had got done eating, Keith put the dishes and the leftovers into his saddlebags. Julli sat there watching him the whole time. He knew how to do a woman's job. That made her snicker, and she made a mental list to make sure that Keith did his womanly duties every now and then.

Julli looked at Keith, smiling. Keith gave Julli a kiss. Julli said, "Keith, I am glad that we got to spend some time together. Today was fun."

"I too thought it was fun. Julli, I love spending time with you," Keith said, feeling extremely happy for she had showed and told him her feelings for him. He only hoped that they were as sincere and as deep as his were. He hoped that time would tell and wished that it would hurry up; he was getting impatient.

"I have to ask why you had Teagrans cook all the good food. Did you put him to extra work?" Julli asked Keith, knowing that Teagrans would have accepted the challenge just so he could show off his cooking skills. Julli was sure that given the chance, Teagrans would have a successful restaurant if he so chooses to go into the cooking business.

Keith shakes his head and says "You know how much Teagrans loves to cook. He was more than happy to make this meal. And told me to make sure I served it the way he told me because he was going to ask you when we got home how I did it. He said that if I didn't do it right he wasn't going to cook any food for me the next week." With that, Keith put on his saddest face. Julli had to laugh. He looked so weird with his puppy dog eyes, pouting lips, and the tipping of his head. He heard her laughing and looked up at her, crossing his eyes, making Julli laugh even more. Keith moved over to lean back against the tree and gestured Julli to go sit with him. She did not sit up against the tree like Keith did but sat on the blanket on the ground in front of him. She wanted to be in his arms, but savoring the moment as she did, she needed to talk to him about something that had been bothering her since he worked on the barn raising several months ago.

"I have always wondered a few things," Julli said slowly. Her hands were hurting, and she didn't want to add more tearing of the skin and taking off of the scabs.

"What did you want to know?" Keith yawned, sighing contentedly. He was enjoying himself way too much. At least he was all alone with Julli.

"Tell me about your wife. What was she like?" Julli nearly faltered in asking him. She was so nervous. She did not want him to think she was prying into his personal life, one that he never spoke of except at the graveside for Pamela and the Cathelroans. And of course Luke's.

Keith froze. His breathing was shallow, and Julli saw pain etched momentarily on his face; then it disappeared. "Her name was Jenney. I had known her only a few months before I asked to court her. She was mellow, nothing could make her mad," he signed, keeping his eyes closed. Then as if the memory was too great, he suddenly opened his eyes to stare past Julli, still stuck in the past. "She absolutely hated my jokes. She used to say I had no sense of humor." With that, he guffawed, signing, "No humor?"

Julli noticed that he was not seeing her, so using her voice, she commented, "I bet she was beautiful."

"She was." With that, Keith blinked his eyes and came back to the present time. He glanced at Julli when he finished. "She was beautiful. Jenney had health problems that she kept from me. I did not know that the womenfolk in her family died in childbirth."

"Oh no."

Before Julli could say anything else, Keith interrupted. "Her pa had warned me not to get her pregnant. She wanted a baby so badly and I gave her what killed her. Unfortunately, the baby came too early and I lost my two girls."

Realization on how tightly his bond was with Pamela, which was the result of him losing his own little girl, Julli started to cry. She had not known, and if she had, she wouldn't have treated Keith that way or said what she had said. She regretted hurting him. Julli wondered why Keith would tell her he loved her after the hurtful things she did to him.

"I am so sorry, I did not know," she admitted, crying. Keith wiped the tears off her cheeks and got out his bandana, which he used to finish the job.

"It was not your fault. I did not tell anyone. The only people who knew were my ma and pa." Julli looked at Keith and considered what he was telling her. "If she would have told me, I would not have gotten her pregnant."

"What did you name your baby?" she asked, signing. Julli wanted to know; they both had lost a child each. She thought that knowing Keith's baby's name, they could mourn their losses together.

"We didn't." At the shocked and confused gasp, Keith knew he had more explaining to do. A lot more. "Jenney's pa came when he found out, took her, and buried her in an unmarked grave." Julli watched Keith's face go from solemn to anger at what happened to his baby. "He did bury Jenney next to her ma." Julli thought that Keith had the right to be angry. She was glad they were able to put the ashes in a grave and Kathrin had gotten the headstones. They were not in unmarked graves.

She had nothing good to say about that as she signed, "Oh my, that is horrible."

"Not as horrible as what he and his family did to me after Jenney's funeral." He rubbed his wrists with the scars and rolled up his sleeves. Julli got a good look at the sickeningly grotesque marks he carried around with him.

"What do you mean?" Not wanting to look at his arms any longer, Julli made it a point to keep her attention on his face. Unfortunately, when he signed, not moving his mouth, she had to look at his hands, which were attached to the scars. Julli felt sadness and rage at the people who had hurt him. She hoped that they got what they deserved.

"Julli, I did it all. All the sins we were commanded not to do, I learned to do them. It was what I had to do to stay alive after I lost my family," Keith told Julli, signing only the words he knew and putting body language to the rest. Julli could understand his signing, but it was what he was implying that she did not get.

Julli stared at Keith apprehensively, not getting what he implied. "What do you mean?" she had to repeat. Julli was getting scared. There was a black, foreboding gloom in the pit of her stomach. She was getting squeamish.

"I killed them all." Julli gasped in astonishment. She never pictured Keith as a murderer. She looked at him with disbelief. If this was a joke he was playing on her, she was going to make him regret it. "They were having a party and planned to torture me later when they were drunk," Keith added, signing "torture" as though cutting his midsection with a knife. "The only thing that justified killing them was the fact they were cannibals."

"Oh my grief." Julli wondered what kind of people could get away with such an extreme crime as the murdering and eating of a person. Julli wanted to throw up, her stomach was getting nauseated, and she did not like this story at all. She was hoping it was just a story, but Keith had the scars to prove it. Her imagination went wild, and she pictured him all bloodied up, wreaking havoc on those who were more than likely not human. It was not a pretty sight, and Julli shivered in the warm sunshine.

"I had to go to missionary confessions. I had to be absolved of my sins," Keith said and signed. He used the sign "saved" for "absolved" since he did not know how to describe it otherwise.

"He let that happen?" Julli pointed upward. Keith knew what she meant. She did not say it kindly. She lacked faith in that subject and would get riled easily.

"No, I chose in my anger to do it," Keith confessed miserably. Julli had to swallow at the pain she could see evident on his kind face. "After a few years I was released and told that I had been forgiven and never to do it again," he declared, dismal about what he had to do to be forgiven for his sins.

Julli studied Keith's expression. She could see and feel the despair coming from him. The story was not just a story; he had the scars, emotional and physical, to prove it. "And you haven't broken that commandment?" she signed while looking at his scars.

Keith waited 'til she was done looking, then replied, signing, "No, I was just released when I decided to go and see Mark and ended up helping you deliver Pamela." He smiled at Julli at the memory of how crazy she had gotten during the quick labor she had. She had not even put any blame on the dog; just said that it had been time for her to come. "I like to think that you and Pamela were the tickets to my salvation."

Julli smiled at the compliment, but she was not going to give up her distrust in the one subject that they were talking about. "You still believe in him after all this time?"

"Oh yeah, I do. He saved my soul," Keith admitted, more or less to himself rather than to Julli. "You and Pamela were the good things I was able to have." Julli blinks her eyes at the fact of what helped Keith; she and Pamela being the good things he was able to have was more of a compliment the way Julli saw it. She did not see herself as Keith's salvation. She had too much hatred in her to be a good person. Or so she thought.

"Oh, I see," Julli signed.

"No, you don't. Even though Pamela is gone, I still have you. Now I have your aunt, Teagrans, Paul and them."

"Yeah, well, you know everyone loves you," Julli said as she started to pat his cheek. She could understand his desire to kill those who hurt him and took his baby before he could name her. So he had suffered probably worse than she had, but he still had his faith in the Deity. Maybe it was because he suffered far worse than Julli could imagine that he was able to have forgiveness in his heart. She did not think that she could forgive those who took Mark and Pamela. Let alone Luke and the Cathelroans. She was going to have to think about what Keith said about his past and what happened. Her feelings for Keith outweighed her fear of his past. Julli had sinned as well; she knew that when Mark had gotten her into the church. She had studied the Bible daily and went to the meetings before Freddie died; therefore she knew some of what she had done wrong.

"Thank you, my lady." Keith got up, grabbed Julli's arm, and asked her, exhilarated, mentally crossing his fingers that she would forgive him and go for a walk with him. He didn't want to talk anymore about his past. It was done and over with. He was only looking to the future and hoped Julli would be a part of it. That would be his salvation, receiving love and understanding from a woman who knew his shady past but did not judge him.

"Would you like to take a walk with me down to the creek? I promise to get you back home to your aunt before dark, that is, if you race me there," he tossed out the dare he knew Julli would not be able to pass up. She loved dares and was always trying to get a joke, or rather a prank, going.

"Why, Keith, I would love to, but first, you must let me go fifty feet. When I get that far, then you may start," signed Julli.

315

Keith looked at her and signed tauntingly, "Then you better get a running start!" And she took off walking as fast as she possibly could without limping looking behind her, making sure Keith stood there 'til she reached the destination.

Getting there, Julli yelled back to Keith, challenging him, "Are you coming?"

With that, Keith takes up the challenge and runs after Julli. But by the time he had caught up with her, she had already won the race and was sitting down on the ground near the riverbank. Julli was happy that he had let her win. She had forgotten all about her scraped knees in the excitement of the dare and the fact they were supposed to walk down the river.

Keith walked over to Julli and said, "You won, so here is your prize." He pointed to himself, and then he leaned down and planted a kiss on her lips. Keith kissed her again, only to go back for another and another. Pulling away from kissing her, Keith said gleefully, "Julli, I let you win, just so I could kiss you."

Julli started to giggle, turning away from Keith; she walked fast toward the bank. Keith hurried to catch up to her, wondering what the heck had gotten into her. Julli peeks behind and sees Keith catching up to her. She turned, not noticing that the ground was wet and slippery. Julli precariously stepped on a few rocks before Keith in his haste to grab her had slipped on some rocks as well, causing him to bump into her. Julli screams at Keith as she falls into the river.

"Keith!"

Keith scampers down, trying frantically to keep his balance. The scream sent cold chills through his body as he saw her go down. When Julli sits, wiping the water off her face, Keith finally gets a sure footing and tries helping Julli up. He sighed, relieved, and smiled at the sopping-we look she portrayed. It was funny, and he laughed at her. Pointing to her, he signs, "You are a wet dog." Julli could only glare at him, splashing the water she was sitting in.

Julli decides that it was payback time, so before he could help Julli up, she pulls him down into the river, next to her. It didn't take much to get him to fall as the ground was already slippery.

Keith sat in the water, shocked that Julli had gotten the best of him. They looked at each other, only to laugh at the fact that neither outsmarted the other. Finally Keith gets up, water dripping off of his wet clothes. He gives Julli his hand and helps her up, only to pull her into a kiss. Julli mutters through it, saying, "Keith, I love you."

Keith answered Julli, "And I, you, my beloved."

They waded out of the river to collapse upon the ground, still laughing. Julli gets up and holds out her hand to Keith, who takes it, using caution not to pull on her scabs. He allowed her to help him up, and walking back to the secluded area where they had their picnic, they had their arms around each other's waists.

Keith helped Julli onto her horse, and he got on his, slowly making their way back to the house. By the time they got there, the only part of Julli that was still wet was the area where she had sat upon the saddle. When they got back to the house, Keith helped Julli down from the horse, and they avoided the knowing gazes bestowed upon them by the other residents, namely, Tom, Jerry, Aaron, and of course Teagrans, who smiled and went back to cooking.

After a delicious supper provided again by Teagrans, the men excused themselves to go out to the stables. Julli offered to help Teagrans, who only shooed her out of the dining room as well as the kitchen. He made it a point as long as he was there that nobody was allowed to help or get anything without his consent. Julli could not argue with that. She did not care for cooking that much; she only cared that Teagrans made delicious foods that she was able to eat and allowed her not feel hungry 'til the next meal.

Since the men and Teagrans were busy doing their thing, Julli decided she was going to go for a walk. The air was cool, so she donned a light spencer jacket and strapped on the four-inch knife that Paul told her to keep on her wrist in case she needed some protection. Julli had understood what he implied. She took a deep breath of cool air as she began her walk.

Sadly, it was cut short as she saw the sheriff riding up to her. He did not take off his hat or greet her the way he usually did. His face was businesslike and troubled. Julli was struck by a sudden fear that her aunt had been hurt. How like her day to go down quickly. She barely started to have fun again.

"Miss, I need to talk to you about something extremely important. Where are the men?" He glanced around when he asked, so Julli was not so sure what he wanted, but it was obvious he would rather talk to the men.

"They are in the stables as far as I know," Julli said, hoping that she guessed right.

The sheriff did not give any indication that he had understood, 'til he asked, "Do you mind if we go to your house so I can talk to all of you?" He finally looked at her when he asked.

"No, sir, I don't mind. Can you tell me what it concerns?" Julli asked slowly, wanting to see how much information the sheriff was going to give to her. He had never really acknowledged her as the owner of the ranch. His attitude was that women belonged in the home and men were the owners of everything.

He looked at Julli, barely seeing her, but he did look her way when he said, "Your aunt. And your ranch foreman."

"Give me a few minutes and I'll meet you at the house. Go right ahead to the stables and let them know I am coming," she tried to tell him, but he took off, putting his horse in a trot. Julli wanted to pick up a rock and throw it at him for treating her like she was a nothing. "Some men need sense knocked into them," she grumbled as she quickly made the walk back to the house.

The men had already been seated in the kitchen at the table. Teagrans did not serve them any water or drinks of any sort 'til Julli showed up. *Score one for Teagrans*, Julli thought. *At least he knows how to treat a woman.*

Keith came over to her and pulled out a chair for her to sit on. None of the men had their happy faces on. Julli could tell that whatever news the sheriff brought was not good at all. He got right down to business without giving Julli a chance to lip-read him. It was Keith telling her what the sheriff said. "Julli, when your aunt was kidnapped, Paul got shot."

"What?"

"Paul is okay for now, he's over at the doctor's. He is being watched. They shot him in the shoulder, leg and then twice in the back." As Keith told Julli that, signing the whole thing, Julli broke down crying. She was so upset that she shoved all the drinks, plates, and silverware onto the floor. The men jumped back, scrambling out of their chairs at the sudden display of anger. Julli was not going to apologize for spilling the lemonade onto the sheriff. He jumped up, swearing at Julli, who took no heed to what he said. All she wanted to know was if Paul and her aunt were okay.

"Is he gonna be okay?" she signed to Keith.

Keith was used to the craziness Julli could show when she was upset or in pain, so he did not react too much about her temper tantrum.

"Hard to tell. The doctor says to pray for him."

Julli tells Keith urgently, "We gotta go see him now."

They got on their horses and galloped over to the doctor's office, with dust following them for miles. Julli was not thinking clearly. She did not think at all. Julli went into the doctor's office and saw Paul, who was lying on the bed, unconscious. Going over to him, she placed a kiss on his forehead and swore revenge on whoever it was that hurt him and kidnapped her aunt.

Julli turns to Keith and begs him to show her how to shoot.

"Keith, I need to know if you would teach me how to shoot a gun." This pretty much summed up what she was feeling—demanding, angry, and not going to back down. Keith was scared at the fact that Julli wanted to learn, not for her safety, but for revenge. He was afraid she was going to shoot herself before they could catch whoever was responsible for the kidnapping. He knew her aunt meant a lot to her as did Paul, whom she had only begun to get to know. Keith did not want Julli to get hurt, especially now that somebody showed that they were not going to stop 'til they had gotten what they wanted. It was dark out, and Keith did not want to show her 'til morning.

Julli was so mad that she could not think straight. All she knew was that Paul lay there dying and her aunt was gone. She had no idea if Bertha was okay or not. Since Keith did not want to help her, she turned to Jerry and asked him if he would be willing to teach her how to shoot.

"Since Keith won't help me, will you?" she had to ask. He was the best shot, and she knew she could use Paul as an excuse as they had been close.

"Well, I don't rightly know if I should." Julli saw him glance at Keith, who shook his head.

"Don't you want to help me bring in the person responsible for shooting Paul?" She had to use Paul as bait to get what she wanted. It tore at her to stoop that low. She was going to avenge Paul's death if he died. She was going to make the person responsible wish that they had never shot him. Oh, she was going to make them pay dearly.

"I guess so," Jerry offered the right answer, saving him from Julli's fury.

"Okay, we will head home and then you can teach me," stated Julli to Jerry, who looked like he had been ordered to jump off the mountainside. He seemed scared of Julli now that she had shown a side he never knew she had.

"Julli, it's nighttime and you should be at home waiting for us to come back. A search party for your aunt and to hunt down the coward who shot Paul is no place for a woman, especially one who can't shoot or hear," interrupted Keith, unaware that what he said was what Julli needed to fuel her anger.

"I see!" she snapped at Keith. She saw the hurt look but was beyond caring. "Well, Jerry has already agreed to help me, so I do not need you here telling me what I can and cannot do, or rather what I should do or should not. Bertha is my aunt and Paul is my godfather." Julli was so angry at Keith that she did not know she was talking and signing too fast for the others to understand her. She did not care. No one, not even Keith, had the right to talk to her like that.

The sheriff came in then with bad news. He looked directly at Julli and sighed, saying sadly, "Paul did not make it."

Julli caught the message plain as day. Paul was dead. That was the last straw. Julli saw blood red, literally red. She glanced at the ranch hands, who stood there as shocked as she was, but they had expected the bad news when they first found out Paul had been shot.

Julli ignored everyone but Jerry, whom she went up to and said, "It is time for us to go home."

Julli shrugged off the hand of Keith and swerved around, facing him, livid that he wanted her to be a weak yet strong willed, but not that independent kind of woman. Julli knew that Keith was trying to stop her from acting out her anger, but she wanted to know who had ticked her off by destroying her night. Another night ruined by a person doing what they should not have done in the first place. She gestured by tilting her head to Jerry that it was time to go. He gave no indication that he was going to pay heed to Keith, who muttered something, which Julli believed was pretty much a no. Good thing Jerry was not listening to him, or he would have seen a side of her worse than he had ever witnessed.

When they got to the horses, Julli saw Keith standing outside by the door, staring at her. She swallowed the bitterness and clicked the reins to the mare as both she and Jerry left town, hurrying home.

Julli did not know that shooting a gun was hard until Jerry tried to teach her. He did not quite have the patience as he too was upset about Paul. Every time Julli messed up, he would flick her on the back of the head and stand in front of her, making her watch over his shoulder, and he reloaded and tossed it at her. She did pick up fast enough to satisfy herself that she could handle it well enough alone, but Jerry was not content to let her just go with the rifle and had her learn about the revolver as well.

Julli thought the first time she fired the rifle that her arm was going to be blown off. She was not prepared for the impact of the gun against her shoulder. Once, she had lost her footing and fell down, shooting it after Jerry had reloaded. The gun had knocked his hat off of his head. He swore at her intelligently, but Julli pushed on. She was not going to let a potty-mouthed old man keep her from her goal. The second time she shot the rifle, he had her on one knee, but again the force of the gun knocked her flat on her butt. Julli did not give up; she got back up and picked up the revolver and aimed it. Julli had to lower the fun as Keith popped up in front of the gun.

"Move out of the way!" she yelled at him. She did not dare point the gun at Keith or gesture to him with it in her hand because Jerry had told her that he would shoot her himself if she treated his babies disrespectfully.

Keith stood there undaunted. He had seen her determination, along with the resentment, when he had tried to keep her from learning to shoot. Julli lowered the gun and pulled back the hammer and released it before handing it to Jerry, who looked glad that she had not shot it.

"Is miss done for the night?" Jerry asked. He was tired, but more than that, he wanted to get away from the woman, who was ticking him off at how poorly she could aim and shoot. Not giving Julli a chance to say anything, he grabbed his guns and ammunition and walked over to Keith, saying, "You need to keep her on a rein. She nearly shot my head off." Showing Keith the bullet hole Julli had put there when she fell down from the blast of the rifle.

Keith burst out laughing at that and, ignoring Jerry's snarl, walked over to Julli, handing her his revolver. She took it from him, checked it, and loaded it the way Jerry had shown her. Taking up her stance, she pointed to the bale of straw and signed to Keith, "Place your hat over on the bale. If I hit it, you will include me in the search for my aunt. And you will also pay for Paul's funeral."

"And if you miss?" Keith could not wait to know what the bet would be if she missed. He looked at Jerry, who pretended to hang himself, showing Keith that Julli sucked at shooting. Julli caught the action from Jerry and told Keith, "If I miss, I will do whatever you tell me to do for a month."

"That is not a bad deal. If I tell you to scrub my back, then you'll come and do it, right?" Keith could not resist smirking at Julli. He had caught her in the deal where she would have to do *anything* he told her to do should she miss the target.

To her shock, Julli peeked over the fence to see that the sheriff, Tom, and Aaron, along with Teagrans, were perched on and round it, watching. She thought it was just the three of them—her, Keith, and Jerry. She wished she had not made that deal with Keith when there was an audience.

Julli saw Teagrans giving her the thumbs-up sign, and her confidence in herself went up. She eyed Keith and said, "You're on." Julli watched as Keith and Jerry laughed at something that was said as they shook hands. She got angrier when she saw Jerry going over to the men and they laughed. She wiped back the strands of hair that had been blown on her face by the breeze. She needed a clear shot and complete focus. Seeing Aaron with all the bandanas in his pockets, Julli waved him over. She watch mischievously as the men gave her a confused look when Aaron went over to her.

"Can I borrow your bandana for a little while?" she asked him. When he looked at her, about to refuse her request, she lifted the revolver a little and nudged it toward him. That action worked better than she thought. He handed his bandana to her and held the gun for her while she tied it on her forehead, with the ends hanging down between her eyes.

Aaron gave her back the gun and took off running back to the fence with the rest of the men. Julli knew that they were making comments about her as well as other women. She was going to show them a thing or two.

"Do you need help?" Keith asked, coming to her side to see what was going on.

"No, I am fine, just getting ready to shoot."

"Well, just wanted you to know that the men and I do not think you should learn to shoot as you will only miss. Therefore I think you better quit before you embarrass yourself," said Keith as stupidly as possible.

"Keith, if you really think that, then it might be in your best interests to not to make me mad. 'Cause it seems that I am the only one who has a weapon," said Julli, joking, nudging him out of the way with the revolver. She had to snicker at her joke when Keith walked hastily back to the men. She saw him peeking at her over his shoulder as if he had actually bought the joke.

Julli looked toward the bale of straw and saw the hat. Julli was not surprised to see that it had been placed in the very middle of the bale. Men never took women for much, and she was going to do her darnedest to prove them wrong. Julli knew that her ma and pa, along with Freddie and Paul, would be proud of her for trying. Prouder if she actually hit the hat.

Taking a deep breath and finding the best stance for her, Julli pulled the bandana down, covering her eyes. She squared her shoulders, cricked her neck, and placed her other hand on the barrel of the gun as Jerry had shown her. Julli took aim at the hat and fired.

Julli mentally prepared herself for the possibility that she had missed. She was not sure if Keith had been jesting with her about having to scrub his back. She waited a few seconds after firing the gun before she lifted up the bandana. But before she got the chance, Teagrans had run over there, picked her up, and swung her around. In the haste of him lifting her up, she had dropped the gun, which Teagrans kicked over to the barn, where it slid under some crates. He was laughing; his face was too small for the smile he was giving to her.

Julli felt other hands pat her on the back. The ranch hands, even Jerry, were congratulating her for her attempted shot at the target. She had no idea if she hit the hat or not, but just having recognition from the men made her feel as if she was one of them. Even the sheriff had come up and congratulated her by tipping his hat to her. The only man who was not in the circle praising her was Keith. Julli looked to the bale and saw him standing there. Smiling at the men and excusing herself, she walked over to where Keith was. He was standing there staring at what remained of his hat. Julli glanced at where she shot and saw that she had actually made a bull's-eye through the hat of Keith. Julli's eyes widened at that. She did not think she would win at all; she had not expected to hit it plumb center. Julli could not believe her eyes, and neither could Keith.

"How did—? You did not even see—!" was all he could mutter through his shock. He had the look of a man who had reached the end of his journey, only to realize he had reached the end long before he started. Disbelief. Shock. Amazement. Julli was not sure what she was supposed to do or what to say, so she stood there looking at Keith in shock first then to the now-destroyed hat.

He turned to her, not saying anything. His eyes told all. They were eyes full of admiration and awe for the woman standing by him.

Finally mustering the courage to break the silence from shock between them, she signed happily, "I won. See you in the morning." Keith barely blinked. Julli cockily sauntered around him and, much to the delight of the men, stood on tiptoe and planted a big kiss on his lips.

After that, she walked in the darkness of the night back to the house. The men turned to watch her, not quite believing the feat she had accomplished tonight. The fact that Julli was blindfolded when she shot the hat plumb center took precedence over the death of Paul. They were going to have a funeral in the morning before the posse sets out to search for the murderers and to find Bertha. However, since Julli won the bet, she was going to go with the men. She had earned the right, thanks to the teaching she had received from Jerry. On the other hand, was there someone there who guided the ball to the hat, thus destroying it with one perfect shot?

In her room, Julli looked out her window, seeing the men moving about in the barn. She could see the dimly lit candles, and through the cracks in the walls, she saw their shadows. The men had been shocked beyond measure, especially Keith, who had for some reason sided with the men about women in general. She was included in the category they classified the female species.

Tonight she received their admiration and respect. Julli had shown them that women were equal, or better if mildly put into words; she also showed that just because she was classified in the "deaf and dumb" quota, it did not necessarily apply to her. She had never had to work so hard to earn some respect. Julli wondered if it was her pa along with Freddie and Paul who helped her to shoot perfectly. That was a feat she was afraid she could not take the credit for. She had aimed and pulled the trigger, but there was a feeling that she had help. Julli glanced up at the sky; in the darkness she could see a few stars hiding behind the clouds. Julli signed a silent thanks to those who helped her tonight.

"Thank you, Pa, for your strength. Thank you, Freddie, for your faith in me. Thank you, Paul, for the respect you had for me, and thank you, Ma, for the courage to be who I am."

Julli saw Keith walking toward her window; she saw him stand there looking up at her. Then he put his fingers to his lips and blew Julli a kiss. Julli smiled at that gesture and left the window, going over to her bed and lying down.

Sighing, it had overall been a hectic day. First, it started out with going on a picnic date with Keith, and then the talk about his past freaked her out. They had fun, only to find out her aunt had been kidnapped on Main Street by thugs nobody recognized. Paul died, and she had to prove she was just as good as the men, maybe even better. Julli sighed and wondered what else was going to happen. She prayed that her aunt was okay and brought home safely. They had a funeral to attend to in the morning; then they were to get the posse together. Julli was ecstatic to be going but also nervous as it would consist mainly of men.

Clatter!

Julli jerked with a start as she felt the windowpanes rattle. Not seeing any shadows, she lay back down, only to have the vibrating panes rattle again. This time she saw a rock hitting the window. Julli got up quickly and walked over to the window.

Seeing the men down below her, she lifts up the window and leans her head out just as Keith tossed a rock, hitting her on the cheek.

Julli yells out in pain as she pulls her head back in the room. She was holding her cheek when Keith came bounding into the room, followed by Teagrans, who lit the candles.

"Are you okay?" Keith asked, but when he saw the blood oozing down Julli's cheek, he swore unintelligibly, which earned him a smack from Teagrans on the back of the head.

Julli felt the sharp pain as she removed her hand, feeling the blood slowly marking a path down her cheek. It hurt, but it was nothing compared to the shock of being hit with a rock.

Looking at Keith and Teagrans, Julli asked, cautiously eyeing them, "Who threw the rock?"

Neither man was willing to take the blame for it. Julli looked at both of them and groaned. So much for looking out the window. Right now they were acting like children who got caught playing ball and breaking a window, then running in fear of being punished for it.

Teagrans grabbed a rag and put it up to Julli's face. He had a gentle way of taking care of Julli. She felt a kinship with him.

"So what did you guys throw rocks at my window for?" Julli asked, bewildered. She was not going to let that pass; she was upset enough. She knew that it had to be Keith or possibly Aaron. Not wanting to put Aaron down, she focused on getting the culprit out in the open.

"Just wanted to let you know that the sheriff sent word for the U.S. marshal to come out to investigate," mumbled Keith, with Teagrans using some signs he had picked up.

"I see. Now who hit me with the rock?" Julli asked, signing again, but with one hand, as she held the rag to her cheek with the other. Looking from Keith to Teagrans, who shrugged and turned his head to Keith, Julli picked up on the telltale sign and snapped at Keith, "Next time just bang on my door!" She started to giggle at the guilty look Keith had but caught herself as she was trying to stay in the moody mode she had just been put in when she got hit. It was endearing knowing that he was caught by Julli and looked miserable at how she was treating him.

"And that when he gets here after the funeral, will probably round up the posse and go out," added Keith, still with the sorrowful look on his face. Julli was about to give in to his misery but the determined look he gave her caused her to withdraw it.

Keith looks at Julli and says, "Julli, you know that it is not safe for you to go with us. I swear that I will bring your aunt back safely. Do not worry please."

"Sorry, you agreed to the deal and I won. I am going and that is the end of it." Getting up from the chair near the window, she went over to the mirror. Looking at her cheek, she decided it was nothing and shrugged, offended that she had to open the window for them to come into the house, into her bedroom, and now they were standing there like idiots. "Get out!" she snapped angrily at both of them. She did not bother to laugh when they hurried out, shoving each other out of their way to get to the door first. She was too upset to care that the men had stumbled down the stairs, nearly trampling the other in their efforts. Neither did she notice that when they had gotten downstairs and out the house, they hollered something at the others, and all the men scattered, running to the barn and stable to hide. She would have been furious if she could have heard what they said.

"The mad woman is going crazy. Run for your lives!"

CHAPTER 17

———◆◆◆———

Finding Aunt and Coming unto Christ, Catfight and Murders Solved

Teagrans had banged on the door in the morning, waking Julli up from a sleepless slumber. She had cried herself to sleep, missing Paul's eyes. She cried that he got killed and there was nothing she could have done to stop it. She beat herself up mentally, saying that if she had not allowed them to go to town, it would not have happened. Remembering the talk she had with Keith after Pamela died, that everything happened for a reason. She was getting the hang of that, but it did not make things easier to deal with. The past kept bringing itself into her present, and she wished that she could just forget it. There was a nagging doubt about what the day was going to bring.

The funeral went the best as it could have, considering the townsfolk were chatting about Bertha's disappearance. Julli looked at the people, not reading their lips. She took in their gestures and their facial expressions and had an inkling as to what they were saying, thinking, and feeling. She was a good judge of character.

Keith had pretty much stayed away from her since she found out the rock that cut her cheek was tossed by him on accident. She wanted to go up to him and tell him that she forgave what he did, but he was nowhere to be found. Teagrans helped Julli as much as he could. He would stay by her side and let her know either by signing or by slowly speaking to her what others were saying. When he told her confidentially what he overheard the marshal and Keith talked about, she left him standing in the sun, intent on finding Keith and confronting him.

Finally finding him in the store, she stomped over to him and hit him on the back so hard that her hand stung. "What is this about you telling the marshal that I could not go?"

As soon as Julli came into the store, he felt her hit him on the back. Wincing at the sting of the slap, he stiffened, dreading having to face her. Slowly he turned and faced her.

"You are not going. It is too dangerous for you," Keith said threateningly. He was not in the mood to deal with Julli acting like a spoiled child.

She was ticked off; after all, it was her aunt who had been kidnapped. Taking in the silence by Keith as an affirmation that he had not planned on keeping the bet they made last night and was not going to allow her to tag along, she turns, stomping off out of the store. She then nodded to Teagrans, who knew that she was mad and quickly brought the horses over. He rode home with her in silence.

Julli saddled the mare and was about to get on when Teagrans came over, carrying saddlebags loaded with food, drinks, and ammunition. Not saying a word, he ties them on and then looks at Julli with remorse. Julli sighed, looked down at the ground, and when she looked back up, Teagrans was offering her a boost up the horse. But before she took the reins from him, he signed, "Please come home safely." Julli nodded and, nudging at the horse, rode out of the barn. She got to the road and urged the horse into a gallop. She was in a hurry to get to her aunt.

Julli slowed down several times, letting the mare rest while she took in the surrounding area where she was at. Julli decided on a direction and followed it using her guts and what knowledge she learned. She was past the boundary of her property and ventured toward the mountains. She had a feeling she needed to head there.

When it got dark later, she decided she had better get a camp going. She had no idea how far she had gone, but she felt good about the distance she made. It was too dark out for her to continue, and the horse needed its rest. Julli got some wood and made a campfire. She looked in the bags and found some grain, which she gave to the horse. Patting the mane, she looked at the eyes of the mare, and an idea came into her head. The mare had brought her out this way; it was as if the horse had an instinct as well as Julli in which way to go. Deciding that she was doing well and that she had a friend, Julli gets out some more grain for the horse to snack on.

Looking around the small camp she had, Julli was glad that the bushes offered some protection and privacy. She had never camped alone. Putting some of the food on the fire, which Teagrans had packed, she waited for the food to warm up so she could eat and get some sleep. It had been a long day. Keeping the mare tied nearby, Julli sits on the ground, glancing at it to alert her if there were any noises Julli had to be cautious about.

She looked about her and noticed that the small campfire was not exactly visible, but it kept her warm. The mare nickers. Julli gets up scared, knowing that there is something out there, but does not hear the coyotes howling. Julli wished that Luke was with her; he would have alerted her, and she would have known what the noise came from. She got out her bedroll and placed it on the ground. Julli was too wound up and knew she needed her sleep, but it did not come easy to her. She was alone out there in an unfamiliar place, not knowing what was out there.

When the horse nickered and startled Julli, Keith walked into the camp, leading his horse. Julli ran into his arms, sobbing. She had been real scared being all alone out there. Keith held on to her and swore that he would protect her come what may. He was so grateful that she was okay. They had seen her fire earlier but had waited 'til now to come see who it was. He could not believe that she had actually got on the horse and rode all that way out there. He had not even known she left 'til now.

"The marshal is coming in. We got lost and could not find the tracks. The posse split up to cover more ground, leaving me with Bill," he finally managed to sign to her when they let go, breaking the hug. Keith looks at Julli with awe and tells her, "It looks like you can handle yourself pretty well out here. I am sorry I doubted you earlier."

"You are here, that is all that matters right now." She looks around and adds, "I thought I was lost."

"No, seems you are on the right path after all," admitted Keith, smiling. His little woman was showing him what he knew was there but did not want to admit to. She was not just a prankster but also a very tough, determined woman.

Julli was so glad that Keith found her. She steps over to the campfire, with Keith trailing her, and starts warming up the food again.

Julli gets busy, knowing that Keith was watching her the whole time. She hoped he did not realize she was wearing his trousers. They were baggy on her but gave her some freedom to move about without having to pick up her skirts and worry about the hem getting ruined.

When the marshal walks into the camp, Julli barely had time to acknowledge his presence, as he and Keith were busy talking about whatever. Julli wanted to interrupt and have them tell her what was going on, but the seriousness of the situation stopped her. Julli served both men and got some tea for herself, sitting down on her bed, near the fire. The men ate heartily like they had not eaten for days. Julli knew that Keith was going to compliment Teagrans on the food when they got home.

Keith gathered up the dishes and washed them out, putting them back in the saddlebags for Julli without her asking him to.

Julli watched as Keith and the marshal got out their bedrolls and lay down, getting ready for sleep. Julli drank the rest of her tea and glanced at Keith, seeing him observing her. Julli got up, put her mug away, and lay down on her bed, facing Keith. The light from the fire flickered across their faces as they took in each other's faces.

Julli remembers the song and signs to Keith, "I remember the song you sang for me a while back. It was beautiful."

"Someday I will sing it to you again. Good night, my love." He turns to his side and soon is asleep.

Julli sighs contentedly, closes her eyes, and is soon asleep as well.

Keith wakes Julli up early in the morning. The marshal
had coffee going and ready, and when he offers her some, she
refuses, shaking her head. "Thank you but I prefer tea."

They saddle up and get ready to go. There was not much
conversation going from what Julli could see. Both Keith and
Bill kept their eyes out, searching and tracking the land. It
was not 'til a little after noon when Bill tells Keith they were
approaching an abandoned shack.

Keith waves Julli over, signing to her. "There is an
abandoned shack just a little over the hill that we are going to
go check out. Do you think you can keep lookout?" he asked,
hating to put her in danger, but she came out this far on her
own and deserved a chance.

Nodding her head affirmative, Julli keeps lookout as Bill
and Keith go check it out. Not long after, Julli sees a man
sneaking up behind Keith. She knows if she yelled, the man
could shoot Keith, and she did not want that to happen. She
got her shotgun out, made sure it was loaded, and took aim.
She fires the gun and flinches when it hit the same spot that
she had a bruise on. She only succeeded in getting his hat
shot off.

He spins around, looks, and sees her. He stood up and
pointed his gun at Julli. She stood there frozen. Her other gun
was in the saddlebag, and she had not loaded it. She forgot to
do it this morning as everyone was in a hurry to get back on
the trail.

Keith shoots and hits him. He spins around, dropping the
gun, and falls to the ground. Julli watched in shock as Keith
reloads behind the ditch and regretted that a man died because
of her. Julli shook that pitying thought out of her mind and
watched as Keith and Bill start shooting at another man trying

to get to the horses. Julli sees him go down, as Keith and Bill run and enter the shack.

Julli reloaded her shotgun, grabbed the revolver, and loaded it as well. Swinging the bags over her shoulder, she waits a few minutes; then out of concern for Keith and Bill, she sneaks down there. Coming up to the shack, she peeks through the window and sees Bill sitting down, holding his shoulder. Keith was on the ground with his hands on his head. Julli puts the flint through the window, hoping that she was as quiet as possible; she did not want any trouble. She took aim and knocked the hat off of the bandit. Keith jumped up, and Julli ducked, missing the fistfight between Keith and the guy.

Julli slinks down the wall of the shack and gasps as she feels thuds coming from the fighting going on inside. She pushes her hat back and crawls over to the doorway, only to have the bandit topple over her as Keith knocked him down. As she went down, her gun goes off, missing Keith, who yelped out. Julli panics and tries shrugging the man off of her, but because of his deadweight, she cannot move him. Keith steps outside, sees Julli, and sighs. He rolls the unconscious man over, getting him off of her. Leaning down, he hauls Julli to her feet and shoves her into the shack.

Once inside, Julli goes over to Bill, who was lying down. She gasped at the sight of the wound and, upon moving his shirt back, swallowed back the bile at the sight of the blood. She without thinking unbuttons her shirt and takes it off, revealing another one under. Luckily, she had worn two. Julli rips the one she took off into strips and helps Keith bandage Bill's wound.

Keith told Julli, "You are doing good." Then snaps at her, holding up the ball that missed him, "You nearly shot me! What were you thinking?"

Julli only stared at him in disbelief. She had not meant to miss the man or nearly shoot Keith when the gun went off during her fall. She was trying hard to do things right. He was probably just upset that things had not gone smoothly on the search for her aunt. It was not her fault.

The bandit woke up and started shooting into the shack. Hearing the gun go off outside, Keith falls onto Julli, who looked at him in shock. She had not known they were being shot at 'til wood splintered off the walls and dust flew in the air. If it were under different circumstances, she would not have minded having Keith jump on her.

Keith looks down at Julli and says, "Wow, nice." He winked at her.

Julli looked around; there was no more shooting, so she swats him off of her. Not entirely mad at him but grateful that he had saved her.

Julli glances at Bill, who was unconscious, his hand placed over his wound, but Julli could see that it was soaked with blood. They had to get him to the doctor as soon as possible, even if that meant putting off the search for her aunt. Julli did not have to wonder whose life was more important. First, she was going to help Keith with Bill, and then she was going to go look for her aunt. She had no idea where to look or if Bertha was okay. It hurt Julli to put her aunt second; she could be okay, treated like a queen, and would rebuke Julli for not taking care of the man who put his life on the line to find her.

Keith shuts the door and checks the windows. He sees four guys out there. He pointed to the window and put up four fingers. Julli nods and takes stance at the window over the side from Keith. Just as she was about to get up and peek through the window, Keith flagged her down, saying, "They left." Julli sits back down on the ground, troubled. She had just gotten up, and Keith had told her to sit back down. What was going on? At least she and Keith could have some time to figure out what to do about Bill.

Crawling over to Keith, she says, "I am going to go look through the shack and see what I can find." Being on her hands and knees with the revolver in her hand made it impossible for Julli to sign. She just spoke it to Keith, who nodded.

Crawling on her hands and knees, unmindful of her scrapes, she goes through the small shack and sees a small trapdoor near the fireplace. Going over there, she opens it and gasps in surprise to see her aunt Bertha there tied up.

Julli yells at Keith to help. "I found her! She is tied up!"

Keith leaves his lookout post, goes over to where Julli was, and bends down, pulling Bertha up. Julli frantically tried untying the ropes and was upset that Keith used his knife to cut them before she could get the notion in her head to do that. Bertha stirs, and Julli offers water from the canteen strapped over her shoulder. Bertha opens her eyes and sees Julli holding her. Julli sobs in relief and gathers her aunt into her arms. She was so glad that her aunt had not been harmed other than the bruising from the ropes and the bandana shoved into her mouth.

Bertha says she was kidnapped because of land. "It is for the land that I was kidnapped. They really want it." Julli watches her aunt mumbling. Even after years of lip-reading, she was having difficulty this time as her aunt's mouth was swollen. "Someone wants the claim. Been using it for thirteen years." Upon hearing Bertha say that, Bill grunts and verifies Bertha's story. Julli could only put words together that she was able to catch from her aunt's mumbling. It came as no shock to Bill or

Keith, but Julli had not thought too much about the land. She thought it was the cattle only.

Julli and Aunt Bertha care for Bill, changing his bandages and giving him water. Trying to get him comfortable as possible was not an easy feat. There was hardly anything in the shack to use. They put Julli's saddlebags under his head, and Julli took off her skirt, tearing it in half, and used it to cover bill as the night went on. Keith could only stare at Julli, who was down to a shirt and bloomers, including her boots.

Julli looks at him and asks, "Do I need to strip some more?"

Keith's face went red even in the darkness. Julli laughed at that. She had managed to make him embarrassed, which was nearly impossible in the time she had known him.

Keith scouted around and provided some adequate protection for them in the shack. While he was doing that, Julli saw her aunt Bertha reach into her bag and pull out her Bible. Julli finished taking care of Bill, who was going in and out of consciousness.

Keith's job done, he came and sat across from Bertha and Julli. The marshal woke up groaning, as Bertha nods to Keith, who bows his head. He said a quick prayer, which Julli could not see. When he was done, Bill breaks the silence by saying docilely, "I am a Christian. Have been for years. It is my job that makes it hard to act like I care, but I do." He looked at Julli in the semidarkness and said, "I am sorry for treating you like you were not good enough."

Bertha signs that for Julli. She nods her head and signs, which Bertha translates, "It is okay. I appreciate you doing your job."

Satisfied that some leeway had been given, Bertha opens the Bible to Luke 7:50, which she reads aloud. Julli follows along, with Bertha using her finger as a guide.

"And he said to the woman, 'Your faith has saved you. Go in peace.'"

Keith bowed his head. As did Bill when Julli looked at both of them. She was feeling uneasy where Bertha was going with the reading. She saw her aunt flip the page and move on to Luke 8:48, which Keith quoted, while Julli followed her aunt's finger along the lines.

"'Daughter,' he said to her, 'your faith has made you well. Go now in peace.'"

"Faith in what? Faith that all I have dies?" Julli asked aloud, but even though she knew that they heard her, they chose to ignore her outburst. She was getting upset. Why did her aunt have to go to that section in the Bible? Were they trying to humiliate her?

Her aunt and Keith sat there paying no heed to her, as Bertha moved on to Luke 17:3-4.

"Be on your guard. If your brother sins, rebuke him, and if he repents, forgive him. And if he sins against you seven times in a day, saying, 'I repent,' you must forgive him."

Julli read the verses, following her aunt's finger. She did not know that her comment got her directed to Keith, who was in the darkness, definitely upset with her. "I forgive who?"

Keith said, signing, "Who sins against you."

Bertha nudged Julli with her elbow and signed when she looked at her. "I don't hold anything against who kidnapped me. Everything happens for a reason."

Julli paused when her aunt said that. She had to come back with a remark that would put them in their place. It was not right to let them get away with bad behavior. "So it's okay for them to hurt you?"

"No, it's not, but having forgiveness helps to make each day worth it," came groaning from Bill, whom Keith got up and sat by, giving water to.

"So I'm to forgive him who took Mark and Pamela from me?" Julli asked Keith.

"Yes, although it was not his doing. He's not the one who does it. It's the person who did it." He gave her the eye and the sign, which Julli knew meant he was not going to give in easily.

Thinking was not hard when Julli was as calm as a thunderstorm. She hoped they could not say much about what she said next.

"Freddie wasn't killed, he died!"

Bertha gasped and looked at Keith, shocked beyond words at Julli's outburst.

"Who did you blame?" Keith signed to her.

Pointing upward, Julli signed instantly, "Him!"

"The Heavenly Father didn't kill Freddie. Neither did he with Mark, Pamela, or Luke," Keith signed, upset that Julli was still stuck in the negative zone. He had tried showing her love and patience. She was making him mad that she was not giving being positive a chance.

"I'm supposed to forgive whoever killed Luke and who set the house on fire that killed Zeke, Mindy, and Pamela?" Julli snapped, irritated. Very irritated. She was getting tired of everybody covering up the whodunit thing. She knew who was responsible, and she knew they had to take the consequences for their actions. Freddie had taught her that, as did her aunt Bertha.

"Yes, justice will be brought to them. They will have that death on their conscience. It will haunt them for the rest of their days," Keith justified his answer, looking at Bill, who confirmed it with picking up his revolver and pretending to shoot.

"They'll remember what they did?" Julli wanted to know; she was not sure she liked the feeling that her hatred gave her. "Will they come ask forgiveness?"

"If they don't, they aren't able to deal with the knowledge that what they did was wrong," admitted Bertha. "And you know that I have done a lot of wrong stuff and it bothers me half the time because it was not the right thing for me to do."

After what her aunt said, Julli looked at Keith as she signed. "What if they don't? Should I forgive them anyway?"

"Yes, it does not help to hate them," he said. She knew he was speaking from experience. His past had taught him a lot, and Julli knew that he had to work for years to be absolved of his sins. If that was the case, he should know where she was coming from.

"It feels good to hate them and want them dead," she signed. Her lie belied what she was really feeling. She did want them dead, but she hated the thought that she was turning into a monster. Julli knew it did not feel as pretty as others made it out to be. She just was not ready to let them get away with hurting her and those around her that she loved.

Bertha tapped her hand and signed what Bill said: "I have shot and killed men who if I had a chance they would have lived life differently."

"But that gives them a chance to do the same deed again without remorse," Julli signed back. She knew that her aunt was not going to use the harshness of what Julli signed when she spoke what Julli had signed. There was something very different in the atmosphere, and Julli was not sure she grasped it fully;

everyone became even more somber when Bertha opened the book and had started reading.

Keith looked at her, not understanding what she signed. "What do you mean?"

"They could kill in a different way," simply put from Bertha, who did understand Julli's signing. She also understood what Julli was implying.

"Yes, but we aren't to judge them," she signed to Julli with approval from both Keith and Bill. The men nodded their heads, agreeing with Bertha, who looked at Julli with compassion in her eyes.

"Who does?" signed Julli derisively. She was getting worn out from them acting so noble in their cause not to allow Julli or anyone to put their beliefs down, not when her questions had made sense.

"Heavenly Father," was all it took for Bill to say before he started coughing. Keith helped him lean forward and gave him some water when he was done. Julli saw the water spill down Bill's stubble on his chin, then onto his shirt. He did not care. Julli caught the glare he tossed her way.

"What about when it takes too long? Does he let them off?"

"No, he deals with them in his own time. Maybe they will suffer and die worse than how they killed. When they do die, he deals with them based on the condition of their hearts, whether it's sincere in repenting or if they close their heart and they don't care, refusing to ask for forgiveness."

"Well, I hope that they choke on their own spit!" snapped Julli, signing to Bill furiously.

"Julli!" admonished Bertha in the darkness of the shack. The light from the moon gave enough for Julli to see her aunt's face.

Julli, not liking the fact that she was rebuked, flung out her hands and said aloud, "Whatever!"

The marshal, being feverish, goes to sleep. Julli's aunt grabs her skirt and bunches its half under her head, pulling the rest over her, and falls asleep. Keith got up and kneeled in front of the window, looking out. Julli was not sure if he saw anything, but when he sat down, he avoided her, keeping his head averted from her. He leaned his back up against the way and placed his rifle across his knees. Julli could feel the tension in the room as Keith kept watch, listening to the sounds inside the shack as well as outside. Julli knew he was worried about the shooters coming back and Bill not faring so good with his wound.

Julli stays up, watching Bill, and ponders what they talked about. They really felt what they were talking about. Even with Bill's job to hunt down those who committed wrongdoings, he had stood by his faith. Keith did that as well. His past was very shady, and he had the scars to prove it. Her aunt had shunned the Gospel for years, and it took Freddie's death for her to open her heart. Why was it so hard for Julli to do the same? Had she allowed the devil to overtake her heart, forcing out all that was good, clean, and pure? Was she condemned?

Julli remembered when Mark had first taught her that night after the party. He had planted the seed of faith in Julli's heart. She had stopped watering it when Freddie died, and no matter how hard she tried to will it to sprout, it wasn't 'til now that Julli stopped willing and let it reveal itself to her. Julli felt a feeling she had not felt for so long. It started in her heart; her mind was cleared of all thoughts, and she felt as if there was this warmness around her, engulfing her 'til she was consumed by it. Julli widened her eyes as she felt the urge to pray. She felt so humbled that she started to cry.

The morning came too early, when Bertha shook Julli, waking her up from her sleep. Keith heard riders approaching and had warned Bertha, who relayed that information to Julli. Bertha went over to Bill, taking his fevered head onto her lap, and leaned over him, providing some protection for him. Julli grabs her guns and is about to stick them through the window when Keith grabs her. He hollers something to the folks outside and sighs in relief. It was the rest of the posse. They had heard shots, and not finding Keith or the marshal, they had banded together and came to check it out as soon as morning came.

Keith opens the door, and several men come in, nodding to Julli and Bertha. They gingerly carried the marshal out to the horses. Aaron came in and offered his arm to Bertha, who took it gratefully. Julli was in shock; her aunt did not try to groom herself before taking Aaron's arm and walking out like she was the queen of England.

Julli saw Tom and Jerry shaking Keith's hand and slapping him on the shoulder. She saw other men outside as well. They all looked as worn out as Julli felt. It was a good feeling to be saved and found.

Keith comes over, takes Julli's arm, and they walk out of the shack. Keith stops Julli, pulls her up to him, and kisses her amid the scattered applause and cheers from the posse.

Julli had not been so glad to be home, to take a long, luxurious bath, scented with rose petals, or to eat the meal that Teagrans made. Julli had nearly fell off her mare on the trek home. Keith had come over to her and tried to make some conversation, but she was so tired that she did not pay attention to half of what he said. What made her happy was that Bill had been rushed to the doctor and he was healing well to everybody's relief. Plus her aunt had been found safely.

Everybody was happy at the news. The only problem remaining was no one had found the kidnappers, minus the one Keith had shot. It was unfortunate his secrets died with him.

She went upstairs to her room, intending to lie down, but saw the journal on top of the chest. She goes over and opens it to where she left off. Julli felt energized and depressed at the same time while reading her ma's journal. The information left in there fit the puzzle that pieces were missing from. Julli knows now that the Jacksons wanted the land but there was no credible proof yet. He was in charge of the rustlers; that much she was sure of. It was easy to convert the Hamperston's brand to Jackson's. It was written there plain as day in the journal. Julli knew her ma would not lie about something like that. In her absence, Timothy Jackson used the land and river for his own pleasure, rustling and hiding cattle.

Bertha came up a few days later when Julli was making notes from her ma's journal. The new marshal had come with more information. He had dropped off some papers that Bertha's lawyer had looked into. The land was worth a lot. She had river rights, which were considered water rights, and it belonged to Julli; the only problem was it was not hers to claim. The law stated that it had to be put in a man's name, and when the man died, the woman could claim it through marriage, unless he, the owner, had any sons; then it would be passed to them. Julli was angry at what she read, until she read more of her ma's journal and found out that she too had to depend on a man to have anything. Her aunt Bertha had managed to scrounge up property by being married three times. There were no male heirs for either of them, but Bertha's last husband had left it to her provided she donated some monies to his favorite cause, the South.

Bertha told Julli, "Melissa Jackson is here. She said that her pa sent her as soon as she got home from visiting some friends. She would like to know if you would come down and meet her."

Putting down her ma's journal, Julli gets up, straightening her skirts. Her aunt looks at her appreciatively. She thought it would be good for her to please her aunt after what she had been through. Not knowing if she would make it or be found. Julli glanced at her aunt and saw the happiness she had at being with Julli. She was with family, and that was the most important.

Going downstairs, Julli gets to meet Melissa. She looked somewhat like her father with her green eyes and nose. She was impeccably dressed as well as her father was when he came calling. Julli got a bad vibe as Melissa she greeted her. It was a feeling of doom, grief, and evilness. Julli was taken aback by the force of her gut feelings. She swallowed the bile that rose in her throat and willed her stomach to calm down. She wanted to make a good impression for her aunt's sake.

Julli was glad that she could lip-read Melissa fairly well.

"Hi, I am Melissa, Timothy Jackson's daughter. He told me to come over and meet you." Melissa offered Julli a quick hug, which Julli accepted. Smiling at Melissa, Julli took in the outfit she was wearing. It was sort of like the one she had seen but never worn. The sea green color did not compliment her eyes, which Julli disliked instantly.

"It is a pleasure to meet you."

Julli watched her glance around the house and back at her; then she said saucily, "Likewise. I like what you have done with the house." Julli took in the snobby attitude Melissa portrayed. Melissa did not seem the least impressed with the house, contrary to what she had just told Julli.

Smiling, Julli took in the compliment, knowing that there was a good chance her aunt was eavesdropping as she had not yet come into the room. "Thank you, my aunt helped a lot." Melissa was walking around, glancing at everything in the room, and did not see Julli signing to her. She could hear Julli well enough.

"I can tell." Melissa sat down in Julli's favorite chair. She gestured at Julli to sit as well. Julli chose to sit in the chair opposite of Melissa so she could lip-read her. "She seems remarkably well after what happened to her. My pa told me when I got home the gory details. I am so sorry about your loss."

Closing her eyes at the mention of loss, Julli could not speak but gathered her strength to say, "Thank you. Paul was a great man."

"Yes, he was," Melissa said, unconcerned. She had heard about Paul and did not pay any interest in regard to that. She had known Paul since she was little, and he never had a kind thing to say to her after Julli had been sent away. The nerve of Colin and Brionna to send her best friend away without a good-bye or any way of contacting her.

Teagrans brought in the tea and saucers. He placed it on the table, faced Julli, and rolled his eyes. Julli, who was being polite, tried so hard not to laugh. She could tell that Teagrans did not care for Melissa either. Standing up straight, he asked, "Do you need anything else, Ms. Julli?"

"Not at the moment. Thank you."

He bowed to Julli, winked, and walked out of the room back to the kitchen slowly and strutted his freedom by cocking his head and flexing his muscles. The action was not lost on either Melissa, who grimaced, or Julli, who smiled. Turning to pour the tea, she paused and gestured to Melissa, who nodded.

"Yes, please and sugar too."

Putting in the cubes of sugar, she hands Melissa the saucer, who takes it and places it back on the table next to where she was sitting.

"I see you give your servant a lot of respect," she said, disappointed. She had hoped that Julli was a lot like her and she could use their friendship to her benefit, even Julli's money if she had some.

"Yes, he is a dear friend of mine." Julli was so used to this. Her aunt had treated her slaves a little better than most, but when Julli put down the rules, Bertha changed her point of view and accepted Teagrans with utmost respect. He had earned it after all.

"I didn't know that Southerners were generous with their slaves." Melissa raised her eyebrow at Julli and drummed her fingers on the table. It was how Melissa acted, so cocky and sure of herself, caring only for herself and herself.

"He is not a slave and I am not like most Southerners," Julli signed. She saw the look of mistrust on Melissa's face and made it a point to sign while she was speaking. If this was her childhood friend, then it was a good thing that she did not remember her.

"Well, that is your choice." Melissa peered at Julli before taking up the saucer and sipping the tea. "You should make sure that nobody else sees you treat him so good or you will have a hard time out here. Most folks like us do not tolerate those beneath us," she added as she took another sip. Julli, watching her and hating what she said, wished she would choke on her own words.

"Oh, thanks for the warning. I'll keep it in mind." Not. She had far too much respect for Teagrans to pay heed to Melissa's warning. She was not about to let some spoiled and snobby brat like Melissa tell her what to do. After all, it was her place, and she could do pretty much whatever she wanted to do.

"Welcome." Clearing her throat, placing her hand on her chest, she sat up prim and proper and popped the question so fast that Julli sat there staring at her. "So, Julli, do you remember anything growing up here?"

"Not really, I was too young when I left," Julli admitted, signing. She did remember Paul's eyes but was not going to say anything and have Melissa ruin that memory.

"That is too bad. We used to play when we were little." She took another sip, placed the saucer on the plate, scooted up closer to Julli, and said, "My ma used to come buy food from your ma and I got to say, you were my first friend." That being said, Melissa reached out and grabbed Julli's hands.

Now not being able to sign, Julli said starkly through a stiff smile, "That is nice. I didn't know that. My ma did not mention that in her journal."

At the mention of the journal, Melissa let go of Julli's hands and asked through clenched teeth, still moving her lips, "Your ma had a journal?"

"Yes, she wrote down a lot of stuff that happened when she and my pa moved out here." At the mention of that, gloominess clouded Melissa's face. She looked like she was going to throw a fit. Julli wondered what was wrong with her ma having a journal.

"Did she mention me?" Julli saw Melissa brighten up in hopes that she was in the book. Julli wished she had not brought up that subject, especially the word "journal," which seemed to make Melissa act like something hit her in the chest.

"I can't remember. She might have. I haven't gotten that far," Julli admitted truthfully. She did not see what the problem was. It would have to be Julli's memory, not her ma's journal, for her to recall Melissa.

"Oh, I see." Melissa got up shakily. She placed her hands on the table and announced, "Well, I got to go into town and meet with some friends. One of them recently had a baby. Luckily she was married or her pa would have made them have a shotgun wedding." With that, she forced a smile. Julli looked at her and thought she would keep her a little longer and play some word games if she could and try to figure out Melissa.

"How old is the baby?" signed Julli. She wanted to know, but on the other hand she didn't as she was reminded of hers.

"Few weeks I think. I left before she had it," replied Melissa, disinterested.

"It?" questioned Julli curiously.

"A boy. Luckily it did not inherit its ma's looks, she is nothing pretty to look upon. I was told the blanket she received was imported, very expensive." With that, she made a statement that Julli had to follow through with a statement of her own.

"I had a baby girl but she died. I still have the blanket my aunt made me before I was born," Julli signed slowly. The pain still hurt.

"You did?" Melissa looked at Julli's hand, which was ringless. "Who were you married to? The gentleman outside with black hair?" Julli caught a few moments in the past and did not catch the knowing look Melissa had when she described the man vaguely whom she had glanced upon on her way to Julli's homestead.

"No, it was his cousin's baby. We were not wed." Julli narrowed her eyes; she was not liking the fact that Melissa seemed to know how to play the question game. In addition, she did not like the way she looked at Julli or treated her, along with her friends.

"I see. What a shame," Melissa haltingly said, sitting back down but picking up her handbag and eyeing Julli with an expression void of emotion.

"Yeah, it was," was all Julli could say, 'til she was interrupted by Melissa, who was now bored of the game. Julli looked up at Melissa and could see something akin to hate and pity on her face.

"It was so good to see you." With that, Melissa got up, swishing her skirts, and yells something, which brought Teagrans over to her. He opened the door for her but did not bow. Julli caught the snarl Melissa directed at Teagrans, and she lost her nerves.

"Don't you ever treat Teagrans like that." Julli stood up and walked over to Melissa, who was standing there frozen with shock. "Please leave now." With that, Julli waited 'til Melissa walked out the doorway; then much to Teagrans's delight and Bertha's dismay, Julli slammed the door with force. The windowpanes rattled, but Julli felt so much better. Her anger pent when she looked at Teagrans, who was smiling at her. His eyes sparkled a silent thank-you.

Julli, ignoring her aunt, went back upstairs to her room. Still upset with Melissa about the way she treated Teagrans, she walked over to the window. She parted the lace curtain and lifted it, allowing her to see the silent scene before her, which turned noisy when she saw Melissa's carriage stopping in front of Keith. Julli watched as Keith laughed along with her. The nerve of the woman to flirt with Keith. Julli saw Melissa offer Keith her hand, which he placed a kiss upon. Julli quickly added, the nerve of Keith to flirt with Melissa on her property. She was sure that she had not dreamt that Keith told her he loved her or called her "my love."

With a grunt of frustration, Julli flung herself onto her bed, hitting the pillows with her fists while mumbling, "How could he? The nerve of them! Oh, she makes me so mad! I should slap him across the face!"

She stayed in her room the remainder of the day. When Teagrans brought her meal up to her, she only thanked him and lay back down, pulling the covers up to her chin.

Julli awoke from her late nap and realized it was dark out. All the lights were out in the hall, and Julli assumed everybody had gone to bed for the night. She lay back down with the covers up to her chin and sighed, just as the door opened and closed just as softly. Julli could sense the silent figure moving down to the right of her. She dared not stir until the shadowy silhouette disappeared into the darkness and out of the room. The door had barely shut when on impulse Julli opened it, following the dark shadow down the hall. She creeps slowly and adjusts her eyes to the dimness of the hallway. As quietly as she could, she hurried across the distance between the hallway and the door to her parents' room, which they used for storage. The door was not shut all the way, and Julli nudged it open as slowly as she could, trying to be as quiet as possible. Looking into the room, she did not see the shape and squinted her eyes, trying to detect any movement.

The stillness was broken by the unmistakable rocking of the chair as it was bumped, causing it to rock back and forth. Julli gasped and covered her mouth quickly, trying to stop any sounds from coming out when she saw the chest being opened and some things taken out. The shadowy figurine heard the small gasp and froze, then sprung into action, pulling Julli into the room so quickly that Julli fell down against the crates.

She saw the attacker going out the door. Anger and fear tore at Julli, forcing her to get up and go after the person. Not thinking, Julli ran a few paces and jumped onto the back of whoever it was trying to get away. She knocked the both of them to the ground and wrestled for the on-top position. Julli felt hands clawing at her hair, pulling it, and she saw red as she felt the pain. Ticking Julli off was not the best thing for the attacker to do, as Julli sat on top and swung with all her might at the covered face of the person.

Lights were lit, and feet stomped up the stairs. Julli was sitting on top of the attacker with a mask covering the face. Julli pulled off the bandana and hat and screamed in anger at who it was.

"Melissa Jackson!"

Keith came and pulled Julli off of Melissa, who was unconscious. Julli had dealt her a heavy blow to the head, knocking Melissa out. Julli flexed her fist; her hand hurt from the force of the punch.

Bertha came scurrying up and gasped, saying, "Oh my goodness!" as Julli got to her feet and bent down, retrieving the things Melissa had tried to steal.

Holding up the journal and blanket, Julli looks at her aunt and says, "She tried to steal my birthright."

Aaron came in, saying, "Someone—!" He stopped abruptly when he saw all who was there and the unconscious form of the neighbor's daughter, Melissa.

"Did Ms. Julli do that?" he sputtered out.

Julli looked at him and saw what his question was and asked, "Would you like some?" Julli's fist pointed up at him, he swallowed and shook his head swiftly.

Keith hauls Melissa into his arms, only to dump her on his shoulder, as Aaron leads the way out of the hall.

Bertha grabs Julli and says, "I am so sorry I didn't see what was going on."

Julli could only look at her aunt. She saw the concern on her aunt's face. Julli had no idea why Melissa would want to take the journal and the blanket. Something was going on, and Julli intended to find out. She just had to figure out where to start. Grabbing her aunt's hand, they made their way down the stairs to the living room, where Keith and Aaron were.

When Bertha and Julli finally came down the stairs, Aaron had dispatched Jerry to fetch the marshal. Teagrans moved the pillows on the couch, and Keith dumped Melissa there and used his bandana to tie her wrists. Teagrans, not satisfied with that, grabs a rope and ties the bandana to it and puts the rope around his waist.

"Makes a nice decoration, don't you think? Also helps hold pants up." Teagrans snickered, showing that the rope tied around his waist did indeed hold his trousers up.

The marshal comes and arrests Melissa, who was groggily waking up, for trespassing and attempted thievery.

"Well, there goes the butter for the biscuits," commented Tom cautiously.

"What do you mean?" Julli asked, rubbing her palms on her skirts. If Tom was talking about food, all he had to do was ask Teagrans, who was always happy to oblige.

"Ya should go talk to her. She knows more than you think," he added warily, much to Julli's puzzlement. Julli rubbed her hands on her face; she was tired. She only hoped that things would work out and she could live her life day by day without all the drama that had happened the last few weeks. It was so much, and Julli wondered what other trials the Lord was going to push her way.

Julli goes to the jailhouse in the morning to talk to Melissa and get some information if she was willing to talk. Melissa was forced to stay the night as her pa was out of town. She gave Julli the most evil of looks when the marshal let her in.

Julli took in the tired and disheveled attitude Melissa had. *Poor girl had to suffer the night without her accommodations.*

"What you want?" snapped Melissa, coming over to the bars. She was not very pretty at the moment, her face scrunched up in hatred. Julli looked at her and mentally ruled that hatred definitely was not pretty; Melissa was proof of that.

"I just wanted to see how you were doing and ask you why you wanted to take my ma's journal and the blanket my aunt made for me," Julli signed, knowing that Melissa would pick up what she had said and signed.

Melissa took her time answering. When she did give her comment, she was not nice in how she answered Julli's unasked question. "Have you not figured it out yet?"

"Figured out what?" asked Julli, signing. She was desperately hoping that Melissa would give her something to go on.

"Never mind, my pa will get me out and you will be sorry," stated Melissa, going back to the cot and gingerly sitting down. She had slept on the cot, and it sure was not soft at all. Neither was the wool blanket she had been covered with.

"Oh, okay. Have it your way." Julli sighed as she signed, dismayed. She had only hoped to be on civil-enough terms with Melissa. It was not to be.

Timothy Jackson comes barging in, demanding that his daughter be released and whoever hurt her arrested.

"Do not you folks know who I am? I want my daughter out of this jail right now," he thundered, yelling at everybody in the room. Julli was included even though she could not hear.

The marshal looked indifferent. He was to do his job, and no one was going to stop him from doing his best. "She has to wait 'til bail is paid," he stated, waiting for the outburst he knew was coming.

Timothy was not known for his patience. He pretty much yelled, "I'll pay the dang blasted bail, just let her out now!"

"She has to show up for the trial. If she does not, she will be sought out and brought to justice. She cannot leave town," replied the marshal, giving direct orders. He took his job seriously, Julli found out. He listened to everyone who came complaining and also to those who were being accused of something. It did not matter if it was little or big; he had a job to do.

Julli noticed that the marshal did not seem scared of Timothy as did some others. He brought out the worst in people but apparently not the marshal.

Turning to Julli, Timothy fumed, "You! You are the one who will pay dearly." He pointed at Julli, and she flinched when she saw the finger coming onto her face. Remembering how the marshal stood up to him, Julli gathered her strength to face her adversary.

"What did I do?" Julli signed as indifferently as she could muster.

"Shut up, you are too much like your ma!" Timothy yelled at Julli. At the mention of her ma, Julli's face paled, and she had a bad feeling. *I am too much like my ma?* she asked herself. Timothy had made it seem like a bad thing, but Julli knew otherwise.

"What do you mean?" she had to ask. There was something Timothy knew that she had to find out. She was pretty much sure that it had to do with her parents.

Keith had gotten tired of hearing Timothy yelling at Julli, so he stepped in front of him and said, "Do not talk to her like that. It was your daughter who broke the law."

Julli saw Timothy turn to Keith and scream at him. "Shut up! You have no say."

"I say because Julli is my woman," signed Keith. He spoke more than he signed since he was talking to a man crazed about something. Apparently, it was about Julli, or rather the fact his daughter was in jail. Julli beamed when she saw what Keith signed. Julli knew that Keith really cared for her and that the other day when he kissed Melissa's hand, it was only his way of being polite. How like him to play with people as her aunt did. They had so much in common; Keith and Bertha.

Timothy saw red at what Keith said, and no one was prepared when he pulled his gun out from behind him and aimed at Julli. Only the marshal had caught the sight of the gun behind Timothy and was prepared for any action on his part.

Julli screamed when Keith turned to her and shoved her out of the way. Julli fell and looked up in time to see Timothy fall down forward to his knees. His gun was no longer pointed at her but at the ground.

"The land should have been mine!" Timothy yelled at Julli.

With her eyes wide, she watched him fall face forward. Keith hurried to her side and helped her up. Keith only shook his head when Julli looked at the prone figure on the ground.

Timothy had died. Melissa was let out, only to find her pa dead. She screamed and tried to go after Julli. Luckily, the marshal and his deputies were there to hold her back. Julli saw the marshal say something to Keith, who nodded. The deputies not holding Melissa picked up the body of Timothy and made way to the coroner's morgue.

Keith took Julli's arm and led her outside. He grabbed her in a hug, placing a kiss on her forehead. "I am so glad that you are okay." He smoothed back some of her curls that had managed to find their way onto her face, out of the bun she had put them in.

Pushing back his hat, Julli ran her hands through his black hair. His forehead was damp, and Julli knew it was because the tension in the jailhouse was a lot for him to deal with. Julli saw the love in his eyes and signed, "So am I. Is it finally over?"

Keith nodded and took her hand. They made their way to the stable, where their horses were waiting for them.

The marshal let Melissa go home to prepare for her pa's funeral and told her that they would be watching her. Julli was told that they had men watching Melissa wherever she went, so Julli was safe for the time being. She had to go to court to be charged and sentenced. Julli was sorry that Timothy had died; she would have liked to find out more about her folks. It was a pity that Melissa was more like her pa than Julli had given her credit for. She was upset that she was not going to be able to find out anything from Melissa either. The marshal had told Keith to tell her that if they showed up for the trial, they would find out more information.

When Keith and Julli got home, she was hauled into her room, where her aunt Bertha had to check her to make sure she was okay. Keith stayed downstairs and chatted with the ranch hands about what had happened. Julli saw her aunt cocking her head toward the doors and knew she was eavesdropping on the men, listening to Keith telling them what happened in town.

Finally being able to pass her aunt's inspection, they went into the kitchen, where Teagrans said that in a few hours he would have a meal ready. One event led to another, and Julli wished for once she could pull her hair out and scream. Maybe then she would feel better.

Her aunt had her sit in a chair in the living room and put her feet up. "Come on, Julli. You need to relax. I'm going to help Teagrans with the tea." At Julli's protest, Bertha looked at her sternly and waved her finger, warning Julli not to dare her.

Bertha walked into the kitchen. Julli laid back her head and agreed with her aunt. She could use some minutes alone to sort through the pieces that had accumulated over the past few days. Julli was looking forward to finishing the puzzle and move on with her life. She was about to have a silent prayer, when her aunt threw the kettle into the room. Julli felt the clatter of the kettle hitting the floor, along with hot water that sprayed her. Julli got out of her chair quickly as she saw her aunt go crashing down against the floor, and she saw the shadow of an attacker.

"Not again!" groaned Julli. She dived behind the love seat and pulled out a revolver that Keith had hidden underneath it. Julli checked it and found it was still loaded, which was good news.

Teagrans was knocked out. Julli could see his boots on the floor not too far from the doorway. Julli peeked quickly toward the door and saw five men coming in. Julli felt their boots stomping on the floor as they split up. Carefully crawling to the edge of the back of the couch, she spied a tall figure dressed in black, with a bandana over his face and a hat way too big for his head. Julli saw that he had a revolver in his hand, and she knew that he was going to shoot her if he found her. Julli placed the gun over her left arm and waited 'til he came into her sight. When she pulled the hammer back, the click was loud enough for him to hear, giving him her location. There was no time; she had to shoot. She pulled the trigger and felt the gun going off.

Not wanting to look and knowing that she had used the only shot possible in the revolver, Julli sighs, leaning back against the backing of the chair. She was emotionally distraught. This was the last straw. She was tired. If they wanted her, she was going to give them a fight worthy of everything she ever was.

Julli was jarred to her knees when she feels footsteps coming and going in the doorway. Taking a chance, she raises herself up to peer over the top of the love seat. There was a man leaning over the person she was pretty sure she had shot. Julli gets up, slowly making her way over to him. Putting the butt of the revolver out, she got ready to give a big whack on the head. Then he spun around, and Julli saw it was Keith.

She dropped the gun and gave a cry of gladness that it was only Keith. He got up and grabbed Julli in a hug, kissing her on the cheeks, neck, and sighing into her shoulder. Julli starts weeping; she was so glad that the Heavenly Father was watching out for her. She had to owe him her life; after all, he had sent guardian angels to keep her safe through all this.

"Aunt Bertha and Teagrans?" she managed to get out between kisses from Keith.

His only reply was to look at her and tilt his head to them sitting up on the floor in the kitchen. Julli pulled out of Keith's arms, ran over to her aunt, and grabbed her in a hug. Seeing Teagrans next to her aunt, she reaches out and grabs him into the hug as well. Thankfully, both of them were okay. Her quick and silent prayers had been answered.

When all the chaos calmed down some, Julli was told by Bertha, signing excitedly, "You shot that one in the doorway. That means Keith shot two out by the stable, Tom shot one over near the barn. Aaron got one as well. Unfortunately, he got shot in the leg. The doctor is checking him out but he should be fine."

Julli sighed, thanking the Lord for the safety of those she had around her. She had gotten to see that he had always watched over her, as did her folks. Her ma would be proud of her, as would her pa. Not to forget to mention Freddie, Mark, Zeke, and Paul. Julli hoped that her baby, Pamela, was proud of her ma. She really missed her.

Twenty minutes later, the marshal and his deputies came galloping to her homestead. He wanted to tell her personally that Melissa had escaped and that he feared for Julli's life. Julli laughed when he walked into the house with a shocked expression. He had arrived too late but early enough to get a statement from one of the attackers, whom Keith shot.

"Well, Ms. Julli, you sure know how to attract trouble." With that, he laughed, then went outside to talk to the posse he had brought with him. Julli smiled. It was not that she attracted trouble; it was that trouble was attracted to her.

The man who was alive managed to tell the marshal who had hired them and where they were hiding. Bertha looked at Julli and finger spelled, "M-e-l-i-s-s-a."

Keith came in to tell Julli something she did not want to know. He was going to go with the marshal and the posse. They had been told where Melissa and some of her hired hands were hiding.

"I'm going to go help them. I want to be there when Melissa is told that she is never coming out of prison," Keith signed carefully. He was not sure how Julli was going to react. It had been a long day, and she did not need another thing to worry about.

"Just come back safely," signed Julli, giving Keith a kiss on the lips for good luck. She was going to say a prayer for all of them to come home to their families safely. Julli was going to pray for Melissa's soul. She was going to need it because she did something that was not good. Julli felt at peace when she made the decision to pray for those who had sinned against her and her loved ones.

Julli went up to her room and fell asleep as soon as her head touched the pillow.

Keith came in with Bertha a few hours later.

"Melissa has been arrested. She and the hired hands surrendered pretty fast. Right now, they are on their way to the county jail pending the court date. They will let us know when it is and we are to go and testify about everything."

"Oh, that is wonderful news. I am so happy," signs Julli gleefully, as she sits up to give Keith a hug. When she looked at her aunt, she sensed there was something foreboding. Julli could not put her finger on it, and she closed her eyes, praying that it was not another shooting.

Keith gets up and tells them, "I'll be outside if you need me." He walks out of the room, only glancing back to blow Julli a kiss, which she caught and put to her heart. She blew a kiss to Keith, and he copied her actions, placing her kiss on his heart as well.

"Julli, I wanted to let you know that I have some news for you. I sent your journal to my lawyer and they found out who killed your parents." At Julli's shocked yet anxious expression, Bertha continued signing, "Timothy Jackson and his wife came out to kill your folks. Your pa had already died from a fever when he was shot. Your ma had been shot afterwards. She somehow managed to put down their names in her journal with her own blood."

All Julli could do was sit there and take in the information her aunt gave to her.

"That is not all. I am leaving to go back East. You do not need me any longer," Bertha signed as calmly as she could with hands that were visibly shaking.

"What?"

"You are finally free. You have shown a lot of courage and faith. Julli, it is time for me to let you go. You are an independent woman and I love you so much." Julli grabs Bertha into a hug. Neither one could cry. There was nothing to be sad about. Julli had proven she could do it with her aunt as much as she could without. Bertha needed to get her own life going, even though it would be far from Julli.

CHAPTER 18

———◆◆◆———

Wedding

Keith took Julli on a stroll; Julli had dressed in a light blue blouse with a darker blue skirt. She wore her dark blue spencer jacket, and her hair had been neatly braided. This time Julli left it down and did not care if the curls were wayward and escaped. She felt so light that nothing could keep her down. There was a candlelit dinner prepared by Teagrans when they got back from the stroll. Candlelit dinner prepared by Teagrans. Keith sang the song again to Julli. She loved the song and wished he would sing it more often. Keith told her that he would sing it every year on that day. Julli was puzzled why that day was of significance.

Keith offered her a present. Before she could open it, he got down on his knee and asked her to marry him. Opening it, she sees a golden ring with three crosses etched on it; it was breathtakingly beautiful. Julli looked at Keith through unshed tears and said, "Yes!"

She was getting tired of Teagrans always chaperoning them. Julli and Keith kept the ranch going with the help of Jerry, Aaron, and Tom. Teagrans was offered his freedom, which he took on the condition that he stayed at the ranch and cooked. Julli had agreed to it, and they never lacked good home-cooked food. Julli was kept so busy that the meals supplied her with the energy she needed to keep going day by day.

Melissa had gone to jail and was transferred to a prison for women. They had found her guilty of theft, attempted murder, and extortion. Her pa had been buried, with only Melissa, the pastor, and a few deputies attending the funeral. Julli had forgiven Melissa and her father for the deaths of her folks, Paul, and using her land all those years.

Bertha surprised Julli with her arrival again. This time she was loaded with her belongings, planning on staying. She had sold the estate back East and decided the West was for her too. To Teagrans's delight, Nicole came as well. Julli watched as their romance blossomed, and they wanted to get married right away. Bertha had arranged their marriage at the ranch, and there Teagrans and Nicole were wed. Julli was happy for her friends and wondered when they, she and Keith, were going to set a date.

Without telling Julli, Keith had asked Bertha to get the wedding plans under way. He wanted the best wedding Julli could ever have. Bertha had gone to the bank and set in motion the financial securities that Julli would have from the ranch. The past thirteen years of debts had been paid, and Julli had transferred the property into Keith's name. She was kind of upset as it had been her pa and ma's ranch, but putting it in Keith's name and marrying him was better than having to move out if she had not had a male take over. Women still did not get many rights.

Julli, Keith, and her aunt took a trip to Johnsville to see Kathrin and the graves. Julli was able to see Mark's grave. She and Keith laid some flowers on there and had a prayer, thanking the Lord for the blessings they had received. Julli added that she had loved Mark and always would. Her heart felt lighter, and she was able to keep the seed growing; it had sprouted but did not yield any flowers yet. She was still working on that.

The new owner of the Cathelroans' property had graciously put a wooden fence around the graves, keeping them undisturbed and well maintained after his ma died and had been buried there. The owner had graciously allowed Julli free access anytime she wanted. She went the first time with her aunt Bertha and Keith. However, the second time was for her alone. She cried and took a nap next to Pamela's tombstone. She missed her little girl so much and knew that she was where she belonged, with the Heavenly Father. Julli would always have the memory of Pamela with her. The pain had eased but was not forgotten. Never would be.

She had gotten a bone that Luke used to gnaw on and buried it there, hoping he liked it. Wishing that she could bear to have another dog, but one was enough for Julli, and that was Luke.

They stayed there two weeks before they headed back to Sonastown. It was not known for its greatness, but it was home for them.

They got back to find boxes in Julli's room. Her aunt had ordered a simple yet elegant wedding dress. It was modestly cut as Julli wanted, with long slender sleeves that had a string at the end, which Julli tied on her middle fingers. The train was long, and Julli wondered how long it was. "Oh, about two feet," was the only comment she got from her aunt. There were little crystal gems up and down the skirt and around the hem. The bodice was all lace over white satin. Julli knew her aunt had spent some good money for it. "You only get married once," belied Bertha.

There were white boots to go with it. Julli wondered why boots, 'til her aunt made the comment that they were out West and boots were a practicality. Instead of a veil placed over her head, she had a white hat that had a veil attached to it. It went all the way down her back, nearly reaching the beginning of the train.

Since the rings were gold with three crosses on them, her aunt had gotten Julli some gold earrings studded with diamonds, with a small cross chained to each of them. Julli really loved all that she had gotten for her wedding.

"Keith, when are we going to set a date for the wedding?" she signed, popping the question mid meal that night.

"Oh, how about Saturday?" he signed, feigning indifference.

Julli had opened her eyes in surprise as she signed, "Are you serious?" He winked at her.

"No, I am happily telling you, this Saturday." There they went again with the word game.

Julli could only run around the table and run into the arms of the man she loved. It was no surprise to anyone but Julli, who had been kept out of the secret.

Cake was made by Teagrans, who instructed Nicole to make it white with vanilla. Teagrans decorated it, much to Julli's liking, with orange peels swirled all around the white cake. He had put white and orange icing on the cake and topped it with more orange peels. There was one large, with a smaller one on top, and two more on the sides. Julli knew that there was not going to be any leftover cake because everyone knew about his cooking, and if it was not for the wedding that they came, it was because of his cooking.

Bertha as well as Keith had invited lots of people before Julli even knew the date. Kathrin had come and was her maid of honor. Julli had begged her aunt to be her matron of honor, for which Julli had not needed to waste time trying to convince Bertha because she had already known Julli would want her there. They had bonded even more the past few months they had been together.

The wedding was to take place that Saturday around seven o'clock. Julli was so excited.

It was going to be outdoors at the front of the house. Her aunt had supervised the whole wedding preparations. There were candles, maybe hundreds to a thousand, lined up along the path that Julli was to walk down on. Julli had asked Tom to walk her down the aisle, and he had choked up. Nevertheless, he was true to his word; he was there dressed up. Julli wondered if her aunt had bought everyone their wedding apparel. Even Teagrans and Nicole were prim and proper.

The pastor had written down for Julli to read what was going to be said during the ceremony. Julli had to reread it several times. Luckily, since she could not hear, she would have the wedding ceremony on paper to keep.

The reception was to be held in the barn, where the band was setting up their instruments. Julli was not sure she wanted music, but her aunt had stood firm, saying, "Keith sang you a song. He played the guitar. What makes you think he wouldn't like some music?"

The blue thing Julli wore was her sapphire necklace. The borrowed was her aunt's lucky bracelet, which she had brought with her from Ireland. Julli swore she did not need anything else; she already had what she wanted. Her whole family was there with her, and she knew that her prayers had been answered.

The first dance of the night was to be Julli and Keith's first dance as a married couple. Julli had expected Keith to sing the rose song that she loved, but this time it was him singing along with the band to a song he titled "Always!"

Since Julli had read what the pastor wrote, she knew when to say "I do" and what was expected of her. She had no problem following along, especially with her aunt and Keith ready to sign at the first confused look she displayed.

The guests had applauded when Keith lifted up the veil and kissed Julli after the pastor told him he could kiss his bride. Nevertheless, nothing had them applaud even more than when the reception came. Julli and Keith had cut the cake together, and after Nicole scooped up the cake for them to feed each other a bite, Julli on impulse shoved the cake on Keith's face. She felt pretty good being mischievous. Nothing could have prepared her for the revenge Keith was going to exact on her. After wiping his face off with the napkin Nicole handed to him, he just shrugged and said, "Oh well, better now than later, which could be a frying pan."

Julli, taken aback by that, asked, "Do married women really hit their husbands with a frying pan?" which she had to sign, and Teagrans, acting like the butler, had to announce what Julli asked, which resulted in a lot of guffawing by the men and tittering by the women.

Shaking his head no, he wrapped his arms around her, and turning her to face the cake, he said as he grabbed her hands and smashed them into the cake, "This is what your husband does to you out of love!" There was a round of applause as Julli stood there with her hands in the cake, which Teagrans had made. Julli looked over to Teagrans, only to see him holding his midsection, laughing and pointing at Julli.

Keith pulls Julli's hands out of the cake and pops one finger into his mouth, sucking and licking off the cake and icing. They stood there 'til Keith had licked each of her fingers clean and handed her a napkin to finish the job. Smiling, Julli edged closer to him while she snuck some cake into her hand. Keith, catching on to her, shakes his head and places Nicole in front of him at the moment Julli shoved cake toward him.

In horror, Julli looked at Nicole covered in cake. She wiped the cake off of her face and flung it at Julli, who sidestepped. There was a splat as it hit Bertha, who stood there in shock. Swallowing, Bertha walked over to the table and grabbed a napkin, wiping off her dress. Turning, she scoops up a chunk of cake, which she aims at Aaron. Hence began the first food fight at a wedding, consisting mainly of cake and icing.

Keith grabbed Julli's hands and helped her out of the cake-tossing war and into the house, where they hurriedly changed. Before they could make their getaway in the carriage, which had cans tied to its every nook and cranny minus the horses, the guests came running tossing rice into the air. Many of them were applauding, waving, and shouting out their cheers to the newlyweds. Julli spied her aunt, blew her a kiss, and then signed the sign for "I love you!"

Julli and Keith were going on their honeymoon finally. Julli was finally married, and she had the Gospel in her life. She had found out that no matter how hard her struggles were, she had someone watching over her. Never again was she going to question the wisdom of the Most Holy Being. She had learned that faith overcomes obstacles, and an abundant quantity of faith she had.

EPILOGUE
WITH
JULLI AND NEW BABY

November 10, 1819
One Year Later

I t was not too bad. The labor had only lasted six hours, but Julli felt so worn out and tired that she wanted to curl up in a ball and go to sleep. But the knowledge of what she had just done helped her to recover her strength, and she was able to put the idea of sleep aside. If only for a moment.

"Here's your little boy," signed the midwife to her.

Looking at the bundle of joy covered with blankets, which she had brought into the world, Julli felt her maternal instincts returning. Her love for the child grew until it engulfed her whole being, and she felt that her role as a mother was indeed God's plan. Julli's faith had been renewed, and she was filled with the Holy Ghost.

Julliannyia reached out and eagerly took the bundle from the midwife's arms and brought her baby to her bosom. She touched the soft little cheek and couldn't believe the little miracle of life was actually in her own arms. She started smiling and couldn't stop as the little boy puckered his lips and turned toward her finger. Instinctively, Julli knew what he wanted, and she was glad that she would be able to give it to him. No one but her, as his mother, could provide that comfort for him.

"He's adorable!" came the booming voice of the proud father.

Frowning when the baby jumped in her arms and started crying. His little face turning a shade of red, beet red. With a look of bewilderment, she turned to look at the shadow by her side, figuring that somehow this shadow was the cause of her son's discomfort. Was Julli ever right!

"Shh!" the midwife admonished the father.

Julli proceeded to place her son in the nursing position, while Keith looked on. After a few tries, the baby finally found what he wanted and latched on. Secure with the knowledge that her son was getting his fill of his mother's milk, Julli turned to her husband and mouthed the words, "He's here. My baby is here!"

"I know," signed Keith with shaking hands before he leaned over to place a kiss on her forehead. His eyes shone with unshed tears as he gazed at both of them, mother and son.

With Keith watching them, she continued to tend to their son. Julliannyia smiled and remembered her daughter, Pamela. Visions of Pamela's smiling face, with her mass of curly brown hair much like her mother's own, her button nose, and puckered lips. She looked so much like her newborn baby brother. A memory worth keeping.

The baby fussed and opened his eyes. Julli looked deep into them and was drawn to the depths of another memory. Then a thought came over Julli, and she must have gasped because

Keith suddenly put his hand on her face and asked, "What? What is it?"

Julli stared for a moment before looking at her husband and replying. "Do you remember when we first moved out here, I met this man whose eyes I remembered?" Julli asked her husband with her voice.

He nodded, and she proceeded to tell him the idea that she had.

"I think we should name him Paul." Keith was quiet for several moments as he pondered the idea. Julli feared at that moment that he would say no to her.

They had still mourned the loss of Pamela even after a couple of years. They also mourned the death of Paul, who only lived a couple of They had buried him not far from the house against the pastor's wishes. His grave had been dug up and his remains had been buried with his feet facing towards the mountains. Again more people that Julli loved died. But the good thing was Julli learned that things happen for a reason; something had to come and take the place of the loss. She had finally learned that.

Keith, struggling to keep his emotions under control, let her know what he thought about her idea.

"Grand idea. Let's go for Paul Ryder Petershire," came the answer.

Looking at her husband, Julli searched his eyes for his feelings and could only see the love he had for her shining in them.

"Goody. It is Paul Ryder Petershire," announced the midwife to the closed doors. Julli knew that the midwife was telling her aunt and their friends the good news. They were going to like the name.

Julliannyia smiled and looked at her nursing son. She knew that her daughter would have approved of the name. It was just one way of keeping her memory alive, and she had a little brother to watch over. Maybe more in the future if it was God's will. Julli knew that her little girl would always be in her heart, but she was able to let her go now. So would she with Paul, the man she considered family. She finally had the strength to survive in this land, and her faith was strong enough for her to keep the man she loved with her forever.

"I'll always love you, Pamela. Wherever you are!" whispered Julli.

Seoithín, seo hó, mo stór é, mo leanbh
Mo sheoid gan cealg, mo chuid gan tsaoil mhór
Seothín seo ho, nach mór é an taitneamh
Mo stóirín na leaba, na chodladh gan brón.

Curfá:
A leanbh mo chléibh go n-eirí do chodhladh leat
Séan is sonas gach oíche do chóir
Tá mise le do thaobh ag guidhe ort na
mbeannacht
Seothin a leanbh is codail go foill.

Ar mhullach an tí tá síodha geala
Faol chaoin re an Earra ag imirt is spoirt
Seo iad aniar iad le glaoch ar mo leanbh
Le mian é tharraingt isteach san lios mór.

Irish Lullaby Irish Gaelic (pg 126 and 127)1/12/2013 7:17 PM

ABOUT THE AUTHOR

J oyce Moon was not always deaf. She lost her hearing when she was at the age of six. Her family had gone to the park for a church picnic, and Joyce climbed up the slide and got knocked down fourteen feet. She suffered a concussion and a broken wrist. A few days later, her mother noticed that she did not respond to loud noises and found out Joyce was rapidly losing her hearing. Joyce did not go to schools for the deaf. Instead she was mainstreamed in normal schools with the use of interpreters signing in SEE and ASL. Joyce grew up on a farm in Colorado, and she still loves all kinds of animals. She has always loved to read and write. Right now, Joyce has eight children, four girls and four boys., ages ranging from eighteen months old to twenty-one years old. She currently lives on the outskirts of Duchesne, Utah, where she resides with her family. Well, most of them.